Silent Suspicion

a Lincoln Keller Mystery

By Lee E. Meadows

Proctor Publications, LLC • Ann Arbor • Michigan • USA

© 2000 Proctor Publications/Lee E. Meadows

Proctor Publications, LLC
P.O. Box 2498
Ann Arbor, Michigan 48106-2498
1-800-343-3034
www.proctorpublications.com

Meadows, Lee E.
    Silent suspicion : a Lincoln Keller mystery /
by Lee E. Meadows
    p. cm.
    LCCN: 00-132551
    ISBN: 1-882792-93-9

    1. Murder--Michigan--Detroit--Fiction
2. Afro-Americans--Michigan--Detroit--Fiction.
3. Detroit (Mich.)--Fiction. 4. Detective and
mystery stories.   I. Title.
PS3563.E1698S57 2000   813'.54
            QB100-900577

Printed in the USA

Dedications

To my wife Phyllis and my son Garrison, whose patience, support and belief have been sources of inspiration in pushing me to write this story. Thank you family.

To Hazel, Don and Kathy at Proctor Publications LLC, for their unwavering support in bringing Lincoln Keller to the mystery genre. You're moving to new heights and I am glad to be along for the ride.

To that growing network of Lincoln Keller fans. Thanks for the plot ideas and character relationships as well as the great feedback about the story. I will continue to keep Keller "human" and the stories fast-paced, real and entertaining.

To the Y2K Michigan State Spartans (Citrus Bowl Champs, Big Ten Hockey Champs and NCAA Basketball Champs). Wow! What a ride! There are no mysteries here gang, just pure tenacity and unwavering belief in your abilities to be champions. A heartfelt congratulations to you all.

To my personal "mole". Thanks for sharing some of your insights on conducting thorough investigations and for being a technical consultant on some of the finer details of *Silent Suspicion*.

To Mayor Coleman Young, Columnist Bob Talbert, Radio personality Martha Jean "The Queen", and social activist Bill Beckham. You all cast a long shadow over Detroit's landscape. Detroit was much better because you called it "home" and we are wiser because of your commitment. Your spirits lives on!

To John Weaver at Page One (every story starts with Page One). Thanks for the "title" idea.

To Rochelle "Shelley" Williams. A special thanks for your cover concept.

Special Acknowledgments

Bookclubs

The lifeline that runs to the soul of an author, sustaining the spirit and promoting growth.

Contact	Bookclub	Location
Leza Roberson	Rare Essence Book Club	Aiken, Sc
Jonice Tenette	Sassy Sistahs Book Club	Altadena, Ca
Veleria Banks	In Good Company Book Club	Ann Arbor, Mi
Lola Jones	First Sunday Book Club	Ann Arbor, Mi
Joyce Hunter	African American Reading Group	Ann Arbor, Mi
Sandy Robinson	Sistah/Friends Reading Group	Ann Arbor, Mi
Alicia Carr	African American Literary Forum	Atlanta, Ga
Rasheda Blocker	Sisters at the Roundtable	Atlanta, Ga
Tanya LaFleur	Sister, Sister2 Book Club	Atlanta, Ga
Carla McManus	Hotlanta Book Club	Atlanta, Ga
Shirley Johnson	Dundalk Avenue Book Club	Baltimore, Md
Phyllis Fuqua	RDBB (Reading Divas)	Birmingham, Al
Gina Milton	Book Divas	Boston, Ma
Troy Johnson	AALBC Book Club	Brooklyn, Ny
Venetia Hays	Sistahs With Vision	Brownsmills, Nj
Barbara Eaves	Sisters Reading Books	Chicago, Il
Vanessa Lipske	Sister Review Book Club	Chicago, Il
Pam Walker-Williams	The Good Book Club	Clear Lake, Tx
Kanitra Brooks	Words of Wisdom Book Club	Dallas, Tx
Lisa Cross	Sistah Circle Book Club	Dallas, Tx
Jennifer Pope	S.O.O.P (Stories Of Our People)	Dallas, Tx
Darlene Ramzy	The Literary Cafè	Dallas, Tx
Marlive & Portia	GRITS Online Book Club	Dallas, Tx
LaRon Wilkinson	Beautiful Women Book Club	Dayton, Oh
Francine Archer	Motor City Review	Detroit, Mi
Brenda Brown	BTS Book Club	Detroit, Mi
A.J. Kyle	Books Are Seeds Of Knowledge	Detroit, Mi
Karen Lemmons	African American Reading Group	Detroit, Mi
Barbara Pritchett	The Sisterhood	Detroit, Mi
Pat Rowbowski	The Phoenix Club	Detroit, Mi
Shelley Smith	Readerís Choice Book Club	Detroit, Mi
Karlyn Singleton	S.I.S.T.E.R	Detroit, Mi
Dr. Harriet Slocum	African American Literary Guild	Detroit, Mi
Dr. Deborah Smith-Pollard	The Bookies	Detroit, Mi
Pat Terry	Terry's Book Club	Detroit, Mi
Dr. Eleanor Walker	Sisters In The Word	Detroit, Mi
Jeanette Wallington	Powerful Women of Purpose	Detroit, Mi
Vanessa Woodward	Journeyís End Literary Society	Durham, Nc
Greg Jourdan	Tender Warriors	Fairfield, Ca
Victoria Jourdan	ITCOMS	Fairfield, Ca
Suzette Perkins	Sisters Of The Written Word	Fayetteville, Ar
Taji Richardson	AA Sister/Brother Book Club	Greenville, Sc

Phyllis Jones	Sistahs Of The Written Word	Houston, Tx
Felecia Smith	Phenomenal Women Book Club	Houston, Tx
Delores Thornton	Sisters With Soul	Indianapolis, In
Jackie McKinney	Powerful Women of Color	Jacksonville, Fl
Linda Neville	Sable Literary Sisters	Jersey City, Nj
Rosie Harvey	Sistahs Who Enjoy Reading	Lake Providence, La
Betty Thomas-Gilkey	Sistahs Reading Books	Lansing, Mi
Paula Cunningham	Sistahs Reading Club	Lansing, Mi
Phillip Brown	African Nation Book Club	Lewisville, Tx
Annette Thomas	Sistahs Reading Books	Long Beach, Ca
Edwina Jackson	Divine Sisterhood Reading Club	Lorton, Va
Andromedia Bowden	Women On The Move	Los Angeles, Ca
Janel Stephenson	Special Thoughts Reading Club	Los Angeles, Ca
Dorothy Simon	Seven Sisters Sipping Tea	Louisville, Ky
Anfra Boyd	You Are My Sister (YAMS)	Memphis, Tn
Likeisha Mills	R.A.R.E Book Club	Memphis, Tn
Annette Breedlove	Sistah Girl Reading Club	Miami, Fl
Joyce Cobb	Black Women Who Read	Minneapolis, Mn
Cheryl Barker	Afrocentric Literary Guild	Mishawauka, In
Ron Murphy	Afro-American Book Discussion	Montclair, Nj
Regina Campbell	The ASWAD Literary Group	Nashville, Tn
Dwayne Jenkins	Books Brothers Reading Club	Nashville, Tn
Karen Johns	Between Sisters Book Club	Nashville, Tn
LaShawn Barber	Sisterhood Book Club	Nashville, Tn
Pat Houser	Ebony Book Club	New York, Ny
Stephanie Twitty	Godyva Chocolates Book Club	Norcross, Ga
Tamara Sims	S.I.L.K Book Club	Orlando, Fl
Sheri Clark-Brooks	Sistah Harmony Book Club	Phoenix, Az
Jacqueline Green	Bourbon Street Book Club	Phoenix, Az
Monique Ford	Circle of Sistahís Book Club	Philadelphia, Pa
Valerie Odom	The "Sistahs" Are Reading	Philadelphia, Pa
Orlanda Thompson	Busara Nayo Book Club	Philadelphia, Pa
Judiann Winston	African American Women Book Club	Philadelphia, Pa
Angelicia Simmons	Elimika Msomajiwa Book Club	Raleigh, Nc
Alesia McMillan	African Jewels Book Club	Reynoldsburg, Oh
Kim Griffin	Sister to Sister Book Club	Rialto, Ca
Addie Armstrong	Black Pearls Literary Society	San Antonio, Tx
Lee Scott	Black Minds Book Club	Washington, Dc

Mystery Book Clubs

Contact	Book Club	Location
Diane Wynings	South Lyon Tuesday Club	South Lyon, Mi
Karen Westlake	Ladies Literary Guild	Wayne, Mi
Laura Carroll	The Mystery Ladies	Minneapolis, Mn
Elaine Munsch	Sisters-In-Crime	Shelbyville, Kn
Suzze Tiernan	Mystery Readers Group	Bloomfield, Mi
Anne Saunders	Mystery Mavens	Farmington, Mi

They're all that and @

J.A Phelps @African American Booksellers, Troy Johnson @African American Literature Book Club, Alicia Carr @African American Literary Forum, Valerie Daniels @African American Mystery Page, Mo and Marty Fleming-Berg @BCA, Betty Davis @Black Book Network, Lloyd E. Hart @Black Library, Kim Griffin @Blackliterature, Tia Shabazz @Blackwriters, Renee Reneau @Blackvoices, Janet Lawson @Bookbrowser,Gwen Richardson @CushCity, Darlene Ramzy @Dallasblack, Pamela Guinns @Imagine, Vanessa Woodward @Journeyís End Literary Society, Ron Kavanaugh @Mosaicbooks, E. David Ellington @Netnoir, John Weaver @Page One, Maxine Thompson @On The Same Page, Darcy Prather @What2Read, PauletteBrown@WriteDirections, T.C. Matthews and Kia D Sidbury @ProlificWritersNetwork, Jim Daniels@Nubianchronicles, Elizabeth Henze@MurderExpress

Bless those Librarians

Ruby Anderson (Indianapolis), Addie Armstrong and Barbara Knotts (San Antonio), Shirley Johnson (Baltimore), Betty Thompson (Ann Arbor), Joyce Cobb, Charles Brown and Jerry Blue (Minneapolis), Hellena Stokes, Meller Langford, Obi Dike Kamau and Sandra Parham (Houston), Dr. Gleniece Robinson (Ft. Worth), Sonja Hayes (Dallas), Ron Murphy (Montclair), Florence Simkins-Brown (North Miami), Marshelle Denson, Judy Bullock and Heather Campbell (Jacksonville), Jennifer Leverette (Panama City), Elinor Williams (Orlando), Patricia Kelker (Philadelphia), Phyllis Green Mack (New York), Samuel Morrison (Ft. Lauderdale), Kathleen Bethel (Northwestern U), Sylvia Sprinkle-Hamlin, (Winston/Salem), Gladys Smiley-Bell (Kent State U), Ednita Bullock (NCA&T), Cynthia Cobb (Fayetteville), Wayne Crocker (Petersburg), Sherry DuPree (Santa Fe Community College), Andy Venable (Cleveland), Ann Bush (Tampa), Jackie Sullen (Detroit), Dorothy Seymore (Louisville), Arnice Smith (Cincinnati), Charlotte Momon (Jackson, Ms), Jamie Turner, Mae Bolton and Veronica Lee (Oakland), Sharon Johnson (Compton), Alicia Antone (East Providence), Lydia Acosta (Bloomington), Monica Lucas (Raleigh), Gloria Creed-Dikeogu (Lawrence), Ruby Hunter (Crofton, MD), Judy Register (Scottsdale), Sherelle Harris (South Norwalk), Merrikay Brown (Lewisville NC), Shirley Miller and Barbara Best-Nichols (Durham), Leatrice Brantley (Rochester, NY), Cissy Lovett (Dayton), Danita Barber-Owusu, Vickie Novak (Calumet City, IL), Deborah Hogue (Denver), Dianne Kelly (Cypress, TX), Sandra Lockett (Milwaukee), Johnnie Dent (Queens, NY), Emily Guss (Chicago), Mildred Nance (Silver Springs, MD), Garland McLaughlin (Boston), Carolyn Allen (Charlottesville), Negla Ross Parris (Brooklyn), Donna Whitner (Kansas City), Vanessa Ramseur (Charlotte, NC), Denyvetta Davis (Oklahoma City), Cynthia Kidd (Austin), Sally Reed (Norfolk), Sherwin Rice (Elizabethtown, NC), Carolyn Barkley (Virginia Beach), Marcellus Turner (Tacoma), Billie Dancy (Pleasanton, CA), Alice DuPuis (Miami), JoAnn Looney (Baton Rouge), Valencia Hawkins (New Orleans) Kelly Richard (West Las Vegas), Cecil Hixon (New York), Gloria Coles (Flint, MI), Eva Poole (Denton, TX), Lucille Dade (Carrollton, TX), Dorcel Thrower (Toledo), Kathleen Bethel (Evanston), Joyce Jelks (Atlanta), Carolyn Garnes (East Point, GA) Darline Carter (West Islip), Teresa Smith (Euclid, OH), Bescye Burnett (Jackson, MI), Mildred Rias (St. Louis), Sandra Williams-Bush (Buffalo), Doris Walker (Orange, NJ), Fannie Simmons (DeKalb), Donnie Griffin (Marietta, GA), Alice McCanless (Morrow), Toni Walder (Dayton), Beverly Kane (Saugerties, NY) Betty Thornton, Dianne T. Scott, Janice Jefferson, Shirley Burks, Ann Marie Davis, Ali Subhanallah, Sylvia Coker, Madeline Morgan, Deborah Peterson and Virginia Fore (Baltimore), Roy L. Jones (Largo, MD), Stephanie Jones (U.S. Army), Barbara Christine (U.S. Army), Arlene Luster (U.S. Air Force), Jewel Player (U.S. Govt.), Kathy Bowersox and Mildred Brown (Southern University)

Silent Suspicion

a
Lincoln Keller
Mystery

1

Deborah Norris had eyes that would draw a confession from the Pope. Almond shaped and tinted brown with finely arched eyebrows, she stared back at me with a look that I could only describe as penetrating. Her flush, copper tone was accented by evenly trimmed, low cut hair. She flashed a daring smile. She wore a black tunic that revealed enough neckline for me to take in a thin, silver necklace with a small diamond resting comfortably around her neck.

She would not have to ask me to bear my soul. I believed she could see beneath the artificial layers of my own self-delusions and hold those secrets deep within the security of her own humanity.

It was a belief I could never test.

A bullet ended that possibility.

Deborah would have been thirty-seven years young had we met today. Eight years ago a bullet changed that annual celebration. Her remains lay buried in a city grave yard on Detroit's east side, tucked away in a corner of a small, grassy incline and marked by a bronze plaque on a marble headstone.

She was twenty-nine at the time of her unexpected death. As a free lance journalist fighting to leave her signature on the stories that helped to shape the beginnings of Detroit's turnaround, she was once described as all 'Fire and Heart'. Insiders said a Pulitzer was a part of her future.

A random act of violence changed that conversation.

I gazed at the picture sitting on the oak mantle of the marble fireplace in the Indian Village home of Judge Warren 'War Zone' Henderson.

On the opposite end of the mantle was a gold-framed color portrait of Judge Henderson and his family. The Judge's neatly trimmed salt and pepper beard covered his soft ebony tone, giving him a professorial look that would be the envy of any tenured faculty member. The evenly trimmed look followed a symmetrical pattern from the bottom of his chin to the top of his low cut, slightly curled hair. Through intense brown eyes, he posed with regal bearing in a dark double-breasted Brooks Brother's suit, red tie and towering like a smiling ornament. Next to him sat a honey-brown toned, full-smiled woman with finely trimmed, arched eyebrows, smooth skin and rectilinear gray strands that complemented her ebony styled hair which curled slightly at her shoulders. Dressed in a blue, full-length dress, her red nailed, manicured hands crossed and resting on her lap, she looked like someone who'd find comfort among kings or kooks. There was something in her manner that enveloped her like an invisible, form-fitting layer of strength. Dignity, I decided. She wore dignity that same way Lena Horne wears class. The kids in the photograph were polished extensions of their parents — standing on opposite ends, the son looking like a younger version of his father and the daughter looking like a younger twin of her mother.

"I'm not sure I can be much help to you, Your Honor," I said, aware of his reputation of never taking 'no' as a final answer.

'War Zone' Henderson didn't suffer fools lightly, if at all. The six foot, nine inch former NFL defensive tackle, turned Wayne County Circuit judge, was a designated combat area. He ruled as a steely-eyed, iron-willed overseer with a tactical understanding of the law, a razor sharp mind and a tongue that could slice through court procedure faster than Patton's Third Army. He was a trench warrior who didn't take prisoners, but was kind enough to mail the remaining body parts back to the next of kin. It proved he had a heart.

He never gave an inch and covered more territory than a drunken crop duster.

Garbed in a dark blue, white trimmed running outfit, unzipped at the neck, he looked like he could still rip the helmets off fleet footed running backs. Age and law hadn't affected his paunch line. He was one of the reasons why I decided that I'd rather be a defensive back. I'd rather give the hit than take one.

Employing the services of a private investigator would have gone against his swaggering, grousing, take-care-of-it-my-way nature.

Or, so I thought.

There's a price one pays for hanging around a war zone. Pieces of you wind up in places you hadn't expected. The innocent go down as quickly as the guilty and with very little fanfare.

"If I believed that I would have never asked to see you," he said in a barrel-toned voice. "Your reputation for the unusual is not, shall we say, without merit. Your brother, Jefferson, says you're a pretty good detective."

My bounty hunting eldest brother is the other half of Keller Investigations. "He said that?"

"I met your brother two years ago at a seminar I taught at the University of Detroit's Law school. He didn't strike me as someone supportive of the legal system."

"He's a born skeptic, Your Honor. That's why he's a bounty hunter."

"Well, he caught Dawson Briggs after he'd jumped bond. I was personally glad to sentence that pervert."

I appreciated Jeff's vote of confidence. Unsolved homicides weren't the kind of cases that flared my nostrils, but Jeff's recommendation meant there was more to the story.

"What makes you think I can help?"

"It happened eight years ago yesterday," he said, ignoring the question. "Deborah worked as a free-lance journalist. Never wanted a full time gig. Her body was found three blocks from where she lived near Franklin Court. We thought she was out of town." He paused. It didn't seem like a good time to interrupt. "I worked in the Prosecutor's office at the time. The homicide detective called to the scene was a friend of mine.

3

Though she was found with nothing that would identify her, he recognized her immediately and contacted me to ID her body. Nothing I ever experienced in the NFL, or anywhere, was as painful as that moment when I looked down and saw her lying on that metal slab."

Eight years ago I was working in Oakland California as a patrol officer and hadn't paid much attention to the unsolved crimes in Detroit. At the time we had too many in Oakland. "The case is still unsolved?"

"It's still an open homicide so technically they have to keep the case open. Realistically, there's very little they can do. Especially given the last round of budget cuts. Homicide detectives are already stretched to the max with their current cases. Not much interest in an eight year old unsolved murder. I'd like to restore the level of interest." He rubbed his massive trench worn hands, momentarily mulling. "I need someone who is removed from the case and has a fresh set of eyes. It would also help if that person can somehow get into the mind of the killer. I think you can do that, Mr. Keller."

"I'm not sure if that's a compliment, Judge, and please call me Linc."

"Linc, my sister-in-law's spirit ..... " He turned toward the slight noise that announced the person entering the room. "Oh, honey, this is Mr. Keller. The man I told you about."

"Mr. Keller," she acknowledged with a tight smile and an even tone.

She also wore a similar running outfit, though her shoulder length hair was pulled back and tied with a thin blue ribbon. If she was over fifty then I was a goalie for the Detroit Red Wings. There was no way that harmoniously trimmed body could have been around for fifty plus years.

I hesitated slightly. Unsure if I should shake her hand, kiss her ring or excuse myself before I said something stupid.

"A pleasure to meet you, Mrs. Henderson," I said without too bad an assault on the King's English.

"Why don't we all sit down," Judge Zone offered.

He found his way around to the auburn colored, leather high back chair behind the desk; she walked over to the casement windows, peering out as if there was something else on her mind.

I eased down slowly into the velvet cushion armchair.

"I have something here for you, Linc," Judge Zone said as he removed a slightly full manila envelope from a side drawer in his desk. "It's every piece of material I could find that's been written about Deborah's death."

He slid the envelope over toward me.

"I've tried to be meticulous, not wanting any information to get by me. I'm sure you'll find it helpful."

The folder contained copies of the original homicide report, statements from witnesses, faded articles from both the Detroit News and Free Press, hand written leads that were pursued, and a wallet size copy of the picture of Deborah that I had just seen. Most of the information would have been obtainable for the average citizen, but as I quickly learned, Judge Zone had his own unstoppable way of doing things that were not mine to question.

A quick review of the first three faded articles revealed an obvious pattern. "Everything indicates it was a robbery." I said. "Her purse was found a couple of blocks away. Anything of value was taken while the other stuff was scattered around. There was no indication as to how much money was taken and her credit cards were never recovered." I sighed. "Your Honor, this could be a real waste of your time."

He ignored my remark and continued, "You'll find copies of the police reports that corroborate the newspaper accounts. Knackton was a Sergeant at that time. He's also convinced it was a robbery."

"And you're not convinced," I said.

"I can smell a draw play."

"Is there anything that says something different?"

"Not back then and not eight years later. That's why I want a fresh pair of eyes looking at this information. It may have been just a robbery. Maybe you can finally convince me."

Sylvia Henderson hadn't stopped peering out the window. Deborah was her sister so I didn't know what to make of it. "What are your thoughts on this, Mrs. Henderson?"

She turned and walked toward the back of the desk and answered my question with a question; "What is your level of experience with this kind of investigation, Mr. Keller?"

"I saw a lot of things when I worked as a cop in Oakland, California, Mrs. Henderson. Most of which was a compelling argument for a second flood minus the Arc. Even when I know why people do what they do, I still don't understand why they do it. I secured a lot of crime scenes, talked with a lot of witnesses and heard more than my share of excuses for conduct even the animal community would find offensive and barbaric. But to answer your question, I'm not an experienced homicide investigator. I was a patrol officer."

"And now?" she asked.

"Robbery homicides don't come across my desk and I don't go looking for that kind of case. People do enough other kinds of things that keep me busy. For those reasons, as I told your husband earlier, I'm not the best person for this job."

"He's convinced otherwise."

Not exactly a ringing show of support for my opinion, but I could live with her apprehensions. There was something in her manner that suggested a reluctance to reopen an old wound, but I didn't doubt that once opened, she'd stay with it until it was over.

Sylvia Henderson's strength, as I would soon learn, would be found in areas invisible to the naked eye.

Judge Zone reached over and held her hand. "My wife loved her sister very much, Mr. Keller. They were fifteen years apart in age but you wouldn't know it to have seen them together. Sylvia practically raised Deborah."

In my mind, that made her loss even more painful. Big sister/mother/ best friend. You never expect to outlive the ones you raise. But she had.

"Your Honor," I said. "We're both professionals here and I have too much regard for you to not emphasize this point. There are far more experienced investigators who'd provide a higher level of service. If this is that important to you, then you need to give it further consideration."

"We'd like YOU to look into it," he replied. His tone was decisive and unquestioning. I'd seen and heard that tone in his Circuit Court room in downtown Detroit when I had to testify in a case he was overseeing.

"Before I commit, there's one other problem." Judge Henderson waited. "This case has Lieutenant Knackton's fingerprints all over it."

Lieutenant Nick Knackton and I had one ongoing problem that seemed to always bring out the alley cat in both of us. Her name is Candy Malone and she's an investigator with the Detroit Police Department Homicide Division. She's talented, ambitious, thorough and sexy. She's also the on-again, off-again lust of my life - and Knackton's unofficial protegee.

"I've heard there's some dissension between you two," The Judge stated.

"We don't send each other Christmas cards."

"I see it as a minor complication."

"If he's a friend of yours, he might take offense," I said.

"He'll respect my wishes," he replied with an even tone and a furrowed brow. "I'm well aware of the unwritten, non-interference code among law enforcement officials.

"I can ease some of the way for you. I do have influence within the police department. Besides the copies of the report I've given you, I can take care of the political matter. Knackton's friendship doesn't change the fact that I'd like your help."

I'd be the one in need of help if Knackton and I crossed swords. "Your Honor, even if Knackton wasn't part of the picture, you know there are territorial complications that happen anytime a private investigator steps on the turf of homicide investigators."

"I'll handle those," he replied in a dismissive tone. "I know a little something about playing on someone else's turf. I just need you to fill the hole."

"That's not filling a hole, Your Honor. That's like trying to stop a Green Bay sweep."

"I've stopped a few in my day."

"But I haven't," I sighed. Hope may spring eternal but reality is often the winter of my discontent. "It may prove to be futile, Your Honor."

"Then we'd be no worse off than I am now. I think having someone like yourself cast a fresh eye on her murder might prove to be more helpful than what's been done so far."

"Still, eight years is a long time," I said hoping he'd thought about the reality of his request.

"Not when it feels like yesterday. I need this thing resolved, Mr. Keller, and I'd like to count on your help. Name your price and bring me results."

"The trail would be ice cold by now, Judge." I continued, "Almost impossible to find any real leads. At this point I can't honestly say my results would be any different."

I took out the contract I'd brought with me. "This is a standard agreement employing me. I'll need a retainer fee of five hundred dollars. I'll put that against the daily rate and bill you for expenses. If at anytime you're dissatisfied with the progress or quality of my work ..... "

" ..... I know a little about how the law works, Mr. Keller," he said as he pulled the contract toward him. "I'll read through it tonight, have it signed and delivered to you tomorrow."

"That'll be fine."

"When can we start?" he asked.

In a few days was an answer that would not have endeared me to him or his wife. "We already have, Your Honor. I'd like to start by asking a few questions."

"Go ahead," he replied leaning back in his chair.

"Can you remember anything about what was going on with Deborah the last time you saw her."

"How can we forget," Sylvia cut in. "That was the night she was murdered."

2

We moved to a screen enclosed back terrace complete with wrought iron furniture, beige patterned cushions and a slate covered floor. Sylvia Henderson brought in lemonade as we settled into our individual seats, the somber notion that Deborah's last encounter with her sister and brother-in-law occurred the night she was murdered didn't do much to lighten the mood.

"She periodically dropped by to have dinner with us," Sylvia began. "There was never any predictability as to when she would. Not that it was necessary. She knew Warren and I enjoy dining at home whenever we can. It's our way of sharing time and going over the day's events. It seemed that whenever we were about to start eating, the door would chime and Deborah would come breezing in, throwing kisses and asking 'what's for dinner?'." She glanced over at Judge Zone, who returned her reflective smile. "We'd just laugh and she'd start right in telling us every-thing that was going on with her and trying to get our take on events around Detroit. She loved being a free-lance journalist."

"Not that she had to," Judge Zone added. "I have friends on the *News* and *Free Press*. I tried to help her secure a full time job with those publications, but she preferred free lance work so she had articles with the *Michigan Chronicle, Citizen, Post, Bulletin* and *City View*. She even had articles published in a couple of national magazines. She was a good writer. She could have been successful with any of those papers."

"But?" I asked.

"But, free lance only partially described my sister," Sylvia said.

The conversation stopped momentarily as The Judge filled our ice-stacked glasses with lemonade from the sterling silver carafe on the glass-topped table anchored between us.

"You were saying, Mrs. Henderson. Free lance only partially described your sister."

"Free spirit is a much closer description."

"Try earth mother," The Judge said.

Sylvia smiled. "My sister was a conduit for earthly and universal absurdities known to mankind. She attracted everyone and everything that didn't have an anchor point and made everyone feel important by asking about their mother.

"She had the uncanny ability to emerge unscathed in situations that would normally wreck anyone else. She called us one night from Police Headquarters because she'd been arrested during a gang raid."

I listened.

"Remember that, honey?" The Judge nodded. "A gang raid no less. You know what she was doing? Writing an article about Visiting Nurses being the true advocates of community outreach. She was shadowing this Visiting Nurse on her rounds. What was that girl's name dear?"

The Judge reflected. "Phyllis Johnson."

"Oh yes. Anyway, Deborah wanted to get a first hand look at how Visiting Nurses do their work, so she followed this Miss Johnson into an East side project to visit with a patient. The area was ripe with gang activity, but for whatever reason no one seemed to bother Deborah and Miss Johnson. Turns out that the patient Miss Johnson was treating also lived in a place where gang members kept stolen items. From what I understand, a door was kicked in, members of the Police gang squad swarmed the area and Deborah and Miss Johnson were taken downtown as part of a gang sweep."

"I asked her if she was alright once we got down to Police Headquarters," The Judge interrupted. "She said 'yeah, I got some great interviews in the back of the paddy wagon'. The gang members kept yelling at the cops that they'd arrested a nurse and a writer. She thought the whole thing was funny."

"Did she have very many friends?" I asked.

"She knew a lot of people ... naturally," Sylvia answered. "But only a couple of close friends."

I made a mental note to get those names later. "Tell me about the last night you saw her."

The Judge started. "She'd stopped by for dinner. Naturally started telling us about some of the story ideas she was working on. She also brought by Sylvia's birthday gift. At least part of the gift."

"What do you mean?" I asked.

Sylvia answered. "That picture you saw of her on the fireplace mantel. I'd asked her for years to have one taken. She said she would, but only for a special occasion. That occasion was my forty-fifth birthday, only she was two days early. She brought the picture by because she said she was going out of town to follow up on a story."

Sylvia stopped. Taking a moment to sip her lemonade.

"What was the story?"

Judge Zone filled the momentary void. "She never said specifically. Just that it was one of those stories that writers follow to the truth."

"Any idea what that meant?"

"No." He added, "But then you had to know Deborah."

"We dined as we usually did that evening," Sylvia said. "Deborah did most of the talking and except for a minute or two when she left the room, dominated most of the conversation."

"Unfortunately, I had to leave the two of them that evening. I had a meeting with potential contributors to my Circuit Court election campaign. I said 'good night' and we'd see her when she came back to town. I told Sylvia not to wait up for me and that was the last time I saw Deborah alive."

"What happened after that, Mrs. Henderson?"

She sighed. "Oh, we girl chatted. Mostly about her life. I probably said some over-mothering things; she probably kidded me about my sometimes stuffy nature. She always kidded me, played jokes on me or set me up for some fun mystery. She said that since I was so mothering, I was an easy mark. She didn't know that I let her do a lot of those things because, well, just because I loved her. She was a lot of fun."

"How much time did you two spend together before she left?"

"Maybe an hour. Maybe a little more."

"And from there?"

"From there she said she had to run and she'd call me when she returned."

"Didn't say where she was going?" I asked.

"No. And I didn't ask. As my husband said, you had to know Deborah." She stopped and looked over at The Judge. "The next phone call we received was from Sergeant Knackton, asking us to come down and identify her body. That was four twenty-seven a.m. the next morning. A homeless woman and her child found her body. She was kind enough to wave down a patrol car." She fought back those tears from an endless well reserved for a lost loved one.

I stepped in. "It still sounds like a robbery."

"That's the official explanation, Linc," The Judge replied. "But rather than bias you, I'll let you sort through the facts."

"What if its true?"

"Then it's a lie," he said evenly.

I didn't see a need to argue, so I let it go. "Well, let's do it this way; I'll look through the information. After that I'll probably have more questions to ask. From there we'll see where it goes. Will the two of you be available?"

"I'm in town for the next two weeks, so just call me at the court or here."

"Mrs. Henderson?"

"Here is fine," she replied.

I thanked them, finished my lemonade, scooped up the folder and they escorted me to the front door.

As The Judge opened the door, I said. "Your Honor, I know how much this means to the two of you and I promise you I'll do as much as I can. But, again, eight years is a long time."

"My sister's soul walks among the restless. She deserves better than that, Mr. Keller. Please do what you can," Sylvia said.

I nodded.

"By the way," I said. "You mentioned that the picture on the mantel was part of your birthday gift. What was the other part?"

Sylvia reached over the collar of her runner's outfit and showed me a necklace; identical to the one Deborah wore in her picture.

"I always told Deborah how much I liked her 'lucky' necklace and so for my birthday, she had one made for me."

"Nice of her to give that to you."

"That's the irony. She didn't give me the necklace that night. I received a phone call a few days later from the jeweler who happened to read the story and contacted me. Turns out that Deborah had ordered the necklace two weeks earlier. He called because he wasn't sure what to do. He was such a nice man. I paid the remaining balance and I've worn it everyday since."

"Was Deborah's necklace taken in the robbery?"

"Yes. It wasn't on her when she was found. I know she had it on when she left me that evening. Whenever she felt she was on to something she'd tap the necklace three times and say, 'all luck is attitude'. I guess the charm finally faded."

I tried a less painful question. "What were the names of those friends you mentioned?"

Sylvia paused. "Sharron Westlake was a friend from junior high and on through college, and the other one I didn't know that well, although they lived in the same townhouse complex."

"I'm sure I can find out who she is. Do you know if they're both still in the city?"

"Sharron for sure," Sylvia answered. "I don't know about the other one."

"There's one other thing," Judge Zone said. "About six months before her death, Deborah had registered for a gun. A small .22 caliber."

"Any idea why?" I asked.

"According to Deborah, it was just the usual city stuff. She wanted to feel a little more protected." Judge Zone sighed. "Unfortunately, ballistics confirmed that it was the same gun used to kill her."

Sylvia sighed. "Who'd want to hurt Deborah?"

Police files all over the country are littered with unsolved cases based on that same question. I opted not to share that insight. "Well, I won't take anymore of your time for now," I said.

They walked with me to my car, said their good byes and began their evening walk through the neighborhood. I fired up the Nova and waved.

As I drove down the half moon driveway toward the street, my head was spinning with a thousand different thoughts. Most of which were about a twenty nine-year-old free spirit whose untimely death altered the life paths of her immediate family and I supposed anyone else she had encountered.

I thought about The Judge and Sylvia Henderson and their rise to prominence as a strong and loving couple, proud of their children, motivated by their accomplishment and mindful of their unique role in Detroit's inner circle.

They'd made their way into the elite and that meant their every move and thought found its way into the local media whether they meant it to or not.

Detroit had its aristocracy and embraced them with idolized passion. There was always the need to believe that they were somehow above the basic human frailties and walked on clouds of opulent perfection. I'd been given the chance to see them in their most vulnerable, human reality. The polish was removed and beneath the surface there was the same tarnish, the same dark catacombs of insecurity, uncertainty and doubt.

I drove away from that castle with a couple of leads and an unshakable feeling that something was out of sync. I'd spent enough time in the trenches to know that people tend to bury more than they reveal. The human psyche is more than a collection of thoughts and experiences; it's a revelation of our own longing for more than the sum total of our being, at any cost.

There was something on the other side of this investigation that lurked just outside of the light. The shadow of things unknown. Those things that are invisible in the light, sinister in the dark and lethal to the touch.

As I motored toward Vernor Street, my internal radar sounded a loud warning. I was being reminded that the real danger on any path is not the moss-covered rocks that we trip over, but the fungus that lies underneath.

3

Twilight began its slow creep onto the city's rhythm and the mild breeze danced like a blithe spirit through the cabin of my Nova. Late summer in the city. A time when unscheduled activity often led to trouble and impatience as a substitute for boredom. The longer evenings provided the perfect excuse for delaying being anywhere but home.

I didn't need an excuse, but I had a good one anyway.

With thoughts of my new case doing the 'Hustle' to the sounds of Stevie Wonder's *My Eyes Don't Cry No More'*, I took the Lodge exit off I-94 and followed the Milwaukee ramp over to Grand Boulevard where I turned onto LaSalle Boulevard. This historically preserved area of artistically designed brick homes of columns, rotundas and linear manicured hedges, reminded me of a place that Frank Capra may have come to in order to film a movie. I suspected that was the reason my brother Rosie and his wife Rae bought their home in this area. Since graduating together from Michigan State over twenty years ago, they've lived and work in Detroit with unwavering dedication — to their alma mater, to their city, and to each other.

I parked behind a sky blue Ford Taurus that had a white sticker with red and blue lettering attached to the left side of the rear bumper. It read *'The Constitution Was the First Union Contract'*. It meant my youngest brother Truman was visiting as well and, in all likelihood, discussing UAW issues in between fourth and fifth servings of whatever hadn't made it into the mouths of anyone in the house who hadn't finished eating. I also spotted Jefferson's Econoline Van parked across the street.

A full house.

The two story, gray-bricked structure with its white columns under the portico had become the unofficial way station for misplaced Keller boys. Rosie and Rae had taken on the role of nurturers and confidants. Their home was 'the light tower on a lonely coastline that shone its eternal beacon of light, leading us through the fog and to home where a pot of chili was always waiting to be served'.

Rosie's quote, not mine.

I pushed the dimly lit doorbell and moments later the large oak door swung open. Truman's thick-bodied outline greeted me, complete with a plate of food in one hand.

"Hey, Linc," he said while crunching on a helpless pork chop. He turned and yelled, "It's Linc!" to nobody in particular.

Realizing that I had a momentary reprieve from a Union lecture, I eased past the carpeted front room where Truman had parked himself in front of their big screen television, laughing at one of those shows on the WB. He had a full tray of food and the remote. All he needed was a naked woman.

Heaven couldn't have had a happier citizen.

"Hi, Linc."

I turned and saw my medium height, mocha toned sister-in-law. Rae was shoeless; wearing her favorite cutoffs and a loose fitting shirt with Michigan State etched on the front. Her sparsely gray medium height Afro was evenly trimmed.

"Hey, Sis," I said. We hugged. "Man, talk about an opportunity to wipe out all the Kellers."

"It wouldn't work. You'd all just multiply," she said. "If there's any particular Keller you want to see, they're all here. Truman just finished off the last cow; Jefferson is upstairs with Ken. He wouldn't go visit with his grandmother because he heard Uncle Jeff was back in town."

"Funny how that little bugger seems to know before any of the rest of us," I said.

"Yeah. Sometimes I think that nephew of yours and Jeff were born under the same star. I should be worried," she said with a smiled. "Rosie's in the den listening to cassette tapes."

"How've you been?" I asked.

"Since the new facility opened, it's been one whirlwind moment after another."

Rae works as a Station Manager for a car rental company. Her office is located at Detroit's Metropolitan Airport and a recent surge in leisure travelers has forced her into some long days and nights. The rest of us have filled in where we could. Especially picking up my niece and nephew from school on the days when both Rosie and Rae are on jam.

"Well, you know we're all quite proud of you," I said.

"That's right!" Truman yelled from the front room.

Rae shook her head. "Have you eaten?" My answer was irrelevant, since she was leading me toward the kitchen. "Help yourself to whatever's left."

Macaroni, green beans, rolls and baked pork chops were the food items in separate glass trays located on the wood top counter. The kitchen had been recently remodeled. Home and garden meets urban renewal with just a hint of African renaissance.

"You here for the meal or is there something else you need to discuss?" she asked.

"I just met with Judge Warren Henderson and his wife, Sylvia."

"War Zone?" she said with genuine surprise.

"The same. Seems he wants to get some closure on the murder of his sister-in-law and hired me to sift through the information."

"I remember that story. What do you think he wants?"

"Answers for one. Overall, just some peace of mind. I told him that the odds don't favor closure. Eight years is a long time. It may have been just a robbery."

"You think you can help him?"

"He thinks I can. Jeff referred him to me."

"Well, Jeff's upstairs probably filling Ken's head with stories of sinister manhunts and Witness Protection Programs."

My seven-year-old nephew had the distinction of carrying on our parents' obsession with presidential names after they ran out of sons. Kennedy Keller had a special bond with Jefferson. A karma that started when they met in the netherworld.

"I'll talk with him later. I need to make a couple of phone calls and talk with Rosie," I said.

"You know where the phone is," she said, and then she nodded toward the den and changed the subject. "Rosie's in there, lamenting over the end of a golden era. His sulking always lead down one path."

I smiled wryly. "What is it now?"

"Only the latest in video camera technology. I'm sure he'll show it to you."

"Should I appear interested?"

"It would sure help me out," she said as she leaned forward and kissed me on the cheek. "I'm going upstairs to read. By the way, how are you and Candy doing?" she asked with a knowing smile.

"We're still talking," I said quickly.

"Consider yourself lucky. You know we can see through that stuff all the time."

"I know," I said. "God gave all women the special gift."

"That's true," she said pointing her finger at me in a mock gesture. "Male cleverness is an oxymoron we've tolerated for thousands of years. That tolerance is a special gift. I'll lecture no more," She hesitated a moment, then added, "Linc, I know asking a Keller to be careful is a waste of precious oxygen, but be careful."

"Always, Sis. Always."

I stepped into their renovated kitchen and picked up the cordless phone.

After punching in the familiar number, I waited for the more familiar response.

It only took a second to call Julie at INFO-SEARCH, knowing she'd work late just to avoid driving in rush hour traffic.

Julie occupies the office across from Keller Investigations and is the primary reason why my brother and I haven't gone the way of cyberspace and the Internet. For a reasonable fee, she takes care of those web walks for us.

Julie reluctantly answered on the fourth ring.

"I should've known it would be you, Linc," she rumbled into the receiver. I heard the keyboard singing its magical phrases in the background. I knew she had the phone cradled while she tapped away on some cyber hunt. "I'm one minute away from getting out of here and naturally you'd call."

"Call it the charm of the beast, Jules."

"I tend to think of it as the pain in the ass. What do you want?"

I began telling her about the case. She interrupted before I could finish.

"I remember that story. Yeah. Pretty sister. Young, did some free lance work. Wasn't she shot?" As she talked, the keyboard tapped out its music of the night. "Why are you interested?"

"Sniffin' mostly. Got a curious itch. Thought I'd scratch it before it grew."

"Yeah, right," she replied. "Anyway, I'll do a quick search and slide what I find, along with the bill, under your door."

"Jules, this obsession you have with paying bills ..... "

" ..... is the reason why I can stay in business, feed my children and support us in a comfortable life style ..... thank you very much."

"We pay on time," I said.

"You pay in time. There's a difference," she remarked.

"Yeah, but without the Keller business ..... "

" ..... I'd turn a profit. I'll dig up whatever's available. I gotta rush. Mom's keeping the kids and I have visions of hot dogs and ice cream being thrown up before the nights' over. Bye."

21

The second call was a little higher on the humility meter, but presented me with a nice excuse to call.

I swallowed and called the Homicide division of the Detroit Police Department's downtown headquarters.

My semi-committed main squeeze, Detective Candy Malone works in Homicide. Though our relationship had cooled over the last month, we still remained friends, whatever that meant.

The detective who answered the phone said she was out but would return shortly. I thanked him, punched in her pager number and left a lewd message.

The phone rang while I was filling my plate.

"Show a little class next time, Linc," she started in. "You said six instead of sex and the message took on a completely different meaning."

"I meant six. The meaning was clear. You got a minute?"

"For six?"

"Funny. No, I need your help with a dance through a mine field."

"What's her name?"

"His name is Knackton and his fingers are wrapped around an old case that's suddenly fallen into my lap."

She hesitated. "What case and how old?"

"Eight years ago. The homicide victim was Judge Henderson's sister-in-law."

"I remember that one," she said. "I'd just moved over to vice so I didn't have direct contact with the primaries on the case. It upset a lot of people around Detroit. I didn't know her but apparently she was one sharp lady."

"I've heard that."

"You also heard it was Knackton's case?"

"I heard a rumor," I said.

"And that rumor lead you straight to me." An exasperated sigh followed. "Linc, it's bad enough that you two are enemies ..... "

"We're not enemies," I interrupted. "The man was promoted to Lieutenant the same year Columbo entered the academy. His life hasn't advanced very much since then and he takes it out on anyone within breathing distance. Especially people who breathe in your bedroom."

"Which leaves me always caught in the middle," she said.

"I can think of a middle I'd much rather ..... "

"...Not now one track mind."

"Look, Candy, all I need ..... "

"I know what you need and what makes you think I will violate policy by showing you the case file?"

I smiled. "I already have copies of the file. What I need is the unofficial stuff. The things left out that the public wouldn't know."

Her sigh was long and heavy. "Look, I'm in the middle of two assignments and I haven't eaten this afternoon. I'll be back at the station in the next couple of hours. I have some papers to shuffle and from there, I'll see what I can do."

"You're the best," I said.

"Yeah. Seems like you would know that," she said with little conviction. "I'll call you later."

It was a subtle dig that I stored. Armed with my plate, I made my way into the den. Ladder-back chairs, a round table, and bookshelves, all in matching mahogany brought a rustic feel to the room where books and cassette tapes were the dominant theme.

The three brown patterned throw rugs that were woven and purchased at a Native American reservation in Upper Michigan blended well with the polished wooden floor. A recently purchased Compaq computer, complete with tower, speakers, microphone and built in CD, on top of a ergonomically perfect workstation rounded out their technology obsession.

Rosie lounged in his favorite brown club chair with his legs propped up on the ottoman, eyes closed, listening to a cassette tape through black wire thin earphones.

As gene pool degradation goes, Rosie had inherited our father's receding hairline. As more of his dome began to show, he compensated by growing more facial hair. He now sported a full beard and mustache with linking sideburns. The sporadic gray strands gave him the look of an aging radical looking for one more cause to defend.

I tapped him on the forehead. He opened his eyes and smiled.

He reached down and hit the stop button on his Walkman. "Our missionary kitchen attracts Keller's from both sides of the equator," he said.

I plopped down in the curved back armchair and sat my plate near the edge of the computer table. "If you started charging the same rates as the 'Top of the Renaissance' you'd get a different crowd."

"I can't afford to have the top of the house rotate so you get a full view of the neighborhood. The kids might like it, but it would shoot the budget."

"What's up?" I asked, pointing to a stack of cassettes.

"For me, the end of civilization as we know it. But for the world, the beginning of a new era in radio broadcasting."

"You're gonna change the station format?"

Rosie ejected the cassette and placed it on the stack. "The last Arbitron ratings sealed it for me. It's change or die."

In recent weeks Rosie's disposition had moved just to the left of cynical. His beloved 'Oldies' format at WHIP was not holding up in Detroit's highly competitive listener's market. The landscape really became heated when everybody's favorite Jazz station, WJZZ, suddenly, and with very little announcement, switched to an 'urban contemporary' format in order to compete with the powerful WJLB. The new station, known as WCHB, fought for their lucrative share of the teenage spending market. Other competitors like WQBX, 'the MIX', had carved out a dominant piece of the adult 'baby boomer' market with an 'oldies, contemporary, no-rap' format. The recent change at WGPR to a similar format had spelled doom for the all 'oldies' format that Rosie cherished. It was all tolerable until WGRV, 'The Groove', exploded into the market. Their play of 1970's classics had baby boomers dancing in their yogurt.

"So what's the next move?" I asked.

He sat up. The earphones hung loosely around his neck and a glint of mischief shone through the turmoil. "I've spent the last few weeks listening to stations from all over Michigan and I think I've finally found the voices who fit nicely into my idea for a new format. I'm calling it 'EnTalktainment' radio."

I stopped chewing and swallowed. "What is EnTalktainment?"

"More than just talk, listener-phone-in and the endless arguments. But something bolder. Talk that entertains. Stories that amuse. Guests from the world of artistic expression. Humor as an opiate for the tumultuous days."

"Rosie ..... "

"Listen up, Little Bro. I've found just the people who can pull it off. Check this out." He started pulling cassettes from the stack. "The six to ten a.m. slot would be handled by David Fair, currently an announcer and news director for WEMU in Ypsilanti. It's part of National Public Radio. David has a powerful morning voice, smooth transition anecdotes and knows enough about Michigan and Detroit to keep listeners engaged in the morning. Now from ten a.m. to two p.m. I'd bring on Andrea Vincent, currently holding down that time slot at WJKN down the road in Jackson. Her style is consistent with mid-morning fun and games, plus she does an excellent job of interviewing guests. I heard her interview a couple of dry authors. She made them sound entertaining."

"Are these folks going to play any music?"

"I don't know yet, the idea is still evolving. Next, the two p.m. to six p.m. slot would be held down by ..... you ready for this? John Arnold."

"You think you can convince him to switch stations?"

"His contract is coming up for renewal. I'm going to sure try. He already knows the afternoon audience. He does enough reading, researching and is wired into the Detroit community. He's a great listening talk show host with a flair for the spontaneous. The six p.m. to ten p.m. slot would go to Doug Massie, currently a newsman and talk show host with WKAR up in the road in East Lansing. His style would be perfect for that end-of-the-drive, time-to-settle-in audience. Then from ten p.m. to two a.m., I'd work that beginning midnight shift audience with Hugh Burrell, Mr. Blue Pig himself."

"Is he available?"

Rosie grabbed a dark blue newsletter. "Look. He's retired from the Police force, he's left the Blue Pigs group and he's doing motivational talks and consulting with youth groups. He'd be great for that audience."

"What about the two a.m. to six a.m. time slot?"

"I haven't decided yet. There are a couple of possibilities. I'd like to try and convince Jeffrey Miller to take on that slot."

"The brother who hosts 'Transition'?" I asked recalling the Sunday night talk show on Channel 50.

"Yeah. I think he'd be perfect although I'm not sure if he'd want to do radio at that time in the morning. Same thing for Lonnie Peek over at QBH. I think he'd be perfect, I'm just not sure he'd want the time slot. But I'll ask the question."

"Sounds good to me."

"It's got some holes, but I think it can be done." He stopped talking, saw what I had to eat and shook his head. "Sorry, Bro. I'm sure you didn't stop by just to hear how I'm going to revolutionize the industry."

"Yeah, that was one of the reasons. The other is this new case I just picked up."

"Oh, yeah? What is it?"

I told Rosie about the Deborah Norris case and all the surrounding information. As he would do with anyone, he listened intently, carefully and without interruption. When his forehead furrows, that's a signal that he's processing the information and connecting it with other pieces of information that he's absorbed over the years.

I told him as much as I knew. Mainly for two reasons; first, I trust his insights and secondly, being able to talk out loud to a confidant sometimes allows for new possibilities to be considered.

After I finished, he sat back and whistled.

"I remember that story. I was working as News Director and Announcer for WQBH eight years ago. Lot of stuff going on at that time. The story didn't stay in the headlines very long. It never occurred to me that the case wasn't solved. Why'd The Judge wait so long to get private help?"

"He says he wanted to support the system since he's professionally and politically connected. Now, he wants questions answered that the system couldn't answer so he and his wife can ease into retirement."

"I might be able to help," he stated mildly. Rosie saying he may be able to help is like Oprah Winfrey saying I might be able to promote your book.

"Help with what?" Truman asked as he pulled out a chair and plopped his stocky body down on the embroidered seat cushion. How he'd managed to ease into the room without either one of us hearing him would be one of life's little mysteries. Plus he was plateless, so I had reason to be concerned about my own food.

"Linc's working on a new case."

"Oh yeah? Something serious or just some penny ante divorce stuff?"

"Don't you have a strike or something you should be organizing?" I asked.

"Maybe. Are you exploiting any non-union people with a less than minimum wage job?"

I suppose it would be unusual for any of us to leave this planet without being tolerant of some form of verbal abuse from family members. The prospect of being trapped with Rosie and Truman in the same room meant that not only would I get my share of verbal abuse, but I'd get it along with someone else's.

I took the efficient route and filled Truman in on what I was doing.

"Wow. I'd forgotten all about that one. What do you think you'll find?"

"I don't know. Maybe nothing. Possibly something that confirms it was nothing more than a robbery." I slid my plate over to Truman and turned to Rosie. "You said something about helping."

"Guy I use to know worked for the *Free Press*. Name's Schaefer. Arlan Schaefer. Used to work the crime beat. It seems like he spent a lot of time hanging out at 1300 Beaubien and the Frank Murphy building. We met at a conference; sat up and drank one night and from then on he used to feed me stories, sometimes long before the other stations got a hold of them. I don't think he worked that story, but he always knew stuff that other people didn't know. He might be helpful."

"I'll call the *Free Press* tomorrow," I said.

"Wouldn't do you any good. Last I heard, he'd left the paper three years ago. I'm pretty sure he left Detroit. I still have some friends in the news business. Let me make a few calls tomorrow. I can probably find him."

"Thanks, Rosie." I checked my watch. "Well, it's getting late and I want to do a little more reading before turning in. Plus I'm expecting a call from Malone."

"How are things?" Rosie asked with a slight grin.

"We're okay."

"So were Richard Burton and Liz Taylor."

"I gotta go." I stood up and turned toward the door.

"Mind taking that with you?" he asked pointing to Truman.

Truman looked up. "I can have all of Local 385 organized and picketing your station for unfair labor practices just like that. Being president of a local has its advantages."

"You're dropping peas on the floor," Rosie countered. "Hey, Linc. I have this great new video camera that ..... "

I waved, eased back down the hall and out the front door. Night had finally set in and the air, though muggy, was comfortable. I fired up the Nova and clattered over to Grand Boulevard, followed the street past Henry Ford Hospital, over the newly repaired bridge and onto the Lodge

Freeway.

Earl Kluge's soft guitar strokes filled the Nova from the smooth Jazz station I'd started listening to at night. I had the beginning of a case that should take no more than a day or two to bring to resolution. I thought there'd be essentially nothing I'd learn that hadn't been revealed in eight years of investigating. After a few days, I'd be able to say to Judge Zone that there was nothing I'd learned that he didn't already know.

Unfortunately, being wrong about these matters had become far too common an occurrence in my line of work.

As I was about to find out, this case was no exception.

4

It was still early evening when I left the Keller Missionary retreat, so I drove over to the office to check on a few things before heading to my apartment.

I traveled the five and a half miles down the three-lane highway until I reached the Livernois exit. Four blocks past the University of Detroit's main campus is the office building where Keller Investigations is lodged with several other small, but growing, businesses on the street that housed more black-owned businesses than anywhere else in Detroit.

I bounded through the door and up the worn carpeted stairs to the second landing where Keller Investigations, INFO-SEARCH, African Artists Gallery and Joe's Collectible Records peacefully co-exist to our mutual advantage.

I keyed the frost windowed door and spotted the manila envelope lying on the floor with my name written in bold, black letters. A red trimmed voucher was paper clipped to the top.

Julie had worked fast and left a bill.

I carried the envelope over to my defaced, institutional oak desk, sat down in the squeaky swivel chair, hit the play button on the answering machine and dumped the contents of the envelope on top of the large desk calendar.

There were three messages for Jeff, the original Stealth Bomber. I wouldn't know if he was in or not unless I visually saw him sitting at his desk. We'd given new meaning to President Clinton's 'Don't Ask, Don't Tell' policy.

I leaned back in my squeaky swivel chair to look through the information Julie had left for me. I held a black and white, slightly faded picture of Deborah Norris at eye level. The reporter who'd written the story laid out the facts in a dispassionate display of journalistic sensationalism. What he couldn't state as fact, he presented through innuendo. Through it all, there were certain facts that he couldn't bend.

Deborah Norris had been shot once with a .22 caliber bullet. Her twenty-nine year-old body was found a few blocks from where she lived. She'd been lying there a few hours and there were no other signs of violation. As if being murdered wasn't enough of a violation. Robbery was listed as the motive.

'Sister-in-Law of City Prosecutor Found Shot to Death'

The grim headline and story didn't read well eight years ago and did little to brighten up the next millennium. I read through the remaining material. All newspaper articles. Each had its own spin on what happened. The police launched an intensive investigation. They'd gone to great lengths for answers that never came to light. I followed the story through its first few days, past her burial and sporadically until the story stopped drawing any attention. It was still unsolved and no longer important enough to warrant headline attention. The story died with her, but lived on with her family.

I glanced at the adjoining picture. The ashened-faxed copy did little to compliment her obvious aesthetic charm. I had no sense of tone, eye color or other radiant qualities. She flashed a smile that seemed to say it all. She appeared confident and certain with nothing in front of her except the world and all its possibilities.

That smile. I wondered what lurked behind that smile.

By the time I'd finished reading all the material given to me by Julie and The Judge, I had scratched out a page full of notes and questions. Trying to connect the dots on an eight-year-old picture would be almost an impossible task. Investigations seldom ran a straight line, up the middle and into the end zone untouched. I knew this one would be an inch by inch struggle on a rain drenched, mud caked, grassy field in Cleveland, down by four points with no time-outs and the clock running. Sometimes it's not so bad if you're on offense and Joe Montana is the quarterback. However, I was a gimp-kneed cornerback trying to run with Jerry Rice ..... and that's all bad.

• • •

I was top and bottom heavy with food and information when I keyed the door and walked up the flight of recently painted, not so creaky stairs to my upstairs apartment.

Living on Livernois Avenue among the many one-storied storefronts had proven to be quite advantageous. The access to services was beyond comparison and the office for Keller Investigations existed just a few scant blocks from where I sacked at night.

I had a bay window apartment located above an accounting service that came with an adjacent parking lot and a semi-conscious security service. There was usually a half-open eye attached to a security guard watching the cars at night and the owner liked the idea of having an ex-cop as an upstairs tenant. Something about it being a great tax write-off.

He went easy on the rent and I didn't shoot people on the premise.

The kind of peaceful co-existence we all strive for.

Unfortunately, one of the half-eyed security people somehow missed catching the people responsible for the tireless, abandoned Ford Galaxy sitting by the curb in front of my door. Three days ago, the car appeared in front of my apartment and after several calls to Detroit's abandoned car removal service, the Galaxy remained a permanent eyesore on a newly paved street. My last attempt at getting the car removed resulted in my being reminded that mine wasn't the only street in Detroit with an abandoned vehicle.

My apartment is a testament to functionality. Four rooms, no waiting. The furniture and few accessories followed me when I made the trek back from Oakland, California.

The answering machine resting on the round-top, three-legged coffee table flashed a digital four to grab my attention as I dropped the folder on my butt condusive recliner located in the front room by the bay window.

Four messages seemed a bit unusual for someone with an unlisted phone number. Despite its professed changes, phone security still paled in comparison to the ingenuity used to obtain information we normally shouldn't access.

The digitally prerecorded voice announced the date and time of each caller with detached indifference.

The first two calls were from Rosie reminding me of the informal get-together over dinner. He was cooking so all Kellers were obligated to show up.

I'd fulfilled my family obligations for that evening.

The third caller was a telemarketer wanting to sell me an insurance package that could be easily charged to my credit card.

Phone security. Another new oxymoron.

Candy Malone's voice rounded out the fourth call. A little more than an hour ago, she'd called to say she had information that might be helpful to my current case. She'd call later.

The call came in at 9:30 p.m. I checked my watch. 10:35.

Feeling full, but not particularly tired, I pulled a can of light beer from the fridge, clicked on the floor lamp, opened the window wider and settled onto my recliner to read through the Deborah Norris folder.

The combined information given to me by Julie and Judge Zone began to shape part of the picture of Deborah Norris. The real issue being; would the information there justify looking any further than a robbery attempt?

'I can smell a draw play' The Judge said when he gave me the file. Who better than a former all pro defensive end would know when not to bite on the obvious.

A draw play. Football vernacular for 'what being shown isn't really what's happening'.

The Judge didn't like the feel or smell of what happened to Deborah and eight years later I'd been hired as his cage rattler.

I began sifting through each piece of information like an original forty-niner. Maybe there was something hidden among the faded pictures, scratchy handwriting and form numbers.

Outside, the fading Livernois traffic provided a subtle distraction as I moved from one form to another.

Background noises were a common part of my concentration as far back as my boyhood years on Russell Street where the physical barrier between my neighborhood and Hamtramck was a set of railroad tracks whose trains roared through the daytime hours unnoticed and drifted through the night hours with calming serenity.

I liked the night noises of city living. Well, most of the noises.

That's probably why the soft ringing from the telephone jolted me out of a restful nod.

As the second ring sounded, I glanced down at my watch. It read a little past midnight. I'd dozed off for about twenty minutes, obviously not entertained by the information in the folder.

I lifted the receiver before the answering machine took over.

Malone's voice filled the noiseless void. She called to make sure I'd returned and she was only a couple of minutes away.

"I don't know how helpful this information is, Linc, but we should talk."

After she disconnected, I moved toward the bathroom to brush the taste of sleep out of my mouth.

We still had keys to each other's abodes, which I took as a good sign. The keys hadn't seen much use over the last few weeks.

I heard the door being keyed just as I'd finished filling the coffee maker with her blend of Vanilla Hazelnut.

I didn't really like the stuff but it helped to keep things conversational.

When Malone opened the door, I could tell it had been one of those nights. For homicide detectives, that usually meant every night. She wore her shoulder length jet-black hair tied in a ponytail revealing the fullness of her almond beige tone and darkly captivating eyes. Tired eyes that had seen too much of the tumultuous dark side of human nature.

She looked haggard and put-upon. For someone who went through great lengths to keep an aerobically toned, five foot eight figure, her shoulders drooped as if Atlas had told her to 'hold this for me and I'll be right back'.

"That coffee I smell brewing?" she asked as she dropped a manila folder on the sofa lounge and eased toward the recliner.

"Got your name on it," I replied.

She sighed as she sat down, leaned back and released the footrest.

After I poured the coffee, adding one teaspoon of sugar and one teaspoon of creamer, I walked in to where Malone sat and tapped her on the shoulder.

She opened her eyes, sighed and nodded thanks.

"Long night?" I asked pulling up the round, orange leather ottoman that didn't match anything in the apartment except the angles of my butt.

"Sometimes I'm not sure where the night ends and the day begins. The things that people do to one another over some of the most petty stuff in the world still leaves me in the dark."

Malone's talents, skills, street savvy and instincts had taken her a long way through the Detroit Police structure in a short time. She'd been labeled a star from the moment she left the academy and everything people said had come true. She had achieved more at the age of thirty-two than most folks had after thirty-two years of employment. A product of Detroit's East Side and Martin Luther King High School, she knew she wanted to be a cop the first time she heard a police siren in her neighborhood on Cadillac Street. Though street wise, she maintained that questioning 'I don't get it' approach to trying to understand the motives of people.

"The only difference between now and a million years ago is the choice of weapons. Other than that, the motives are pretty constant."

"Thank you very much, professor," she replied sarcastically. I held my hands up gesturing that I was sorry. "Don't mind me, Linc. You know how this work can be sometimes."

"What happened?"

While holding her cup of coffee, she moved her right forefinger around the edge of the cup's circle. That usually meant she'd been thinking long and hard. "We got a call about six o'clock this evening. Major disturbance over on Sheridan, between Charlevoix and Kercheval. This strung out nut, no-account-idiot, had gotten mad at his two stepchildren. He threw the five-year-old girl down the steps and threw the six-year-old boy out the top front window onto the sidewalk. The boy died." She stopped and glared at me. "You know why he did it?"

I didn't say anything.

"The kids had mistakenly thought that the white powder he left on the kitchen table was baking soda. They were trying to fix themselves something to eat because their mother wasn't home. Meantime, this fool wakes up out of a nod, notices them putting ingredients in a mixing bowl, asks about the powder he left on the table. They told him what they did and he went berserk. Now an innocent child is dead."

There was nothing I could say. I'd seen similar incidents from my cop days in Oakland. It was one of the reasons why I returned to Detroit and took up private investigation.

"Wasn't your fault, Candy. Human frailties weaken in direct proportion to the strength of the addiction."

"We're suppose to be better than that, Linc. We're suppose to be better."

"And we aren't. So there."

She faked a smiled. "Yeah, so there. Let's talk about your involvement with this case."

Actually, we needed to talk about many things. I just wanted to lengthen the amount of time I had with Candy. Our relationship had suffered a blow. Nothing as devastating as the last Holyfield/Lewis fight, but it was strained. Despite our busy schedules and informal socializing agreement, I missed her. For reasons far beyond her obvious sensuality and sexiness.

Although those reasons couldn't be discounted.

"Technically," she began, "everything points to robbery."

"That's what you think?"

"Based on the facts, I'd say yes."

"But based on your instincts?" I asked.

She leaned forward slightly. "Something feels out of sync. The Medical Examiner's report lists her time of death as sometime after ten o'clock and before midnight. It's believed that she was meeting someone."

I didn't know if The Judge had heard this possible conclusion. I made a mental note to ask him. "Any idea who?"

"No, but it fits the facts," Malone said. "But it doesn't give the motive."

"What's even more intriguing is that she was suppose to be headed out of town," I added.

"Yeah, we know that. But we don't know why. You have any ideas?"

"Pure guess work right now. She didn't tell her sister or the Judge. She just said she was going out of town for a couple of days but she'd be back in time to surprise her sister with the rest of her birthday gift."

I told Malone about what I had learned at my meeting with The Judge and Sylvia earlier that evening.

"What they told you is pretty much confirmed. Of course, there were other people interviewed, but none seemed to know where she was going or who she was supposed to meet." She sipped her coffee, making me wish I was a coffee cup, before continuing. "Phone records were checked and there was nothing unusual there. Her appointment calendar didn't tell us a lot. I have the impression that she didn't write down anything."

"But she was obviously going somewhere to meet someone about something," I said.

"That much we do know. We just don't know the other stuff."

"So you believe it was more than just a robbery," I said.

"I'd bet my badge on it. We don't have enough facts to support any other conclusion."

I stood up and walked over to the bay window. Staring outside, I noticed a group of teenagers, clad in their summer sleeveless basketball jerseys, baggy pants and Nike, Adidas and other well known footwear, strolling down Livernois Avenue, laughing and moving like specters across the concrete landscape.

"That's what The Judge meant by 'I can smell a draw play'."

"What do you mean?" Malone asked.

"He believes there's more to it."

"Anything he can prove?"

"No. That's why I'm in the picture," I said.

She stood up and walked over to me. "Linc, I'm obligated to tell you, professional to professional, you need to walk away from this case. The Detroit Police Department does not take kindly to citizen interference in its work unless it is to provide helpful information. Naturally, I can't tell you how to run your business, nor would I try. But, you need to be careful. You're walking on the turf of someone who doesn't like you anyway."

I smiled. "If I left you alone, Knackton would leave me alone."

"Probably, but don't forget; he's a cop. A veteran who knows a lot of people who owe him favors. On any given day, he can be a good investigator. Most days he chooses just to put in his time with the least amount of trouble. And he knows a lot about trouble. He's a smart cop who knows how to make trouble. Once he finds out that you're investigating this case, and he will, he'll do everything short of killing you to get you out the way. Don't underestimate him. There are a lot of people who did and right now they're sitting in Jacktown trying to keep a tight butt until their parole hearing."

"Well, fortunately, I'm not breaking the law."

"Doesn't mean he won't make trouble," she said firmly. "Just watch your step."

"I'd rather watch you."

She smiled. "I'm sure you would. Look, I'm out of here. I desperately need some sleep before my pager goes off."

"You can sleep here," I offered.

"Normally I'd say okay."

"But ..... ?"

"But ..... I know you had an intimate relationship with Erotica Tremane. I saw that look pass between you two at her husband's funeral. At first I thought it didn't bother me, but since then I've learned that it does."

She stopped to breathe so I tried to interrupt.

"And don't bother trying to explain it away or justify it as 'helping a client during a difficult time'. Quite frankly, it wouldn't matter what you said. I know we've had this loosely defined relationship in the year we've been seeing each other. And we never really voiced expectations. You didn't pressure me and I didn't pressure you. That made it fun. But during that time, it never dawned on me to worry about those nights we weren't together if you'd be sleeping with someone else. I knew I wouldn't, but I just assumed you wouldn't either. When the reality of that assumption hit me, I had to stop and reevaluate what I want."

Funny how men and women think differently. "Shouldn't I be a part of that discussion?"

"I'm not sure. Should I have been a part of the discussion when you slept with Mrs.Tremane?"

Silence seemed to be the best answer to that question.

"No answer? Probably just as well. My problem, of course is I've never cared about someone the way I care about you. In my mind, the foundation we had has been shaken."

Loosely defined relationship? "Shaken beyond repair?"

"Shaken, not stirred," she quipped.

"So, as the one being denied the pleasure of your ..... company, what do I do in the meantime?"

Candy smiled. "Work your case, take two cold showers and call me in the morning." She put her arms around my neck, kissed me hard and slowly worked her tongue around the outer layers of my lips. Like I said, I normally don't care much for that Vanilla Hazelnut, but it sure tastes good like this. She pulled away, looked down and then gave me a hither stare. "Better make that three cold showers."

"Maybe we could negotiate ..... "

"Bye, Linc."

Despite my assertions, Candy insisted on leaving without the pleasure of my company. I stood in the bay window and watched as she wheeled her Pontiac Grand Am down Livernois.

As I headed to the shower, I knew that the best remedy for an excited libido would be to plunge myself back into the Deborah Norris case and not think about what Malone had just done to me.

5

Throughout the night, I tossed and turned so much that I could have easily been mistaken for the main course at a cookout. Just stick an apple in my mouth and serve me along with the spinach salad. Maybe the restlessness came as a result of Malone's visit or the cerebral, unfocused shadows that danced in and out of my head throughout the night. More than once, it seemed like the images were reaching out to me.

When the radio finally kicked on, I welcomed the morning knowing I'd have a fixed activity to occupy my mind. Those fading images moved further to the back of my thoughts as radio personality Johnny J stumbled through reading the weather as his lead into a sixties tune entitled 'Open The Door To Your Heart' by a one hit wonder named Darrel Banks.

Looking at clear skies and temperatures in the mid-eighties, I opted for a casual look. I donned a light blue, short sleeve shirt, dark blue Levi Dockers and black shoes. I grabbed my all purpose blue sport coat and the dark tinted, gold trimmed sunglasses I've owned since my days as a defensive back with the Raiders.

I made it out the door and into my Nova in just under twenty minutes. Though the Keller Office is only several blocks up Livernois from where I live, I decided to drive since my activities wouldn't be limited to the office.

Livernois Avenue was in the midst of its own revitalization. It's lifeblood are the scores of services offered by the majority of black business owners who've formed a healthy alliance to preserve their way of life. The rows of one-level storefronts is reminiscent of a scene out of a Jimmy Stewart movie, complete with people sweeping their front sidewalk, the University of Detroit/Mercy main campus and the new bicycle patrol service being offered by the local police precinct. The two-person patrol was part of the new 'Community Policing' program I'd read about in an article written by a Dr. Garrison Brock, a professor of Criminology teaching at the State University at Detroit's downtown campus.

After I'd crossed Davison, I pulled into the parking lot next to the three-story building that served as an incubator for several small businesses needing a place to start.

Among that illustrious crew is INFO-SEARCH, the information search and seizure creation of Miss Julie Block. Her office sits across from Keller Investigations. Jeff and I liked that advantage. She did too, only she'd confess to that fact during the final stages of torture.

I bounded up the two flights of steps, ignoring my office and heading straight to Julie's.

Opening the clear glass door, I was greeted by Mary Cooper, the office receptionist and Julie's first line of defense. Mary sported multi colored beaded dreadlocks that Julie grudgingly agreed to in fair trade for efficiency. A twentyish college student with chestnut skin, Mary's standard greeting line left little to her imagination and quite a bit to mine.

"Hi, Mr. Keller. How goes the dick business?' she giggled. Like always.

"Mostly up and down," I deadpanned. "Is the boss in?"

She continued giggling. "Yeah. Go on in."

I thanked her and opened the door to Julie's office. Mary was still giggling as I caught sight of Julie leafing through several printed articles.

Julie has the kind of bosomy, hourglass figure that was bequeathed to her by a fan dancer from King Arthur's court. She knows she has the figure, so she dresses to accent what's there and leaves you to imagine the rest. Her style draws you in and her mind holds you at bay.

She's a businesswoman. Make no bones about that fact. Dressed in a gazelle silk jacket and belted dress, she's a five foot, five inch survivor with a cat's charm and panther's sense of purpose.

She peered up, looking over the edges of her reading glasses. "I heard Mary giggling. Another dick joke?"

"What can I say, Jules. Always leave them wanting more."

"Don't book yourself at an open mike just yet. Mary giggles while reading diet books."

"Who wouldn't?" I strolled over to her glass- topped desk as she clipped the articles together and slid them into a large envelope. "I need a favor," I said.

"Then run for office. This is a business," Julie said as she turned toward her computer monitor. She slid the keyboard onto her lap and began tapping information onto the screen.

"That information you downloaded for me yesterday on Deborah Norris was helpful. Thanks."

"Mmmmm. And?"

"And I want to pursue another angle. Just as a way of giving me some sense of who she was."

Julie kept tapping. "What did you have in mind that you can afford?"

I liked Julie. She's the big sister I was denied the privilege of picking on. "I want to get some sense of Deborah's work. Can you put together a collection of the articles and other pieces of work she did?"

"That's easy enough. Can you pay your bill?"

"I do have a client," I said.

"Fine," she said. "Leave a retainer with Mary and I'll get started this afternoon."

"Thanks, Jules. You're the best."

"I know. But, it'll still cost you," she replied pointing toward the door.

I'd almost made it through the door when Julie called out. "By the way, Linc. How're things with you and Malone?"

"Okay, I guess. We saw each other last night."

"All night?" she asked slyly.

"I refuse to answer on the grounds that it might stimulate me."

"Men and their two heads." She pulled open her desk drawer and began writing down a phone number. "Here. This is the phone number to 'Terry's Enchanted Garden'. It's a flower shop, boutique and book-store. Pat Terry is the co-owner with her mother. They're down Livernois between Outer Drive and Seven-Mile. Send Malone a bouquet of flow-ers."

"Flowers? To a police station?"

"Why not?" she said handing me the slip of paper.

I thanked her and told her I'd return later on that afternoon.

"Where're you headed?" she asked nonchalantly.

"It's sniffin' time. I have to pay the bills you know."

•   •   •

I stepped across the hall, opened the door to Keller Investigations and caught sight of Jefferson; my glossy domed eldest brother, sitting at his corner desk filling out some paperwork.

"How's Pittsburgh?" I asked easing around to my desk.

Jefferson didn't bother looking up. "A lot cleaner."

"Found who you were looking for?" He didn't bother answering, just held up the standard looking, yellow-paged carbon forms he fills out when a fugitive has been apprehended. He probably found the question insulting. I changed the subject. "I have Judge Zone as a client. He says you recommended me. I didn't know you two knew each other."

Jefferson stopped writing, picked up his sunglasses and began clean-ing the dark lenses with a white tissue from a box on his desk. "The Judge is a good man. It's too bad what happened to his sister-in-law. It ain't a secret. His disappointment with the lack of progress is well known in certain circles."

"Unfortunately, Knackton is part of that circle," I said.

Jeff shrugged.

I opened the folder and leafed through its contents. "According to the paper, the motive was robbery."

"According to the paper, Dewey won," he replied nonchalantly.

"You think different?"

"Doesn't matter what I think. Only what The Judge believes."

I rubbed my eyes, suppressing a yawn. "Why'd he wait so long to have someone else look into it?"

"Detroit politics," he muttered. "Try not to get too close. You'll get burned."

I stood up and stretched. "You think there's more to it than just robbery?"

"I think The Judge thinks there's more." He turned slightly toward me. "It may be nothing more than a robbery. Who knows? A good man wants answers to a bad situation. Maybe you can help, maybe not. You do what you can and let the rest fall where it may."

"Why didn't you look into it?" I asked.

"I don't like searching through gray areas," he said while sliding his forms into a manila envelope. "Did enough of that working for the government. What I do now is easier. Man breaks the law and runs. I get hired to find him. I like things straightforward and simple. No gray."

It wasn't the first time he alluded to his previous work as a United States Marshal. There were stories he seemed unwilling to tell and I know better than to ask.

"You in town a while?" I asked.

"A while." His hand was on the doorknob.

"Hey, Jeff." He turned; his sunglasses hid those brown eyes people say he stole from our mother. "Thanks for the recommendation."

"We need the work," he said. "The overhead is killing us."

He eased that carved six foot, two inch frame out the door like a silent predator. He rarely made time for small talk. I looked around the office of Keller Investigations. The two wooden-top desks were cast-offs from the offices of some nameless administrators within the Detroit Public School system. The phones were early touch-tone, the copy machine whistled and the fax machine left a long vertical black line from the top to the bottom of every faxed page. Our chairs swiveled in name only. Creaked seemed a better description. We had two institutional green file cabinets and the unmatching chairs for clients should have been designated for only starting fires. Our office was in a building owned by a lawyer named Uhlander Means. He had the building labeled as an incubator for new businesses and received a tremendous tax write-off.

"Yeah. The overhead's killing us," I said. A long time ago, I gave up trying to sort out the mindset of Jefferson, the eldest brother of the Keller quartet. I decided that as the eldest he had certain inalienable rights that I, as the third oldest didn't deserve to have clarified. At the age of forty eight, retired from the United States Marshals Office and a full-time Fugitive Recovery Agent or bounty hunter, Jeff had mastered the subtle art of talking through his actions.

His departure left me with a vacant, quiet office and no urgent messages. I had a couple of clients to contact and some unrelated work that I needed to finish before I hit the streets to search for answers to an eight year mystery.

6

After two solid hours of undisturbed work, I stretched and glanced at my watch just as the phone rang.

"Keller Investigations," I answered.

"Mr. Keller. This is Sylvia Henderson. I hope I'm not disturbing you."

"No problem Mrs. Henderson. What can I do for you?"

"There's some additional information I'd like to share with you about Deborah. Do you have time available today?"

"I can always make time Mrs. Henderson. Where and when would you like to meet?"

I heard pages being turned during the momentary void. "I have two morning appointments and lunch with some committee members. I expect to be finished by two o'clock. Say ..... two-thirty?"

I agreed. "Where?"

"On the corner of Kercheval and Yorkshire, there's a storage facility. I'll meet you in front of the building."

We agreed on the location and rang off. She wanted to share some additional information about Deborah and we'd meet at a storage facility and without Judge Zone.

I let it go. Whatever was there, I'd find out later.

What I needed were answers. Answers to questions about a free lance writing free spirit named Deborah Norris. I hoped my first stop would help.

According to the information in the folder, Deborah lived in the

Silent Suspicion

Franklin Court townhouses located near Chene and Lahser only blocks from downtown. The dumpster that served as her temporary coffin was located three blocks from her address.

I thought I'd do some asking around. Though eight years is a long time, sometimes there are people who hang around an area long enough to become experts on its history and culture. Not dissimilar to the front porch mothers who kept a watchful eye on the sights and sounds of the neighborhood back during the Keller adolescent days.

The Franklin Court townhouses were part of a renovation scheme that took place in the late 1970s. It's concept of middle class housing for single working professionals worked well enough. During the 1980s the area attracted many new professionals who were just starting to carve out a career in entry level professional positions with the Big Three and several merged banking operations. I'd only seen the area in passing during one of my infrequent trips back to Detroit from Oakland. It was hailed as a successful housing attraction. Which meant that people rotated in and out of the area as they moved up the corporate ladder.

Hopeful seemed to be my best option.

Despite the fact that several of the carports were filled, I didn't think I'd find too many people at home.

Back when I was a cop, canvassing the neighborhood was a critical preliminary step in an investigation. The idea being; you never know who happened to be looking out a window or who consistently tracks the movements of their neighbors.

My field supervisor would say, "Sometimes you get lucky."

However, eight years is a long time.

I parked in someone's reserved spot, locked the Club onto the steering wheel and slid on my jacket as I strolled up the sidewalk to the door where Deborah used to live.

I pushed the black doorbell several times, knocked, waited and finally gave up. My first suspicion had been confirmed. No one home. I walked over to the next townhouse and repeated the process. Knowing

I wouldn't be mistaken for a Jehovah's Witness or a recruiter for the church of Latter Day Saints, I figured it wouldn't hurt to tell the truth. The only problem being; I didn't have much success finding someone home who'd listen to the truth.

After ninety minutes of doorbells, taps on windows and people peering through curtains, the final tally of people who answered their door came to four. Three of whom had lived in the area less than two years and the fourth threatened to call the police if I didn't go away. Hot, tired and completely frustrated, I heeded the advice of the fourth person and decided to go away.

I'd slung my jacket over my shoulder and had made it within a few steps of the Nova when a red and white Pontiac Sunbird parked in the adjacent spot.

A medium height, cinnamon tone man in a black striped-suit stepped out of the car, complete with a black leather brief case.

I asked if I had parked in his spot. He nodded that I hadn't and moved with a determined pace toward the townhouse where Deborah used to live.

As he pulled the door key from his pocket, I moved up behind him, calling out as I approached.

He turned. His eyes and general manner conveyed a this-better-be-good attitude.

I stopped several feet from him.

"Sorry to bother you my man," I said. "My name is Lincoln Keller and if you don't mind, I'd like to ask you a few questions."

"You a cop?" he asked in an impatient baritone.

"Not anymore," I replied. I removed one of my business cards and gave it to him.

"A private investigator huh? A regular Sam Spade."

"More Sam than Spade. Mind if I ask you a few questions."

"What if I do mind?"

"Then I move to plan B."

"Which is?"

"Ask you nicely," I said flashing a mock grin. He was all of five seven, stout, late thirties, clean-shaven and trying to sneer me into going away. "Won't take but a couple of minutes."

"First let me ask you what you're investigating?" he said not giving an inch.

"A murder that took place around here about eight years ago. In fact, the woman who was murdered, lived here."

He hesitated for just a moment. "Deborah Norris?"

I nodded and stepped closer. "Did you know her?"

"You might say that."

I grinned. "Well, I might say a lot of things. Did you know her?"

He turned toward the door, slipping his key into the lock. "Yeah, I knew her."

"How did you know her?"

He peered over his left shoulder, staring with eyes that could melt a Minnesota winter. "We were lovers."

7

We sat in beige colored director chairs on the small back deck looking onto the grassy courtyard of the similarly built townhouses. A simple, round glass top table with rubber coasters provided the support for the two bottles of light beer that forged the initial bonding.

His name was Winston Hill. A former middle manager with one of the Big Three auto companies and currently unemployed ..... again.

Divorced from his wife of eleven years, he returned to Detroit two years ago after being downsized from an automotive supplier in central Ohio. He'd been through three downsizing experiences in six years. The last one took its toll on his marriage. He returned to Detroit, hoping to recapture some of the luck he lost when he moved his family across the industrial Mid-West. He didn't believe that he was out after three strikes. As long as he could keep fouling off the pitch, he still had a chance.

"I'm not the only one pounding the beat looking for a job," he said after downing a large gulp. "Most of the people out here are living the lie. Trying to maintain the front while their back is being blown away."

"I didn't realize it was that bad."

"You don't know the half of it. These outplacement firms are a joke. Most of the people in my so-called network are also unemployed and companies who place want ads don't even have the common courtesy to send you a note saying they at least received your resume. When I'm not job hunting, I'm doing Temp work through a local agency that specializes in placing managers with organizations that need someone to fill in during someone's vacation or sick leave. It feels like a meat farm out here.

Smile for the man and hope they'll lend a hand. The great corporate promise huh? What a joke?"

"It's not that I'm not interested, but how'd you know Deborah?"

He nodded. "I don't blame you, homeboy. Most of the time I don't like listening to me either. "Another beer?"

I declined.

He twisted the top off a beer pulled from small, ice filled cooler next to his chair. "Deborah used to live in this apartment. My ex-wife and I lived right across the courtyard. We'd been married just over a year. She worked for a software company and I was a first line supervisor on the afternoon shift at the Connor plant. She worked mornings. It wasn't the best arrangement, but we were young, eager and stupid."

"Sounds like love to me."

"Did to me, too. Anyway, Deborah would sit out on this deck, writing articles for different papers and magazines. Whenever I got up during the latter part of the morning, I'd want to sip my coffee outside on the deck. We started out waving good morning to one another. Not every morning, but on those mornings she came out, I made sure I came out as well."

"How long did this go on?"

"Bout a month or so. Finally, one morning she waved me over and invited me to have coffee with her" He stopped. "On the deck."

"At first."

"Yeah, at first. So I found out she was a free lance journalist, she loved writing, she was unattached and a stone fox. Now, having said that, you know what was really her most attractive quality?"

I didn't answer.

"Her ability to embrace the moment and squeeze it for all it was worth. She was an interesting dichotomy. On the surface she gave this illusion of being disorganized, but underneath, her mind and sense of information compilation was like nothing I'd ever seen. She could sit and write for hours at a time. Pulling details from her head like faster than a

Pentium processor. Complete concentration. Serious and precise. Then she'd go party with the same amount of dedication. Don't let her get together with any of her runnin' buddies. They could dance, drink and party all night. Seems like there was always a celebration whenever Deborah had a story or an article published."

"You remember any of her runnin' buddies?"

"There were really only two." He scratched his head and rubbed the front of his chin. "Sharron Westlake for one and MiShaun Lucas was the other."

"Any idea where I can find them?"

He paused. "Not really."

His answer had all the ambiguity of someone trying to avoid an honest answer. "Did you try keeping in touch over the years?"

"Naw, not really."

He gave me the proper spelling of MiShaun's name. I sipped my remaining beer while Winston continued his confessional.

"Couple of times when my wife went to St. Louis to visit her family, I stayed here. Usually because I had to work on the weekends. But each time, it was during a celebratory weekend of some sort. So when I'd drag in and turn on the light, I'd notice her light was on and there'd be music and laughter drifting out of the window. So I'd invite myself over. Just for a drink, nothing more. That's how I met MiShaun and Sharron."

"Any idea if they're still around?"

He thought a moment. "I would imagine so. Eight years is a long time. I ..... I haven't given much thought to eight years ago."

Death either brought people together or pushed them apart. Winston didn't seem anxious to talk about the separation.

I switched to another subject. "How'd you end up in here in Deborah's old place?"

"Luck, coincidence, the curse of the Pharaohs. I don't know. I hoped being back here would change my luck. The place was clean and available, so I jumped on it while I had the chance."

I stood up and stretched. "After she was found, I know the police canvassed this area and talked to a number of people. I don't recall seeing your name on any of their lists. Why didn't you tell the cops what you told me? For the record anyway."

"Because nobody asked me," he said in a mocking tone. "You see, we'd moved out a month earlier. I was promoted to middle manager and transferred to a plant in Kokomo, Indiana. Nine months later, I was thrown my first strike. Downsized like a big dog. I didn't know Deborah had been murdered until two or three months after the fact. I just found out in passing."

"Must have been rough?"

He paused. "It should have been. But about that same time, I got wind of the downsizing rumor. I felt bad, but I had more real world concerns. The second time it happened, I figured everything would be all right, but the third time was too much. My wife and I called it quits and I came back here." He took another sip of his beer. "You know, I was raised by a strict father and mother. They believed that hard work and effort was its own reward. Put in your time, do your work, treat people nicely and rewards would be forthcoming. Lord knows I bought into that crap and look where it got me. Divorced, back living in Detroit, looking for full time work in between part time gigs, in debt and not really qualified for anything. I'm a shining example of the American dream turned upside down. So where's my reward? What do I get for those years and hard work and effort?"

He wasn't looking for an answer from me and I didn't offer one.

"I'll tell you what I got." He put his hand behind his back and made a jabbing gesture at his butt. "Know what I mean? I won't let that happen again. When I find the right hustle, I'm going to milk it for all I can and to hell with everybody else."

I'd never been downsized, but I had been screwed. I imagined one was just a fancy way of saying the other. I didn't have a good response, so I decided it was time to leave.

"Winston. I appreciate your help. I don't want to take any more of your time."

"Time I got plenty of. You want to borrow some? I can let you have it cheap."

"Next time I'm running short on sleep, I'll call you."

I stepped off the deck, choosing to follow the sparsely grassed path around to the front.

"You know something, Keller?" Winston asked. I stopped. "You never did ask me about the sleeping episode with Deborah."

"Along the way, I decided it was none of my business. It was a shared time between you and her. That's probably where it should stay."

"I cared about her. It was fun being around her. And for a time or two we took the fun past the line. I never regretted what happened. If anything, I regretted that it didn't more often. I think we just happened to catch each other at a weak moment. After a while we acted like it never happened. Then three months later, I was transferred. Fortunately, my wife never knew."

But she probably suspected. I decided not to give him a lecture on how most private investigators earn their money. I could build a business on what wives suspect ..... and know. After working a few of those cases, it seemed clear to me that I didn't want to add to the misery that reasonable people inflict on themselves. If his wife never mentioned her suspicions, then as far as I was concerned, he could live with the illusion.

"Thanks again Winston."

He walked me to the front of his townhouse, we shook hands and I eased into the Nova, unlocked the 'Club', fired up the engine and followed the side street onto Lahser.

Sometimes you get lucky.

My mind spun like a gyroscope. Thoughts moving symmetrically around some centrifugal core. I played through my conversation with Winston, the documents I'd read the information given to me by Judge Zone and Sylvia, just trying to make sense of what I knew and who

Deborah Norris was.

One night, eight years ago, she had dinner with her sister and brother-in-law. From there, she left to go out of town to 'follow up on something we all take for granted' and several hours later her body was discovered by a homeless person who had the decency to call the police. The papers got hold of the story and wrote that it was a robbery and the killer was never found.

Why?

Who was she meeting?

What lead was she following?

If a bolt of lightening strikes a tree and the tree falls on a house, destroying most of its structure, insurance companies call it an act of God. The lesser informed among us call it a random occurrence. Knackton and the other officers involved with the Deborah Norris case knew it wasn't random and clearly not an act of God.

I knew there was more going on than what I'd read or heard, but what?

There was a corner gas station at the next exit so I pulled up next to the kiosk with the white lettered, blue sign where a working phone is implied to exist.

The sound of highway traffic made hearing the dial tone a little difficult, but not impossible as I punched in a phone number.

I gave the operator the name. She told me the phone number was unlisted and couldn't be of additional service.

It was customer service at its highest point.

I punched in the number of a more reliable service.

While the phone rang, I scanned the area, checking out the street traffic, pedestrians and the panoramic view of the Golden Arches, billboards and other scenic beauties that fill the visual void when moving along the highway.

"Hello. INFO-SEARCH," Mary answered on the second ring.

"Hi Mary. It's Linc."

"Hi Linc. How's the ..... "

"Only when we see each other Mary. That's when I'm at my wittiest. Is the boss in?"

"Hold on, Linc," she said suppressing a giggle.

I spent more time on hold than a seventh inning stretch. Julie finally answered.

"It's me. Jules. You busy?"

"Would saying 'yes I am' make you go away'?"

"No."

"Then what is it?"

"I need a location and phone number for a name I'm about to give you."

"Call an operator."

"I did."

"Use a phone book."

"Now why would I expect to have a phone book at a phone kiosk?"

"When are you going to buy a cellular phone?"

"I don't want to be reached that badly or talked to that much."

She sighed. "What's the name?"

"MiShaun Lucus. I'm not sure of the spelling."

"You need it now?" she asked as I heard her fingers working the keyboard.

"It would help since I'm out and about."

Julie has access to more software programs that do so many different things that sometimes I wonder if she hacks into government offices and reads confidential mail. Her ability to instantly access information, going into the right databases at the right time is primarily why she's become increasingly successful. I once kidded her about becoming a professional hacker since she was so adept at accessing databases. She peered over her reading glasses and said, "I have two children to raise." A freight-hauler roared by drowning out all other sounds for a few moments.

"Did you hear me, Linc?"

"No," I yelled back. "What did you say?"

"I have a MiShaun Lucus, that's M-I-S-H-A-U-N on Dickerson Street near Mack. I did a cross-reference with the Detroit High School database and found her as a 1976 of Cass Tech. I did a quick run through the local periodicals and found her name in a picture with Trevor Stallings. She's referred to as his Assistant Director."

"Trevor Stallings? Where do I know that name?"

"Stallings has been a real mover and shaker on the Detroit scene over the last decade. Acquired their family wealth through a string of Cosmetology schools. Big time activist and community organizer, served on several commissions for Detroit and Wayne County."

I rolled the name around in my head while Julie kept reeling off his resumé.

"Real big in Detroit politics," she continued. "Comes from a politically active family."

Nothing Julie said seemed to click until I happened to turn away from the noise being made speeding tire treads and looked across the highway. Then it all came together.

"Never mind, Julie," I said interrupting her monologue. "I know who he is. Slide your bill under the door, okay? And thanks."

I hung up and walked to the edge of the sidewalk, fixed on what had just become an interesting complication to the case.

There it was. Larger than life, displayed like a smiling salesman on a billboard over the Largo Lounge and Grill and up from the Lodge freeway. The face of Trevor Stallings, community activist, politically wired and the person for whom MiShaun Lucus served as an Assistant Director.

Trevor Stallings. The man with a new vision for Detroit. The man with the courage to make change happen, was currently running for one of the two vacated seats on Detroit's City Council.

"It figures," I said.

8

Realizing that no investigation ever runs a straight line to the heart of the matter, I needed a few minutes to rethink my strategy and satisfy my growling stomach. My beer brunch with Winston hardly qualified as a nutritional pick-me-up.

The visible evidence of the approaching noon hour could be seen in the lines of cars crammed into the drive thru lanes of Detroit's best known service employers. The fast food giants had drawn in their daily addicts with all the marketing skill of an illegal pharmaceutical supplier. They lined up like weaning drug users at a methadone clinic. Tempted as I was to join the other dependents, I recalled the unsolicited grief I'd received lately from Malone, Julie, Rae, Mary Cooper and even Rosie. They were all convinced that my late thirties arteries were going to become permanently clogged with the remains of Big Macs, Whoppers, Double-deckers and a large order of fries. So I vowed to adapt a healthier approach to nutritional pleasure.

I replayed the morning events over a Taco salad and a small order of fries.

Before rolling back on the streets to meet with Sylvia Henderson, I did manage to get Trevor Stallings office address and phone number. As the Executive Director of 'Empower Detroit', he held one of the four most visibly powerful public service positions in Detroit and Wayne County.

Where he worked was no secret, however my phone call to his office told me that getting an audience with anyone on his staff qualified as one of the twelve labors of Hercules.

Despite my urgent lie, the woman who answered the phone said that the earliest appointment I could get with MiShaun would be the middle of next week.

So much for serving the people.

I considered another approach during my cruise from the Lodge Freeway over to I-94 where I made a hasty exit on the pot hole ramp.

Once on Kercheval, I followed the storefronts, small businesses and service agencies to the U-Store-It facility that sat off the main street and north of a recently cleared out lot.

Sylvia Henderson is a class act in sling-back heels. The calming wind in an urban storm. Dressed in a blue-belted cotton jacket and slim pants, she glided from the driver's side of a mint green Lexus. She walked with a protective aura of grace that would stop the mounted charge of warring factions.

"Mr. Keller, I'm so glad you could meet me on such short notice."

"It's my pleasure, Mrs. Henderson. Please call me Linc."

"Ah, yes," she said. "My husband has informed me of your family's presidential references. You have a brother named Jefferson. Am I correct?"

"Eldest of the four. My second eldest brother's name is Roosevelt and I have a younger brother named Truman."

"The reason behind the names?"

"My mom's favorite President's. Blame her."

"She only had four that she liked?"

"Actually there were five. After Truman was born, my old man noticed a mounting food bill so he decided to stop making boys. My brother Roosevelt decided to finish off the quintet by naming his son Kennedy."

"Will there be other Keller men whose first names are the last names of former presidents?"

"I'm not sure. In my limited lifetime that leaves Nixon, Ford, Carter, Reagan, Bush and Clinton."

Sylvia smiled. "Well, you could always work with Washington, Adams,

Jackson or Coolidge."

"Or Taylor, Fillmore, Harrison, Wilson or Cleveland."

"Cleveland Keller? Could work. What do you think?"

"I think I'm glad mom only had the five favorites."

"Yes, me too," she motioned toward the front of the building. "Walk with me Lincoln. I have something I want to show you."

We walked past several blue painted, white tinted metal doors with black numbers spray painted in the lower left corner. The lack of dissimilar design and color of the doors impressed me. Sylvia stopped in front of one of the doors, keyed the lock and pulled the door up.

The cedar block room contained a number of brown boxes that only varied in size. Taped closed, marked and stacked to maximize efficiency, there was little doubt as to the previous owner. Sylvia clicked on the overhead tube light.

"I couldn't bring myself to throw away any of her things," she stated. "Somehow it seemed I'd be giving up on knowing the truth about what happened. Rather than torture myself with the daily reminder of not knowing, I decided to bring her things here. That way, I'd at least know they were safe until ..... "

" ..... Until what, Mrs. Henderson?"

She sighed. "Until I could bring myself to some peaceful resolution."

"Why are we here?"

She moved slowly around the room, checking the side markings on each box. "There's a box of her materials that I thought might be ..... ah, there it is."

She pointed to a medium sized, rectangular shaped box sitting on top of a larger box. I grabbed the box by its open-end handles and carried it over to the door.

The box was a little heavier than it looked and I could only carry it comfortably by lifting it up to my left shoulder. Large, black felt pen letters spelled out the word FILES across both sides.

Sylvia closed and locked the door while I waited for an explanation.

I set the box down on the yellow lined tarmac. "What kind of files are in here?"

"From what I can tell, these are all the stories Deborah worked on during her free lance career. I thought they might be helpful to your investigation."

No doubt the files would tell me something about the nature and character of Deborah Norris, but the real information would have been in the place where she lived. The style and arrangement of furniture, the clothes bought and how they hang in a closet, the books, magazines and newspapers and their location in the home. Even the location of the toothpaste, soap and other cosmetics in the bathroom would have told me a lot more, a lot faster about the nature and character of Deborah Norris.

Unless there were pictures somewhere in the police file, I'd never know the orderliness of her home environment. Interviews and files represented the next best truth.

"They'll probably be helpful, Mrs. Henderson. I'm assuming you have already gone through everything."

"I did. Everything is accounted for except her music box."

"Music box?"

"Deborah found an antique-looking music box during her trip to New Orleans. She used to store pieces of jewelry and other things. It was a cute box that she kept on the stand by her bed. When I went to move her things I noticed it was gone and for the life of me, I have no idea where it could have gone."

"Did you mention it to Knackton?"

"Yes," she sighed. "But he didn't seem to make much of it."

My own experience with Knackton said just the opposite. Despite our fur raising, mark-out-my-territory experience concerning Malone, I knew him to be a pretty thorough investigator, when he put his mind to the task.

Of course, that was eight years ago.

Sylvia and I walked back to her car. She talked more about Deborah's work.

I listened.

After she keyed the driver's side door, she stopped before easing behind the steering wheel. Behind the eyes of that first class woman burned a restless soul. The need to know outweighing the sadness of her loss.

"Lincoln, I just want you to know how grateful I am to you for looking into this matter for us."

"Thank your husband," I said. "I've learned that it is not wise to refuse a request from The Judge."

"War Zone has been my lifeblood," she said in amusement. "His gentleness would be surprising to those who don't really know him."

"I think he likes it that way, Mrs. Henderson." With my hands placed on the open window, I gently closed the door as Sylvia sat comfortably behind the wheel. "Mrs. Henderson, does the name MiShaun Lucus mean anything to you?"

Her hesitation was momentary. "Why, yes. She was the other friend I couldn't remember. A real Mutt and Jeff combination if ever there was one. MiShaun was medium height, a bit on the chunky side with red hair and freckles. They lived together for a while. I only met her a couple of time. I could tell that she admired Deborah. You could see the admiration in her eyes. Deborah had something that she wanted. I don't doubt that their relationship was built, in large part, on what Deborah could teach her."

"What did Deborah get in return?" I asked.

"Knowing Deborah, probably very little," she replied despairingly.

"It was probably more than either of us could realize." I leaned forward stopping just short of the open drivers' window. "You believe there's more here than meets the eye. Don't you?"

"Yes I do. I don't profess to know everything, but I do know that Deborah wasn't careless. Carefree, yes, but not careless. She would have never put herself in a position to be robbed and killed the way she was. No, not her."

"Life has a certain randomness Mrs. Henderson. We don't know why the good die young or the evil live so long. Coincidence is sometimes nothing more than that. As we say in football, sometimes the ball takes a funny bounce."

"Not in this case. Not Deborah," she said firmly.

"How do you know?"

"I know because from time to time, Deborah tells me." She keyed the ignition and put on her sunglasses. "I don't expect you to understand." She adjusted the rearview mirror. "But I am grateful that you're helping."

I nodded and stepped away from the car.

Sylvia slipped into traffic while I picked up the box and carried it over to my Nova. I threw the box in the backseat and checked the time.

It was still early afternoon, so with Sylvia's statement looming in my head, I decided to visit the offices of Empower Detroit. My hope being that MiShaun had a few minutes to talk about a close friend.

9

'Empower Detroit' was carved in large, gold plated letters on top of the archway of a three level, gray gothic building on Third Avenue near the Masonic Temple close to downtown Detroit. The area was a combination of urban renewal and urban refuse located in one of Detroit's designated 'Empowerment Zones.'

Good fortune allowed me to find a parking spot in front of the building and spare myself the suicidal parking rates of the parking lot across the street. The steep angled walk up the concrete steps added to the symbolized authority common to gothic architecture. The once visually stunning lobby, complete with marble floors was now a dusty shadow of its once proud self.

I checked the marquee and found the listing for the office of Trevor Stallings on the third level. The allure of a creaky elevator did little to instill me with a sense of safety, so I opted for the curving marble stairs that led to the third level.

The top floor was an open area with cushioned seats and a circular, mahogany desk where a woman sat and answered phones, wrote messages and look as harried as a mother of eight children on a rainy Saturday afternoon.

The receptionist, moon faced with vertical laugh lines, and a horizontal grimace, spoke in a commanding tone to someone foolish enough to call on the phone and inquire about some kind of service. The wood carved nameplate on her desk read Helen Barnes.

I stood in front of her accidentally kicking the leg of the desk to get her attention. She looked up, having to stop her lecture to the unworthy caller and pointed toward a set of perfectly aligned armchairs just across from her desk.

"No, thank you," I said. "I have a set like that at home."

"Excuse me," she said lengthening her grimace.

"Is MiShaun Lucus available?"

"Do you have an appointment?" she asked holding the phone receiver like a weapon.

"Will my answer to your question determine your answer to my question?"

If looks could kill, my face must have been the best target she'd had all day. "Hold on. I'm in the middle of a phone call here."

"I'll wait." I flashed my best-dare-to-be-charming smile.

She finished the phone call and turned to me with her most put upon glare. "Now just what is your problem, sir?"

Condescension, I thought. One of the twelve stages of lingering low self-esteem as quoted by some psychologist I heard on WPON. "First, there isn't a problem, there's a conversation I need to have with MiShaun Lucus and I'd like to know if she's available."

"And what's the nature of the conversation?"

Impatience, another stage. "It's a personal matter." I gave her one of my business cards.

A beast of burden couldn't have released a more exasperated sigh. It was another stage in the process.

"Private Investigator." She returned the card. "Miss Lucus can't see you right now."

"Shouldn't she make that decision?"

She snorted, as if to say, Shouldn't-you-go-to-hell? "Just one minute. Have a seat."

Ordering people around, another phase. Watching all of these stages unfold in front of me meant that I'd be approached by a producer of a nationally syndicated television talk show. 'I saw all the stages of declining self esteem...and lived!' The receptionist and I weren't on the right path to a mutually bonding experience. In my mind I'd finally met Hell's icy twin sister. And her name was HELLen.

I silently complied as she picked up the receiver and buzzed someone's office.

Knowing that what was about to happen would fall short of my goal, I eased comfortably into one of the perfectly matched armchairs and began the wait-there-until-I-decide-to-get-to-you game played by people whose perceived power only rivals their lack of competence.

Illusion of power was another stage in the process.

I'd seen the type before. Driven by a consuming self-importance and an independent derangement. Snake eyes of the deadliest combination in a position to inflict harm. Prone to acting out their insecurities by undermining the stability of the rest of the world.

Thoughts of Helen's character danced for a few moments before being interrupted by the peripheral presence of someone who I figured was their version of the Sergeant-at-Arms. He physically filled the visual area between Helen and me. He stopped a few steps from where I sat, his arms folded across a barrel chest.

Years spent wrestling with two older brothers and coming out on the short end had long since short-circuited my easily intimidated gland. I stood up to greet the latest contestant in the look-at-me-I'm-important contest.

Ignoring my extended hand, the bronze bomber with his fu manta moustache and tint shaded gold trimmed glasses carried all of two hundred and twenty plus pounds on a frame that matched my height evenly.

He wore a light green, short-sleeve shirt and dark green tie with a gold tie clamp. His perfectly ironed black pants and the gloss on his tasseled shoes would make a Drill Instructor orgasmic. I'd seen his type before. He was just biding his time until one of the states that had the death penalty posted openings for executioners. He seemed to be the type who believed in keeping a sharp axe in case there was a power outage.

"May I be of help to you, sir?" he asked. I sensed more condescension. Obviously the declining low self-esteem trauma had reached epidemic proportions.

"Maybe," I replied. "Are you MiShaun Lucus?"

"Certainly not."

"Then you can't help me. But I suspect you knew that before you walked over here."

He unfolded his arms and did the best fist-on-hips stance I'd seen since the late Yul Brynner in the King and I.

"The Assistant Director is quite busy right now. Whatever you require, I'm sure I can handle."

"And who are you?"

He puffed up his chest. "I'm Miss Lucas's Executive Assistant. Now what can I do for you?" His impatient tone was almost amusing.

"Wow, the Executive Assistant to the Assistant Director. Should I kiss your ring now or wait for your halo to stop glowing?"

"All right, my man. That's it." He started to move his left hand toward me.

"You don't want to do that ..... my man. For two reasons, one it's completely unnecessary and two, if it were necessary, this isn't the time or place. Now be a good little gopher and go buzz your boss. Tell her a private investigator needs to see her about a personal matter. Meantime, go find a mirror and impress yourself."

He stopped, did a reevaluation and put the errant fist back on his hip.

"Between you and Queen Grimace over there, I've caught nothing but grief since I walked in the door. If this is how Detroit reaches empowerment, then we are hurting. I have a matter to discuss with MiShaun Lucus that's none of your business." I nodded to Helen. "Or hers. Now, either let her know I'm out here or let me make an appointment for sometime before the new millennium ends."

"As I said earlier ..... "

"No need to be rude," said a soft voice from behind Helen's desk.

He turned and I stood aside to see a svelte, ebony haired woman, medium height looking slightly annoyed. Her finely manicured, red nailed hands were clasped in front of her.

"My name is Lincoln Keller," I said stepping around Mr. Big Stuff and walking over to the desk. "I'm a private investigator here to discuss a personal matter with MiShaun Lucus. My hope is that these two don't represent your best attempt at community relations. Is there any way you can put me in touch with MiShaun Lucus, Miss ..... "

She walked over and extended her hand. "MiShaun Lucus. Won't you come in, Mr. Keller?"

10

The plush green carpet, glass top desk complete with Hewlett-Packard computer, digital clock radio, gold plated, engraved pens and a leather high back chair seemed too ostentatious for an Assistant Director of a non-profit agency, but my only comparison were the offices of the Oakland Raiders key staff members.

There was no comparison.

My most surprising fixation was MiShaun. The description I'd heard from Sylvia was red-haired and chunky with freckles.

The freckles were visible.

"Have a seat, Mr. Keller." She pointed to a low-back, black leather armchair. "I'm afraid I don't have much time. Ten minutes at most."

"I'll meet you half way and only take five," I said.

MiShaun was no chunk with red hair. Her dark blue, steel high twist polyester fraille belted jacket with matching trousers clung to her svelte figure like a second layer of skin. The top opening of the jacket revealed a white silk crewcut top. She topped off the outfit with a matching white scarf tied loosely around her neck. I caught a glimpse of her initials embroidered in blue.

Thin faced with just a hint of cheekbone, she looked taller than her medium height description even without the matching high heels. Her gracile figure spoke of fad diets and trendy spas.

The Nineties had wrapped itself around her transformation.

My staring used up valuable seconds in a short interview.

"Your executive assistant is very protective of your time."

She was non-plussed in her reply. "Tyler Cain is very protective of all of us. He takes his duties seriously."

"And just what are his duties?"

She ignored the question. "To what do I owe a visit from a private investigator?"

"This visit is brought to you by someone who's interested in what happened to a friend of yours. About eight years ago."

"Deborah?"

I nodded.

"Have the authorities found something new?"

"Nothing that I'm aware of. That's why I'm poking around. I'd like to ask you a couple of questions."

She leaned back in her chair, swiveling toward the window. "Deborah's death is a nightmare that never goes away. One moment we're talking about men, careers and power shopping and the next moment I'm watching her being lowered into a shallow grave. My best friend taken from me and I still don't know why."

"No one else seems to know why either."

"Can I interest you in some mineral water?" She opened the door to a small, mahogany-lined refrigerator that sat on the floor next to the matching glass top credenza.

I declined. "When did you last see Deborah?"

"It seems like yesterday that I answered that questions and others by the officer in charge of the case."

"Knackton?"

She nodded and poured water into a white cup with a flowery silver pattern. "I saw Deborah the night she was killed. She stopped by my place to firm up some plans we'd made for the weekend. She said she was going out of town to check out some story." She paused. "Did you know she was a free lance journalist?"

"Yes, I did."

"She was always chasing some story. Never wanted to work for any paper or magazine in particular. She loved pitching ideas and selling stories to whoever would pay."

"Did she say what the story was about?"

"No. She rarely talked about the stories while they were being researched and written. She liked waiting until the story was in print and then we'd celebrate."

"Any idea where she was going?"

"That also remained her secret."

"You'll forgive my misunderstanding, but that doesn't sound like the relationship of best friends."

She sipped and smiled reflectively. "That was part of Deborah's character. She loved mysteries and pulling others into her way of thinking and having fun."

"What do you mean?"

"You know how every high school has a class clown or prankster? And no matter what happened, you always knew who was the culprit?"

"Willie 'Pooh Pooh Face' Green was the culprit at my high school."

MiShaun smiled. "Well, Deborah operated a lot higher than that. She loved creating little mysteries around you, pulling you in and then springing the unexpected surprise at the end. Once she had me convinced I'd inherited a million dollars from someone who remembered a good deed I'd done when I was seven. I wish you could have seen the detailed paperwork. I looked at documents I would have sworn were from a law office. God knows how many people she pulled into that charade. It was a work of art. When I finally showed up at this law office for the supposed reading of the will, the office receptionist escorted me into this large office filled with lawyer looking books and furniture. I sat down just as this stuffy looking old guy came waddling in. He introduced himself as Frankfort T. Bankington and said before he could read the will, he needed proof of who I was."

I liked Deborah's imagination.

"So I showed him my license and social security card. He looked at both ID's, checked me out and then pulled this large folder with more legal documents. He starts whereforeing, be it known, and other stuff I didn't understand before finally handing me a small folded piece of white paper. I opened the paper and there was a hand scribbled note that read 'Hey girl. I hope you like your surprise birthday gift'."

"Surprise birthday gift?"

"I once mentioned in passing how I thought it would be fun to have an elaborate office birthday party. I wasn't serious, but Deborah thought it would be fun. So the moment I caught on to what was happening. Thirty people came from out of nowhere yelling 'Surprise' and 'Happy Birthday'. I don't know how she did it, but Deborah somehow convinced over thirty people, that I didn't know, to join in and celebrate my birthday with her."

"Sounds like she was pretty special."

"She was." MiShaun glanced at the digital clock. "Sorry Mr. Keller, but I do have to go. I'm about to be late for an important meeting."

"I understand." I stood up. "I don't know if anyone can ever get over losing someone special, especially given the way she died."

"Her magical lucky necklace just ran out of power. She'd always tap it three times and say 'All luck is attitude.' Tapping it three times that night certainly didn't save her life."

"Any chance I can ask you some questions later on?"

"Sure. Just make an appointment with the office receptionist."

"If I go through her, I won't see you until Y3K."

She pulled a business card from the black, silver-lined cardholder on her desk. "This is my home number. Please try to be discreet with its use and mindful of the time you call."

"I'll introduce myself to whoever answers," I said as I slid her card into my wallet.

"If I don't answer, then the conversation will be one sided. Just you and my answering machine."

I paused just before opening the door. "By the way MiShaun, I understand there was a third member of your group. A Sharon something?"

"Actually its Sharron. Emphasis on the 'ron'," she replied while looking through a folder. "Sharron Westlake. Last I heard she was working at a child care center."

"You two haven't been in touch for a while?"

"A lot of things died with Deborah's passing. Sharron and I drifted apart." MiShaun kept sorting through the folder. The lack of eye contact told me more than what she wanted known.

It was a dead subject.

I thanked MiShaun and found my way out where I waved to Helen as well as the Tyler, the Angel of Death, still hovering around her desk looking for a carcass to devour.

It was all I could do to suppress a chuckle. "The Executive Assistant to the Assistant Director. I'm impressed."

I didn't need to read minds to know what he was thinking. His face had the look that said 'We'll meet again, chump. And next time I won't be so nice'.

If I hadn't been schooled in the Oakland Raiders philosophy of 'Just Win Baby', I might have been worried.

11

I lugged the remains of my mind, body and spirit back to the office to check for messages and gather any additional information Julie might have found on her cyber hunt.

There were four messages for Jeff. All had that urgency that comes when bail bondsmen invest in the good nature of people only to have them miss their day in court.

Rosie left a message asking me to call him at the station. Truman called wondering if I'd like to join him and some his Union brethren at an afternoon Tigers game. The Yankees were in town and there would be hell to pay.

It was too late to call Truman, so I called Rosie.

Having his direct line saves me the indignity of being put on hold. He answered on the second ring.

"Hey, Linc. That friend of mine I told you about last night."

"Arlan Schaefer."

"Yeah. Turns out he did retire from the *Free Press*. He lives in Lansing now. I have his number. Call him and tell him you're my brother."

"Will that endear me to him?"

"A little. The rest will come when you buy him two rounds of a perfect Manhattan."

"At once?"

"Well, he did work for a major daily."

I jotted down the number and thanked Rosie.

"By the way, I'll be out of town for a couple of days. I'm headed to a conference on Michigan State's campus. My old mentor, Dr. Larry Redd has pulled together some of the top people of color in the broadcasting industry to discuss issues and trends. So I'm going to sit in and get reenergized. I'll be staying overnight at the Kellogg Center."

"Rose. C'mon. East Lansing is only ninety miles away. You can get there and back in a little over an hour. Why the need to stay overnight?"

"Oh. Did I mention Walt Conyers, Ernie Betts and Earl Robinson, Frank Grant, and Otis Buchanan?"

"No, but that says it all. Have a good time."

"Unavoidable at best."

Rosie and Rae were the only black people I knew with Spartan green and white temperaments. Any loss to the rival maize and blue University of Michigan team was taken personal. Rosie usually made up excuses to hit the campus and hang out with his undergraduate buddies from the 'good old days'.

I sifted through the mail. Sent out a few invoices and paid even fewer bills. A large manila envelope was perched on the corner of my desk with the familiar blue label and white letters that spelled out INFO-SEARCH.

Jules at work again. I opened the envelope, removed the invoice and looked through the contents.

There were copies of articles from various Michigan papers and a couple of regional magazines. All had been written by Deborah Norris.

I counted seventeen all together. Sequenced from the earliest date to the most recent, varying in length. A quick skim of the titles revealed a diverse journalistic interest.

Deborah Norris didn't just hang around one arena.

It meant a little more nighttime reading to go with the box Sylvia had given me. Were there secrets to be revealed in that box and the articles?

Damned if I knew.

Before leaving the office, I punched in the 517 area code and Arlan

Schaefer's number in Lansing. What I got was an answering machine that cryptically told me to leave a message or get lost.

I left a message. I scanned the Ameritech phone book for Sharron Westlake and found a listing for her on Wisconsin near Outer Drive. I punched the number and was rewarded with another answering machine.

I didn't leave a message.

Feeling like I was in the valley of a long day, I grabbed the envelope of articles, locked up and headed back to my Nova.

It was that time in the late afternoon when things changed with the direction of commuter traffic.

Frogs looking for a princess to kiss them so they could shed their outer skin to unleash the 'player' inside moved toward the liquor castles to buy the three rounds of an elixir with a beer chaser. Deaden the brain, relax the senses and distort reality.

Just for a few hours. Harmless braggarts looking for an unsuspecting audience in a tunnel where dreams were just over the next horizon.

Everyone had his or her spot. Mine was Artie's. The last bastion of social relief where most of its denizens were a day late, a dollar short and a mile off and on the wrong side of town. Artie's was known as the last stop on the road to nowhere.

That's where I headed to welcome the night. But before leaving, I paged Malone.

12

Artie's brimmed with the usual bunch of lovable losers. The last place dreamers covered their personas and insecurities with enough cigarette smoke to hide the Titanic. It was a great place to hide from what people wanted and revel in what you didn't know. Artie's was the perfect training ground for con men, swindlers and political spin masters.

Despite the robust atmosphere and loud taunts, the place was held in check by two unyielding elements: Ada, the gap tooth, sassy, red haired take-it-or-I'll-give-it-to-you waitress held center court on any and all who violated the second unyielding element; her ten commandments for social living. Her machine gun tongue could rip through a person's outer layer faster than a hyperactive ninja. Whatever she missed, the twelve-gauge shotgun that Frank kept behind the counter could easily hit.

Parked in my favorite booth and listening to the informed elite of the group argue about the six year contract the Detroit Lions had extended to popular running back Barry Sanders made me long for the those two-a-day workouts at the Raiders training camp. Usually, before the nostalgia becomes too hard to handle, I'd rub my hand along the scar on the side of my left knee. Back before orthoscopic surgery could put a athlete back on the playing field in six weeks, some of us were born a little too early, to be spared the old 'snap and sew' approach to knee rehabilitation. Maintaining some of my speed and predicting rain were the only benefits I derived from the old approach.

I hadn't been too far along on my second light beer when Candy worked her way through the clattery herd.

Though dressed in the casual covering of celery wool plaid jacket with a leather trim, black spandex top, Chino flat front cotton pants and low-heeled brown loafers, the beauty that she carries so well could lull a man into a self-aggrandized rap. So much so that she could shoot the periods off his sentence and he'd never know why he couldn't finish a conversation.

For me, sleeping with a homicide dick had taken on new meaning.

"Inviting me to this sewer hole isn't my idea of a quiet place where we can talk," she said motioning to Ada.

"I thought you'd appreciate the atmosphere."

"The same way I appreciate a morgue. The only difference between this place and the morgue is that the people in the morgue know they're dead."

Ada lumbered over, took Candy's order and mumbled something about her being too skinny where it counts.

"If I didn't like her so much I'd arrest her for having an indecent personality." She picked up a miniature bar pretzel from the aluminum bowl in the center of the table. "I hate these things. So what's happening with your case?"

I replayed the day's events, telling her everything that happened, including my meeting with MiShaun Lucus.

Candy listened just as her training required, choosing not to ask questions until I finished my monologue.

"Well, that's some progress," she said.

"Maybe. I can't be sure just yet. Most of what I've learned supports what's already in the file. The question of why? and what was she doing? is still a mystery."

"Everything we know suggests she was meeting someone," Candy said matter-of-factly. "Knackton has already confirmed that information."

"But who was she meeting?"

"A source?" Candy offered.

"Possibly. How about a secret friend?" I added.

"Possibly, but who?" she sighed. "Maybe she had a snitch."

We played with a few more possibilities while waiting for Ada to bring Candy's order. The conversation with her, though helpful, only disguised what I knew were my true intentions. The original chemistry that simmered in our relationship was off. We were out of sync and the road back to a workable equilibrium rested with my own haphazard attempt at reconciliation.

If you could imagine a bear trying to play the opening to Phantom of the Opera on a harp, then the humor of this not-so-pretty picture was understandable.

"So, what's your shift like for the rest of the week?" I asked.

"I'm on the afternoon rotation until the end of the month. You know what that means; my day ends when the month ends. Why do you ask?"

"I just thought maybe we could find some time to do something."

"Like what?" she asked as Ada finally returned with Candy's soft drink and fries. She used the silent moments after Ada's exit to play with the arrangement of the plate and glass.

"Oh, I don't know. Dinner, movie, dancing, maybe a weekend out of town. Chicago has a lot to do. There's a police commander there I know named Larry Cole who really knows the city."

"It all sounds nice, Linc. But with this current rotation, it's difficult to plan."

I swallowed the remains of my beer and leaned forward. "You're enjoying this aren't you?"

"Enjoying what?" she munched a French fry in a halfhearted effort to suppress a smile.

"This personal groveling which you know is uncomfortable for me, but I'm doing anyway."

"And which you are doing well I might add, but it needs work."

"But is it working?"

"Let's just say that I'm appreciating the effort."

I had a witty retort all lined up when her pager signaled. She checked the message, removed the cell phone from her pocket and called in.

It didn't take a genius to figure out what was going on, especially if it's a call to a homicide detective.

"Got a triple homicide," she said glancing at her watch. "Probably gang related. Duty calls." She slid out from the booth. "Thanks for the snack." She leaned over a planted a kiss on the cheek. "I like the way you grovel. See you."

"I'll call you later," I said as she eased through the crowd.

I sat for several minutes, oblivious to the noise, eating from the plate of fries Candy left behind. I realized I had two choices. I could sit there and wallow in self-pity or I could get back on the case.

Or I could do both. I paid the tab and headed for my Nova.

It seemed a good time to drive and focus in much the same way Louie, Melvin, Ralph, Rollin and I would cruise Second Avenue during the early hours as teenagers jammed in a 1960 Catalina. We were full of hormones with no interested outlet. A drive was a form of mental cleansing and should be used wisely.

So, full of hormones with no interested outlet, I motored over to Woodward Avenue hoping the city's rhythmic beat would help me sort through the malaise.

"Here's where I miss WJZZ the most," I muttered to myself and the City of Detroit, remembering the jazz station that was suddenly yanked off the air and replaced with urban contemporary nonsense.

I would have gladly substituted one funk for the other, if not for the unmarked car that had been following me since I left Artie's. Ordinarily, I might have been concerned, but the driver was too good to be an amateur and the car was too plain to be rented by a pro. I changed lanes again, just to see what would happen.

The car moved with me.

"I don't have time for this," I said.

There was a fenced, vacant lot located just to my right, so I pulled over and parked on the side street, waiting for my shadow. The unmarked car pulled in behind me, leaving the lights on for effect.

Stepping out of my car, I half shielded my eyes to fight off the hibeam light being intentionally flashed in front of me. My .38 was cleaned, oiled and ready, if needed.

The illuminated burly outline of the person walking toward me added a Twilight Zone effect. As he moved closer to where I stood, I slowly began putting features to the outline and took solace in the fact that I wouldn't have to use my gun.

"Evenin,' Lieutenant," I said. "And what brings one of Detroit's most celebrated investigators to this spot? As if I couldn't guess."

Lieutenant Nick Knackton, hog jowled with a granite face and barrel chest, stopped a few feet from me, looking up from his most intimidating stance. My one wart in an otherwise stable universe arched a salt and pepper eyebrow and then spat on the ground.

"We got a call that someone was down here exposing himself to the rodents," he said in a gravel tone. "Now that I see its you, I can tell the caller that there's nothing to worry about. You can't expose what you don't have."

"Wow, Lieutenant. A person would have to go all the way to a seventh grade boys' locker room to find original lines like that one."

"What are you nosing around about these days, Keller?"

"This vacant lot. Some investors I know want to build condos, but were concerned about the security. You looking for work?"

"Don't play me for stupid, Keller."

"It's not a play."

He snarled. "I know damn well what you're up to."

"Then why ask?"

Knackton pulled an ugly, fat cigar from his shirt pocket, bit off a piece of the end, lit the thing and blew the first cloud of smoke toward me.

"I'm still the investigator of record in the Deborah Norris case. Any inquiries have to come through me. I don't need help from some two bit P.I. who couldn't find an elephant in midnight traffic on the Lodge."

"Is the elephant driving or a passenger?"

"Go take pictures of men in jerk-off booths," he said with breath that smelled like sewage. "I don't need your help."

"I wasn't hired to help you."

"Who hired you?" he asked while chewing the end of his cigar.

"I exercise my right to say none of your business."

"It didn't take long to figure out it was The Judge."

"Judge who?"

"I told him time and time again that I'll find out who did it."

I shrugged.

Knackton stepped closer and pointed a stubby finger in my face. "Then let's get one thing clear." He moved closer, going for stronger intimidation. "You keep your nose clear of this case. I don't want you screwing up any of the work I've done. Some cases take a lot longer than others do. You tell that to The Judge." He turned and walked toward his car.

"Seems like more than just a robbery to me," I said. He stopped and turned around with a look that would have frozen a steel mill. "That true?"

"Conclude that all by yourself, did you?"

"It came to me in the night."

"Probably while you were peeping through key holes. Stay the hell out of it, Keller or I'll have your license."

"Hmm. Threats, intimidation and general surliness. Not exactly three of the seven habits of effective people."

"Stay away from it Keller. Find something else to do. I hear Farmer Jack is looking for security guards."

I called out. "One thing, Lieutenant."

He turned, still snarling. "What is it?"

"Any suspects?"

"Some P.I," he said. "In an open homicide, no one's above suspicion."

Knackton strolled to his gray Chevy, slammed the driver side door and screeched his tires making a fast exit.

Someone at police headquarters dropped a dime to Knackton and told him of my involvement with the Deborah Norris case.

Not surprising. The walls of police precincts are the worst places for secrets to hide. If Knackton knew, it also meant he knew how I got the information. It was no secret, but it could make life a little uncomfortable for Malone.

Having seen enough of the area and too much of Knackton, my investigation so far hadn't told me a great deal. But at least I felt like I was considering all the angles.

The drive back to my apartment was leisurely despite the information in my head and a box of material in the back seat. Somehow I'd convinced myself that I'd actually stay up for a while and read through Deborah's files.

I carried the box upstairs, dropping it on the floor near my recliner. Opting for my Raiders workout shorts and a sleeveless muscle shirt, I parked my tired body, pressing the play button on the answering machine to hear the three waiting messages.

Arlan Schaefer, Rosie's friend now living in Lansing, returned my call. He said he'd be around during the latter part of the evening.

Truman called and said he'd call later.

Judge Zone called and asked if I'd stop by his office the next day.

Since it wasn't quite ten o'clock yet, I picked up the cordless receiver and punched in Arlan's phone number. Anticipating the answering machine, my patented answering machine response was thrown off when a raspy voice male answered.

I introduced myself, used Rosie's name as the icebreaker and told him a little about my investigation.

"I moved back to Lansing because I got tired of working the crime beat for the paper. You see so much over time that you start to go numb."

I asked if he remembered the Deborah Norris story.

"You like baseball?" he asked.

It was an interesting question to my question. "It's been a while."

"I'm not talking about that major league hype that comes through Comerica Park. I mean real baseball. The way it was meant to be played."

"Then it's been a longer while."

"Good. Tomorrow, you come on up to Lansing and we'll take in a Lug Nuts game."

"I'm pretty busy right now. I thought we could talk ..... "

" ..... Lug Nut games. Nothing like 'em. Come on up. You got a pen and paper handy?"

I did. And told him so.

He gave me the address of a place where he worked.

"Try to get there by four o'clock so we'll have time to talk before the game."

I agreed, thanked him and rang off.

Still clutching the receiver, I decided not to think about my conversation with Arlan Schaefer. A veteran, Detroit based P.I. named Amos Walker once told me that during an investigation, just follow where the case leads you ..... no matter how wayward the path. In this case, the path lead to Lansing and a minor league baseball game.

It seemed like a good time to call Sharron Westlake. She answered on the second ring.

I avoided a lengthy introduction and moved right to the point of my call.

"Has Deborah's case been reopened?" she said in a weary voice.

"It was never closed, Miss Westlake. Nothing new has been discovered so far. I've been asked to give it a look."

"How can I help?"

"If its not inconvenient, I'd like to meet with you just to ask a few questions. I'll try not to take too much of your time."

She hesitated. "Well, I do have tomorrow off. Tell you what; I have a hair appointment at nine thirty tomorrow morning. There's a hair salon in the Fisher Building called 'Distinctive Styles'. It's located in the corner of the building facing Second Avenue. How about if we meet outside of the salon at about eleven?"

"I can be there, Miss Westlake. I sure appreciate your cooperation."

"Don't mention it. Deborah was a friend of mine. I miss her a lot."

I thanked her and placed the receiver back in its cradle.

What lay ahead was my looking through Deborah's files to get some sense of the kind of work she did.

I hung in there until just after midnight.

13

Despite the one interruption during the night, I managed to carve out a decent night's sleep. Normally, the interruption would have been Truman calling to discuss his latest idea for preserving union solidarity. However, it was a dream filled with distilled images and shadows moving through a mist that broke my sleep into two distinct times of the night.

I hit the office early, awakened by 'Free Ride', the cat of a thousand lives, scratching on the bedroom window and in need of shelter after a long night of ..... who knows what?

A glass of juice and a bagel served as the much needed breakfast as I zipped through the growing morning traffic, trying to sort through the mountain of information sitting on the back of my brain stem.

If appearances are true, then Deborah had been one orderly person. My trip through her files gave me a great sense of the importance of her work.

Deborah's first professional article was a 1984 in-depth article in the *Michigan Chronicle* that highlighted the growing number of African-American children in the foster care system. She went on to talk about the problem adoption agencies were having finding African-American parents to serve as adoptive parents. The article was poignant, moving and a call to action. The article also served as a hallmark for what would be her writing style. As I went from one file to the next, reading the articles that showed up in the *Monitor, The Michigan Citizen, The Detroit News* and *The Detroit Free Press, The Flint Journal*, as well as a number of local and regional magazines, it became obvious that Deborah loved her profession. Though writing proved to be her love, I surmised that her real strength was the meticulous way she went about collecting and documenting her research. Every piece of information she gathered that pertained to a story she was writing had a written code number. Articles, pictures and notes were given a sequence number, hand-written on the top right hand corner. The information for the first article written for the *Chronicle* had an A-1 through A-14 sequence. The same pattern followed for her second publication and continued on, ending with her last article written for *Crain's Detroit Business Magazine* in April of 1992. She'd made it all the way to the letter Y before her life was cut short. On the whole, the files weren't very revealing. Deborah wrote great stories, but nothing that would suggest that she had actually gotten under someone's skin. However, there was one thing I couldn't shake. Not during the night, not during my drive to the office and not during the few quiet moments I had behind my desk before the rest of the tenants showed up to open their businesses.

Deborah had a habit of sticking a note, article or some reminder of her next story in the folder of the story she was currently completing. Right after A-14 of the first article was a hand-written note that said 'Downsizing, employee buy-outs, blessing or curse' with a big red letter B scratched in the top right hand corner. Her next file was an article written for the *Michigan Citizen* on corporate downsizing, complete with all the research labeled B-1 through B-17.

The pattern stayed consistent through all of her files except at the end of the Y files, there wasn't a note, article or anything to suggest there would be a Z file.

Maybe she hadn't put together an idea for the Z file.

It was possible even though it didn't seem bloody likely.

The unlikeliness had nestled somewhere in the back regions of my brain and slowly chewed on the cells. Deborah didn't strike me as someone void of ideas for stories.

So where was the Z story?

I had leaned back in my noisy swivel chair when I heard Mary Cooper, across the hall, opening the door to INFO-SEARCH.

I called out to her.

The multi-colored beads she wears at the ends of her dreadlocks, clicked and clacked as she turned her head to greet me with a full mouthed smile.

"What is it Mr. Keller?" she asked.

"What time is Julie due in?"

She glanced at her wristwatch as she stood outside my office door. "Not for a while yet. She's downtown making a proposal and presentation to the Independent Grocer's Association. I'm sure she'll be in later on this morning. Is there anything I can do?"

"Yeah," I said as I jotted down some names on a post-it pad and ripped off the sheet. "Ask her to run a search on these names. I'm interested in knowing something about their background."

Mary sauntered over. She took the paper and read both names out loud. "Tyler Cain and ..... Wow! Trevor Stallings. You mean, like *the* Trevor Stallings? Mr. man-about-Detroit and next council member?"

"The same."

"What do you want to know about them?" she asked.

"Whatever Julie can find out. See that she gets that for me okay? It might be helpful."

"What about this name here? It looks like Windham Hall."

"That's Winston Hill," I said suddenly remembering that I'd scratched his name on there. "I'm not sure if it's worth her time, but check him out just for the record."

"You're the dick," Mary replied giggling as she walked over to her office.

I shook my head, noting that there is a price one pays to keep good help these days.

The next hour was spent following up on a few inquiries and reviewing my notes for a case that I'd recently completed. I had the goods on a couple of alleged incapacitated people believed to be putting the screws on their insurance carrier. One woman, who said her left ankle would never heal and thus prevented her from working or standing during long periods of time.

Three straight mornings of her out for a jog would be verified in the pictures I'd taken.

The other claimant alleged that his back ached every time he bent in the slightest manner. The pain wasn't as apparent from the pictures I had of him playing nine holes of golf for ten straight mornings.

Stupidity is one of the reasons why I stay employed.

A call to Judge Zone's office caught him before the nine o'clock court start up time.

He asked me to join him for lunch in his office.

Jeff strolled in not too long after I rang off. His dark glasses and shaved head added to the menacing demeanor that came with his muscular tone and blue Jean outfit.

He plopped down at his desk, punching the button on the answering machine.

There were three messages, all for Jeff.

The first two were people who used his skills before and it sounded like they'd need those skills again.

The third message was odd ..... by comparison. The low toned, nasally voice only said "J Keller. It's me. I got something you can use. You know where to reach me."

"Sounds like someone from a grade B 1940's movie," I said.

Jeff folded his dark glasses and slipped them into the pocket of his shirt. "Just a snitch who owes me big time. From time to time, he gets wind of something. Calls me and if the info is good, I slip him a few duckets."

"This sounds like one of those times."

He shrugged. "We'll see."

Jeff made his follow-up phone calls. I finished my own work.

There was still some time before my meeting with Sharron Westlake, so I decided to do what any investigator would do with some spare time.

I hit the streets.

The fresh smell of coffee flowed from the Coffee Cafe located directly across from our office. Like many of the businesses residing in the one-level store front buildings that make up the gist of Livernois Avenue's economic base, the Coffee and Cream had found its niche as an early morning quick stop. It's a great place to grab a cup of coffee, a doughnut and any one of several different newspapers. The coffee, doughnuts and newspapers all varied in size, flavor and content.

On a clear sky, breezy morning during the workweek, a cup of flavored coffee was the great equalizer.

I ordered two large cups of a special blend, made sure the lids were sealed tight and slid into the Nova. I had a reliable source of information whose usually sour disposition was made easier by a token gift of hot, flavored coffee.

Once I merged with the traffic going east on I-96, I aimed my chariot of filth toward downtown Detroit and the fabled fortress at 1300 Beaubien known as the First Precinct.

•   •   •

My paunchy friend with the hip replacement who worked the front desk in the lobby of police headquarters was in the middle of another one of his long winded instructions to a elderly woman about the proper way to file a complaint.

Sergeant Manfred Stovic, known as 'Gabe' because his ears protrude out like Clark Gable's, managed the first line of defense against all citizens who walked in the door looking for help. A veteran of twenty-five plus years, with a fair complexion and tired eyes from having seen too much, rarely had anything nice to say about anyone or anything. He measured the success of his day by the number of times he was tempted to draw his gun and didn't. Most people tried to avoid Gabe. Which is exactly what he wanted. I'd learned rather quickly that Gabe often knew more than he was willing to say and heard more than he cared to admit.

I ambled up to the desk, waving off the initial inquiry of one of the younger officers assigned to work the desk.

"Got no time for you now, Keller," Gabe said as he pointed the elderly woman toward an office door.

"That's too bad, Gabe. And after I drove all the way down here to bring you a cup of coffee."

"Like Hell." He bent down to make a notation on a form as his half moon reading glasses slid down his drinker's nose. "What flavor?"

"Mocha Delight. And a cup of French Vanilla creamer to lighten the load."

Gabe turned toward the young officer who initially tried to help me. "He wants something. Every ex-cop with nothing but time on their hands always wander through that front lobby door looking for something."

The young officer grinned and kept working.

"Front steps in five minutes, Keller." I nodded. "And the coffee had better be hot."

"Hot as a summer day in Hell." I replied.

Going back outside served two purposes: It allowed Gabe the chance to break, but not too far from the desk and; I could keep an eye on the time on the meter.

I had too many instances of being one minute late just as the meter maid was driving off, smiling at my futile efforts to reverse time for only a minute.

Gabe wandered out as I took notice of a short, walnut-toned middle age man who look like he'd gone thirteen rounds with life, lost every round, but stayed on his feet. He headed up the steps, brushing by Gabe, who hardly took notice.

"The coffee doesn't change the fact that you want something, Keller.

I accept your bribe with the stipulation that I can tell you to piss off."

"The pissing off option remains," I said as I handed him the cup.

Gabe ripped off the plastic lid and slowly sipped, stopping to savor the taste before depositing the nectar into his gut.

"What's on your mind, Keller? And make it quick."

"Eight years ago there was a robbery/homicide case involving the sister-in-law of one of our now prominent judges. Does it ring a bell?"

Gabe stopped and looked toward the passing traffic on Beaubien Street. "Yeah, it does. It's the burden of Knackton's unfinished legacy. Why do you ask?"

"Let's just say I have a professional interest."

"Let's just say you shove your professional interest and go find something else to do with your time."

"Why?" I asked.

"For Christ's sake, Keller. Didn't you learn anything during your cop days in Oakland? Cops have a rule about meddling. Especially in old cases that determine whether they go out in style or just go out."

I understood. Once you've worn the blue you learn that cops have a thousand unwritten rules ..... many of which you learn by accident. Those that you don't learn fast enough can get you killed.

"The Oakland PD had their share of rules."

"Then you know that for any plainclothes investigator, their case is their case, no matter how long it sits open. That case belongs to Knackton and if it is solved, he'll do the solving. Not a dollar-an-hour P.I.'s like you."

"My rates have gone up some."

"Find two other people standing here who give a damn." Gabe continued his savored sipping. "I remember that case along with a million others that sit in our files waiting for someone to step forward or some clue to shake out. A lot of things didn't come Knackton's way because he couldn't bring that case to a close. No arrests. No prosecution. No glory. No precinct commander position."

"He's solved a lot of other cases."

"This one was a headliner, Keller. It has all the politics and drama of a Greek tragedy. Our former Chief of police put a lot of pressure on Knackton to find the killer. After all, 'War Zone' was a prosecutor at the time. So he was part of the team. We had to do more than we normally would. But the leads took us nowhere. Knackton kept looking, but a number of other people were murdered along the way. Homicides didn't stop just because The Judge's sister-in-law was killed. Over the years, other cases had to be solved, resources were drying up, but the work still needed to be done."

"So, the case fell down on the priority list."

"The department's list, not Knackton's. He already has a hard-on for you and that bounty-hunting brother of yours. And it sure doesn't help that you're slammin' Malone."

"She's a big girl."

"Go sell it in Seattle, Keller." Gabe finished his coffee, taking the last dregs with one gulp. "If you're poking around this case, you're asking for trouble."

"I can cover the deep routes," I said.

Gabe smiled. "You're playing football and Knacton has a baseball bat."

"I'll wear a helmet."

As he crumbled the styro foam cup, Gabe turned toward the front entrance. "I gotta go, Keller. Some of us still work for a living. Anybody ask me about you and this case, I don't know you and I don't know nothing."

"Not easy to deny, us standing here on the front steps of the First Precinct."

"I'm having a cup of coffee listening to you ask questions about things I can't answer. Piss on all of 'em."

"Thanks for what you didn't tell me." I did a quick glance at my watch. "Now, if I hurry I can just make my hair salon appointment."

Gabe shook his head. "You're a real killer, aren't you, Keller?"

I strolled down Beaubien Street to where my Nova sat parked by a meter that was slowly moving toward zero hour. I jumped in and wheeled into traffic as my meter reader nemesis tooled around the corner looking for victims.

There was just enough time to jump on the Lodge freeway and zip over to the Fisher Building in the New Center area to keep my appointment with Sharron Westlake.

14

The Milwaukee/Grand Boulevard exit off the Lodge freeway leads right into the heart of the New Center area. The revitalized area is the brainchild of the former Mayor's administration and represents part of Detroit's resurgence.

I made the right turn onto Grand Boulevard, mercifully avoiding the construction work on the closed overpass that forced the westbound traffic to be rerouted. The three lanes were modestly clear as I swung over to the third lane, anticipating the left turn onto Second Avenue. A black Toyota Camry had just inched its nose into traffic, abandoning a cherished-metered parking spot in front of the multi-leveled New Center Building.

As a new building in Detroit's revitalization, the New Center Building was designed to look like the left corner of the Pentagon. What it lacked in uniformed personnel, it made up for in stylish, cosmopolitan dressed people who looked like money.

After I popped in enough quarters to play a boxed number in the first race, I jaywalked through the light against the northbound traffic on Second Street and passed under the skyway that connected the New Center Building with the Fisher Building. The monolith, historical structure is home to a number of businesses, but it primary recognition is for being know as the place where Detroiters came to show their furs, jewels and black ties at the numerous plays and musicals that grace the Fisher Theatre.

Once inside the tiled lobby, I looked to my left and saw the words

'Distinctive Styles' hair salon painted in bold letters across the window of the door. A display of African-American women wearing various hairstyles caught my immediate attention in the otherwise vacated lobby.

I was ten minutes early for my appointment with Sharron Westlake. I grabbed the brass handled door, intent on venturing in and asking for Sharron.

Instead, I opted to stroll down the lobby, past the security guard's desk and take in the gothic tone and style of the Fisher Building. Several small shops lined the corridor that lead to the grand lobby area outside the paneled doors of the Fisher Theatre. I noticed a coffee-and-snack stand right across from the box office. A row of colorful flags on gold colored poles angled sequentially along the base of the upper mezzanine.

By the time I'd wandered down to the marquee to see what theatrical plays were coming to town and caught a glimpse of several modernistic painting in the window of Art shop, more than ten minutes had eclipsed.

I turned the corner leading back to the salon and noticed a honey-toned woman of medium height, wearing a blue jean skirt, light blue blouse, black stockings and black, low heeled shoes standing in the lobby, looking out the doors to Second Avenue.

She was willowy with the kind of sculpted long legs that men think about under the cover of darkness with only the stars to light their imagination.

If this was Sharron, then our timing was perfect.

I waited until I was close enough to be heard before calling out.

She turned, momentarily squinting her eyes as I eased closer.

"Miss Westlake?"

She nodded.

"Hi. I'm Lincoln Keller," I said extending my hand. "I appreciate your meeting with me like this."

"Mr. Keller. I hope you won't be offended if I ask you for some identification."

I took out my wallet and showed her my P.I. license.

Sharron held the wallet, looking at the picture and then to me.

"I've looked better," I said.

"It's a nice picture," she replied. "So you really are a Private Investigator." She returned my wallet.

"Licensed and bonded by the state. Can we find a place around here where we can talk?"

"If we go around the corner to this coffee stand, there's a sitting area behind it."

We didn't say anything during that brief walk, filling the silent moments with the usual awkwardness of first encounters. This particular awkwardness was magnified by the reality of a conversation about a friend of hers whose eight-year-old murder still remained unsolved.

Sharron motioned to the coffee stand. I declined. While she ordered, I found a round, marble table in a corner by the doors of the dimly lit sitting area. There was just enough noise from the lobby traffic to shield our conversation from predatory listeners, but not make it difficult for us to strike a conversational tone.

She joined me at the two-seat table. She carried a medium sized plastic cup filled with coffee in one hand and in the other hand, enough packets of sugar and creamer to soften the taste of battery acid.

She sat down on the wrought iron seat, angling away from the table so she could cross her legs comfortably.

"I love the smell of coffee, but I hate the bland taste," she said as she ripped the tops off three packets of sugar.

"Why not drink tea?"

She smiled. "Because I hate the smell of tea."

Sharron had crescent brown eyes shielded by razor-trimmed eyebrows, a peach face and lips to die for. Sporting a medium cut hairstyle with the ends curled and covering her ears, she looked like a commercial for black woman entrepreneurship.

"As I said Miss Westlake ..... "

" ..... Sharron. Emphasize the 'ron'."

"As I said, SharRON, I'm looking into Deborah's death."

"Why?" she asked.

"Because I've been asked to."

"By who?"

"That's confidential and I thought I was asking the questions."

She sipped and shook her head. "Don't mind me. I work with preschoolers all day so I'm use to asking questions. It's the only way you can find out what's on their minds."

"It's not too much different with adults," I said.

"Except children are more honest with their answers."

There was nothing I could say to that universal law of human development.

"I'd like to talk about Deborah."

"Will it help find her killer?"

"I honestly don't know. I'm asking questions. We'll see where it leads."

"Deborah was the best friend a person could have, under any set of circumstances. And I miss her."

Sharron spent the next several minutes talking about her relationship with Deborah. She discussed their history from the time they met in middle school through their time at Pershing High School, the years at Western Michigan University as roommates, up to their return to Detroit. She fondly recalled their entrance into the work world, all the fun times in between and up to the moment where she stood over the grave that marked her friend's untimely departure from this world.

She really missed Deborah.

"There were only three of us still standing at her grave long after the preacher had finished. Her sister, brother-in-law and me. That had been one of the worst times of my life. There are still moments when the phone rings and I hope it's Deborah calling to say she's back in town after chasing some lead for a story."

From time to time, Sharron referred to Deborah as if she had only gone out of town and would be back momentarily. She sipped her coffee and talked fondly of a relationship that now had a void as big as eternity and just as lasting.

I asked fewer questions during her catharsis, opting to listen for the unspoken.

"I started seeing a counselor a few months after she died," Sharron continued. "I just couldn't shake the fact that she was gone. Lots of sleepless nights and bad dreams."

"How long before the dreams stopped?"

"Several months. It took a while, but they finally stopped."

"When did you last see Deborah alive?" I asked.

She leaned back, sighing as she recalled the moment. "Two days earlier. She was pounding away on her keyboard, working on some story, naturally, and I stopped by to see if she wanted to run over to the Fairlane Shopping Center. Lord & Taylor were having a big sale. I figured we could both use the therapy."

"Why?"

"Oh, she'd been working pretty hard lately and so had I. Armed with a few extra dollars, it seemed like the right thing to do."

"And was it?"

Sharron glared at me. "Had I known that it was going to be the last time I saw her alive, I would have stretched the time as long as I could."

"I meant no offense, Sharron."

"I know," she sighed. "I'm sorry. It's just that talking about her brings back a lot of pleasant memories."

It seemed like a good time to get specific. "Sharron, did Deborah say anything to suggest that she may have been in trouble. Or that something was strange? Phone calls, letters, people following her, a story she was working on?"

"Nothing that I can recall. She was always excited about the stories she wrote though she never went into detail until after the story was finished. It was her way of doing things. I'd seen it in high school, college, throughout our friendship. As to that other questions; if something strange was going on, I would have known about it."

"Deborah had dinner with her sister and brother-in-law the night she was killed. She told them she was going out of town to get background information on a story she was writing. Did she happen to mention where she was going?"

"I'll tell you the same thing I told the police; I didn't even know she was headed out of town. Though I wasn't surprised. She loved calling me and announcing that she was currently in hotel whatever in a city somewhere working on a story. And would I water her plants?"

Deborah's flair for the spontaneous was proving to be an exhausting character trait. "Did she have any enemies? Did she have any jealous former boyfriends? Some guy she met in a bar who wouldn't leave her alone?"

"No. In all likelihood, something like that would have happened to MiShaun, not Deborah."

"That's the first reference you've made to MiShaun. I had the impression that the three of you were a pretty tight trio."

"MiShaun and I were friends because Deborah and I were friends. Deborah was the reason we were together. Once she died, there was no reason for MiShaun and I to continue. We both knew it."

"You didn't like MiShaun?"

"I was uncomfortable around MiShaun. She was wild. Partied a lot, drank too much and prowled more than I cared for. When the O'Jays sang about 'Living for the Weekend', they had MiShaun in mind."

"That's odd. I spoke to MiShaun and she told me that the three of you partied a lot at Deborah's place."

"Only because Deborah decided that MiShaun was killing herself with those wild weekends of too much drinking and men who loved her for the moment. Must have been that red dye job she used to wear. I've heard men say that after a couple of drinks even a bear looks good."

"You weren't friends?"

"We weren't enemies. You see, MiShaun wanted more than she was capable of handling. She felt that the best way to make it to the top was to be on top of the right man at the right time. She tried to hit all the social spots where the brothers from GM, Ford and Chrysler hung out. Always believing she'd meet the right person who'd give her the right job. Provided that she did the right job   if you hear what I'm saying."

"I hear. So, Deborah tried to protect her from herself?"

"As much as she could. But MiShaun really believed that all she had to do was meet the right person and she'd be on her way. I always thought people-hopping was pretty risky business. I remember one week-end; I had to go to Indianapolis for a conference. When I got back, I found out that Deborah had spent the whole weekend playing nurse-maid to MiShaun. I was told by Deborah that MiShaun had really gone overboard with her drinking. Something happened that scared MiShaun senseless. Apparently Deborah really laid into her. Threatened to shoot her with her gun. Just kidding of course. But really read her the riot act. Three snaps, around the world, back hand slap."

"With a ring finger?"

"You know it. Anyway, after that weekend, MiShaun began to settle down some. She joined AA, started working out, rinsed out that red hair look, moved into her own place, but   "

" ..... But didn't give up the search for Mister Right."

"No, not really. She just changed where she looked. It must have worked. Last I heard she was working with Trevor Stallings as some kind of executive assistant."

"Actually she's the Assistant Director."

"Figures. I guess there are ways to get around having a college degree."

"I noticed that she had a number of framed certificates on display in her office."

"Again, I'm not surprised. I know she started degree programs at several colleges around the city, but never finished."

"College isn't meant for everyone. Sometimes that knowledge we amass between our ears is more precise than what comes from the formal classroom. We know what we know."

"What MiShaun knows isn't based on what's between her ears," Sharron said in a cryptic tone.

"Like I said; we know what we know."

"I'm sorry. I'm probably feeling the rush of memories. I'm really happy for MiShaun."

"But not enough to stay in touch?"

"I said I was happy, not joyous. Anyway, I don't think I've been very helpful. I didn't know what story Deborah was working on that supposedly took her out of town. I don't know of any enemies and I'm not sure if it was nothing more than her being in the wrong place at the wrong time. It happens you know. The energy from her necklace must have been on recharge that night."

"MiShaun suggested the same thing."

She rolled her eyes. "That stupid necklace. Deborah bought that thing from a man in New Orleans. We went there for Mardi Gras during our senior year. She met this brother who said he made the necklace and blessed it with some Cajun chant designed to bring good luck to the wearer."

"Deborah found a jeweler who'd make an exact copy for her. She wanted to give it to Sylvia as a birthday present."

"That's Deb. Loved her sister. Teased her like hell. I know Sylvia always expressed an interest in having a similar necklace."

"Well, now we know why it took so long."

Sharron glanced at her watch. "I hate to be rude Mr. Keller ..... "

" ..... Linc."

She smiled, just slightly. "Linc. I have several errands to run on my supposed day off. I don't know how helpful I've been, but feel free to call me if you think of other questions."

I handed her a card. "Feel free to do the same if you happen to think of something I should know."

We both stood and shook hands. Her touch was warm and her eyes had that look of emotional irresolution. She really missed her friend and talking about it may have been therapeutic, but it wouldn't bring her friend back.

"Thanks so much for your time, Sharron," I said.

She hesitated. "Deborah used to do with me what you just did. I'd banter on and on, and she'd listen. She was such a good listener. Talking with you reminded me of how much I missed that about her." I noticed a slight watering of her eyes. "I hope you can find out what really happened, Linc. I just want her soul to rest comfortably."

"I'll do the best I can."

Sharron headed back through the lobby while I used the revolving door exit back onto Second Avenue. I entertained a reflective thought about relationships as I jaywalked across the one way street.

It seemed to me that every relationship represented the opportunity to move somewhere, emotionally, physically, whatever. That movement helps to define the character of who we are and what we wish to become. In a world where our existence is measured in exact seconds, time spent in a relationship is a clear choice in the use of time. Deborah chose to invest her time in friends who didn't like each other and stories that might make a difference. There's something in the relationship of things that determines the direction of events.

In Deborah's case, that event took her away far too soon.

As I fired up the Nova, to head back downtown to meet with Judge Zone, I knew it all meant something.

I just didn't know what.

15

The court clerk directed me to Judge Zone's inner sanctum. He had just cleared the courtroom for a needed lunch break with strict instructions for everyone's prompt return at one fifteen. Though it was ten minutes into the noon hour, I didn't get the sense that he thought I was late.

Judge Zone was simplistically impressive. The oak paneled walls held his academic achievements and a number of plaques honoring his service to several organizations. Several floor-to-ceiling bookshelves were neatly jammed with enough leather bound law books to educate a small country in South America. His glass-topped desk had all the functional and ornamental trappings common to elected power, including a computer, printer and modem. The law meets the Internet in cyberspace. There were also several pictures of him posing with teammates from various years in the NFL.

He sat hunched over his desk, consuming a chicken salad sandwich on toasted rye bread and a small fruit plate. His black robe was partially unzipped and a message moved across the blue screen of his computer monitor.

He pointed to the armchair adjacent to his desk, opting not to talk with his mouth full.

I appreciated the gesture.

"So," he said while wiping his mouth with a napkin. "You making any progress?"

"Well, I know a lot more now than I did when I started, but I'm not sure if it's anymore than you already knew."

"Let me hear what you know."

I detailed my movements since he and I last talked, going over the things that seemed to make sense and those that didn't. He listened in much the same way he would sitting in his judicial chair or standing inside a huddle. Hear the facts, cut to the chase and take action. It was basic survival philosophy for any jungle.

"Also, I had a rather chance encounter with Lieutenant Knackton. Seems he'd gotten wind of my sniffing around his turf. He didn't like the smell and, as a matter of fact, neither did I."

"I'm not surprised. The man has ears everywhere."

"Most of which he cut from the heads of people caught sniffing around his turf."

The judge leaned back; a slight smile fought its way up from the corners of his mouth. "He got you worried?"

"I'm an ex-Raider, Your Honor. We only worried about not being in on the next play. Knackton I can handle. It's the people in the shadows around him that might give me some trouble."

"I have some pull within the department. I'll make sure you don't experience any undue interference."

"Appreciate that. Now if there's nothing else ..... "

" ..... Just a couple of other things," he said motioning me to remain seated. "My wife seems to think you're going to find the answers to why Deborah was really murdered."

"She's hopeful. I told her I'd do my best. Of course, you know asking me or for that fact, any investigator to look into it, would raise her hopes more than just a notch."

"If I wouldn't have hired someone, she probably would have. It means that much to her."

"How much does it mean to you, Your Honor?"

He steepled his fingers underneath his shaven chin. "I'm going to assume that your question is an attempt to get at information and not to piss me off."

"I've witnessed what happens to people who piss you off, Your Honor. Jumping off the top of the Renaissance Center would be an easier way to go."

He pumped up his massive frame, leaned forward and glared at me like I was fresh meat hanging from a branch somewhere in central Africa. "Then know this; from the moment I met Sylvia I knew that she and I were destined to live a lifetime together. She's been the joy I needed to counter balance the brutal paths I've had to walk. Through it all she's been the one absolute, unconditional constant in my universe. What makes her happy makes me happy. She has the most irritating, but humorous, giggle I've ever heard. She's classy enough to converse with Presidents and can laugh at the Three Stooges. For the last eight years, that laugh has been lacking in our lives. Part of who she was lies buried in that grave with Deborah and I want her back. She can't handle not knowing and I can't handle what it's done to both of us." He paused, staring off for just a few seconds. "I can no longer wait for the political forces-that-be to resolve this thing. Had I followed my true nature, I would have hired someone seven years ago. But I decided to play the political game and support the system in which I'm a member. Well, that time has past." He paused and sat back reflectively. "I plan for closure. When one event ends, I move on to the next. It's why I like being a judge. I can bring closure to some of the crap that slides into my courtroom."

I kept quiet.

"I'm fifty-five years old, happily married for thirty years. My son graduated from law school at the University of Michigan and my daughter just started Medical school at Stanford. My wife and I are pretty well off. Given our investments, we could retire tomorrow, buy a condo in the Caribbean and sip coconut juice from now until we became too fat to walk." Judge Zone stood up. "Mr. Keller, I have spent a great deal of my life fighting battles from my side of the line. During my football days I became very good at getting past obstacles that stood in the way of my goals. I transferred that same commitment to law and in a short time became one of the best prosecuting attorneys ever employed by the city. I never lost a case. As a judge, the legal system helps guide a lot of my decision making, but the decision is still mine to make. I'm used to doing, not watching. Deborah's death has forced me to take a sideline interest and it rubs against my nature. I'm a public official and I can't be seen operating outside the law. Through my own ways and means I've collected a lot of information, but I can't do much about what I've learned. That's why you're here, Mr. Keller. Please keep that in mind."

Feeling properly chastised; I nodded and told The Judge I'd be in touch.

I stopped just short of the door. "You said there were two things, Your Honor. What's the other?"

"Four years ago I tested the waters to see what kind of support I'd have if I decided to run for City Council. There was enough there to suggest I had a better chance than most. As I began to organize, my campaign was unexpectedly side tracked by an unsubstantiated rumor that would have put my candidacy in serious jeopardy."

"What happened?"

"That's unimportant. You just need to know that I haven't been able to prove how it happened, but I have every reason to believe that the whole thing started in my opponent's camp."

"Who were you running against?" I asked.

Judge Zone stopped and looked at me as if I'd asked a silly question. "Oh, that's right. You were out of town at the time. I was running against Trevor Stallings."

I sighed. The deeper you look, the more complicated things become. "Will that information affect my investigation?"

The Judge glanced at his watch and picked up a trial folder. "It shouldn't."

'But it might' was the statement left unsaid between us.

He turned toward his computer as I opened the door to leave.

The Judge knew I'd have to find out what the rumor was that detonated his possible run for City Council. It was four years later; there were two vacancies and a host of unemployed politicians interested in trying to become city policy makers. I didn't remember seeing The Judge's name among them.

Rather than tell me what happened, he assumed I'd find out on my own.

And I knew just who to ask.

16

The folder containing all the information gathered so far lay spread out on Julie's desk. I was arranging every piece by date and time. Julie stared stone faced at her computer monitor as her fingers pointed and clicked their way through one database after another, searching for information on what caused a warrior like Judge Zone to drop out of a race before the race started.

"There wasn't a lot said about it," she mumbled. "The field was wide open at the time, so any number of people may have dropped a dime to the press about some allegation."

"Unfortunately, everyone had something to gain. The Judge hinted that maybe Trevor Stallings may have been involved."

"Doesn't make sense," Julie replied. "With his family and their connections, he could practically walk into a city council seat. He wouldn't need to hint at an allegation. If anything, I'd wonder why he hasn't tried before now."

Julie pointed and clicked her way into another two or three places while I sat reviewing the information she'd gathered on Tyler Cain.

His story read like a Leave It to Bubba paperback novel. He'd had a busy and interesting thirty-two years.

The product of a broken home, it even started like a paperback novel. Mr. Cain had become a real student of the juvenile system having studied it from the time the doctor smacked his butt and he retaliated by assaulting the man with his own stethoscope.

He was eight years old when he had his first run in with the law and as he got older his wearisome mother left the gist of his home train-ing to the more creative teachers who make the streets their castle.

Petty thefts were his thing for a while, followed by some strong-arm collection work, selling stolen goods and other habits that reflect a growing felon's interests.

He moved in and out of juvenile detention like a joyous New Year's Eve celebrant in a revolving door, usually spending just enough time to learn a new skill.

As an eighteen-year-old adult, the picture became less clear, though the pattern was evident. It was hinted that he was involved in a stolen car ring, although in all four cases the charges were dropped due to lack of evidence. He continued his assault on the scales of justice until a funny thing happened on the way to becoming a full scale criminal.

He found religion.

He was saved and his life took a new path. However, his savior didn't come by way of the Bible's teachings. His savior had a more earthly orientation. His savior's name is Trevor Stallings.

Six years ago, Trevor Stallings took Tyler Cain under his wing at 'Empower Detroit Inc.' and since that time it looked like he walked the path of saints.

"Found it," Julie said. "Right there, tucked away on the back page of one of the suburban newspapers." She clicked the print icon and the page jettisoned it way through the printer.

"Thanks, Jules."

"Need anything else?" she asked.

"Not at the moment. I have more than enough info to sort through, especially Tyler Cain. I wonder how a guy clearly headed for the Jacktown, managed to turn himself around before the cell doors are locked behind him."

"People change," Julie said non-chalantly.

"Your enthusiastic response just underscore the fact that you don't believe it."

"I don't believe in miracles. If properly motivated, people have been known to experience remarkable changes."

"You sound like a late night infomercial."

She shrugged. "So sue me and pay your bill."

"This stuff on the Stallings is even more interesting," I said trying to change the subject. "The old man, Wayne Stallings, taking a chance by breaking from his line job in the plant and starting his string of Cosmetology schools. His story reads like Horatio Alger. Worked his way up despite the obvious barriers that come with being a black entrepreneur in the Sixties, married a woman ten years his junior and became quite a player on Detroit's business front."

Julie went on to explain how Wayne Stallings was quite a Renaissance man of sorts. He dabbled had seats on the Arts council, the public television advisory board, started a scholarship fund for deserving high school students to attend Wayne State University, was a frequent attendee at Detroit political banquets, and was a collector of art, jewelry and crafts from South Africa.

"He also has two sons; Trevor and a younger brother named Pernell. There's quite a bit here on Trevor's accomplishments, but very little on Pernell."

"Some people don't like the spotlight, Linc," Julie said while glancing at her digital clock. "Now, if you don't mind, I have work to do."

I lifted the page from the printer's tray and placed it in the folder.

"Try to keep it in order, Linc. It will make your life at lot easier." Julie glanced at the photo of Deborah on top of the folder. She picked it up, leaned back in her chair and sighed. "She was pretty, wasn't she?"

"In more ways than one, from what I'm learning."

"You called 'Terry's Enchanted Gardens' yet?" Julie asked.

"Just getting ready to do that very thing," I said as I stood up.

"Liar," Julie sighed. "I don't even know why I bother. If Candy had any sense at all, she'd shoot you and save herself some additional heartache."

"Yeah and then who'd you have to come and annoy you everyday?"

"Ask me after I've had the opportunity to experience such a rare occurrence."

"By the way. I'll be headed to Lansing this afternoon. I should be back late this evening."

"Then leave the folder. I'll probably have added a few more things by the time you return."

Since I only needed the article she'd just printed, I agreed and headed for the door.

The path back to my office was made easier due to Mary's absence to run an errand.

Once I had my feet propped up on my desk, I read through the article. It started with highlighting the strengths Judge Zone would bring to a political leadership position. The reporter hyped his accomplishments as a football player and as a tenacious prosecutor before becoming a prominent judge. There was also mention of his comfortable life by way of investments in real estate and a few growth companies. Further into the article, the reporter began to explore Sylvia's background, assessing her worth as the wife of a future politician. Her charitable work was unprecedented and she'd been given several awards for her work. Though she'd never held a full time job, it was also pointed out that thanks to Judge Zone's career, she had the opportunity to raise two wonderful children and contribute to Detroit's social scene in ways others couldn't. The article went on to suggest that the pressures of campaigning, and being in the political hot seat would be things that would really test her mental stamina and political savvy.

I put the article down and leaned back in my chair with my arms locked behind my head.

On the surface it didn't sound like that big a deal. At least not important enough to cause Judge Zone to back down from something he wanted to pursue. I scratched a few notes to myself, checked the time and had started to stand up when I spotted the business card for 'Terry's Enchanted Gardens' lying on my desk.

I shrugged and punched in the number.

After the genuinely polite greeting, I asked to speak to Pat Terry, assuring the greeter that I was a referral.

After spending very little time on hold, Miss Terry's voice broke the silence.

We minimized the introductions and began talking about the ritual of sending flowers to someone. Without missing a beat, she engaged me in a dialogue that made me feel less inept at mending relationships.

As she talked me through the process, I realized that she had the kind of soothing manner that someone about to jump off a building would need to hear.

I think I would have told her anything.

She convinced me to go with a tropical arrangement as opposed to the always-steady roses.

"Women really know that they're special when a man sends them roses," she assured me. "If you send roses, everyone will know she has a love interest. However, if you send a tropical, everyone in her office will come to see what it is and ooh and ahh."

Miss Terry didn't know that when cops ooh and ahh it takes on a level of kidding that only the strong could endure.

We finally decided on a 'Bird of Paradise' arrangement.

"Guaranteed to get you out of trouble," Miss Terry said with conviction. We also decided that my statement on the accompanying card wouldn't be mushy.

"How about something like 'New Beginnings'?" Miss Terry suggested.

Focused and unmushy, just the way I liked it.

I gave her Candy's address down at the First Precinct and my credit card info. Miss Terry convinced me to set up an account.

She probably knew that the road to forgiveness was both long and winding.

My next stop was Lansing; the capital of Michigan and a meeting with a former crime beat reporter named Arlan Schaefer.

17

Detroit to Lansing on westbound I-96 is an abrupt perceptual reorientation from the sprawling monolithic buildings of the city's core, down past the glass-encased, postmodern structures of regional automotive suppliers and into the uneven landscape that connects one small city with another.

The drive usually takes about an hour or ninety minutes, depending on where the construction was taking place. Naturally, it was westbound just past the Brighton, Michigan exit. There was no doubt in my mind that the one-lane traffic was the direct result of someone knowing I'd gotten out on the road. Unfortunately, I ended up trailing a school bus loaded with elementary school kids waving at me and holding up hand scribbled notes on the back window. Their parents wouldn't have been amused by their enlightened observations of the human anatomy.

Though I was.

I rolled into Lansing an hour and fifteen minutes later, exiting onto Grand Avenue and motored toward the core of downtown Lansing.

Other than Sacramento, I hadn't visited many capitols during my earthly tenure. The few times in Sacramento occurred during my years in Oakland, but that was mostly to hang out with a congressional aide I'd met whose long, shapely legs should have been designated two of California's natural resources. With legs as long as a cold winter night and a passion that burned Texas summer, she liked politics and power. I liked her legs. There were no career conflicts.

Lansing looked liked Sacramento, except for the lack of palm trees and consistently mild weather. The large concrete, pillar structure that resided at the end of Grand River could have been grown or dropped in any state capital anywhere in the country and who would've known the difference.

Arlan Schaefer directed me to a light brown, two-story building that could've easily passed as someone's Norman Rockwell home, minus the picket fence and dog. The building sat on Grand Avenue at an angle from the more modern looking building that housed the *Lansing State Journal*.

I turned off the one-way street and onto a recently paved driveway with visitor parking for anyone visiting the Grand Avenue Capital Building. The wooden marquee on the front lawn listed three businesses occupying the space. The one I wanted was the *Lansing Community Advocate*, a weekly newspaper that focused on the Lansing scene. At least that's how Arlan described his newly found passion.

Once I entered the wood-paneled door, a sprightly looking receptionist, fortyish with green eyes and laugh lines, directed me up the stairs to the office of the *Lansing Community Advocate*.

Had any of the steps creaked, I might have been concerned about what waited at the top.

Before I hit the top stair, I heard the distinctive sound of country music being played and someone's voice hummed along in rhythmic rapture.

I entered a high-ceiling office of wood paneling and matching floor. Set off in brown, light for the walls and dark on the paneling, a white haired man with a short coif, sharp nose and a ruddy profile sat in front of a computer screen moving images around while sipping a green looking concoction.

"Mr. Schaefer?" I queried.

He turned around and stared at me with deep-set, crystal blue eyes. "Who's asking?"

"Lincoln Keller, Mr. Schaefer."

"Roosevelt's kid brother?"

"Actually, next to kid brother." I extended my hand.

He stood up and moved from around the L-shaped desk. He wore a plain gray sweatshirt, blue jean shorts that exposed his pale, hairy legs and sandals. Excess casual and proud of it. "Glad to meet you, Lincoln. Grab a spot over there and I'll be right with you."

There were two-pillow cushioned, curved-back chairs sitting by a window, so I parked my carcass and watched while he moved more images around on the computer screen.

His office looked liked a journalist slept there in between stories. Piles of magazines were stacked next to, and around the six, black four-drawer file cabinets. There were several pictures hanging on the wall which seemed to capture the Arlan Schaefer crime beat years through photos taken with Detroit and Michigan celebrities. Several stacks of news-papers were piled according to city and a mini-fridge sat precariously balanced on a three-legged chair.

"All set," Arlan said several minutes later. He turned off his com-puter and moved toward a green and white windbreaker on a hanger behind the door. "Where's that wild brother of yours?"

"Attending a conference on Michigan State's campus. I thought he might have called you by now."

"No need to. We talk when we talk. Besides, he went to school here so he's probably destroying the city with some former campus friends."

I thought of how little I knew of Rosie's Michigan State Spartan buddies and opted out of further comment. "He sends his best."

"I don't need his best. What I need is to get to the Lansing Lugnuts ball game before they exchange the line up cards."

"Mr. Schaefer ..... "

"Arlan. Please."

"Arlan. I won't take too much of your time. I just wanted to get some background info on Deborah Norris."

He hesitated. "Damn shame what happened to her. She was one of the good ones. Had good journalistic instincts."

"I thought maybe we could ..... "

"We'll talk on the way. Baseball is the only sport that lasts long enough for a person to purge the daily toxic grime from your system and start the night on a good note. C'mon Keller, I'm buying."

"It seems I have no choice."

"It seems you don't," he said smiling impishly.

●　　●　　●

Lansing is a mixture of small town and big city with just enough of each to offset the other. As the state capitol, it's hallowed, stone pillar halls are abound with elected state officials and their staffs who do everything they can to appear sleek and glitzy, yet its downtown has a home spun appeal that rivals a 1960s sitcom. There's a peaceful coexistence of automotive practicality and political one-upmanship. Somewhere in the middle of all that maneuvering, the City of Lansing decided to enhance its down home image by constructing a baseball park for a Class A team known as the Lansing Lugnuts. The game is played in what is suitably known as Oldsmobile Park, since the car manufacturer and the city had enjoyed a long-standing partnership.

General Motors' consolidation of its corporate staff changed the nature of the partnership.

It seemed to me that the lesson was; whenever a business moves out of town, start a minor league baseball franchise.

Inside the impressive red brick structure, the seating was designed so that everyone in attendance had a good view of the evenly manicured field of dreams.

"Great day for baseball. This is how God intended for this game to be played. Close to the people, under an open sky, a grassy field and players not quite good enough to be obnoxious."

Arlan spent most of the time talking about his sudden departure from Detroit. He'd had a steady diet of murder, morgues and maligned personalities, too much booze and too little sleep. Three bad marriages and an assortment of affairs with lovers whose ages were diametrically opposed to his.

"It's the way I spin an adjective and apply a verb. Drives 'em crazy." The raspy-coated laugh told me enough about the now defunct four-pack a day habit that drove him to using the arm patch.

"Moving here saved my life," he admitted as we sat down on the steel bottom benches. "I started this community paper and thanks to a bunch of stringers and work-at-home moms, I cover all the light stuff that the area news stations miss. It's much better for my declining ulcers and the ten thousand or so who pick up the paper at local outlets are happy to see pictures of themselves, family members and friends. I should have moved here twenty years ago."

The reminiscing served some higher purpose I suppose, but wasn't telling me what I wanted to know about Deborah. As the enthusiastic crowd began to take their place within the newly constructed baseball field, Arlan talked unendingly about everything that ran through the cyber cells in his head.

"She had good instincts. Could smell a story better than most."

"Deborah?" I asked having tuned back into the conversation.

He sighed. "I met her at a press conference in Detroit. She walked up to me like she'd known me all my life. Said she admired my work and insisted that I be her mentor. I thought she had a lot of nerve."

"You were impressed?"

"Better than that; I was inspired."

I let him fill in the gap.

"I'd seen a lot of them come and go. College pricks looking for the big story that would send them to New York or Los Angeles. No commitment to developing their writing style. Just do what you have to do to get to the coasts."

"Detroit's no schlock journalistic market."

He snorted. "No it isn't, but there's still New York and LA." He paused. "Deborah was different. She wanted to write good stories; insightful stories that made a difference. She never talked about leaving. All she wanted was to be a good journalist."

"Why didn't she try to get on with the *News* or *Free Press?*"

"Too many editors, too many rules. No room to do what she wanted to do. She valued her independence too much and I don't doubt she would've made a decent living as a free lance." He turned toward me. "You ever read any of her stuff?"

I nodded.

"She did her homework and she never tried to write over the reader's head." He stopped and watched as members of the Lansing Lugnuts ran out of the dugout to begin their warm ups. "Unfortunately, Deborah never got a chance to work through the bug."

My squint told him I wasn't tracking.

"Crusader bug, young man; the curse of all journalists looking to change the world. The desire to make a difference, to find and expose the truth at all costs. The public has a right to know," he said mockingly.

"Isn't that journalism?'

"No. That's youth. The unwavering belief that the truth is pure and absolute. Tell it like it is and the public is better off."

"You say different?"

"I know different. The longer you hang around, the more you realize that the world changes whether you write about it or not and the truth depends largely on the number of papers sold and if it rained."

"Cynicism in place of idealism?"

He whistled when one of the ballplayers launched a pitch over the center field wall. "Reality in the face of deadlines. Most of us make it through that phase. Deborah never got the chance. She died believing in the purity of the truth."

"You were still working the crime beat then, weren't you?"

"Yes," he said in an even tone. "I couldn't write the story since I was a part of it."

"Did your sources confirm that it happened just as it was written?"

He shrugged. "Pretty much. I know we were instructed to leave out the part about being killed with her own gun. Though we could never figure the motive."

"You don't buy the simple robbery motive?"

He stared up at the cloudless sky and sighed. "The truth is rarely simple. Something else triggered her death." He stopped. "No pun intended."

I asked several more questions, hoping that he'd seen or talked to her prior to her death. They hadn't talked then, but for the times they did talk she hadn't mentioned any boyfriends or problems, and he had no idea what story she may have been working on.

By now the teams had finished their warm ups, batting practice and posing for the crowd. The line-up cards had been exchanged and the cry to 'play ball' was announced on the field and repeated on the loud speakers.

As the first batter strolled to the plate, I asked, "Who knew she carried a gun?"

"Far as I know, no one. But my guess would be her close friends, most likely Judge Zone and me, of course. Beyond that, I don't know." The first pitch was thrown and cracked inside the catcher's mit, momentarily distracting Arlan. "Good pitch! Yeah!" He leaned back. "You gonna find her killer?"

"I don't know. I'm asking a lot of questions."

"You should be a journalist," he said while watching a batter double off the wall.

"So should you," I replied.

He smiled and cocked an eyebrow. "I enjoy what I'm doing. The stories I write are about decent people trying to live a good life without too much hassle." He paused. "It would take one hell of a story to pull me back into that madness."

"Well, you never know," I said.

"Maybe." He replied. "This search for Deborah's killer; may I offer a bit of advice for you, young man."

"I'm listening."

"Just look for the truth."

"Pure truth, or the real truth?"

He paused. "Whichever one got her killed."

18

Long, uninterrupted drives back home have a way of allowing time for the mind to sort through its gray matter receptacles and piece together information that appear to have no relevance.

Despite the annoying slow-downs for construction, my return trip down I-96 gave me some needed sorting time.

My talk with Arlan was helpful, though not as revealing as I'd hoped.

Luck and hope are what keep a P.I. searching.

Arlan Shaefer had seen the light that flowed from Deborah's spirit. I gathered that he saw in her what he wanted to be when youth, time and energy were elastic concepts that stretched across an endless spectrum of experiences.

He'd missed his shot at the brass ring. Deborah's unfortunate death had denied him his last chance at immortality.

Like himself, Deborah had gotten the investigative bug. Like himself, she wanted to change the world. The only difference was he'd been given the chance to hang around long enough to see the futility in that belief. Deborah had died still believing in the possibilities.

I rolled those thoughts around in my head for the duration of the trip, stopping only to take note of the fact that I had already changed over to the Lodge freeway and had made the exit onto Livernois Avenue.

For me, it was too early for bed and too late for dinner. The chilidogs, fries and beer I consumed at the ball game worked my system like falling meteors.

Feeling bug-eyed awake, I drove over to the office to check for messages. I keyed the alarm pad, punched in the security code and drifted upstairs to the Keller office.

I clicked on the overhead lights, noticed Julie had left the folder on my desk and hit the play button on the answering machine. There were two messages; one for Jeff and one for me.

Sharron Westlake called, asking if I would get in touch with her this evening. She said she needed to see me right away. She remembered something and wanted to tell me about it. Mary noted the time of the call. The message came in at 7:59.

At 10:47 I could only reach her answering machine.

Though it wasn't the proper time at night to go calling on a woman you'd just recently met, I decided to throw decorum out the window. The Goddesses of Social Etiquette would just have to deduct some merit points.

I locked the office, walked downstairs and noticed a familiar Econline Van parked behind my car.

Jeff's shadowy outline waved at me.

The passenger side window was rolled down when I peeked in and saw someone who appeared to be sleep.

"Do you know him?" he asked.

I looked at the unconscious figure, clad in cord jeans and a black sweatshirt "No. Can't say that I do."

"You sure?" Jeff flashed a thin light across his face.

"I don't know. That flow of blood coming from his nose makes it hard to say."

"I gun butted him harder than I thought," he replied. "Name's 'ST', 'Street Time' to his friends. Mostly a small time, penny-ante operator who's too stupid to know that you don't stalk the people walking behind you."

"What's he doing here?"

"Word has it that he was looking to move up. He was trying to make a name for himself. So he put the word out that he was looking to do contract work."

"Contract work?" I said not liking the drift of the conversation. "You mean like; tearing down abandoned buildings on Woodward, installing windows in the new Condos down by Belle Isle? That kind of contract work ..... right?"

Jeff shrugged. "Anyway, you remember the call I got earlier from that snitch?"

"Yeah."

"Somebody dropped a dime that he happened to overhear. Turns out somebody wanted to get rid of a Keller."

"Wait a minute. What about ..... "

Jeff wouldn't let me interrupt. " ..... I already checked. Rosie's in East Lansing at the home of his buddy, Ernie Betts. According to Ernie's wife, Greta, when last heard, Rosie, Ernie, Walt and Earl were in their basement playing Miles Davis albums and recalling some of their protest marches. Truman's working late. He's involved in an all night marathon bargaining session to prevent a strike at their plant. That left you and me."

"And it couldn't have been you because ..... "

Jeff smiled evenly. "Because there's no one in Detroit that stupid."

"Why me?"

"That's what I'm going to find out."

I stared at the unconscious figure. "Is he any good?"

"If he was, you'd be having this conversation with mom and dad, not me. So we have an advantage because whoever hired him made two mistakes: one; they didn't hire the best, two; they came after a Keller."

"Jeff, I realize that as the eldest you have certain rights. But you could have just told me."

"You'd already left for Lansing by the time I found out. Now we need to find out who hired him and why."

"Need any help?"

"No," he said with indignation in his tone. "I'll take him to my place and talk to him for a while. I'll call you once I know."

I walked out with Jeff. He peeled away from the curb and onto Livernois like a man on a mission.

I sat behind the wheel of my car convinced of one thing; the so-called contract on my head had something to do with my investigation of Deborah's death.

Somebody really didn't want me nosing around.

Why?

I fired up the Nova and checked the lateness of the hour.

"The hell with social etiquette," I said to myself and the Goddesses of Social Etiquette and headed out to see Sharron.

19

Twenty minutes later, I rolled off Outer Drive and onto Wisconsin Street in search of Sharron's residence. The modest, two-level brick homes on this middle class residential street were made similar by the black-poled lawn lights being used as the first line of defense against the possibility of burglary. Despite the obvious use of driveways, traveling down the two-way street was an adventure in dodging parked cars.

Sharron's home was a two-level brick with a white wooden front and black shingles. I found a parking spot two cars down from her house, latched my 'Club' onto the steering wheel and walked up the short, lawn-lit walkway. The doorbell was also dimly lit as I did the push-and-wait tango for what seemed like several minutes.

Someone did peek through a curtain before the voice behind the door asked. "Who is it?"

I recognized Sharron's voice and hoped she recognized mine.

"Just a minute," she said reluctantly.

The door slowly opened and I moved cautiously, stepping on a plastic throw rug.

Shadows from a moon lit sky stretched across the darkened area as Sharron's outline closed the door behind me.

"Watch your step," she said turning away from me and walking toward an open area.

"Sharron, I'm sorry I didn't get back to you earlier, but I've had a strange evening."

"That makes two of us," she replied angrily.

She flipped on an overhead light and I immediately saw part of why she was angry.

The observation led me to two conclusions: either she was Detroit's female version of the Odd Couple's Oscar Madison, or; her home had been burglarized.

Whoever turned her home into a self-contained pit had done a thorough job. Furniture had been turned over; books, magazines and CDs lay scattered on the carpeted floor. Sharron stood in the middle of the mess, her arms folded and shaking her head.

I glanced around, choosing not to step too far. It reminded me of similar scenes I'd witnessed as a patrol officer back in Oakland. I'd experienced the general feeling of helplessness and personal violation felt by the victims as they tried to sort through why someone, anyone, would take what they'd worked so hard to achieve.

The view into the next room didn't get any prettier. Overturned dining chairs and a broken vase of artificial flowers added to the debris. A metallic grey CD player had been wrenched from its corner and lay several feet from the table it rested upon.

That observation altered my conclusion.

"Sharron. This wasn't a burglary, was it?" I asked.

She shook her head, too angry to cry and too vulnerable to hold it in. "No. It wasn't."

I spun Sharron toward me and that's when I saw the other part of her anger. She'd tried to cover the welt under her right eye with some facial powder that did nothing more than highlight the fact that she'd been hit.

"Sharron! What the hell's going on here?"

"I wish I knew," she replied still fighting the tears. "I wish I knew."

"Have you called the police?" I asked while looking around for a telephone.

"No. I haven't and I won't. I ..... I can't."

"Why not?"

"I've been warned not to ..... "

I turned the couch upright, put the three pillows back in place and helped her sit down. "Warned by who?" I looked around the scattered remnants of Sharron's home. "What happened?"

"I don't know how they got in, but I'd just turned in just a little after eleven. I couldn't have been asleep more than twenty minutes when I felt a gloved hand over my mouth and I was dragged from my bed and down to the living room."

"Was it one person?"

"Two who dragged me downstairs. The other had already started messing up my home."

"Did you see their faces?"

"No. They wore black outfits and black ski masks. It didn't disguise the fact that they were black."

"What did they want?"

She stared up at me. Her eyes burned with anger. "They wanted to know what you and I had talked about. What I had told you."

"What you told me? Why?"

"How the hell should I know. They think I know something, but I don't know what it is they think I know."

"You think it's connected to Deborah's death?"

"I can't imagine what else it could be. I'm not that important a person. I don't have a lot of money and I work for a living. Why would anyone want to threaten me? It's Deborah. I know it. But I don't know what."

"Describe the men who attacked you."

"What can I say? They were disguised. Two were about medium height. The other one, the one who slapped me, was a little taller, maybe a little bulkier. I don't know."

There was rotten smell at the fragrance counter. Sharron had been slapped, threatened and her home ransacked while I'd made number one on someone's hit parade.

I knew there was no such thing as a coincidence, so I told Sharron about my near fatal encounter. "Don't suppose I can talk you into reporting what happened here?"

"The only reason why you know is because you just happen to show up. You want to help?"

"Of course," I said.

"Then help me put my place back in order."

"Sharron."

"That's as much help as I need right now. Okay?"

I spent the next couple of hours helping Sharron. It was a good excuse to hang around to make sure no one backtracked to add to her misery. She moved around methodically, only conversing when I asked about the placement of certain items. About half way through I had picked up several pictures that had been knocked down from the mantel above the fireplace. It was the usual assortment of family, graduation and self-portraits, common to most homes. The only exception was the gold-framed picture of Deborah. It was an exact duplicate of the one on her sister's mantel.

Deborah had signed the picture in the bottom right hand corner, just as she had on the other one.

Sharron must have noticed me staring at the picture.

"Something wrong?"

"No. This is exactly like the one I saw at her sister's home. I guess she really liked the portrait."

"It's a good likeness. Really captured the physical and inner beauty of my friend."

"When did she give you this picture?"

She hesitated. The tears she fought so hard to keep in check, began to work their way down her face. It was a slow descent for the first tear bubble. "About a month before she was killed. She had copies made for MiShaun, her sister and me. She said it was the only picture she'd ever taken that told the complete story."

"It's a good picture. Wish I could have met her."

"If she liked you, she would have found a way to victimize you with one of her elaborate practical jokes."

"Did she get you?"

"More time than I care to count."

The undamaged, miniature grandfather clock chimed at half past two in the morning. We'd done about as much as we could, given the circumstances.

I checked all the windows and doors to make sure that all was secure. It seemed futile given what had happened, but I knew I had to do something. I had a friend who'd give her a good deal on a more sophisticated security system, but I also needed someone to look after her for a few days while I continued to dig.

There was no doubt in my mind that I'd have to keep digging. Dig deep and wide, until I found whatever it was that laid buried beneath the surface of Deborah's murder. Someone had gotten nervous and careless. They'd taken the first shot and missed. Along the way, an innocent person had been slapped, threatened and her home turned upside down.

Threats thrown at me were easily discarded. Hell, I'd played for the Raiders.

However, I was impatient with the weak that preyed upon the innocent just to assert their strength.

That made me mad.

She declined my offer to stay; stating that she would not live in fear in her own home.

I didn't like the answer, but respected the posture.

I left Sharron with two assurances; my home and office number. She could reach me anytime. I told her she'd seen the last of this harassment.

As I sped down Wisconsin Avenue to Seven Mile Road, I had two phone calls in mind once I reached my apartment.

20

I ignored the two waiting messages on the answering machine as I punched in Jeff's unlisted phone number.

Not knowing what he was up to had become a way of running Keller Investigations that seemed to suit both our styles. As the eldest brother, he made himself available in that elder brother kind of manner. As a partner in Keller Investigations; he met his part of the operating expenses. I hoped he had information to share on the world's newest contract killer.

The answering machine kicked in with his usual short introduction. 'Leave a message'.

I asked him to call me soon.

I punched in the second number, expecting to hear an answering machine only to hear Tank's gravely, sleep soaked voice echo through the receiver.

"Yes, I'd like to place an order for a floral arrangement of Tiger Lilies."

"Linc? That you man?" he asked.

"Yeah, big man. What are you doing home at this hour?"

"Trying to sleep. It's been a long three days and, what the hell do you want at this hour?"

"Got a job for you."

I gave him a quick overview of what I was doing, moving quickly onto Sharron and what happened to her home.

"What do you need?"

"Just keep a watchful eye on her. At a distance until I can figure out what's going on here. What do you think?"

He yawned. "Sure. I could use the field experience and the extra cash."

When we first met, Tank and I almost became adversaries. Since that initial meeting, he's helped me on a couple of cases and has decided to move his career on a path of law enforcement. After meeting Jeff, he decided to become a bounty hunter. He takes on odd jobs from time to time as a way of learning his craft. He hopes to move out of the floral arrangement/delivery business by the end of the year. I neglected to mention my placing an order through Terry's Enchanted Garden.

I gave him Sharron's address and description.

"Sounds like a neighborhood where I'll stand out," he chuckled

"Yeah, but everyone will be too frightened to tell you."

We agreed on when to touch base.

I plopped down in my recliner, stripped down to my red silk under-shorts and propped my feet up on the footrest. I should have gone to bed, but my body and mind were out of sync.

"What the hell have I wandered into?" I mumbled while pressing the play button on the answering machine.

Jeff's voice slithered out of the speaker. "Stay loose and watch your back. I'll be in touch."

I'd already adopted that posture.

The second message played.

"Nice touch with the flowers, Linc. It's working." Candy's voice in seductive E minor brought some relaxation.

More than I thought since it's the last thing I heard before nodding off.

• • •

It was the combination of unsettling dreams and semi-comfortable sleeping conditions that contributed to my inability to find the deepest point in the sleep cycle.

A cacophony of voices and meaningless images zipped through my mind like children on a merry-go-round. Whirling by my mind's eye just fast enough to blur the landscape. In all likelihood, the ringing phone was a welcome relief from the mental drama.

I answered the phone, croaking out the formal hello as the fading dreams and the bright morning fought for visual dominance.

The woman's voice had that official morning formality I'd come to associate with telemarketers.

The blurred images interfered with my usual song and dance routine to get her off the phone.

"Mr. Keller," she pressed on. "Trevor Stallings would like to meet with you today. He has some time around noon. Would it be possible for you to join him?"

"Where?" I asked.

She told me.

I said I'd be there.

The sound of traffic moving up and down Livernois Avenue gave me a pretty good clue as to how late in the morning I'd slept. I glanced at my watch for verification. Given my rather unusual late night, sleeping past ten in the morning seemed justified to me.

I stood and stretched, eased my way to the bathroom while thinking about why Trevor Stallings wanted to meet with me. It seemed to me that someone in the middle of a political campaign for a council seat had more important things to do with his time than meet with a private investigator.

"Must be important to him," I mumbled to the tube of toothpaste I was squeezing. "Or else why would he have tracked down my unlisted number?"

It was one of those questions I'd have to ask Mr. Stallings.

I fumbled through my closet looking for just the right outfit; casual with just a hint of class. After all, the twenty-sixth floor of the Renaissance Center wasn't an average bar and grill.

●   ●   ●

The seven-tower, glass-shielded monument to modern downtown living known as the Renaissance Center was built on the shoreline of the Detroit River and stands as a architectural landmark to the revitalization of downtown Detroit.

Those architectural silos recently became the world headquarters of General Motors, thus solidifying the notion that the downtown area would experience a major face-lift. It's home to several corporations, numerous law, accounting and consulting firms, shops, boutiques, fast food joints, a movie theatre and a major hotel. There are also places for the jet-set crowd to sit and relax with an overpriced, watered down drink and engage in social intercourse.

Now that I was 'decked out' in my blue, double-breasted sport coat with silver buttons, a dark blue turtleneck shirt, neatly pleated blue pants and my black casual shoes with tassels, I felt much more in sync as I rode the observational elevator to the 26th floor.

When the elevator doors opened, I stepped onto a casual lounge area with several people standing around, drinks in hand and looking rather upbeat for a lunch crowd.

There was a circular lounge that sat in the middle of the spacious red carpeted area. A hand-carved, horizontal bar sat unobtrusively in the back of the room. Its tall, leather-cushioned seats were all occupied and the spaces between them were filled with others seeking conversation or other social amusements.

I worked my way through the conservatively attired crowd, taking in the various fragrances generated by the expensive perfumes and cheap colognes.

A white-jacketed server cruised by with a tray of beverages and offered me a choice of soft drinks. I thanked him and walked near the entrance of the banquet room.

I peeked in, not certain as to whom I was suppose to meet, though I did spot a familiar face at the speaker's podium that was apparently lambasting some poor technician about the sound quality of the microphone.

I walked around the scattering of round tables with the sparking red tablecloths and six-person-servings until I reached the podium.

"Hello, Tyler. How's everybody's favorite executive assistant this morning?"

He stopped his ranting momentarily, glared down from the podium, motioned me forward and dismissed the technician all in one movement.

"Mr. Stallings is in the back," he said. "He's going over parts of his speech."

He led me along the elevated dais, past a closed curtain that led down a hall to a corner room.

He knocked twice and opened the door.

The room was decorated to look like a small luxury hotel room without a bed.

Trevor Stallings was sitting at the hardwood desk, turning pages under the soft light of a desk lamp. He made a few notations as Tyler cleared his throat.

Stallings looked up.

"That P.I. you wanted to see is here, Mr. Stallings," Tyler announced.

"Ah, yes. Thank you, Tyler. Come in, Mr. Keller. Please have a seat." He pointed to a curved back chair that had green back and seat cushions. "Tyler, please see that we aren't disturbed."

"Yes, Mr. Stallings. However, I must remind you that you should be out mingling as quickly as possible."

"I know. I won't be long," he replied with an assuring wave. He waited until Tyler had closed the door behind him. "Mr. Keller, can I offer you a drink?" He'd already stood up and was walking toward the refreshment cabinet.

"No, thanks," I said. "But please indulge yourself."

He took out a small bottle of mineral water and poured it over the waiting glass of ice. Stallings was the Nineties version of polish and style. He was American Express platinum in a three-button, wool Brooks Brothers suit and silk tie. He walked like someone certain of his destiny and unwilling to accept anything less. He radiated focus and confidence. A bulky six feet even with brown eyes and a carmel tone, he could have been mistaken for a loud mouth if his glossy enamel smile wasn't so silencing. Evenly coiffed of hair and mustache with matching blues that a color coordinator would envy.

"So, what did you want to see me about?" I asked.

"Well, you don't waste time," he replied instead of answering.

"You don't have much to waste," I said nodding toward the speech.

"That. Oh, yes." He walked back over to the desk and sat down. "Well, when I got word that a private investigator is looking into the background of one of my key staff members, you can understand why I'd be interested."

"I can understand, but I'm afraid you've been misinformed. I'm not looking into a key staff-members background. I specifically spoke with MiShaun to get information about a case I'm investigating."

"Oh? And what case would that be?" He swirled the drink around so that the ice rattled and took a quick sip.

"Let's not play games, Mr. Stallings. You don't have time and neither do I. Tracking down someone's unlisted home number suggests more than just a passing familiarity with what's going on. I'm sure that reclamated gopher of yours told you more than you're letting on, although his information is inaccurate."

"Tyler's a very loyal employee."

"Despite his rough beginnings," I added.

He nodded and smiled in that way people do when they're surprised and impressed. "People can change, Mr. Keller."

"So I've been told."

"Well, since we're not playing games; yes, I do know that you're investigating the tragic death of Deborah Norris. A truly gifted writer, so I've been told." He hesitated momentarily. "From what I understand, that was eight years ago. That's a long time."

"For some people it was yesterday. The case is still unsolved."

"That is tragic indeed. MiShaun has mentioned her from time to time. I guess they were quite close."

"That's why we talked."

Someone tapped on the door bringing a momentary pause to our immovable dialogue.

The person who entered was a slimmer, younger version of Trevor. Not quite as flashy, but with similar tone and matching eyes.

"Mr. Keller," Trevor said while standing. "This is my brother Pernell."

I stood up, hand extended, just the way we were taught in grade school.

Pernell returned the gesture, although with less enthusiasm. "Mr. Keller, you here for my brother's speech?"

"No," I said. "I'm here to clarify some misinformation."

"Mr. Keller is a private investigator recently acquainted with MiShaun," Trevor said. "I asked to see him. Turns out my concerns were off center."

"Is MiShaun in some kind of trouble?" Pernell asked.

"None that I'm aware of," I replied.

I left the sentence hanging, waiting to see who'd jump in and fill the gap.

"Well, MiShaun is a valued employee and a great asset to our organization," Pernell quickly offered. "I hope whatever you're investigating won't distract her from work."

"It shouldn't," I said.

Trevor chimed in. "Mr. Keller, I hope you're not part of that huge majority of people in Detroit who don't vote in critical elections."

"Every election I vote in is critical."

"Good. Detroit is in the midst of a great transformation. But it can only happen when voters exercise their constitutional rights. This city has been plagued too long by people who represent a political and moral philosophy which I feel is counter productive to the long term interests of Detroit." He stopped for a moment. "Where were you raised, Mr. Keller?"

"Russell Street, on the North End."

"And based on that little information, I know more about you than you'd care to admit. The North End of town is basically blue collar, factory labor, the little which still exists. You were raised in a staunchly democratic district in a city that functioned under twenty years of a backroom, hardball-playing democratic Mayor. You've probably voted along democratic lines most of your voting life. How am I doing?"

"Not bad. Not perfect, but not too bad. Why are you telling me what I already know?"

Trevor half smiled. "I represent the new breed of voting African Americans. In some ways I'm a foreigner in my own home city. But I believe that it's the way we have to go. I'm a Republican who can see that Detroit's future doesn't lie with old line political ways, but in the investment of the new wave of political conservatism that has swept the country."

"I don't mind what's sweeping the country. What I object to is the people who fall through the cracks. Your becoming a republican councilman in a democratic city would be quite a feather in your cap."

"I have a higher aspiration than councilman. I think the 13th district is ready for a new, younger congressman with new ideas about leadership." Trevor spoke more to himself than to me. "The problem will be helping the African American voters see and understand the new vision."

There were three rapid knocks on the door and Tyler hurriedly entered. "Mr. Stallings, I hate to disturb you, but its getting close to that time."

He shrugged knowingly. "Sorry, Mr. Keller, but duty calls. This is an influential group of voters. My speech, 'Investing in the Future' should really hit home. You can stay and listen if you'd like."

"I'll wait for the movie."

We both stood up and shook hands. "Nice to have met you. Good luck on your investigation. I hope you can bring it to some resolution."

I looked into those confident eyes. "I should be able to as long as I stay one step ahead of whoever's hiring people to kill me."

He didn't flinch. "I do hope you're joking, Mr. Keller."

"Not about life and death," I said. "Thanks for your time, Mr. Stallings."

He walked me to the door and I stopped just at the entrance. "Mr. Stalling. Why did you really want to see me?"

He stopped and stared at me for just a moment. "I wanted to find out for myself what you really wanted. I needed to see what kind of man you are."

"Satisfied with the answer?" I said.

"For the moment," he replied. "But we'll see what the future brings."

We exchanged good byes and I strolled into the hallway.

I walked across the main dining room, taking in the array of people, colors and backgrounds sitting earnestly at their tables, preparing to dine and listen to a speech by a young political player who has a long-term vision for Detroit.

Trevor Stallings may have just been spitting in the wind, but I'd see what the future held.

During my wait for the elevator I thought about why Trevor Stallings contacted me. I was inclined to believe that there was some sincerity in his overture. Maybe he had been misinformed, but he deliberately moved the conversation from my investigation to my politics, topped off by what he thought was best for the city. I didn't believe he was that interested in my politics.

On the surface, it was nice and neat, but underneath it felt like torrential waves moving in an unstoppable direction toward a smashing end.

And it was my face I saw on the end of that smashing.

Healthy paranoia ..... I hoped.

I was so engaged in speculation that I didn't notice the woman standing next to me waiting impatiently for the elevator. Mocha-toned with brown-streaked hair worn at shoulder length, she wore a double-breasted, spotted chiffon jacket that tied at the waist, black pants, matching platform shoes and carried a bamboo handle bag. She folded her arms across her chest, staring at the elevator, the carpet and then the banquet room.

Pernell Stallings momentarily cast his eyes in our direction and I knew it had nothing to do with me.

The woman held the stare and turned toward the elevator just as it chimed and opened its doors.

She chose to gaze out the glass barrier at the city as the elevator descended non-stop to the lobby area.

Malone had made a comment some time ago that suddenly popped in my head; "It's a look that passes between two people," she said in describing the reason behind our current cooling off period.

When the doors opened, she walked out, turning sharply toward the nearby exit.

I had nothing else to go on but 'the look that passes between two people'.

Sometimes, nothing is all you have to pursue as a lead I thought while I cleared my throat to get her attention.

She turned around, puzzled but with her urban caution in full display.

"My name is Lincoln Keller." I handed her a business card and opened my wallet to show her my license. "I'm a private investigator and if you've got a minute, I'd like to ask you a few questions."

She glanced at my pictured license and closely read the business card. "Well," she said clutching the card like a cigarette. "You certainly don't look like a private investigator."

"I've been sick," I replied. "Seriously, just a few questions."

"Questions about what?" she asked.

"Not what as much as who."

"Go on," she said impatiently.

"Well, I couldn't help but notice an exchange that went on between you and Pernell Stallings."

"Is that any of your business?"

"Only if you want to talk about what's going on," I said.

"He's a bastard," she replied cryptically

"Would you care to elaborate?"

"Only if you're buying," she said nodding toward the open lounge area near the cascading wishing well.

21

Her name was Jocelyn Kilgore and after our drinks arrived, she offered a toast to all the bastards she'd known in her twenty nine-year history. She was polished edges with an urban slice, having started her career with a local phone company and now held the lofty position of Unit Manager for Technical Sales of Region 3.

It probably meant something and one day I'd ask the question. But not today.

She clinked her rum-and-coke against my lime-water, sipped and leaned back against the cushioned lounge chair. There were stories behind that flush round face and the one that I wanted to hear was right there on the surface.

We sat in an open lounge area complete with leather surface seating and a circular view of people moving steadily about in the recently purchased headquarters of General Motors.

Her story began with a chance meeting, which is where they usually began.

"I met Pernell several years ago at 'Flood's' downtown. I had recently graduated from Wayne State and wanted to celebrate my accomplishment. My friends and I decided to go 'night clubbing' the way we wanted to, but couldn't during those poor student years in college." She looked away for just a moment. "You go to college?"

"Prarie View State down in Texas. I had a football scholarship."

"Nice. Anyway, so I'm dancing, partying and just having a good time when this brother comes over to our table and asks me to dance."

"Pernell?"

"Mr. Bastard himself, although I didn't know it at the time. I'm thinking, now here's one fine brother. If his act is halfway together, this could be a fun night."

"Was it?"

"His act or the night?"

"Both," I said.

She sipped. "His act was smooth and the night was fun ..... somewhat."

"What do you mean?"

"I ended up leaving with him. We drove his car around the city and then on the outskirts. The boy had a light blue Nissan 300X and a lead foot. But I didn't care, I was having a good time. We sped down some back areas that I didn't know existed out there in Oakland County. Just one long night of fun."

"So you two have been together ever since?"

"Not together really. I've just been one of many whom I'm sure he's taken on that same ride. My problem is I kept thinking he'd change. He slowed down some, thanks to his brother, but not completely. He's still a dog who likes to sniff around."

"What happened upstairs?"

"Me being stupid. I knew he'd be here with his brother so I thought I'd come here and see if I could talk with him. He's been avoiding me."

"Did you talk?"

"No! That damn Tyler saw me and warned Pernell. Seems like he's always looking out for him."

That comment surprised me. "Always? Doesn't Tyler work for Trevor? Or, at least his assistant, MiShaun Lucas?"

"Doing what? That thug doesn't know anything but the life. Pernell would've been the same way if not for his brother. Tyler's there because Pernell wanted him there. They're two of a kind. Pernell may not go speeding down back roads anymore, but he's nothing more than a dog in a silk tie and I've had enough."

"Funny. I had a conversation with Trevor not too long ago and he seemed quite happy with how Tyler had progressed from his previous life."

"He wears a suit during the day, but Mr. Stallings don't see him at night," Jocelyn said as she finished her drink. "Look, I've stayed longer than I planned and I need to get back to work."

"You gonna be alright?" I asked nodding toward the empty glass.

She gave me a dismissive wave. "Oh yeah. This isn't strong enough to do any damage. Besides, I've probably burned off the alcohol." We stood up and I extended my hand to thank her. Her touch felt smooth and warm. "You're probably seeing someone, aren't you?"

I nodded, not feeling a need to elaborate.

She sighed. "That figures. Try not to be a bastard with her ..... okay?"

"Okay."

"Nice meeting you, Mr. Keller."

I watched Jocelyn leave, walking briskly across the tiled floor, her steps being muffled by the endless flow of people moving through the lobby. She disappeared into the crowd as I signed the bill.

I took the exit across the skywalk that led to the parking structure next to the Detroit River.

"Investigations seldom run a straight course," I said to my reflection in the rear view mirror.

The parking attendant ignored my comment and collected the city's parking ransom.

I sped away from downtown not sure what my conversation with Jocelyn meant in the overall scheme of things, but it came in the course of my investigation, so it must have meant something.

Call it a stretch, but its what I believed.

22

Keeping up with Jeff's whereabouts was like trying to find microbes in a sub-atomic universe. You know they are there, you just can't see them.

I'd tried his unlisted number, his pager and would've tried a carrier pigeon if they weren't so committed to not missing their free meals down at Hart Plaza.

He'd left no messages at the office or bothered to show up, so I was left dangling with the knowledge that an amateur had tried to take me out and consequently had been left in Jeff's capable hands.

I pictured bamboo shafts underneath his fingernails and immediately dismissed the picture.

The McDonald's on the corner of Mack Avenue and I-75 was my next stop. I needed to use the phone and munch an order of fries. The lunch crowd had petered out, so that the only noise came from sporadically placed teenagers enjoying a hot afternoon inside the air-conditioned walls of the golden arches.

Several of them displayed the current youthful scowl, or grimace, designed specifically to frighten women, children and anyone who might mistakenly say 'Hello'.

Trends are such an interesting occurrence among the young and uninformed. And more often than not, the two are one and the same.

Since I hadn't been able to reach Jeff, I thought I'd call the fourth key player over at 'Empower Detroit'.

But the unexpected in my unexpected visit was something I wasn't expecting; MiShaun Lucas wasn't unavailable.

Helen "the Barn" Barnes seemed pleased to tell me that.

"From now on? Or just for the rest of the day?" I asked.

Helen Barnes 'humphed' and disconnected. She could humph with the best of them. She had the body for it.

Call it a hunch. I removed MiShaun's business card from my wallet and punched in her home number. I anticipated four rings and an answering machine. I heard three rings and a feint "Hello."

"MiShaun? It's Lincoln Keller. We met the other day."

"So?" she replied in early-afternoon monotone.

"So, I'd like to ask you a few more questions about Deborah. It won't take ..... "

" ..... I'm working very hard right now to meet a deadline. Call later."

"How much later?" I asked ignoring her abruptness.

"Much later!" she replied and rang off.

I called Julie. McDonald's is known for a lot of things and an Ameritech phone book isn't one of them.

Mary patched me through to Julie. When she answered, I told her what I needed. "Remember that glowing report you gave me on Pernell Stallings?"

"I don't remember the report being glowing. There wasn't a lot there."

"But that doesn't mean nothing exists?"

"As long as a person has a social security number, then something exists. There are other databanks I can cross check if you want."

"I'd appreciate it."

"Your appreciation doesn't pay my overhead. I'll leave whatever I find in your office along with a bill for service."

Love that Jules.

I checked the time and strolled back to my booth where my fries hadn't gotten cold and the ice in my drink had melted. I stuffed a few more fries, cleared off my table and headed to the parking lot.

Silent Suspicion

MiShaun was at home working against a deadline. Seemed like a good time for a surprise visit.

• • •

The East side's version of Detroit's renaissance had taken the shape of modern two-level Tudor homes erected on newly sodden land with planted trees, a two-car garage and cathedral ceilings with a sun window. This revitalized hope for the future attracted the urban pioneer willing to stake their claim in Detroit's future.

MiShaun's address was pasted on a mailbox in front of a brick front, two-level home with a pitched roof, large front window and a two-car garage.

She had stepped up quite a bit from the old partying days of Franklin Court. The red brick walkway separated the deep, green grass and multicolored flowerbeds as if it were leading me to the door of a saint.

I rang the amber-lit doorbell and waited until the front door was slowly pulled open.

MiShaun stared back, clad in a loosely tied, light blue terrycloth robe, matching slippers. On first glance it looked like the only thing under her robe was a gold necklace.

Working at home has it advantages.

"I'm busy," she snarled.

"Won't take a minute," I said inching my foot over the landing.

"I started not to answer this damn door," she continued.

"Won't take a minute." I repeated.

She moved away in an attempt to slam the door in my face. The door hit against my shoe bouncing back just enough to startle MiShaun.

She glared.

"Won't take a minute," I said.

"What else do you want to know?" she asked impatiently.

"I can ask a lot better if I'm out of this hot sun. What do you think?"

"Oh, come in," she finally relented. "For all the good it'll do."

She led me through a small carpeted foyer into a spacious living room made bigger by the cathedral ceiling and hanging eight-socket, glass chandelier. The corner of the room was done in oak and a gas-lit fireplace done in artificial red brick with an equally artificial oak mantel said a lot about MiShaun's move into the world of power walks and paid advertisements in Detroit's local magazines.

She'd invested in a teal leather sectional with a right facing chaise and enough pillows to accommodate the Detroit Pistons should they happen to stop by for a photo shoot. A glass-topped oval cocktail table with a wrought-iron base, textured bronze finish and gold plated accents sat comfortably on the large square patterned throw rug that covered most of the hardwood floor. The companion end tables held matching gold plated reading lamps. Their kidney shaped base, bar and shade were also gold plated. Underneath the lamp on the right end table was the same picture of Deborah I'd seen at both the Henderson's and Sharron's home.

MiShaun had come a long way from Franklin Court.

Though I was impressed with the sophisticated layout of her home, I was less impressed by the three quarters empty, opened fifth of gin sitting on a flowered blue tray with matching ice bucket, glasses and a small dish of limes cut in small quarters.

Working from home has its advantages.

"What are we celebrating?" I asked.

Gin, like most liquors taken in quantities exceeding one shot, has a staggering effect on one's physical movement. It's only distinguishing trademark is that it doesn't smell as bad as the others do. I figured that's why I didn't smell it right from the beginning.

"WE aren't celebrating anything," she replied firmly. "I'm working from home today."

"How long has this ..... work, been going on?"

"Not long enough."

"It was my understanding you were off the sauce. Rehab, the whole bit. Was I misinformed?"

She leaned back against the back of the couch, propping her matching footwear on the cocktail table. "Not that it's any of your business, Mr. Private Detective, but I've gone through some Rehab and I'm a member of AA."

"Where's your sponsor's phone number?"

"I don't know." The initial strength she showed at the door had started to wane. She seemed more listless. "I haven't had to use it for quite a while. I haven't had a drink for a while."

"Why now?"

She pointed a shaky finger at the picture of Deborah on end table. "Her." She then pointed to me. "You. Everything."

"I'm not quite sure I follow you." I really didn't.

Mishaun signed deeply. "She left me. She left me just as I was starting to be somebody. Just as I was starting to show her and Sharron that I was just as good as the both of them. I didn't have any college degree, but I had street smarts. I knew how to work people, especially men."

Seemed like a good moment for me to keep silent.

"You don't always have to be book smart to get somewhere," she said pointing to the walnut bookshelf in the corner adjacent from where she had plopped. "I'm smart where it counts. You see these?" she pulled open her robe, exposing her firm but unstimulated breasts. "Do you know how many men have wanted to get their hands on these? A whole lots more than you know. But you know how many have actually touched them?"

"Only the ones that count," I answered.

"Damn right." She started to pull her robe together, stopping halfway. "You'd like to, wouldn't you? You'd like to touch them, wouldn't you?" Her tone became more daring. Defiant the way people who've had too much to drink are when trying to appear sober.

Welcome to the uninhibited mood swing world of the Nineties drunk, I thought. "What I'd like is a cup of coffee." I stood up. "I suppose you keep some in the kitchen."

I strolled past her.

"Hey, where are you going?"

"I'm going to make coffee. You sit there and think about why you leaped off the wagon."

She started to stand up, but I grabbed both her shoulders.

"I said sit down!"

She withdrew, tucking her legs underneath her as she settled into a corner of the couch. She didn't appear surprised. Knowing drunks, she was probably relieved.

Even the postmodernist kitchens have similar elements that require very little skill. Brewing coffee still consisted of measuring, pouring water and pressing the on button for the coffee maker. The rest is waiting.

I measured out six cups.

While the coffee dripped, I heard MiShaun mumbling and sighing heavily. I pulled two cups from an overhead cabinet, poured the hot nectar into gold lined cups and eased back into the living area where MiShaun sat somber, staring through blank eyes.

"Drink this," I said. "It'll slow down the death march you're on."

Slightly swaying, MiShaun reached for the cup while stretching out across the couch.

She didn't say anything. Just sipped slowly and closed her eyes with each swallow.

"I don't usually drink it black," she said.

"Are you usually plastered in the afternoon?"

She didn't appreciate the humor.

"The last time I came close to being this bad, Deborah took care of me. I'd really had a bad night."

"Was that the night of the accident?" I asked.

She hesitated. "You know about that?"

"Word gets around. What happened?"

She sighed. "Too much partying with someone I should have stayed away from. I partied a lot back then. Driving home from a club in Southfield, I dozed off for just a second and bounced off that concrete wall on the James Couzens between Seven Mile and McNichols. Hit my head and shoulder. Fortunately no one saw me and the damage wasn't bad enough to keep me from driving. I managed to make it home."

"That's when you two were living together?"

She nodded. "She saw what I'd done. I couldn't say a word. She was right. I'd gone too far. I cried, threw up and felt sorry for myself. Deborah stayed with me the entire weekend. Healing my wounds and my spirit. I probably talked her ear off. If I wasn't sleeping, I was talking or trying to put down her home made soup."

"Where was Sharron?" I asked as if I didn't know.

"She'd gone somewhere for the weekend. Indianapolis, I think. Not that she would've cared. Deborah did. She's the reason why I sobered up. She helped me. I've stayed sober as a tribute to her kindness and belief in me."

I nodded toward the near empty fifth of gin. "You may require additional assistance."

"I'll be fine," she insisted.

"You'll be dead if you're old demons have their way about it."

"It's none of your business!"

I shrugged. "That's true. So how'd you get the job with 'Empower Detroit'?"

She yawned, her eyes slightly watering. "I saw the position posting in *The Michigan Chronicle* for an Administrative Assistant. I applied, got called in for an interview and was offered the job. Since then I've worked hard and become an invaluable right hand to Mr. Stallings. I'm an excellent Assistant Director."

"I'm sure you are. If Trevor Stallings becomes a city councilman, that will open up the Executive Director position for you."

"I've earned the right to be considered." Her righteous tone masked a subtle strand of insecurity.

"Assuming Trevor believes in management succession and not blood rights. There is Pernell you know."

She yawned again and wiped her eyes. "Trevor wouldn't give him the job and Pernell isn't interested."

"That may be true. Let's hope loyalty is thicker than blood," I said.

MiShaun dismissed the possibility and recanted her years of experience, insights, hard work and everything else she thought I needed to know in order to be impressed with what she'd accomplished.

I listened. Partly because she needed to talk, but mostly because she started to drift off. Minutes later she'd slid down to where her head rested on the corner pillow, rolled over to her right side and gone to sleep.

Best way I knew to calm a storm.

I stood up, placed my cooling cup of coffee on the table and walked over to Deborah's picture. I picked up the gold embroidered frame and looked again into Deborah's still eyes. It was the same picture, highlighted by that mischievous smile of confidence, that Sylvia and Sharron owned.

I wished Deborah could tell me what happened. I wished that picture would talk to me for just a moment. There were so many things I wanted to know and no one could fill in the missing pieces.

The older sister still grieved at the loss and hadn't moved on, her closest friend received a visit from some persons who thought she had something they wanted. She went back to living in fear. Now the other friend slipped from her mantel of sobriety and became reacquainted with her drinking demons. And someone decided that my life wasn't worth the apparent trouble I'd caused so far and hired a cheap hood to take me out.

Deborah had a way of creating puzzles.

My digital watch signaled 3:30.

Content to let myself out without MiShaun's assistance, I placed Deborah's picture back on the mirror-top end table, making sure it rested firmly on the rear prop when I happen to catch the reflection something wedged between the back cover and the front of the photograph.

It appeared to be the edge of some kind of paper. I would've dismissed it as thin cushion paper between the picture and the back cover, but the outline looked like something you'd see on a newspaper.

Since my host was two sheets to the wind, I overlooked getting her permission and rationalized that I was just trying to help.

Helping is the sacred code of good investigating.

I picked up the picture and gently pulled the back cover down from the frame. I'd gotten about half way when a newsprint article did a slow descent down to the carpet.

The part of the paper that faced me looked like part of an article for someone having a giant blowout sale.

Assuming that wasn't important enough to be stored in the back of a picture frame, I lifted the newsprint and turned it over.

There was a small headline acknowledging the tragic death in a car accident of a teenage couple on their prom night. I avoided the details of the article because I was initially drawn to the date of the article.

It was dated eight years ago.

There appeared to be a small coffee stain on the paper, but the hand-printed notation in the top right hand corner was unmistakable.

"I'll be damned," I muttered.

Z-1.

I'd found Deborah's last story.

23

I was trapped in an immovable flow of time and matter. Held rigidly in place by the yellowing newsprint in my hand. The story had occupied a small column in the corner of a newspaper printed in a city close to Detroit.

The importance of the story was magnified by the fact that Deborah had taken an interest. The two teenagers were an item as far back as middle school. Morris Shaw and Daphne Connor had planned to marry after high school, attend community college together and begin to carve out their piece of life on a path of unrealized potential and love. That path was cut short when their 1988 Buick Skylark skidded off the road and ran headlong into a tree. They were killed instantly. A Medical Examiner confirmed that there was alcohol in their system, but not enough in either to qualify as legally drunk. They were driving home from their senior prom after having spent the evening laughing and dancing. It was the last dance they shared together.

As a cop in Oakland, California I'd seen similar accidents and worse among senior prom attendees. Despite our best preventative efforts, we always lost a few. I knew Michigan wasn't exempt from these kinds of accidents.

However, Deborah Norris had taken a special interest in this story. Why?

I slid the back cover back in place and Deborah's picture back on the end table.

MiShaun hadn't budged. Her slow ride back to sobriety started the moment she went unconscious.

Now I had more questions and she wasn't in a position to answer.

Recognizing the futility of initiating a conversation with an unconscious drinker, I used MiShaun's phone to call Sylvia Henderson, hoping she might know something.

The Judge answered. When I asked to speak with his wife, he replied very succinctly that, "Mrs. Henderson is at the place she always visits at this time of the month."

He was in a hurry and told me where I would find Mrs. Henderson.

I punched in the 994, free information number for Alcohol Abuse. When the recorded voice kicked in, I pressed the off button. In the event MiShaun happened to press the redial button, I wanted her to hear the right message.

I pocketed the article and tiptoed out the door like a philandering john who'd just had his afternoon delight.

I eased behind the wheel of my Nova, piecing together what I'd heard from MiShaun and what I'd found in her home.

There were any number of possible explanations for why Deborah's newspaper article had been wedged between her picture and the back cover. Only two seemed worth exploring.

MiShaun put the article there. And if she did, why? Or Deborah put the article there. And if so, why?

I peeled away from the curb, followed the winding street around to Jefferson Avenue and wheeled into traffic just missing one of those orange and white striped rubber barrels used to block off lanes during construction. Since early spring, the Michigan Department of Transportation had declared war on Detroit's numerous potholes and after a long hard struggle we were finally seeing some results.

Persuading Julie to run down any more information on the deaths of Morris Shaw and Daphne Connor would be an easy enough request. However, my conversation with Sylvia would be a little harder, especially since she was visiting with Deborah.

The path I was on had just taken a strange turn.

•   •   •

The drive over to the Detroit Memorial Gardens triggered memories of the Kellers and Taylors who transitioned ahead of us. It had been a fortunate while since we'd gathered to say good bye to a family member whose place at the Thanksgiving feast would be forever vacant.

Six years ago was the last time. When we laid Reynolds Keller's remains to rest, it was said that the old man had run out of people with whom he could have a good argument. So, he decided to go after the ones he hadn't met yet.

The Keller boys knew better. He really just missed his better half. Lilly Keller promised to stay with him forever and came up short by a year. Pop figured she shouldn't get off so easy, so he went after her.

I made a mental note to contact 'Terry's Enchanted Gardens' about a floral arrangement.

Driving through the pillared opening of evenly manicured Detroit Memorial Gardens, I rolled along side a green suited attendant pushing a wheel barrel.

I told him whom I was trying to find. He gave a knowing nod and pointed me to an area near the back. Sylvia was a regular visitor.

The drive along the pebbled road revealed a spectral display of grandiose and simplistic artistry designed to make an individual's final resting place a tribute to the fact that they were here. The variety of horizontal, flat stone markers to large mausoleums with penitent archangels guarding the doors struck me as guilt-tributes for what we didn't do or say (or what we *did* do or say) to people that we love while they walked among us.

I was struck by the apparent calm and silence that surrounded the area despite its parallel proximity to the ceaseless backfires, car horns and burglar alarms of the cars that frequent Gratiot Avenue.

Silent Suspicion

Finding Sylvia was easy enough. I spotted her Lexus parked near an area close to a wrought-iron fence that encased the spacious Memorial Gardens.

As I pulled to a stop, I spotted her sitting in a director's chair and staring at a bronze, marble headstone. Despite the invasion of her privacy and the feeling running rampant through me, I moved slowly and silently to where Sylvia sat calmly lost in her thoughts.

From a distance, she was all regal bearing. Perched like a saint giving audience to the needy, Sylvia appeared very comfortable among the headstones and replenished flowers.

I waited until there was only a few feet between us before calling out.

She turned and motioned for me to come forward.

"Mrs. Henderson," I started. "I'm sorry to disturb you like this ..... "

" ..... It's alright Mr. Keller. I've been expecting you." She held up her cellular phone. "Warren called and told me you'd be coming by. I come out here pretty routinely to say hi to Deborah and to be with her. It gives me a feeling of calm knowing I can still touch base with her."

There was nothing I could say. Instead, I offered my hand to assist her as she stood up. She wore a steel, high-twist polyester faille belted jacket with a matching skirt and a light blue silk blouse. She held both her cell phone and a pair of silver framed sunglasses in one hand.

Sylvia slipped her free hand underneath my arm and held on as if comforting me through a trying time. I was overwhelmed by the irony.

Not wanting to say anything that would blow the mood, I took note of the markings etched on Deborah's headstone.

Deborah Jewell Norris

March 3, 1961 - June 30, 1990

Loving Sister and Good Friend

I let the silence drift around us, not knowing when the moment would be right to show Sylvia the newspaper clipping.

"She talks to me sometimes," Sylvia stated.

There are times when knowing when to shut up demonstrates a wisdom beyond the ability for most talk-show hosts to comprehend.

Sylvia turned to me and smiled. "Don't worry, Mr. Keller. You're not hearing the ranting of a woman driven crazy by the voices in her head, I assure you."

"I'd be inclined to trust the voices in your head more than I would the ones driving our current policy makers."

"I suspect that's a compliment."

"Best one I can offer under the circumstances," I replied.

She nodded. "I come here sometimes just to let Deborah know that I'm thinking about her. Every now and then I feel as if she's trying to thank me for spending the time. Sounds silly, huh?"

"I played pro football for four years. Believe me, I've heard sillier."

"Warren used to say that as well. Anyway, you didn't come all the way out here to talk about my voices and football, did you?"

"No, ma'am, I didn't." I unfolded the article and showed it to Sylvia. "I found this article with its special notation on the top right hand corner."

Sylvia stared hard at the handwritten Z-1 and looked back at me. "That's Deborah's coding system. Where did you get this?"

"Read the article and tell me if Deborah ever mentioned an interest in this story."

She quickly read through the Morris Shaw and Daphne Connor accident. "No. I don't recall Deborah ever mentioning this story. But that's not unusual. Sometimes I never knew what she was writing until it actually came up in print. Other times she'd chat my ear off about a story she was developing." Sylvia glanced again at the article. "No. Deborah never mentioned this story."

"Well, I wanted to be sure before I pursued it."

"But where did you find that article?"

"Stuck in between some file folders," I lied. I wasn't certain how the article found its way in the back of MiShaun's Deborah picture and I couldn't risk Sylvia possibly calling MiShaun and asking her before I had some answers. "Just happened to find it today."

"What do you think it means?"

"I don't know, yet. But I'll ask around and see where it leads."

"Mr. Keller, please don't lose that article and return it to Deborah's files when you're done."

"That was my intent, Mrs. Henderson. I'll be in touch."

Sylvia sat back down in her chair while I lumbered back to my car. Since Deborah hadn't shared the story with Sylvia, I had to consider other possibilities.

I drove away with Sylvia Henderson in my rear view mirror still perched in her chair, staring at the headstone of her younger sister.

"I'll find out what this means Sylvia. I promise you," I whispered.

I stopped at the edge of the driveway before turning onto Van Dyke Avenue. "You too, Deborah."

24

As the answering machine played out the four waiting messages, I dropped down in my swivel chair, half-listening to long-winded requests for the services of Jefferson Keller. His reputation among bail bondsman as a 'finder of people who miss their court appearances' contributed to more than half of the revenue earned by Keller Investigations.

My own need to think through the interesting discoveries coming from this romp through the life of someone I didn't know outweighed getting involved with anyone needing information on a spouse they wanted to sue for divorce.

I couldn't have generated the energy.

The unfolded article lay flattened on my desk, held down by a stapler while I quickly zipped through the afternoon mail, discarding all the junk and stacking the bills.

Julie searched on the Internet while I opened the folder of information she'd managed to find on Pernell Stallings.

Leafing through the few handwritten pages told me most of what I needed to know.

His spotlight shone, but from the top of a different circus tent.

He'd been quite the pistol.

At sixteen, he'd been convicted of two counts of malicious destruction. At seventeen, he'd graduated to three counts of assault. Two of the victims were women; the other was a man trying to assist one of the women he assaulted. For his gallantry, he received a broken nose and a financial settlement. There were no obvious mishaps during the eighteen-year-old boy-to-man years. At twenty, he was cited for reckless driving, and again at twenty-one. There was a noise complaint filed against him, which resulted in him and some friends being arrested for disturbing the peace. Apparently, a party being held at his parents' home had gotten out of hand. The last page in the folder was a copy of an insurance claim for his Nissan 300 Z. The car had been stolen one night while he slept and that after a routine investigation, the claim was paid.

"Probably one of the neighbors," I said.

As far as the world knew, after the 1990 insurance claim was paid, he mellowed. Apparently he went to work with his brother and has been a model citizen ever since.

Obviously no one asked Jocelyn Kilgore.

"Found it," Julie said as she waltzed into my office. Dressed in an evergreen silk military jacket with matching pants and a striped silk blouse, she was the essence of cute with a business bearing. "It was the first article in a three-article piece in the *Macomb Daily*. I copied the other two."

"Thanks, Jules."

What she gave me was a more detailed story of the two high school sweethearts who'd known each other since before they were born. They'd been friends before becoming sweethearts and talked of how they were going to make a difference in the world. Both sets of parents talked about how fond they were of each other's kids. The second article was the obituary. The sum total of their lives had been captured in two summary columns.

Maybe that's all any of us deserve.

"Well. Is it helpful information?" Julie asked standing with her arms folded.

"I don't know ..... yet." I replied. "I do know that it was a story that triggered Deborah's interest and I need to know why."

"You think it's connected somehow?"

"That's the sixty-four thousand dollar question."

"Good. You can put it toward your sixty-five thousand dollar bill."
Julie glanced at her watch. "Well, I have to go pick up the little ladies. It's
pizza and movie night. I promised them a reward for keeping their rooms
neat for two weeks. They did; so I have to pay up. They're both so
demanding about people paying their obligations."

"I can't imagine where they'd get that trait."

She smiled and nodded toward Jeff's desk. "Where's the manhunter?"

I shrugged.

Julie shook her head. "Boy, you two."

"By the way ,Jules. Thanks for this info on Pernell. But why didn't
you just download it and save all that writing?"

"Because that information you have is unofficial. I didn't pull it off
a database because it doesn't exist. You remember that Sheriff I told you
I'd been helping to find books and articles for the classes in his Masters
program?"

I nodded. Sheriff Paul Goodman of Missaukee County near the
Upper Peninsula helped track down a lead for me in a previous case.
"How's he doing?"

"Fine. Anyway, I asked him if he'd do some checking around. I
guess he tapped into his cop-world network and came up with all that
information. Apparently some friends of his called some friend, who talked
to a few court clerks in the area. Court clerks are walking information
banks that retain information even when it's not written anywhere. Next
thing you know, I'm getting phone calls from court clerks who knew that
Pernell had gotten into his own brand of trouble, but the cases were
usually dismissed or waived off with a light fine or community service.
Obviously the family lawyer did a good job of keeping his conduct unofficial."

"I didn't mean for you to go through all that trouble, Julie. I could've
just asked Malone."

"Yeah, I suppose you could have. But given that bone in your head
which disorganizes your thinking, Pernell would've been Mayor of De-

troit by the time Malone got the info to you."

"He would've had to wait until after big brother Trevor finished being Mayor."

"My point exactly. Anyway, I gotta go."

Julie's 5:45 departure happened just as the phone rang. When I answered, Tank bellowed his greeting, practically shattering my eardrum.

"Just wanted you to know that Sharron had a pretty normal day for someone who runs a day care. Nothing out of the ordinary happened. After work, she stopped by a grocery store, bought a few items and came straight home. I think she's preparing dinner for two. I noticed she bought a bottle of red wine and some candles."

"Romance?"

"It has that feel. Anyway, I'll wait around until her date shows and I'll go grab a bite and change clothes."

"Sounds like a good plan, Tank."

We rang off and I propped my feet up on my desk, pulling the articles about Morris and Daphne over to me.

As I read through the articles, I knew that I had a task ahead of me that only a sociopath would envy and a priest would welcome.

I'd have to contact the parents of Morris and Daphne and encourage them to talk about what happened.

A forearm under the chin by a pulling guard would have been more pleasurable.

That thought didn't keep me from punching in the number for the information operator.

25

Mount Clemens is a small bedroom community northeast of Detroit, up Gratiot Avenue. As small cities go, it was also experiencing controlled growth as one of the recipients of Detroit's growing commuter population.

Given the time of the day, I'd rather have been a low flying projectile fired from a circus cannon than face the torment of the stop-and-go eastbound commuter traffic on I-94, or the less appealing stop-and go-traffic on Gratiot.

There was no circus in town, so I tried my luck with timing the lights on Gratiot Avenue.

I must have used up my daily supply of luck when I found the newspaper article since I seemed to catch every red light on Gratiot, including the ones supposedly not working until some of the construction had been completed.

The signal for John Arnold's talk show soon faded from the radio, so I then switched over to 'BookBeat' on WPON. Both shows helped ease the pain of driving with tightly wrung commuters moving fast on a slow trip to manicured lawns, picket fences and brick-front one and two level homes.

The Parents of Morris Shaw and Daphne Connor lived on a quiet residential street five blocks down from where I turned off Gratiot. Tree-lined streets with double-sided parking and homes with white aluminum siding gave their street a small town, home and garden look that people run to for peace and run from for entertainment.

I parked in front of a two level brick home with a small front porch and narrow paved walkway. The reluctant voice of Eleanor Shaw still flowed through my ears as I moved toward the front door. It took some convincing before the now widowed Eleanor Shaw agreed to meet with me to discuss her son's untimely death.

A locked screen door was the only barrier between me and the life inside the Shaw home.

I tapped lightly and seconds later was greeted by a chocolate toned, fiftyish looking woman, full figured with an oval face, laugh lines, ebony curled hair that was graying at the temples.

The introduction was made more awkward by the fact that I had to press my ID against the screen and slip my business card through the slightly opened door.

Mrs. Shaw motioned me in and I followed the blue jean outfitted host into her quaint and ordered living room.

"Have a seat, Mr. Keller," she said pointing to a crimson and blue leather loveseat that matched the sofa and armchair. On the pine finished cocktail table sat the usual assortment of Ebony and Jet magazines as well as a leather-bound Bible. A mid-sized television on a pine finished stand rounded out the homey room adorned with pictures.

Framed pictures of various sizes placed on the end tables, and the built-in wall shelves captured the life of Eleanor Shaw and all those who may have passed before her.

Morris Shaw was pictured in a green graduation outfit, smiling at the life ahead and gripping the fake diploma as if it held the answer to all life's questions. Pictured next to him was the man whom I assumed provided answers to the other questions his son sought through the first eighteen years of his life.

He looked to be a no nonsense, big man for whom the only question to the statement 'jump' would have been, "Is this high enough?"

"My husband died three years ago, Mr. Keller. As a result of one of those stupid accidents out at the plant. Between his pension and the settlement, I lead a comfortable life."

I nodded.

She sounded tired. Not the kind of physical tired brought on by the daily grind of constant motion in overheated places with circular fans and a boss who is making the world pay because he was always the tenth guy picked on a nine man team.

Eleanor Shaw was emotionally tired. Despite the comforts of a home and financial security, she'd been stripped of her early life dreams, content to wait out the rest of her life.

"I appreciate your meeting with me, Mrs. Shaw."

"I still don't understand your interest in what happened to my son," she said as she eased down slowly into the corner of the sofa. "I'm not sure   Oh dear. Please excuse my manners. Can I offer you something to drink?"

I declined. "Rather honestly, Mrs. Shaw, I'm fishing right now. I came across an article referring to the accident actually by accident because of my involvement in another case. I came here to see how the two might be connected."

"Susan and Raymond Connor are at their cabin up north right now. They take the rest of their family up there for the last few days of summer, they'll be back after Labor Day."

"And how are you spending your last days of summer?" I asked.

"Me? Oh I spend a lot of time at the church. My sister comes to visit two or three times a week. A group of us play cards every Wednesday and I read a lot. It hasn't been one of the warmest summer's on record."

"No, ma'am. It hasn't."

"Michigan's like that." She stopped abruptly. "I'm sure you didn't come by here to listen to an old woman talk about the weather."

"If you were an old woman, Mrs. Shaw, listening to you talk about the weather would be one of my daily passions."

"You're very kind, Mr. Keller."

"And quite truthful, I might add."

She smiled. "Morris wanted to leave Mount Clemens, make a name for himself and one day come back and run for Mayor. He always believed he could be mayor. He once told my late husband and me that if Coleman Young can run Detroit, Morris Shaw can run Mount Clemens. He was our only child."

"Was Daphne going with him?"

"Such a lovely child she was. They grew up together. Been friends since before they were born. They lived right across the street. I knew they would marry someday because she always bossed him around and he'd just go along with the program."

"He was wise for his age."

"Yes. He always knew, even when she didn't. They were juniors in high school before she finally saw the light."

I waited.

She sighed. "You should have seen how nice they looked on the night of their prom. They were just darling. He wore a black tux and Daphne was lovely in her pink dress. I watched him drive from here to across the street, to pick her up like a gentleman. Can you believe that? My husband and I thought it was the funniest thing. So did the Connors. They drove off in my car on what should have been one of the best nights of their life."

"Yes, ma'am."

"Oh don't worry, Mr. Keller. I'm all cried out. There are no more tears left in this old body. I've emptied the well on both my husband and son. I'm not sure which phone call was worse. The one from the police, telling us about the accident, or the one I received telling me of my husband's death. They're both painful in ways you can't imagine."

"Was there anything unusual about your son's accident?"

"Not according to the police. Their car ran off the road and hit a tree. They hadn't been drinking heavily or driving way over the speed limit."

"Were they being chased? Perhaps racing with someone?"

She folded her arms and sighed. "The police checked as much as they could. There was nothing to indicate if they'd been racing. Besides,

Morris would have known better. We raised him right."

It did not explain Deborah's interest in what happened.

"Mrs. Shaw, did any reporters outside of Mount Clemens contact you about what happened to Morris?"

"Other than the one who works for our local paper. No. None that I can recall."

"How about the Connors?"

"Not that I know of. I can't speak for them, of course, but I can always ask. Is it important?"

"It was important to the person who clipped the article from your newspaper. Based on what I know, that would've only been done if this person thought there was something significant about the story."

"Why would anyone outside of Mount Clemens be interested in Morris and Daphne?"

"That's what I'm trying to find out, Mrs. Shaw."

We spent the next few minutes talking about Morris, her husband, the Connors and other topics that seemed important to her. I'd invaded the sanctity of Eleanor Shaw's life, asking her to recount tragic moments for the sake of trying to find out why Deborah was so interested. The least I could do was to sit and listen.

The hour seemed to go by too quickly and I didn't feel any closer to the truth. Mrs. Shaw agreed to contact me whenever the Connors returned.

I thanked her and returned to my car, sighing at what seemed to be a lack of progress.

The pieces were there and the answers hung out somewhere in the gray areas. I understood why Jeff liked the black and white of things.

It was that focus on colors that caught my attention two blocks from where Mrs. Shaw lived. Those were the red and white flashing colors of a police cruiser that had pulled in behind me.

26

I found an open area several feet from a corner stop sign and pulled over. I knew the routine, having been on the other end on more than one occasion.

I turned off the engine and pulled out both my driver and investigator license as well as my permit to carry and my insurance certificate. I watched as the officer stepped out of his cruiser and did the slow walk toward my car.

This standard, rehearsed routine was primarily designed to give the approaching officer as wide a view of the driver as possible and a hard angle in the event the driver is something less than agreeable.

He was a big man. Tanned with dark tinted glasses and a dour manner and most likely on loan from the World Wrestling Federation. Despite the Nineties, most police departments tried to recruit big people, regardless of gender.

"May I see your license and insurance certificate, sir?"

I showed him everything I'd taken out of my wallet. He read through the laminated material. Slowly, liked they're trained to do. It adds to the tension.

"Where's you gun, sir?"

"Back at the office ..... ," I said, glancing at his name badge. " ..... Officer Tanner. I only carry it if I need it."

He said nothing and walked back to his cruiser.

As the seemingly endless moments dragged on, I used the time to think about everything I'd learned so far. It was like trying to glue clouds together. No matter how I angled the information, they seemed to flow through one another.

Officer Tanner returned, having checked my name through his on-board computer. I couldn't tell if he was happy or disappointed that there was nothing noteworthy on me.

I was one of the many black men who didn't have an arrest record.

"Mr. Keller," he said returning identification. "Is this   car capable of moving without too much trouble?"

A nod seemed enough of an answer.

"Good. Then follow me and try to keep up."

It was not a request and my input wasn't required.

• • •

I followed the police cruiser back up to Gratiot avenue and then east until the street narrowed into a one lane road with nothing but one-level homes and tired business store fronts as a clue that some form of life existed beyond the shopping plazas and fast food stops.

Officer Tanner swerved onto a dirt side-road and after driving several yards stopped near a grassy incline where a nondescript brown sedan sat parked near a partially wooded area.

Ordinarily, I would've kicked myself for not bringing my gun, but the car had that same functionally barren look common among local, state and federal agencies. It was just a question of which one.

While I entertained the question, Officer Tanner had walked over to the car and leaned into the driver side window, apparently having a conversation with the driver.

He motioned me to come forward.

'In for a penny, in for a pound' I thought to myself remembering that I hated stupid sayings during moments of duress.

Tanner eased back to his cruiser as the driver of the other car, an auburn haired woman with high cheekbones and a doughnut hole for a waistline slipped out of the driver's seat. Medium height in a plaid jacket and pants with a black blouse open at the collar, she walked with a confidence common to models on stage or power suits on the corporate rise.

"Mr. Keller?" she said extending an evenly manicured hand minus any nail polish. "I'm Detective Wendy Brewer. I'd like to know why you're snooping around my neck of the woods asking about a case that took place eight years ago?"

"Lincoln Keller, and since you already know I'm a private investigator, I'll stay with the direct approach you've already established. Can't tell you."

Brewer didn't smile or frown. Her crystal blue eyes remained unrevealing. I didn't have a sense of what she might be thinking.

"This way," she said motioning toward an area just past her car.

She led me down an incline where the grass and weeds seem to grow taller and finally a partial clearing. We walked along the foot of the incline until we reached an area where several trees sat like sentinels on the road to Oz.

She stopped at a larger tree that stood in front of the others like the lead pin in a bowling alley.

"This is where it happened," Brewer said. "I was working night patrol when the call came in. A witness saw their car go off the road ....." She pointed up where the traffic zipped by ignoring the forty-mile an hour speed limit. " ..... tear through this area in front of us and crash into this tree. They were killed instantly. They were my first ones."

Doesn't matter if you stay four years on a police force or forty. No matter how much you see, you never forget the first one.

She stared at the tree as if the whole incident was being replayed in her mind.

No doubt it was.

"Mine was a hit and run," I said. "Night patrol in Oakland, California. Two men were arguing over ..... "

" ..... Something stupid," she stated.

" ..... What else is there? Anyway, one guy pulls a gun; the other takes off running down the street and darts into traffic. Unfortunately, while he was looking back at the guy chasing him with the gun, he didn't see the car speeding down the street. He was thrown to the sidewalk on the other side. The driver took off. My partner and I were first on the scene. Sometimes I can still see his eyes, wide open and lifeless."

"You find the driver?"

"Yeah. We had enough witnesses. Found him a couple of hours later."

"This one's still unsolved," she said leaning against the tree. "So in the spirit of cooperation, why the interest?"

"Detective Brewer, how much have you dug up on me so far?"

She removed a small notebook from her jacket pocket. "Enough to know that you're a private investigator, you worked as a police officer in Oakland, California and you once played for the Los Angeles Raiders."

"Oakland Raiders."

"I know," she said. "Anyway, you're part of Keller Investigations and your partner is a former US Deputy Marshall, now bounty hunter named Jefferson Keller. Your older brother from what I understand."

"You know enough."

"So why the interest?" she asked again.

"You also know I can't tell you a great deal because of client confidentiality."

"I hoped that in the spirit of ..... "

I interrupted. " ..... However, I can tell you that it's possibly related to another case and I'll call my client and see if he'd be willing to tell you why I'm snooping. Fair enough?"

She nodded. "Fair enough."

We climbed up the incline and back to our cars. Along the way, we filled the moments with social fodder as a way of easing some of the uncertainty and building on the spirit of cooperation

We stopped at her car.

"Mr. Keller, Morris and Daphne were good kids. Both from nice families, less troublesome than some teenagers and better than most. I don't like the idea of their deaths being unsolved. This town has its own share of problems, but it's a good town with good people. We don't get all the banner headlines of our big sister just west of here and we prefer it that way. Morris and Daphne deserved better."

"I understand, Detective Brewer."

"I'd like to put this case to rest. I'm trusting the fact that you're not holding back information that could solve this thing."

She opened the car door. "Because if I thought you were, I'd have your license pulled and bust you down so fast it would be years before you knew what hit you. Don't play me for small town, Mr. Keller. I live and work here, but it's not where I grew up."

"You may consider me respectfully intimidated, Detective Brewer."

She smiled slightly. "I'll bet."

"By the way," I said. "You mentioned that there was a witness. What did that person see or say?"

"When I hear from your client, you'll hear from me," she said as she keyed the engine.

"In the spirit of cooperation," I said as she drove away.

She suddenly stopped and looked back at me. "By the way, the Raiders have improved their offense, but quite frankly their defense won't stop water from running much less a decent halfback."

Nice shot and it hurt me to agree with her.

I eased back to the Nova and U-turned back toward Gratiot. Now that I had some idea of what was going on, I got over the fact that Mrs. Shaw had obviously contacted Detective Brewer after I called her. Just playing it safe, I'm sure.

As the lure of late summer dusk began to settle onto the landscape, I headed back to Detroit.

Before making the turn onto westbound I-94, I caught a glimpse of the sun's orange summer rays reflected against the clear blue sky.

"Deborah," I said looking at the sky. "What the hell were you on to?"

27

I took time to satisfy my hunger by stopping at Steve's Soul Food on Grand River Avenue. The soul buffet and general noise was enough of a distraction so I could eat and concentrate without being social.

I returned to my office just as the lure of the night opened its doors to its waiting patrons.

The contents of my interviews with Eleanor Shaw and Detective Wendy Brewer were transferred to a notepad with certain passages circled or highlighted. I had more information, more confusion and more questions. It had the makings of a relationship gone bad, only without the subtitles.

I called Judge Zone and gave him an update on what I'd accomplished, also mentioning my encounter with Detective Brewer.

He assured me that he'd take care of the situation.

"Anything else I should know?" he stated, more than asked.

"Knackton's on to me as well."

"Problems?"

"Mostly posturing and bragging about whose is bigger."

"I'll speak to him," he said.

"Not necessary right now, Your Honor. Just wanted you to know. I'll be in touch."

I finished what little work I had, checked the clock and decided to head back to my apartment. Though nine o'clock seemed early, my body felt like midnight in the year two thousand and one.

I had just set the locked the gate and set the alarm on the front of the building when a horn blew twice.

The familiar Econoline Van with the engine idling belonged to Jeff, last seen heading off somewhere with the hit man who couldn't see straight.

"What's up, Bro?" I said stepping close to the van. "Where you been?"

"Get in," he said.

It wasn't a request.

"Why? Where are we going?" I asked.

As I locked in my seat belt, Jeff handed me my .38 and shoulder holster. "You may need this."

"Who are we going to see?"

"We're going to see a man about a contract," he said as he U-turned onto Livernois.

•   •   •

We parked half a block down from a three-level, light brown apartment building, so we had a clear view of the people coming in and out of its shadowy front. A two-level paved stairway led to a similar looking front landing where people tended to sit and converse.

Normally, it wouldn't have been that big a deal, but normality took on a different look down in the Cass Corridor. What looked normal would have offended most people, most of the time, most anywhere.

Every shattered dream and sad story found its way onto the Corridor. There among the numerous social services, small businesses and apartment buildings, the Corridors habitants lived out their final chapter waiting for the grim reaper to point a bony finger from underneath a faceless hooded robe.

The Corridor's forty-year run at being Detroit's self-avowed skid row was about to come to an abrupt end-of-the-century existence. Only the grim reaper wasn't wearing a dark robe and carrying a scythe. He wore Brooks Brother's suits and carried a cell phone. Developers had cast a greedy eye toward the area that drug addicts, prostitutes and transients called home. Wayne State University continued its expansion from the north, while the lure of Casinos, Stadiums and Orchestra Place pushed south from downtown. The Corridor was caught in a progressive squeeze for the land and a stiff-legged boot for its dwellers.

The invisible would just have to be invisible in another location.

During the ride over, Jeff explained why we were sitting under a burnt out streetlight watching a place where the last bastion of society's discards sat waiting for the end.

"Nothing happens in Detroit without it being brokered. The guy who brokered the contract comes here when things get tight at his usual stops. He's got a girlfriend he keeps in food, clothes and drugs."

"Not exactly the Westin," I said.

Jeff said, having adjusted his seat to a more comfortable position; "He ain't no Donald Trump, either. Small time player named Marvin Turner, street name's 'Gold'. He hired ST to pull the trigger on you."

"You figure we'll talk to him and find out who approached him about me?"

"Something like that," he said.

"Where's ST?" I asked.

Jeff glanced at his watch. "Well, if he knows what's good for him, he's about two hours out of Raleigh, North Carolina on his way to a new life."

My silence said a lot about my puzzlement.

"Guy I used to partner with in the Marshall's Office runs a half-way house down there. He retired with a disability. Took a bullet in the back and lost partial use of his left leg. Started a half-way house that he contracts with the state and he gets good results. Most people mistake the partial immobility in one leg as a weakness. He can still out-tough the most street-wise gang member."

"Why'd you send ST to him?"

"He would've been killed had he stayed here. Either the person who hired him or me."

I stared ahead at the building. "Would you have?"

"That's what I told him. I gave him a choice. Get a new life or I'd kill him. After I finished putting the fear of God in him, he chose wisely. So I bought him a one way ticket on a Greyhound, gave him some food money and sent him on his way."

"God know you're doing this?"

"God's a busy person. I'm his emissary."

I never know when Jeff's being serious or not. "You sure 'Gold' will be here?"

"Pretty much. One thing's for sure; people are creatures of habit." He spun his dark sunglasses around as a momentary distraction. "We had this informant that we brought into the witness protection program. He dropped a dime on his drug-runnin buddies when he found out they were going to cut off his hands and scatter the other parts of him some-where over the Atlantic."

"Was he skimmin'?" I asked.

"Big time. So he came running to us and we took him in. He be-came a federal witness, sung like a flat tenor and forever changed his worthless life. We got him a new identity, relocation and protection. He only lasted a year. Gave the team the slip one night and took off. He didn't have to go through all that since we don't force people to stay in the program. Anyway, he made contact with an old girlfriend and they agreed to meet and take off together."

"Why do I think there's no happy ending here?"

"Depends on how you look at it. The guys he busted watched her every day while he was in witness protection because they knew some-day he'd contact her and they had all the time in the world. They con-vinced her that turning him in was a far better alternative than watching her youngest son lose his ability to give her grandchildren."

"And he showed?"

Jeff nodded. "Caught him coming in the back. Two days later our office in D.C. received an anonymous package addressed to our bureau chief. We did the usual screenings. Turns out they mailed us his hands. I imagine the rest of him is lying in the belly of some of those bottom feeders in the Atlantic. People are creatures of habit. That's how I catch most of my bail jumpers. I just go to where they're most likely to show and I wait. The rest is easy." He stared impassively at the night. "Gold will show. All we have to do is wait."

So we waited. Talking very little, if at all. I passed the time watching the Corridor's denizens move from spot to spot in an attempt to be somewhere while going nowhere.

Jeff had already scouted the area and determined there were two ways in and out of the building. Since 'Gold' would be in a ground-level apartment, he could always slip out the window. Jeff also paid the man in the apartment across the hall to turn on his light the moment 'Gold' came to roost.

Money can buy a lot of loyalty.

"How's the case coming?" Jeff asked.

I yawned and gave him a quick summary of what I'd learned since I'd last seen him. He watched the window and grunted to let me know he was listening. I welcomed the chance to talk about the case out loud. Usually some point of clarification would make itself known.

It didn't happen that way.

The time rolled by slow enough and I fought a losing battle with the dream merchant. Two or three times I caught myself waking up, while Jeff just sat and waited.

"She'll be his downfall," Jeff said when I snapped out of another nod.

"Who?" I said stifling a yawn.

He pointed at the building. "The girl 'Gold' keeps locked up in there. Her habit will get worse, as will her looks. The time in between hits will decrease and she'll start stealing from him. He'll get rid of her and if she doesn't die first, she'll find someway to bring him down."

"So why does he do it?"

"Men like control."

"And women?"

He ignored the question. I guessed the idle chatter was his way of bringing me back on full alert.

The blue digital clock showed twenty minutes past midnight.

"Light's on," Jeff said nodding toward the building. "Let's roll."

I kept my .38 holstered as we eased out of the Van and moved toward the building.

"Alright, Linc let's do it just like I told you. He'll probably try to ease out the back and I'll be waiting. This ain't no Schwartzenegger movie, so just knock on the door and stay clear."

"I was a cop in another life, Jeff."

"Just stay smart in this one."

We eased down the quiet street until we reached the front of the building. Jeff moved around to the back to cover the window. I walked up the steps and pressed the buzzer of the apartment where our paid observer would buzz me through.

Once inside the crumbling foyer, the smell of mildewed carpet and rotting wood attacked my senses in a futile attempt to overshadow the other equally nauseating aromas. I gazed down the narrow hall just as an apartment door creaked open.

A gray-haired man with hanging jowls and a sullen face quietly motioned me down the hall. Despite the surrounding noises that filled the air like fanatic specters, it seemed too quiet for what was about to happen.

The old man met me half way down the hall. He reeked of years of beer and other cheap forms of liquid amusement. He was a walking advertisement for what's left when you have nothing.

He whispered through rotting half teeth; "Boys in there with that no-account crack hefer."

"Thanks, pop," I said. "Does she usually answer the door when someone knocks?"

"If she ain't too cracked to heah she might. Usually she just yells something nasty unless'n it's that man friend of hers. Boy ain't worth the nut it took to give him life. Always spittin' at me."

"Okay, pop. I'll take it from here. You just ..... "

" ..... I'll help you boy."

Before I could stop him, he turned and waltzed back to the apartment door. He was standing in front of the door knocking before I could stop him.

I got to the door's edge just as I heard a meek voice ask, "Who is it?"

Instinctively, I pushed the old man away from the door and crouched down just as three shots splintered through and bore holes in the old man's apartment door.

A high pitch voice within a wheezy laugh yelled, "C'mon on in and join the party." Another two shots followed, splintering more wood. The wheezy laugh became louder like something fighting to be heard over the noise.

I held my .38 up near me, glanced over and saw the old man crawling away. He didn't appear hurt.

Standing with my back to the wall, I gave the door a strong backward kick and it swung open. I crouched back down and peered inside. The apartment was dark and I could just barely see the outline of furniture.

A flash from a corner near the window signaled that a bullet hissed over my head. More laughter followed. Higher pitched and a phlegm cough filled the darkness.

"We're having a party! It's party time, Big Man! Come join the party!"

Shooting in the dark could have meant the life of an innocent bystander and I had no desire to make myself an easy target. My heart raced like a chased rabbit as I thought about my next move. I gripped my .38; slowly exhaled and quickly rolled across the floor to the where the old man had crawled away.

As I came out of the roll, I glanced up and saw 'Gold' step out of the shadows, his gun pointed toward the door opening. I cocked the trigger just as the sound of breaking glass took his attention away from the door.

I rushed in and leveled him with a perfect forearm smash designed to stop agile wide receivers. He dropped like a bad habit.

As he fell to the floor, I kicked his legs out from under him to speed up his flight and brought my left elbow down on his Adam's apple.

He landed hard.

A light came on and I turned and saw Jeff standing by the light switch, his twelve gauge shot gun looked like an extension of his left arm. He'd smashed the window open as a distraction, crawled in and found his way to the light switch while I was occupied. His right hand held onto the elbow of a blond, slack-haired woman who'd somehow managed to cram a hundred years of living into a early twenties body.

She had that look. Reddened eyes corrupted by what she used, loose fitting clothes, red painted eyelids, a gold stud in her nose and a cinnamon tone that once commanded attention from the shy and the slick. A one-time looker with fading spirits and dyed blond hair.

She quivered. Although I'm sure it wasn't from Jeff's animal magnetism. Jeff brought her over and gently pushed her down in a flower patterned armchair. His grimace said it all.

"Like the man said, welcome to the party," I said between short breaths.

"Looks like we were expected," Jeff replied. He bent down and picked up the gun 'Gold' used to let us know he gave at the office. "A .38 Special. Not the current weapon of choice in these sophisticated times."

He reached down and pulled the bloodied 'Gold' up and flung him over to a rumpled two-seater couch. "Yep. I think Mr. 'Gold' knew that we were coming his way."

I walked over and closed the door though strangely enough, the commotion hadn't drawn a crowd. What's common depends on where you live.

Jeff had lightly slapped 'Gold' several times to pull him out of his stupor. "What'd you hit him with, a hammer?"

"Once a Raider," I said.

As he groaned his way back to the real world, I saw why he'd acquired his name. Inside that bloody mouth was the world's second largest gold deposit. Most of his top and bottom front teeth were gold plated. Full tooth, not capped.

It seemed inconsistent with the sleeveless blue jean outfit he wore, but then I never was a fashion expert.

He finally came around. He stared up at Jeff's stoic face and my wily grin.

"Hey man, I ..... "

Jeff slapped him hard. "Listen to me, 'Gold'. I'm going to ask the questions and you'll give the answers. I'd better like the answers or ....." Jeff took out a knife from the pocket in his pant leg, opened the blade and waved it under 'Gold's' nose. " ..... I'll start prospecting for gold, one tooth at a time."

A look of hesitation and reluctance crossed Gold's eyes, so I crouched down to eye level. "Don't try him, my man. You wouldn't be the first one to receive his brand of surgery. He's cut the tail off a hundred show-boating peacocks like you."

I could see that youthful, streetwise defiance begin to take over his reasoning capacity.

Jeff saw it too. He backhanded 'Gold' hard enough to crack a jaw-bone. "Killing you would be the least important thing I've done today."

"What do you want?" he asked breathing hard.

"We ask the questions, 'Gold'," I said. "Now, who paid you to arrange the hit on me."

"I don't know ..... "

He didn't finish the sentence as Jeff pushed the knife blade toward his mouth, stopping micro inches short of a front gold tooth. "Wonder how much this one will go for?"

"Some guy finds me and says to take down some private dick named Keller. I told him my price and he paid."

"And free enterprise being what it is, you subcontracted, right? Only your subcontractor is the same guy calling strikes at a hockey game." I shook my head. "You should have done it yourself, 'Gold'. That way you wouldn't be sitting here looking at me."

"Who made the buy?" Jeff asked.

"The Anti-P.I. League," he said defiantly.

I heard the sound of approaching sirens and knew the night was about to become longer.

Jeff squeezed 'Gold' around the neck. "Who made the buy?"

"I tell you and I'm out of business."

"You don't tell me and you're dead," Jeff replied squeezing harder.

"And out of business," I said.

'Gold' quickly thought through his options. "I don't ask the questions. I get a phone call, give a price and collect when the job is done."

"From who?" I asked.

"Don't know until the job is done."

"How'd you know we were coming after you?" Jeff asked.

"Man don't do his job, he suffers the consequences." The defiance still filled the room.

Jeff pulled 'Gold' forward. "What do you mean suffers the consequences?"

"He got to go. Boom. Bang."

Jeff snatched up 'Gold' with his left hand, grabbed his twelve gauge and pulled him toward the broken window. "C'mon, Linc. We don't have time to wait for the cops."

We slid out the window, dragging 'Gold' with us. We eased across the street and behind an abandoned store just as two blue and white cruisers screeched in front of the apartment building.

"One word out of you and I'll cut you where you stand. Clear?" Jeff whispered to 'Gold'.

Gold said nothing.

"Jeff, where are we headed?" I asked.

"That's what mother lode here is going to tell us," he said as he pushed 'Gold' toward the van.

"Tell us what?" I said sliding into the passenger side.

Jeff pulled 'Gold' into the back and handcuffed him to a bar welded on the inside of the van. He uses it for holding bail jumpers while they're being brought back to jail.

"Where ST is being held."

28

Jeff drove with a racer's speed and daring down I-94 until we reached an exit that took us south of Detroit's Metro airport through the city of Romulus and onto Huron River Road. We followed a one lane back road along the Huron River until we came to a sparsely populated area of one level homes, uneven lawns and dirt driveways.

'Gold' reluctantly nodded to a dirt road that led us past a few more homes until we approached a house that sat several yards back from the dirt road. I guess he was tired of being slapped. Jeff knew to kill the headlights and pull the van off the road and into a tall weeded area.

"How many are in there?" Jeff asked nodding toward the dimly lit house.

"Three, maybe four. Depends on what's going on. They use the house mostly for their own kind of parties. You two would never be invited," 'Gold said with an air of pride.

"And after all that money we paid to our PR Firm," I said.

Jeff reached under the driver's seat and removed a roll of duct tape, quickly cut off a piece and taped it across Gold's mouth. "That's to insure your personal safety should you suddenly decide to run your mouth. You keep quiet and for you tomorrow will be more than just another day."

'Gold' saw meaning behind Jeff's icy stare.

We eased out of the van armed with the twelve gauge and my .38. We followed a dirt path up close to the house and could barely hear noises over nature's night music and the occasional plane heard soaring into the sky.

The house was a one-level, peaked roof with a small front porch, two shielded front windows, separated by a wooden front door. There was a Buick Regal and a Ford Taurus parked in the driveway.

As we moved closer, we heard disparate sounds coming from different parts of the house.

I pointed to a small, ground-level window that led to a basement. We moved silently toward the side of the house, where I crouched down to peek inside. The window was also sealed and from the outside, the room appeared dark. Suddenly there was a concentrated flash of light, followed by darkness then a burst of laughter.

I looked at Jeff as he leaned forward concentrating on the sounds coming out of the basement.

The same concentrated flash of light, followed by the darkness and again laughter. The mixture of noise sounded like three men, all-laughing in various stages of mirth.

Jeff's eyes grew big at a sudden realization. He quickly stood up, surveyed the outer part of the house and said, "Let's Go!"

"What's the plan?" I asked as he quickly ran around to the front.

Jeff tiptoed up the steps, looked at the unscreened door, stepped back and kicked the door open.

"Oh, that's the plan," I said rolling behind Jeff with my .38 in hand.

Jeff's twelve gauge was already sweeping across the front of the room while I quickly checked both sides. Though dimly lit by several lava lamps, there was no one sitting in the room filled with furniture bought at fire sales around the Metro area. The usual assortment of drug paraphernalia lay scattered on a wooden coffee table and an expensive looking CD unit filled the air with somebody screaming about a man's penis and Mt Everest.

Jeff moved quickly to an open door just past the living area. Someone came running up the steps. Jeff stepped to the side, waited and as soon as the youthful looking male peered into the area, he saw me standing in front of him. Before he could say anything, Jeff cracked the back of his head with the barrel of the twelve gauge. He picked him up, turned him around and pushed him back down the steps, holding the back of his collar and using him as a shield.

My brother's blatant action focus caught me completely by surprise.

I followed behind, my .38 drawn as we quickly descended the steps as someone shouted "Hey, A-man, what's happening?"

Jeff pushed the hapless 'A-man' in the direction of the voice and I heard a loud crash. I rolled along the side of the wall until I caught sight of a bulky man standing up, with a blowtorch in his hand.

The sight of him standing there with a surprised look on his face was less sickening than the sight of ST strung up by his wrists, his feet dangling inches from the floor and bleeding from the burn wounds on various parts of his body. The immediate sight and smell of burnt flesh in that confined basement almost gave him the moment of surprise he needed. He leaned over to pick up a gun sitting on an end table.

"Leave it alone!" I yelled as I leveled my .38.

He stopped just as Jeff pulled his two not so menacing looking partners together and pushed them toward the third member of the group.

"Cut him down now!" Jeff yelled.

No one moved. Jeff cracked one in the jaw with the twelve gauge and moved toward the other. I kept an eye on the larger one as he glared back at me.

"Now!" Jeff said to the second, the more willing, twentyish looking loser who saw the barrel of the twelve gauge pointed directly in his face. He quickly moved a table next to ST, jumped on top and began unraveling the rope that held his body in suspension.

I walked toward Mr. Menace, my gun still drawn while watching the other guy cut ST down from his elevated torture rack.

"Help bring him down," Jeff ordered.

They both eased ST onto the floor just as the first guy Jeff leveled slowly stood up.

He'd been spot burned like a piece of metal on an assembly line.

Jeff motioned for the three men to back away as I knelt down and pressed my fingers against the vein in his neck.

I felt a pulse and his breathing appeared sporadic. The burns hadn't killed him although the treatment probably would.

"I told that idiot to stay on the bus," Jeff said to no one. He reached in his jacket pocket and took out a cell phone. "I'll call for an ambulance. Take these keys, uncuff 'Gold' and bring him in here with the rest of these losers."

"What about ..... ?"

" ..... They won't give me any trouble. Will you boys?"

Their silence was the only answer needed.

I'd just made it outside and was halfway to the van when I caught sight of a pair of headlights coming down the road. I moved into the shadows just as a green Volvo came to a stop in front of the house.

Once the engine stopped, a youthful looking man climbed out, clad in an all leather outfit, his hair was corn-rolled to the back and he carried a twelve pack of beer. As he leaned forward to lock the car door, I moved quickly.

I stuck my .38 into his back and pushed him against the car. "Shut up and don't turn around," I said. I frisked him, checking for weapons and an ID. He was unarmed, so I took his wallet out of his back pocket.

"Man, what's this all about?" he asked.

"Shut up!" I yelled as I opened his wallet and looked for his license. It was lodged in a plastic compartment. I removed the license, looked at the picture and read the name.

Maurice Grimes, age seventeen.

I spun him around and aimed my .38 into his face. "What are you doing here Maurice?"

"Just partyin'. My man told me they were having a party. Just a party."

"These your 'homies'?"

"Naw, not really. We just started kickin' it a few days ago. I just met him at a house gig my old lady threw. We talked and decided to hang."

"You just gettin' here?"

"Who are you to ask?"

I grabbed his collar. "I am the patron saint of idiots, fools and losers. Glad to meet you. And the answer to my question is ..... ?"

"Yeah. I'm just gettin here."

"Maurice, what you're about to hear is a one time only shot at saving your worthless life. So listen close. You take that twelve pack, pile your butt into that car and take it back to the city. Don't come down this way ever again. Stay away from this house."

"You can't tell me what ..... "

I pulled him closer. " ..... march your butt over to Tabernacle on Beechwood and ask to speak with Reverend Sampson. Read the Bible. Go to the number one mosque and join the Muslims. Read the Koran. Go to a bookstore and buy a somebody's tell-all book on how to stop being an idiot. Those are your life saving choices. Tell Reverend Sampson your soul is in desperate need of salvation. Tell the brothers at the Mosque that your life needs a focus. I don't care which, but two weeks from now when I come looking for you, I'd better see you in a white robe singing in the choir or in a suit and tie selling the Final Call and bean-pies on Greenfield and Seven Mile. What I don't want to see is your face around here again or a front and side picture of you with numbers underneath. Anything like that happens and I'll take that as a personal dissing and nail your butt so tight that your lifelong job will be as a clown who walks on his hands for a traveling circus. You got that!"

He nodded.

I released him and watched as he fumbled with his keys to open the car door. As he climbed in and started the engine, he asked. "Who are you, man?"

"Lieutenant Knackton of the Detroit Police Department. Call downtown and check it out. God's in your corner tonight because you've just been given a miracle. Get out while I'm still feeling forgiving."

He gunned the engine and backed out without saying thank you.

"Maybe it'll help," I said as I walked to the van to get 'Gold'. The night air was pierced with the sounds of distant sirens ..... again.

29

The night dragged on like a bad sermon at the funeral of a relative you didn't like. It seemed like everyone with a uniform had questions for Jeff and me. The local cops, the Wayne County Sheriff's department, officers from Detroit investigating an earlier shooting incident in the Cass Corridor and the paramedics. At one point it seemed like one of the guys who uses the orange signal cones for airplanes taxing into a gateway stopped by to ask questions.

When the mess was finally sorted, the light that closes the night and welcomes the day signaled to everyone that enough was enough.

There were a series of follow-up interviews scheduled and when Jeff finally drove me back to my car, there weren't very many of my body parts left to throw in bed.

When what was left of me finally made it back to my apartment and fell out on the bed, sleep was my only priority. Unfortunately, like teenage sex, the gratification was instant, but the satisfaction didn't last very long. My body was an amphitheater where each muscle throbbed to its own rhythm, accented by the drum solo pounding in my weather predicting left knee. My insides pulsated like a simultaneous broadcast of a Rick James and KISS concert that dragged me into an exhaustive, but troubled sleep.

It started with a kaleidoscope of faces fading in and out of a senseless dream. Images I chased, but couldn't catch and voices that echoed across a bottomless canyon.

Next came the radio alarm, slipping music into the dream and turning it into a nineteen seventies O'Jays concert at Cobo Hall. The radio was on an hour before I realized I'd forgotten to turn it off.

Morning laid on me like an anvil.

The phone calls followed with equal annoyance.

Rosie called to say he was back in town and why did he have the feeling that the unidentified bounty hunter and private investigator involved in preventing the torturous death of a known felon were related to him.

I told him I'd call him back.

Truman called wanting to know why we hadn't invited him along on our stakeout.

Ditto on the call back.

A telemarketer called with a deal on long distance service.

I told her I didn't speak English.

Detective Wendy Brewer called and said she'd heard from Judge Zone and he confirmed that I was investigating a case for him.

"He's quite a legend. My dad said he reinvented defensive line play," she stated.

I heard papers rustling in the background as she cuffed the phone receiver to speak to someone.

"You said there was a witness," I said as I sat up and checked the clock. 9:35 a.m. Five interrupted hours of sleep will certainly keep a person sharp.

"Yes, there was," Detective Brewer said. "The problem is his credibility. He's a local legend and semi street vagrant. He has family in Mt. Clemens; he just hates living with them on a regular basis. His name's Nelson Thom, a.k.a. Nellie. Fifty six year old male who tells stories about the places he's been and the people he's met."

"Spins a tall yarn does he?"

"In a manner of speaking. The man's never left Mt. Clemens. Anyway, on the night of the accident, he was sleeping behind a mechanic's shop just off the road. Said he heard a car coming down the road at a high speed, but didn't see anything until the driver suddenly turned on his headlights. Apparently the driver was on the wrong side of the road moving fast. Morris and Daphne were coming in the opposite direction just as the driver swerved over to their lane and flicked on the lights. Morris tried to avoid hitting the car and the rest you know."

"This Nellie say what kind of car it was?"

"Nope.' She sighed. "He thought it was a sporty model because it looked low and long."

"Color or make." I asked.

"Negative on that as well. It was dark. He says it could have been black, blue or brown. The driver never stopped to see what he had done, so we're left to bury the dead and speculate on the living."

"Would you mind if I had a copy of that report?"

She agreed to fax a copy over to our office.

"Keller, you find out anything, I want to know yesterday."

"On my honor as an Eagle Scout of two weeks."

Once she rang off, I managed a feeble thirty-minute toss and turn to recover my lost sleep.

Futility and a recharged mind drove me out of bed and into the shower. There were other questions I wanted to ask and no one volunteered to come to my apartment and provide answers.

As much as I hated the idea of a bright morning sun against a cloudless blue sky lighting up the front area where I sat in my recliner, drinking coffee and staring at the construction work on Livernois, the vitamin D stimulation brought on by the sun rays probably did more to recharge my engine than that sludge slithering out of my mug.

The Deborah Morris pot was stirring. Though my approach seemed slow and somewhat antiquated, I had a feeling of progress, though uncertainty about the end result.

I had a mystery within a mystery and no one to tell me how it ends.

Deborah Norris had an interest in the crash-related deaths of Morris and Daphne. Why?

MiShaun Lucas fell off the wagon one day after we talked. Why?

Sharron Westlake's home was ransacked again by persons unknown and she refused to report it to the police. Why?

Trevor Stallings, in the heat of a campaign to win a seat on the City Council, takes time out to meet with me. Why?

Pernell Stallings has an unofficial track record with the court systems and like Tyler Cain found happiness as a promoter and supporter of the 'Empower Detroit' movement. Why?

Another question had started to germinate when the phone rang.

The gruff, recognizable voice said. "Keller?"

"Sorry Lieutenant," I continued. "His dance card is filled today. But we have a lovely substitute named 'Pain'. Will she do?"

"Open the door cowboy or I'll create a new way to pull your license."

"You got a warrant?" I said in a mocking deep tone.

"This is a social visit."

I buzzed him in and listened as he ascended the steps like a Grizzly Bear stalking the scent of blood. Knackton hasn't had reason to pay me a social visit, especially given our blood feud for the attention of Candy Malone. I figured he wanted to give in and acknowledge me as the winner, warn me off the Norris case again or shoot me and plead temporary insanity.

When I opened the door, the disheveled public servant lumbered in, stopping momentarily to check out the apartment.

"It looks worst than I thought."

"The apartment or your reflection?" I answered while sliding back over to my recliner.

Knackton wandered and plopped down on the ledge of my window. "Several agencies burned the oil last night thanks to you and your brother."

I yawned. "I'll mention it to the guy with the burn marks."

He glanced outside the window as if quickly collecting his thoughts.

"You got lucky. You stumbled onto something you normally would've found with the help of a pack of bloodhounds and an orbiting satellite."

"Lieutenant, you're such an inspiration first thing in the morning. Are all your social visits so uplifting?"

"Last night's house party have anything do to with the Norris case?"

I reveled at being able to tell the truth. "As a matter of fact it didn't."

"But as a matter of fact, you're still sniffing around," he stated.

"Those are the facts, Jack."

He stood up and placed his hands in his back pockets. The elbows had that triangular shape common to people about to become lecturing and authoritative. "Look, Keller, I don't like politicians who use their muscle to squeeze me into doing something against my better judgement. Judge Zone's been riding the Chief about the lack of progress related to his sister-in-laws death and I've got a backlog of cases that won't go away because the new cases roll in and require immediate attention. We're all stretched tight down at the brickyard."

"Your point being what, Lieutenant?"

He snorted. "I'll be real clear about this. You might have the political protection of a Judge and his grieving wife for now, but sooner or later when all this blows over, he'll still be a Judge with a grieving wife and you'll go back to being a two-bit P.I. with a gimpy knee. The Judge will drop you like a frigid lap dancer."

"You gonna be there to catch me, Lieutenant?"

"Just long enough to bury you so deep that they'll have to sacrifice a soul to Hell just to find out if you're able to see visitors."

"Nice touch, Lieutenant. Consider me happily intimidated."

He snorted again. "Whoever iced the Norris girl is probably dead or doing time in a correctional facility somewhere and it's just a matter of time before someone drops a dime on him in order to look good for the parole board."

"I'm not crazy about you either, Lieutenant, but I know you're smarter than that. You've had a suspect in mind all the time, but no proof. So the real waiting game is for that suspect to make a mistake."

"Stay away from this case, Keller or I'll have the licensing board take a serious look at the way you conduct your business."

"You ever notice how people in authority positions always threaten a person's livelihood when they've got nothing else to fall back on?"

He huffed and turned toward the door. "I can be your worst nightmare Keller."

"Not unless you wore a tutu, a red wig and called yourself Enni."

He stopped and turned back to me. "Enni?"

"Enni thing goes, Lieutenant."

He gave me a look that told me what I could do with my comment and slammed the door behind him.

I looked toward the closed door and said, "Come visit anytime, Lieutenant. It's a spiritual uplift." He ignored me, but I continued. "By the way, Lieutenant, can you use your influence to have that abandoned car removed? It's really an eyesore."

He turned and said, "So are you."

•　•　•

The mush that sloshed around in my head didn't take to early morning riddles, even after a much-needed shower and system cleaning wheat toast.

Since the night was gone and the morning had been ruined, it seemed like a good time to mess up the rest of the day. I made it to the office just before the lunch hour crowd did their push and shove into the local eateries. I didn't expect Jeff to have logged any office time that morning and I wasn't disappointed. Thankfully, Mary and Julie had departed for lunch and the customers moving in and out of the other shops had little use for my services.

I checked the answering machine and what messages there were could wait until my head and tongue agreed to work together again.

As much as I liked the idea of taking losers and other psychopaths off the streets, last nights excursion didn't change the fact that I still had a lot of questions and few answers about what happened to Deborah. Some kind of movement was my preferred option, but I had little to go on and no trees to shake.

Using my fists as props to support my head, I leaned forward on my desk, yawning and wiping the water from my eyes. There was one clear fact that stood out like plaid on the American Flag; something triggered Deborah's interest in the unsolved deaths of Morris and Daphne. So much so that the article was hidden behind a picture she'd given to MiShaun.

Why hide the article?

Why does anyone hide anything? So it won't be found except by the person doing the hiding?

But why hide anything? Because there's something about it we don't want people to know?

Why hide an article? And why hide it behind a picture you've given to a friend as a gift?

Why? ..., Deborah.

Yawn and think. Wipe the eyes and think. Yawn and think. Wipe the eyes and think.

Deborah was a clever planner. She was mischievous, but not in a harmful way. Loved to create an elaborate ruse where the outcome was funny, but not demeaning. She could keep a variety of facts in her head, loved being independent, was in the truth-above-all-else' phase of journalism, a good listener, caring almost to a fault, a good writer and a free spirit.

So why the newspaper article behind the picture?

"Wait a minute," I said sitting erect in my chair. A red tipped laser beam seared through the cobweb gray matter in my head pushing through a thought left sleeping on the edges. "Why did Deborah give MiShaun, Sharron and Sylvia the exact, same size picture in the exact kind of frame?"

Maybe I was truly fishing, but that just didn't seem to equate with me.

I'm the first to admit that men don't think like women, but based on what little I'd come to understand, my present situation with Malone notwithstanding, women are more personal about gifts and men more practical.

Giving three people I like a similar picture sounds like something I'd do for my brothers, but not something Rae would have done with her three brothers-in-law.

Deborah enjoyed creating a mystery as a fun way of getting at people, but I wondered if there was more to this case than just the coincidence of three similar pictures given to three people.

I moved papers around until I located Sharron's phone number under one of the file folders.

I reached to pick up the receiver just as the phone buzzed.

"Keller Investigations," I answered.

"Linc! Why the hell don't you return phone calls," Tank bellowed.

The barrel-voiced yell of my part-time operative served as a reminder that I'd asked him to keep an eye on Sharron. "Sorry, Tank. I've been unusually busy."

"Tell me about it. I have to hear stuff second hand. You alright?"

"Yeah. Nothing I won't get over."

"You want to hear about Sharron's visitor or are you too busy being newsworthy?" he asked.

"I'm all ears, Tank."

He coughed away from receiver, then cleared his throat. "Damn pollen. Anyway, this guy stops by to see Sharron. Looks like they enjoyed a nice dinner and late night fun. Once the lights went out, I went home. Got back in time to see him leave just before the breakfast crowd jammed up the highways."

"Who was the guy?"

"Well, had you listened to your messages you could have ran his plates for me, but since you were busy, I gambled, figuring Sharron would head to work, so I followed him. This guy's good. He spends the night with Sharron, but the day with another lady who lives off Greenfield. Near as I can figure, this lady works nights."

I sighed. "And the guy's name is ..... ?"

"Hill. Winston Hill. Lives over on ..... "

I uncrossed my legs and moved them abruptly from the top of my desk. "Never mind," I said. "I know where he lives."

30

If a bolt of lightening strikes a tree, the tree falls on a house, destroying the roof and wipes out a group of homeless people trying to find shelter from the rain, I'd reluctantly call that a coincidence. However, a bolt of lightening strikes a tree, the tree falls on a house, destroying the roof, the roof caves in and wipes out a group of terrorists plotting the destruction of a building full of innocent people, then I wouldn't call that a coincidence.

I'd call it dumb luck or maybe even justice.

Winston Hill and Sharron Westlake; coincidence or dumb luck?

The Hill/Westlake combination raised a lot of questions and the remaining fodder in my head wasn't connecting the dots.

I made that notation on a pad. My desk now looked like the last dance at bureaucracy central. Notes, articles, pictures, interviews and other info I'd accumulated lay scattered in front of me like strewn litter in need of an alley. And now I had this new twist.

He'd really underplayed his relationship with Sharron.

Why?

Maybe the Sharron and Winston connection was just a passing coincidence and had nothing to do with what I needed to know. Since it was moving onto the afternoon, I knew Sharron was logging in her hours at the child care center, so I'd catch her later.

Apparently, Winston was into something better than temp work, and with a little patience, he'd return home to roost. I saw no harm in doing a little background check.

"That's a lot of steam coming out of those ears. You thinking deep thoughts or trying to heat the place?"

"Hey, Jules," I said as I yawned and leaned back in my chair. "If I have any thought at all, it left on the last bus out to Maryland."

She strolled in, dropping a brown bag on the desk. "Heard you had a long night. You and the man-hunter okay?"

"My body feels like its been dragged through a sausage grinder. Another two weeks of sleep and I just might be able to regenerate any missing parts."

She breezed behind the desk. "Certain parts of the male anatomy shouldn't be regenerated without licensed certification from the state of Michigan. How's the case coming?"

"It's all right in front of me, Jules." I waved across the desk. "New twists, new turns and none of it is connecting." I picked up the newspaper articles about Morris and Daphne. "I think this is my strongest lead. Deborah was interested in this accident. Somebody ran these kids off the road and never came forward to admit their sins. Maybe Deborah was onto something and it got her killed."

"Maybe she didn't get far enough to find out."

"Maybe," I said. "But so far nothing else makes any sense. So I have to follow this lead."

"I don't see how you can follow anything in this mess," she said and she moved a few of my notes around.

I put my hand down. "I'm visual. I have to see what's in front of me in order to get the picture."

"You're messy and there is no picture." She sighed. "You know, I can organize this ..... mess. I can scan everything you have, create a case file and keep it on my computer."

Julie's attempts at info-teching Keller Investigations started when we all moved into the building. I never doubted the truth of what she said, but Jeff never showed an interest and surfing the net never appealed to my recreational interests. Still-

"Before I forget, how about doing a background check on someone for me." I gave her Winston's name, address and license plate number. "See what you can find on this guy."

"Anything in particular?"

"What he's been up to the last few years."

"Done. Now, what about organizing this mess?"

I held up my hands in mock surrender. "Okay. Listen I've got some rounds to make anyway, so see what you can do. If it looks okay ..... " I peeked over at the burgeoning file cabinets. " ..... Maybe you can take on that sleeping giant."

She smiled. "You won't recognize your efficiency."

I picked up the Morris and Daphne article and slid from behind the desk. "Thanks, Jules. I appreciate the favor."

She waved a dismissive hand. "You're gonna love the bill."

It figured. "I'm outta here."

"Where you headed?"

I stopped just outside the door. "The hell if I know."

•   •   •

The truth, like a rubber band, will break when stretched too tight. I didn't know where I was headed because I had too many places to go.

I had no desire to spend my few waking hours going over statements with the local constabulary about last night's events. Maybe Jeff had already taken care of that activity, but I didn't really care.

I needed answers.

That need drove me out of the office and back on the streets, where I fired up the chariot. It seemed to me that nothing was more revealing than a look of surprise, so I decided to surprise MiShaun.again.

In the pristine bare reception area of 'Empower Detroit', I was about as welcome as a pimple on a reconstructed nose. Helen was particularly short and abrupt as she pretended my existence was a fluke of the gods.

"Miss Lucas is not available at this time," she said through tightly clenched teeth.

"Well, what about at another time. Say an hour from now?"

Her grimace deepened. "Not now, nor in an hour or for the rest of the day for that matter."

"How about tomorrow?" I asked.

"How about you find something else to do with your time?" Tyler's recognizable baritone echoed across the lobby. "Miss Barnes has stated clearly that Miss Lucas is not available. What part of that statement is unclear to you?"

"The part where you think I'm talking to you, Mr. Executive Assistant to the Assistant Director."

Tyler rolled across the lobby like he wanted to play the dog and hydrant two-step on my face. I rose up from the reception counter where we stood inches from each other's space, eyeball to eyeball. Seemed like we'd already played this scene.

"You and me ain't making it, my man. We ain't got time for your crap slide all over the rug."

"You ain't?"

He furrowed his eyebrows. "I've had just about enough ..... "

"Cool it, lamp brain. My patience is running thinner than an anorexic dietician, and when I'm sailing along on a few hours sleep, I can be out and out mean. Since MiShaun is currently unavailable, I'll just check and see if she's still working from home. All it takes is one phone call."

"She's not home either," Helen blurted.

Tyler flashed a look that would have melted stone. Helen looked down at her desk and began moving papers around.

"Is she somewhere on this planet?" I asked the now busy Helen.

"Miss Lucas is tending to important personal matters and will be unavailable for a few days."

"So where is she?"

"Attending to personal matters," Tyler repeated slowly diverting the attention back to him.

"Any chance you mentioning to her that I have a few questions I'd like to ask?"

I already knew the answer. His half-curled smirk told me all I needed to know.

"Try not to miss me, Tyler," I said half turning to the door. "You know I'll be back."

I'd left MiShaun stretched out on her couch, calling in Moose from Montana and oblivious to the world. Now, she's attending to personal matters, not related to work.

I checked the time. The workday still had a few hours from being complete, so I rolled the Nova onto a parking lot just across from the 'Empower Detroit' offices.

The matted-haired, haggard-looking parking attendant was reading a physics book and half believed my story about being too cheap to stay in a motel. My request to sleep in my car was met with the most subtle of shrugs. I told him there'd be a tip for him if he woke me up a four o'clock.

He shrugged. That universal motion for dispassionate disinterest meant I'd have time to recharge the body clock.

I parked my car so I had a view of the 'Empower Detroit' building, rolled back my seat and idled my carcass.

• • •

A tapping on the driver side window awakened me. My walking alarm clock pointed to the watch on his wrist, noting the time.

I nodded, rolled down the window and slipped him a rumpled looking Hamilton.

He shrugged.

After paying for the time, I pulled onto the street.

The service station just down the block had enough juice and chips to appease my growling stomach and a bathroom to relieve my overfilled bladder.

Now, fully alert, I pulled into a space across from the 'Empower Detroit' building. The absence of an adjacent parking structure made my surveillance easier. My choice of who to follow was based on degree-of-reluctance to talk to me. Given my growing popularity among those office patrons, I banked on one remote possibility.

Even as the sun set while a mild temperature and the wind blew a gentle breeze, Helen Barnes end-of-the day grimace looked no different from her beginning-of-the day grimace.

She slid her Toyota Tercel into the ongoing traffic, practically pulling along side of me as she motored toward the stoplight.

I pulled in three lengths behind her, hoping that she had someplace to stop before going home.

We drifted along easy enough, stopping and going to the rhythm of the commuter tango until she exited the Lodge Freeway onto Nine Mile Road, crossing over the service entrance that lead to the parking lot in front of Hudson's in the Northland Mall.

She managed to find a spot close to the entrance, while I drove further down, finally parking near the end of the lane.

She didn't appear to be in a hurry, which served my purposes well.

Easing past the valet parking and through the glass paneled doors; Helen stopped momentarily and then moved to the left of the entrance, stopping at a yogurt stand to place her order.

Strolling past her and staying just out of her peripheral vision, I took a spot just to the right of the line. I decided to wait until she was ready to pay for her cup of strawberry yogurt with chocolate topping and then make my grand appearance.

"Hi, Helen. What a coincidence meeting you here."

A momentary look of uncertainty moved across her face as she saw me out of the context of her office. Then she glared. "I do hope you're not following me, Mr. Keller. I'd hate to have to call security."

I'd already anticipated her suspicion. "Nope. A friend of mine manages Hudson's book department just around the corner. I always stop in to see what's new in the Mystery section."

To her credit, she wasn't buying my explanation. "I'm sure I don't believe you."

"Helen, as long as we're here, may I impose on you for just a moment? Granted, our introductions so far haven't qualified as 'magic meeting moments, but maybe we can start all over again. If you'll let me pay for your snack, I think you'll find that I'm not that bad a person. The fact of the matter is, I'm just doing my job."

She hesitated. "I suppose that puts you one step above being completely worthless."

"It's a big step." I nodded toward the vinyl-covered booths in a far corner. "I promise not to take too much of your time."

"Oh, all right. But not too much time. I enjoy my shopping time alone."

I felt adequately chastised. While she slid into a nearby booth, I paid for her snack.

Now that Helen wasn't behind the reception desk, there was a different look to her style and manner. She was taller than I thought, medium height and marrowy, with a pine green skirt and jacket to compliment a silk white blouse.

I knew I hadn't completely won her confidence, so I thought I'd go with a basic icebreaker. "How long have you worked with 'Empower Detroit'?"

A dollop of yogurt balanced delicately on the plastic white spoon as she stopped mid flight to answer my question. "As I said, Mr. Keller; I don't have a lot of time. So, why don't we move past the small talk? You ask me what you really want to know and I'll decide if it's any of your business."

"Fair enough. No sense in hanging out in the gray areas."

She gazed coolly, undeterred by my ill-timed humor. "I know you're a private investigator, you used to play for the Oakland Raiders, went to Prairie View State University, worked as a police officer for the Oakland Police Department in California and you have an office on Livernois."

"And what did I have for dinner last night?"

She ignored the sarcasm. "You're investigating the murder of Judge 'War Zone's' sister-in-law and since MiShaun is an old friend, you've come around asking questions."

"You look that up on your own or did someone ask you to?"

She snorted. "Mr. Stallings was understandably curious as to the nature of your investigation. So he asked me to pull up some background information. I found you in several databases and shared the information with Mr. Stallings."

"Which Stallings?"

"Trevor Stallings, of course."

"Of course." The information highway has no moral off ramp. Despite its alleged advantages, the information age is really nothing more than a large cyber keyhole in which any mouse can peep into your world and stare at your naked life without any regard for those parts which you'd just as soon keep hidden. Helen hadn't said anything that couldn't be accessed from any number of sources; I just didn't like the idea that she knew without really knowing me. "Why is he so interested in my investigation?"

"MiShaun does work for him." Her tone was laced with indignation. "He always takes an interest in things that may upset his staff members."

Her pronouncement sounded like a rehearsed line for a five-second sound bite. "He sounds benevolent. How'd MiShaun get the job of Assistant Director so quickly and with so few credentials."

Helen didn't look up from her yogurt. "She's a hard worker."

"And God don't make the little green apples."

She glared for just a second and then her face softened. "Is it that obvious?"

"You're wearing it on your sleeve."

"My personal feelings for MiShaun have nothing to do with how she works."

"But it does affect how you work." I leaned forward. "Look Helen, I'm not trying to get any dirt on MiShaun, the Stallings or anyone else for that matter. I'm trying to find out why Deborah Norris was murdered. Some say it was just a robbery. I say different. I think MiShaun knows more than she's letting on. I don't mind getting stonewalled 'cause I'll just try digging underneath."

I recanted as much of the case as I could without giving out specific names, dates and relationships. Helen listened, but reserved the right to appear uninterested. "So, now do you see why I need to talk to MiShaun? When I saw her yesterday, she had a looser tongue, but an incoherent outlook. I hoped today would find her more willing to share information."

Helen sighed. "I'm afraid you're going to find her less willing and less available."

"What do you mean?"

"Maybe you mean well Mr. Keller ..... "

"Linc."

"Linc. Everything seems out of place since MiShaun came on board. I never liked the idea of Mr. Stallings working with so many of his brother's friends. We should be about helping people who want to do something with their lives, not those ..... " She paused, then stared off into the crowd of people moving across the lobby. "Last night, Mr. Stallings received an emergency phone call from Pernell. He called from the emergency ward at Henry Ford Hospital." She turned back towards me. "MiShaun tried to commit suicide."

31

I froze.

Helen's mouth moved as it had throughout our conversation, but the words danced slowly through my head, unable to land on a cell that would trigger the full comprehension of what I just heard.

She held up a reassuring hand. "She's okay. She didn't take enough sleeping pills or drink enough alcohol to completely do the job, but she's going to be all right. We were lucky that Pernell just happened to stop by to leave some paperwork."

"What happened?" I asked.

"Apparently she fell off the wagon and had been tying one on all afternoon. Then something upset her."

Or someone, I thought.

"Mr. Stallings arranged for her to be put in a private room under the care of his family doctor. She's resting and not taking visitors." She waited a beat. "I'm surprised you're just hearing this. I expected to see you hanging around the lobby at Henry Ford last night."

Last night blurred by me. "I was busy."

"So was MiShaun." She stopped, reflected for a moment, then said. "I'm sorry. That caustic comment was uncalled for. MiShaun is hurting and all I can think about is how nice it'll be to not have her around the office for a while."

"What will make it so nice?"

She waved dismissively. "Oh, what the hell. MiShaun is a daily reminder that the job I wanted the most was filled before I had a chance to compete. I gave my blood to help make 'Empower Detroit' a special place and yet she waltzes in and leap frogs over me to the Assistant Director's office."

"Some might call that tenacity," I offered.

"You might. Me? I call it; knowing something that no one else knows."

I thought a moment. "Or maybe it's something that someone else wishes you didn't know." I slid out from the booth. "Thanks, Helen. You've been helpful. I don't know if we'll talk again, but if we have to, I'll be a lot more courteous."

She nodded gently, choosing to finish her yogurt.

I strolled across the tiled lobby, past the furniture displays, the down escalator until I reached the book department. I looked on the table of display books, picked up a copy of Walter Mosley's 'Always Outnumbered, Always Outgunned' and paid the cinnamon-toned woman with bedroom brown eyes.

"Thank you," she said. "We appreciate your business."

"My pleasure, Pat," I said glancing at her nametag.

Now, at least I hadn't completely lied to Helen. I did buy a book. Not wanting to be a further nuisance, I tooled out of the Hudson's parking lot and crossed the bridge over the James Couzens freeway to get back on the Lodge. The pieces of this disassembling puzzle were starting to fall off the table.

•　　•　　•

MiShaun's attempt at self-elimination rubbed against the grain of my sensibilities. She'd discovered a measure of success despite the standard barriers thrown at someone lacking a university degree. So why the need to suddenly board the 'A' train to Arcadia? Had I shown a little more concern for her, I might have stayed around until she woke up or until Pernell stopped by. Maybe this pills-and-alcohol episode could have been avoided.

"Don't second guess the first reaction," I quipped.

I knew I wouldn't get much out of MiShaun and didn't want to push the issue   just yet.

In most complex cases, where the FBI, CIA or the local 'blues' are investigating, there is a standard and timely lament that usually brings some focus and clarity. 'Follow the money', if there is money to follow. So far, nothing seemed to suggest a money trail. The only true lead was the accidental deaths of Morris and Daphne. If there was money trail linked to that accident, then maybe Deborah stumbled onto it and that knowledge got her killed.

Maybe cats will fly, mice will sing and more than fifty percent of the registered voters in Detroit will cast their ballots in the next election.

MiShaun was out of commission and Morris and Daphne were my best leads. Maybe Sharron could provide some insight, if she weren't busy with Winston.

32

I motored over to Sharron's home on Wisconsin Street and was pleasantly surprised at seeing Winston's car parked in her driveway.

The luck of the Irish was a statement that didn't play well with an African-American who attended Prairie View State University, but I'm sure the folks at Notre Dame didn't mind that I borrowed it for the moment.

I parked and looked forward to knocking on the door.

Sharron didn't appear surprised to see me, more like disturbed.

"Lincoln, I'm surprised to see you again."

"I have a few more questions and I wanted to see how you were doing since the break in. I promise not to take more than a few minutes."

She didn't have time to formulate an answer, so she beckoned me in to the sound of a champagne cork being unplugged. The living area had been restored. No hint of the mess I'd last seen. However, the startled look on Winston's face as he whirled around with the Champagne bottle in hand, suggested that another mess might be ready to unfold.

Sharron started the introductions. "Honey, this is ..... "

"We've met," I said. "How's it going, Winston?" I extended my hand. "Small world, isn't it?"

"Sometimes too small from where I sit," he replied while giving a passive handshake.

"You two know each other?' Sharron asked.

"We've had a few beers together," I said. "Actually, we met by way of this investigation. I stopped by the old stomping ground and it turns out that Winston lives in Deborah's old place. Told me they talked on a few occasions, but really didn't know her that well."

A look of puzzlement crossed Sharron's face, then vanished. "We were just about to have dinner and celebrate Winston's new job."

"Oh? Well, congratulations, Winston. ..... I know it's been a long haul. Where's the gig?"

"It's not important, man. What brings you out this way?"

I unfolded the newspaper article and showed it to Sharron. "As far as I can tell, this was the last story that Deborah had started to pull together. Does it look familiar?"

Sharron read through the article and shook her head. "No, it doesn't look familiar, but you never really knew what Deborah was working on until it showed up in print."

'How about you, Winston? Any chance Deborah might have mentioned the story?"

He glanced down, half reading the article. "No, she never said anything about this. 'Course, I'd left Michigan by the time she really started getting her articles published."

Sharron's mouth straightened like a hairpin. There was a tiny circle between the clasped lips. Like the previous look of puzzlement, it also vanished. "Well, you'd seen a few. Remember, we met at one the those weekend bashes that Deborah always had to celebrate having an article published." She turned toward me. "He just wandered over one night and joined the fun. We drifted out of touch when he left Detroit, so imagine my surprise when he called and said he was back in town and living in Deborah's old place."

I smiled. "He's lucky to have a friend or two he could call on to help ease his transition back to the city."

He ignored the comment. "How's the investigation going?"

"Slow," I replied. "Right now I'm casting a wide net to see what gets pulled in. This one lead might tell me something and it might not. When the dust settles, it might turn out to be nothing more than a robbery."

"I'd hate to think that Deborah's life came to an abrupt end because some thief couldn't be satisfied with just robbing her," Sharron stated.

"By the way," I said. "Did Deborah ever mention carrying a gun?"

"No. She never mentioned a gun around me," Winston replied.

Sharron hesitated. "Well, she never mentioned her gun, but we all knew she had one. During one of our celebrations, Deborah wanted a take-out order from Mi Ling's Garden, but didn't feel like driving. Her car was the closest to the condo, so since MiShaun couldn't drive and Winston didn't dare, I got elected. Deborah said her keys were in her purse. I looked in and that's where I spotted the gun. I removed it from her purse, held it up and asked why was she carrying a gun."

"What was her reason?" I asked.

"She played it off. Just said that from time to time she needs to feel protected when she's investigating certain stories." She paused. "I didn't give it much thought. It seemed to make sense, so I put the gun back in her purse and never talked about it after that."

"So both of you, as well as MiShaun, knew she carried a gun?"

The both nodded.

Winston spoke first. "Look, Linc, my man, where does this take us? Deborah's gone and we can't bring her back. Everyone says it was a robbery and the thief is probably long gone, dead or residing up I-94 in Jacktown. It doesn't matter now. It's eight years later and she's still very dead. We all miss her, but life goes on."

I thought about Sylvia Henderson. "For some, it does. For others, it sticks to an unmovable moment and consumes their energy." I glanced at the setting on the table. "I certainly don't want to interrupt your celebration with this downer talk about a former friend."

Sharron sighed. "I wish that necklace of hers would have protected her life. Even though I knew it was silly, I enjoyed watching her tap that thing three times and say 'All luck is attitude.' Sometimes I thought it did possess magical properties. When she stopped by that night to say she was headed out of town in pursuit of a story, I remember her saying, 'if all goes well' then she pulled on the necklace, tapped it three times and made her usual statement." Sharron pinched the bridge of her nose. "Deborah said she was going after the truth."

I stared at the Morris and Daphne article, wondering what was the truth. Or was it this story? Maybe she uncovered something from one of her other stories. I wasn't in the mood to play guess-what's-behind-clue-number-whatever, but something lead me to the Morris and Daphne article and that's where I needed to hang out.

"Linc?" Sharron called out. "Was the information about Deborah's gun important?"

"Yes. It probably doesn't make a difference now, so you might as well know; Deborah was killed with her own gun."

Sharron gasped. "She was killed by her own gun?"

"Yeah. The police left it out of the report just in case the killer happens to mention it to a friend or cellmate. It also kept every loony looking to confess to something from jammin' up the system.

"By the way, you said that you drove to get the food because Winston didn't dare and because MiShaun couldn't. I assume Winston couldn't risk the possibility of being seen driving another woman's car, especially since he didn't know Deborah that well, but what was MiShaun's reason?"

Sharron eased next to me, talking to my profile. "Her license had been suspended. It was the second time she'd been stopped driving under the influence."

"How long was the suspension?"

"Ninety days, I think. Maybe longer. Why?"

I didn't answer. "What kind of car did she drive?"

"Well, after she totaled her Pontiac, she didn't own a car for a while. Usually borrowed or rode the bus. The suspension came after she was stopped driving Deborah's car. She'd borrowed the car without Deborah's permission. Fortunately, she didn't hit anyone or anything and Deborah, naturally, didn't press charges."

"Any idea when it happened?"

"That was years ago. I'm not sure when ..... "

Winston had walked over and stood on the other side of me. "Look, man, why don't you ..... "

"What kind of car did Deborah own at the time?"

"A blue Miata. Sporty model," Winston replied with increased impatience.

I smiled, left the question hanging and eased out the door. Once I'd jumped behind the wheel of my Nova, I hustled along the residential streets until I reached Outer Drive. Early dusk and a bright orange setting sun greeted me as I worked the unfolding scenario in my head. This case had an ominous feel and my own speculations were running off the map.

What really got me going was the thought of MiShaun driving a blue Miata owned by Deborah. Someone driving a blue sports car ran Morris and Daphne off the road.

It wasn't fast-food gas that caused my stomach to churn.

33

Connecting pieces and trying to eliminate coincidence or the obvious. There was no reason to believe that the supposed car seen by the one witness to the accident that killed Morris and Daphne was the same one being driven by MiShaun.

Having read the reports shared with me by Detective Wendy Brewer, I knew the exact night of the accident. What I'd have trouble proving would be whether or not MiShaun was driving Deborah's car at that time.

A long shot.

But that's why Judge Zone was paying the bills.

Now I had an even stronger reason for talking with MiShaun, though I was pretty sure her memory would come up short.

I placed a call to Sylvia and caught her in between errands.

After the pleasantries I asked, "Whatever happened to Deborah's Miata?"

Sylvia thought for a moment. "We sold it to a young couple from Toledo. Why?"

"I'm just following a lead. It may not go anywhere, but I thought I'd check it out."

"That was a few months after Deborah's funeral. It's the one thing I decided not to keep in storage. I think I have their number if you want it."

I wrote down their names and number in case I decided to follow the lead a little further.

"Tell me, Sylvia; did Deborah have any accidents with her car?"

"Not that I'm aware of. She always took meticulous care of that car.

'Course, I didn't know everything. It's possible."

"Do me a favor. Ask The Judge to check with his contacts in Motor Vehicles, plus the local and state police departments. See if there's any report of an accident of any kind involving Deborah's Miata."

"May I ask ....? "

"I'm not sure if it means anything or not. Like I said; I'm just following a lead. It might not go anywhere."

Sylvia agreed and said she'd leave the information on my answering machine.

After I rang off, I put in a call to Jeff, not sure if I'd even catch him at his loft.

I was stunned when he answered. "Jeff? I didn't expect to catch you at home?"

"I didn't expect you to catch me at home. You been down to give your statement?"

"No. I've been busy, but I'll get around to it. How's ST?"

"Dead. Didn't last past this morning. Burns were too severe."

"Sorry, Bro."

"He made his choice. Live or die."

Jeff could be pretty matter-of-fact about a lot of things. I changed the subject. "Listen. Do you have a contact or two in the insurance industry?"

"I know a few people," he replied.

I told him what I needed and why.

"I can make a few calls. You at home or the office?"

"Office. No reason to go home this early."

He rang off.

On the way to the office, I stopped at a local 'chew and choke', bought a take-out order of fried shrimp with biscuits and returned to the solitary confines of the office. It was late enough for me to have an undisturbed moment or two. Sometimes the quiet is all the mind needs to decipher the noise.

The two messages on the answering machine were from potential clients. Both sounded urgent and emphasized that someone they knew had referred them to me.

More work.

More desperate souls looking for answers that would keep them from jumping off a roof or sharing a cell with someone named 'Killer'.

I left the messages on the machine, content to listen again ..... later.

The mess I'd left on the desk had been replaced with a manila folder, a case number and a computer disc. A little yellow post it on the disc had a scribbled note from Julie;

'Welcome to the 21st century detective'

My chaos was organized, dated from the first piece of information to the most recent. Placed in segments and attached. The story of Deborah's life had been turned into a sequence of events. With fixed points in time.

I checked under the folder for a bill.

As much as the organization helped, I didn't cruise through the information. It was the sound of fried shrimp crunching in my mouth that broke up the prolonged quiet. I had leaned back in my chair, propped my feet on the desk and muddled through the day's revelations.

I closed my eyes and let the names and faces bounce off the four mental walls, hoping that something would connect.

MiShaun and Sharron with Winston added to the mix. Tyler Cain with the Stallings Brother, Trevor and Pernell. Helen Barnes. Morris Shaw and Daphne Connor. Jocelyn Kilgore.

Malone.

We hadn't talked lately. No calls from her and vice versa. I'm sure we were both too busy.

Too busy to connect. The Nineties excuse for social rudeness and personal protection.

I picked up the receiver, ready to punch in her office number and stopped.

Maybe when I finished with this case.

Yea though I walk in the valley of melancholy, I shall fear no regrets. Except those caused by my own pigheadedness.

Focus on the case.

So I did. For the next hour and a half, I went back over every detail my mind could absorb. Rethinking possibilities and getting back to the one conclusion.

It was more than just a robbery.

So what was in the hole of the doughnut?

Nothing, or was there a deeper meaning?

The night moved to its dance of the nocturnal and I had no other angles to pursue.

"Damn Deborah!" I yelled. "What the hell were you onto?" I gazed down at the open folder, my hands clasped behind my neck to rub away the cramp. "What the hell were you onto?"

No one answered my whispered question.

34

The office offered no additional insight, so I cruised back to my apartment, watched some evening television and decided to crash.

Sleep seemed to be about as far away as the answers to my nagging questions. What substituted was the mental picture of Deborah Norris, journalist, good person and prankster moving across my conscious like a digital image on a computer screen. I knew there had to be something that sat right there in the image, seemingly invisible, but as obvious as a broken nose.

Deborah aspired to be a first-class journalist. She pursued the truth and, based on her articles, didn't fear where that truth may have lead. Ideally, I guessed that was the benchmark of anyone who wanted to walk the path of a journalist.

I sat up quickly.

"Journalist." I whispered. "Journalist. Journal. Journal! Damn! Did Deborah keep a journal?"

I glanced at the clock. It was well after the witching hour, when all sensible people would be asleep, except for senseless private investigators.

Who would know if Deborah kept a journal?

I hadn't noticed anything like a journal when I searched through the box Sylvia left with me, but then I wasn't searching for a journal.

Would Sylvia know? Maybe Sharron or MiShaun would know.

Who is the most likely person to know if a woman kept a journal?

I reached for the cordless phone and punched in a phone number.

The croaky voice that answered is not who I wanted, but it was a good start.

"Hey Rosie, it's me."

"Linc? What the ....? What time is it?"

"It's time to put Rae on the phone. Is she awake?"

He groaned, whispered to Rae, and her voice finally lulled into the receiver.

"Linc? What's up? Is everything alright?"

"Just fine, Sis. Got a quick question; who is the most likely person to know if a woman kept a journal?"

She paused. "I know I'll wonder about this in the morning, so for now I'll just answer the question; the woman writing in the journal."

"Would a best friend know?"

"Not always. Journals are private."

"Colleague?"

"I doubt it. Why keep a journal if someone else knows about it?"

"Where would a woman hide a journal?" I asked.

Rae yawned. "Someplace special to her and the last place you'd look."

"Now what does that mean?"

"It means it's late and I'm sleepy. Good night, Linc."

She beeped off before I could say anything.

Rae's statements raced through my head and I pinged on an obvious place to look. The lateness of the hour prevented me from immediately acting on the answer, but it would be easy to check out in the morning.

When I fell back on my pillow, I breathed deeply knowing sleep was a few moments away.

35

I greeted the overcast morning with renewed curiosity and vigor. I'd gone through the night with no memory of shadowy outlines or distant images.

After the morning shave and shower, I threw on casual attire and placed a call to Sylvia Henderson.

We exchanged formal greetings and I explained to her what I wanted.

"Why do you need the key to that storage room?" she asked.

"I'll answer that by asking you a question; do you know if Deborah kept a journal?"

She thought for a moment. "Not that I'm aware of. But if she had I'm sure I would have known."

"Not necessarily, Mrs. Henderson. I'd like to look through Deborah's things. I believe she kept a journal. If she did, it might be helpful to my investigation."

She thought a moment and said I could stop by and pick up the key.

"You'll be careful going through her things, won't you?"

"More than you'll know, Mrs. Henderson," I said reassuringly,

"Oh, and Mr. Keller," she said before hanging up.

"Yes?"

"If there is a journal and you should find it, I would appreciate being the next person to read its contents."

I gave my promise and rang off.

•   •   •

Inside the cedar brick storage room, I looked through the carefully numbered boxes that Sylvia had meticulously arranged and labeled.

Underneath the tube lighting, I read through the list of items stored, alphabetized, numbered and packed according to size and weight. Organization and detail must have been part of the Norris family genetic code. I didn't really like the idea of going through Deborah's personal items, but I hoped she understood.

My search was driven by the belief that Deborah, being both a woman and a journalist, the odds were more that good that she kept some kind of journal, so as I read through the list I kept in mind Rae's statement.

"Someplace special to her and the last place I'd look," I said as I began eliminating obvious items.

I crossed off clothing still on hangers, all kitchen and dining utensils, folded clothing, underwear and paperback books. Deborah had a fondness for historical romance. Her stereo system and 19-inch color television seemed unlikely places, as did the wall-mounted pendulum clock. I did check behind the head and base boards that came with her box spring mattress. The other mattress leaned against the wall and there was nothing visibly taped on either side.

As I continued to check off items, I mused myself with the often-quoted Holmes lament; 'Once you've eliminated the impossible, everything else, no matter how improbable, is the truth.'

So what was the truth about an assumed journal and its assumed hiding place?

Rae's statement about the privacy of a journal suggested a private, possibly intimate place where it would be hidden. I guessed the hiding place would be unseen, but simple to access. I stared at the various items of wood-paneled furniture draped with a plastic covering. Sylvia probably looked through all drawers and cabinets before bringing Deborah's last material possessions to this man-made purgatory. I figured I owed the furniture a perfunctory check-over.

After checking underneath the drawers, looking in the corners and feeling around the bottom of Deborah's furniture, my suspicions were confirmed; there was no journal taped on the furniture in some discreet corner behind a loose drawer.

As the morning wore on, I focused on smaller items that could be seen as intimate and accessible. In box number 4, Sylvia had noted the things Deborah had kept on her bedroom dresser. There were two silver based lamps, a flower painted storage tray and two jewelry boxes with a complete list of each piece of jewelry stored in each box.

I pulled the box down from its perch, pulled back the tape and rummaged through its contents. Finding both jewelry boxes was easy. Sylvia had stored each in matching white slipcovers. The jewelry boxes were simple mahoganies paneled with silver ornaments with a glossy finish. I opened each box, figuring Sylvia had removed all the jewelry. There was nothing inside or underneath the boxes that hinted of a journal.

I resealed the box and placed it back on top of the other boxes.

Sighing deeply, though not exasperated, it seemed I was running out of possibilities. The idea of a journal seemed to make sense, but it did come to me on a whim. At least I thought it did.

Though investigations rarely run a straight course, they can often times be steered way off course by a red herring.

I hoped I hadn't bitten on one.

There were still other items on the list worth considering so I stood under the lighting, eyes growing tired and looked over the remaining couple of pages.

What remained seemed unlikely places to keep or hide a journal. As I read over the last few items, noting the box of white-out, canister of multi-colored fine point pens and music box, I stopped and noticed the half looped mark next to 'music box'. It looked like a half-finished question mark, but I wasn't sure.

If it was a question mark, did Sylvia mean she wasn't sure if it was a music box or that it was a music box but she didn't know where it was located?

I needed an excuse to break, so I turned off the light, locked the door and drove to the main office, where a thirty-something receptionist with platinum hair grudgingly allowed me two minutes to use the phone.

Sylvia picked up after the third ring. She inquired about my search and I told her it hadn't generated anything so far.

"However, Mrs. Henderson, there is one thing I'd like to ask you. I think you have a question mark by the item listed as a music box; what does the question mark mean?"

There was a hint of anger in her answer. "Deborah had a beautiful two-level music box that she bought during one of her trips. I think she found it in New Orleans at the Mardi Gras."

"Same place she bought your necklace."

"Yes. Anyway, she always kept the music box on the end-table by her bed. It played the most soothing harp music, which she adored."

"Where's the box?" I asked, though I was pretty sure of the answer.

"Gone. It wasn't among her things. I didn't really notice it until I started packing up her bedroom."

"Any ideas about what may have happened?"

"Someone must have taken it. I remember seeing the music box on her table when we were allowed to go and claim her things. Two days later, when I returned with the movers, the box was gone."

"Any hint of a burglary?"

"Nothing obvious, but that doesn't mean anything."

"Did you file a report?"

"Yes, but the police weren't optimistic. Since it didn't appear to be a burglary, they said there was very little they could do."

In my mind, it only left one other possibility. "What else did Deborah keep on that end table?"

"Besides the box and that can of pens, nothing really stands out."

"That can of multi-colored pens which you've written here?"

"Yeah, that's the one. Deborah always called those her 'mood pens'."

I thanked her and said I'd check in later.

After graciously thanking the receptionist for the use of the phone, I slid behind the wheel of my Nova and eased into the traffic.

Assuming Deborah's former residence didn't house a poltergeist, it seemed to me that someone came into her place and took the music box.

It had to be someone who had access with a key. Which meant there were two possibilities. It was someone who was her friend ..... or someone who was her lover.

I thought I'd start with the friend.

36

I waited as Sharron rolled the question around in her head. Sitting across from her L-shaped desk in the office where she directed the activities of her child development specialists, I knew it wasn't the question she was expecting.

She flushed in that way when people find themselves mentally debating the consequences of telling the truth or letting the unspoken lie serve as the focal point of the conversation. Asking her if she knew what happened to Deborah's music box saved a lot of posturing.

"Sharron, let me save you a lot of moral reasoning. Deborah owned a music box. You spent enough time in her condo to have seen it at one time or another. You must have had access whenever she was out of town. You mentioned taking care of her plants. At the time her furniture was being moved, the music box came up missing. As far as I know, nothing else was stolen and it happened sometime after her death. I'm guessing that in your grief to preserve the memory of Deborah, you mistakenly picked up the music box and in the interim, forgot to return it to Sylvia."

Now that I'd given her a way out, I hoped she'd follow through.

She sighed and leaned back in her swivel chair. "It wasn't fair. Deborah was taken away before she really had a chance to live. She was my best friend and no amount of proclamations and mournful statements could ever change that simple fact."

"Or bring her back," I added.

She nodded. "Or bring her back." Sharron rubbed her eyes and looked at me. "Yes. I have her music box. I took it because I couldn't imagine anyone else who'd cherish it the way I would. So I used Deborah's spare key to go into her condo. We had keys to each others place. I sat in the living area and cried until there was nothing left. Once I realized the finality of it all, I resolved to keep something of hers that would act as my on-going link to my best friend. I knew how much she loved that music box, so I took it and haven't shared its existence with anyone."

"May I ask what was in the box?"

"Nothing much. A few felt tip pens of assorted colors, some small post it notes and a few other odds and end."

"Any jewelry?"

She shook her head as she answered, "No. Jewelry never really had a place with Deborah. She loved that lucky necklace, but that's about as far as it went."

"I'd like to see the box, if you don't mind."

"I'm not sure if ..... "

"Don't worry. Your secret is safe with me. I just need to see the box."

"Do your close friends consider you trustworthy?"

"My boy-scout merit badges are a matter of public record." I answered while demonstrating the scout salute.

She leaned forward and pulled open a bottom drawer. "Just make sure that you touch nothing other than the music box."

She placed a black leather shoulder purse on the desk, unlatched the cover and removed a plastic hoop key ring. "Here's the key to my front door."

After receiving instructions on how to shut off the alarm and where the box was located, I thanked Sharron and told her I'd return the key within the hour.

"Lincoln," she said as I stood up. "You never really said why the music box is so important to your investigation."

"I don't know if it's important or not. It's a detail that I need to check out."

"You'll tell me if it is important?" she asked firmly.

"Without hesitation."

•   •   •

Though my entrance into Sharron's home was completely on the up and up, I couldn't help but feel that somewhere on that middle class block, an elderly woman was peering out a closed curtained window, watching me go in while dialing 911, assuming she didn't have a cell phone.

As I made my way up the stairs to Sharron's bedroom, I didn't hear the sound of distant sirens approaching.

There was great comfort in that knowledge ..... for the moment.

Inside the meticulously ordered room, I worked my way around the brass-lined foot board, to the floor-to-ceiling mirrored closet, where I pulled open the double doors and glanced up past two rows of perfectly folded sweaters until I spotted the box with yellow trimming.

"That's it," I said.

I eased the box down from the shelf and gently placed it on the bed so as not to wrinkle the comforter. The box felt heavy enough, so I removed the square lid and pulled back the white wrapping paper. Sharron had taken great care in making sure the box was protected from dust and curiosity.

The music box spoke of gaiety. It looked like it belonged to a time when courtships happened during the early night hours on a porch swing where young couples stared at the night, breathing the crisp night air and swatting away mosquitoes. The music box's polished oak exterior had silver trimming around three sides and a silver latch to seal off its contents. Sharron had assured me that the only jewelry it contained belonged to her, only I wasn't looking for jewelry.

I unhooked the latch and lifted the lid. Given the neatness of Sharron's home, the orderly music box came as no surprise. However, I was immediately struck by the music. Though I was never a fan of harp music, it chimed serenely from the inside and I visualized Deborah laying on a corner of her bed, listening to the music, finding her own moment of peace, unconcerned about work, friends or missed deadlines. Somewhere within her own mosaic, she'd found the time to let the music surround her being while she .....

While she wrote.

Deborah sat, or lay, on the corner of her bed and wrote. She used multi colored felt tipped pens to transfer her thoughts, but there was no doubt that she wrote.

I removed the various pieces of jewelry until the box was empty. There appeared to be a few inches of space underneath the burgundy-lined bottom. After feeling along the edges, I found a spot in the left corner with just enough space to slip a fingernail underneath. Once the bottom was removed, it revealed a small, metallic space.

You couldn't miss it if you tried.

There was a black leather covered notebook with the gold embossed initials DN in the lower right corner.

Part of Deborah's world was about to be revealed to me. A part she hadn't shared with anyone other than her own conscious. Those inner thoughts that governed her head, heart and secret passions had found their way into the hands of a stranger.

I opened the journal to its first page and read the date on the first line in the top left-hand corner.

Jan 1, 1992

'And so another year has begun for me and I look forward to its possibilities .....'

She began that passage in black ink and as I flipped through the pages, I noticed that certain entries were written in different colors. She'd chronicled each day up until her last entry. Curious to know what was going on in her world before she was taken from ours, I read her last written words.

'Though I have to give Sylvia her birthday gift a little earlier than planned, at least she'll have it in her possession while I'm out of town. I'll stop by for dinner tomorrow, have a pre birthday celebration and then excuse myself. Unfortunately I have to keep this appointment if I'm finally going to get these questions answered.' What questions? 'After all, I am a journalist.'

"Yeah Deborah. You were a journalist," I whispered.

I closed the journal and returned the box to its spot on the shelf. The alarm was reset and I left with what would prove to be the most critical piece of evidence needed in identifying Deborah's killer.

37

I'm not sure how much of my story Sharron believed after I returned her keys. The idea of lying about what I'd found didn't sit with my upbringing, but I couldn't be sure what the journal would reveal, or who it would implicate.

"Some leads work out, others are just a brick wall waiting to be hit," I said to fend off her question.

"Nothing I need to know?" she asked returning the keys to her purse.

"Scouts honor." I turned toward the door. "By the way, Sylvia does know the music box is missing and it's upsetting to her to not know where it is."

Sharron turned toward the window, but stared into space. "It would be embarrassing to admit ..... "

" ..... Mrs. Henderson is a classy lady," I said. "The truth might help you both rest a little easier."

After thanking her, I made a hasty retreat to my car.

As I motored back to my apartment, I briefly thought about the fine line a person walks when working an investigation. I don't enjoy lying and I figured I'd enjoy it even less had I really been in the boy scouts.

Though happy to finally have something tangible to work with, my insides reeked havoc with my conscious. What I had with me was not the latest Robert Greer mystery novel, but the private thoughts of someone who's earthbound openness masked a quiet side not known to even her closest friends.

It felt like a sacred trust.

I was the keeper of the scrolls. The one pledged to keep its secrets even beyond my own demise. Hopefully, if Deborah were watching from above, she'd understand and forgive my intrusion.

After adjusting my recliner, I started reading through her journal, searching for any piece of information that would help with my investigation. It didn't take long to see the obvious pattern that defined Deborah's nature.

She wrote according to her moods. The different colored pens helped her to sort out what she was feeling.

Deborah's anger at MiShaun for borrowing her car and returning it with less than a quarter tank of gas had been captured in red.

Deborah's disappointment at having an article rejected stood out in blue.

Her momentary envy of a dress Sharron had purchased was quickly noted in green.

She chronicled normally fluid days in standard black.

She used brown to express her relief with having completed an article.

Her happiness at locating someone to duplicate her lucky necklace was written in purple.

Despite my growing affectionate interest in Deborah Norris, I tried to keep a dispassionate, objective distance between the words and its writer, hoping that a clue was somewhere in those pages.

"She's just a case and nothing more," I said.

'Sylvia is going to love this surprise!' She noted in orange.

After making arrangements to have Sylvia's necklace designed, she had a few days of normal activity and then made reference to MiShaun being asleep on her couch after a late night binge.

'I was glad to finally get her calmed down. I don't know why she continues to destroy herself like that, but I'll help her through this mess....' She'd stopped writing and then returned some time later. 'I'm not sure about what I heard, but MiShaun muttered something about an accident. She seemed regretful about something. She doesn't own a car. What accident is she talking about?'

I had the same question.

'MiShaun woke up screaming I'm sorry, I'm sorry. It was an accident. Oh my god. It was an accident. She was sweating and finally heaved into the plastic bucket I placed next to the couch. She looked wild-eyed and I didn't have to see her heart racing to know that it was. What happened tonight? She hugged me tight and wouldn't let go. She cried very hard and muttered something about wanting me to forgive her. Forgive her for what? She finally went back to sleep. Tomorrow, she and I are going to have a serious talk about her drinking. She's going to get help if I have to personally take her to every AA meeting in the city. She's my friend and I can't continue watching her self-destruct.'

A month before her death, Deborah was still trying to help a friend.

I turned to the next page. 'MiShaun seemed open to getting some help although she denies that nothing happened last night. "Girl, I was just drunk" was how she played it off, but she didn't see what I saw. There's more to this than a drunken binge. She'll never really turn her life around if she doesn't understand how close she is to turning it off. So I guess I'll have to help her confront that reality.'

"Just how were you going to do that Deborah?" I said. "What does one do to help a person with a drinking problem confront reality?

During the years I played in the NFL, there was a loose structure in place for helping those players with a substance abuse problem. Unfortunately, confronting reality usually occurred after the athlete had wrapped his prized automobile around a tree and managed to walk away with only his bruised pride. On the police force, drinking was an acceptable way of letting off steam. Our union made sure a substance abuse program was in place to help fellow officers deal with their problem, but we lost some. Confronting reality is usually why the police officer engages in substance abuse. I knew enough about the structure of social service programs designed to help the average citizen overcome the common addictions.

I leaned forward, almost oblivious to the police siren screaming down Livernois. I recalled a story I'd seen on a local chapter of the Students Against Drunk Driving. They placed the remains of two wrecked cars on the front lawn of their school to remind their graduating seniors as well as the entire student body of the risks that come with drinking and driving. It was their way of confronting reality.

Show the reality and let the reality speak for itself.

•• What was the reality that Deborah would use for MiShaun to confront?

My eyes widened as the possible truth took root.

"Morris and Daphne! Oh damn! Is that the reality, Deborah? Is MiShaun responsible for the deaths of Morris and Daphne?" I asked out loud. Keep reading.

•• I read through several more pages and sensed Deborah's remorse at her sad discovery. She'd looked through the accident reports of several newspapers in the area; specifically those papers printed the morning after MiShaun's binge. There were a number of accidents in Detroit and its surrounding communities during that crucial night and Deborah managed to follow up on each one. She discreetly and meticulously looked into each accident, gathering as much information as possible. In some cases, she was able to eliminate MiShaun right away, while others took a little more time. Every page listed the accident and eventually why it was eliminated. It was also pretty evident that Deborah had a tough emotional struggle with what she was doing.

'MiShaun stopped by this evening, to retrieve her last few items for her apartment and to use the phone. I know she's trying to ignore the entire incident. She saw the newspaper clippings on the kitchen table and asked if I was working on another article. I told her she inspired me to look into the impact drunk drivers have on the family's left to grieve. She didn't think it was funny and I told her I wasn't kidding. I thought it would lead to an argument, but she suddenly changed the subject. When she left, she tried to appear light-hearted, but I knew she was troubled. I said something that got to her. She needs help and doesn't know how to ask.'

Deborah spent the next two days gathering information from several sources, tracking down leads and talking with accident victims. Though her tenacity was evident, I sensed a subtle shift in her tone.

Three days before she died, Deborah wrote; 'I'm almost convinced that MiShaun may have been responsible for the deaths of Morris Shaw and Daphne Connors. The two high school seniors were killed the same night MiShaun cried for forgiveness. I need to check it out, although for the life of me, I can't figure out why MiShaun would be out in Mount Clemens. It doesn't make sense, but it seems to fit. Tomorrow, I'll see what I can find out. I hate what I'm thinking, but I have to know. Is my friend responsible? I can't let my speculations tear into me until I have the facts. I hope my fears are unfounded. Anyway, Sylvia's birthday is coming up and the necklace isn't finished. I called the designer, but he hasn't returned my calls. I'd be so disappointed if I can't pull off Sylvia's birthday surprise the way I want.'

She believed MiShaun was responsible for the deaths of Morris and Daphne. According to Detective Brewer, the only reliable witness thought he saw a sports car careening down the road without the lights on.

MiShaun didn't own a sports car. Deborah owned a blue Miata. Sometimes Deborah let MiShaun borrow her car, but not on the night Morris and Daphne died.

I gathered that Deborah became increasingly reluctant to let MiShaun borrow her car, especially after having her license suspended. It didn't seem likely that MiShaun would have driven Deborah's car that night. My initial idea of MiShaun being behind the wheel of Deborah's Miata seemed far-fetched.

"So much for that theory," I said.

Yet Deborah pursued the idea. If it was true, there were a few unanswered questions.

When I turned to the next page, Deborah had already outlined the questions that ran through my head. She'd written the questions in red with exclamation points for emphasis.

'How did MiShaun get around that night? Did someone pick her up? Did she ride with other friends? Did she ride in a cab? Did she meet someone at one of the bars? Where did she go? Given how she acted, how did she get home? Did someone drop her off at home or at my door? If so, then who? Is that person connected to Morris and Daphne as well? How much time elapsed between the Morris and Daphne accident and her showing up at drunk and rattled?

"Exactly what I was thinking Deborah," I said. "Exactly what I was thinking."

The next line was written in red and I felt its chilling impact.

'I received a phone call today from someone with information about the accident. Call it dumb luck, but I stumbled onto something that I believe will bring all the pieces together. I have to follow this lead.'

"What phone call?" I said "From who?"

The afternoon had zipped along and unlike Issac Newton, I decided not to sit around and wait for an apple to fall on my head. It seemed my best course of action was to shake the tree and see what falls.

First, I left a message for Malone, and then I called the hospital where MiShaun was recovering. The chirpy-voiced-receptionist quickly spouted off that she'd already checked out.

I thought it was a speedy recovery for someone who'd walked close to death.

After dabbing water on my eyes and quickly brushing my teeth, I hurried down the steps ..... and not sure of my next move.

38

Helen Barnes wasn't any more pleasant with me despite our civil talk in the mall, however she did inform me that Trevor Stallings did wish to see me.

"Why?" I asked.

Her tone was firm and impatient. "He didn't tell me why, just to get in touch with you and to tell you where he'd be over the next few hours."

She gave me the information and rang off.

I motored off the Southfield freeway and made the left turn onto Joy Road. As I crossed over the bridge, I spotted the Herman Gardens projects just off to my left. The two-level brick row houses in which the poor and disenfranchised would live in dream-like harmony along the industrial belt, was now an abandoned nightmare. Boarded windows, broken glass and weeded walkways were all that remained of the once great housing projects movement.

My curiosity as to why Trevor Stallings wanted me to meet him there was quickly answered when I turned into the main driveway and saw several television satellite vans parked side by side.

"Photo-op time," I said as I parked my car behind the vans.

The legion of photographic talking heads had gathered in the area that once served as a courtyard, armed with their hand-held microphones and their plastic smiles. Standing in the middle of the pack, basking in the lights and looking politically correct, Trevor Stalling was holding court as he grimaced and pointed like he was rehearsing for the pulpit.

I eased behind the reporters, keeping my distance as I quickly assessed the crowd. There were several familiar faces and a few not-so-familiar. Of course, I took great delight in making eye contact with my old friend Tyler Cain. His returned icy stare told me that he also harbored similar warm thoughts for me.

There were other members of Trevor's entourage in a half circle around him, including younger brother Pernell.

I had to hand it to these brothers; if nothing else, the boys looked sharp.

Since it was the early news part of the evening, I assumed the reports were going out-live to an eagerly awaiting audience just home from their work-until-your-butt-falls-off-day.

"And it is the sad neglect of communities ..... " Trevor bellowed, " ..... that has led to this on-going despair and ..... "

And blah, blah, blah, I thought as his words burned with volcanic contempt.

"The current administration has overlooked the ..... " he continued.

When the noise finally ceased and the questions ended, the reporters and camera people retreated to their vans while Trevor and his entourage quickly debriefed how the staged event came across. A sandy-haired woman in heels taller than Danny DeVito, held a yellow legal pad and wrote down comments as quickly as they were being thrown at her.

I leaned against a rusting basketball pole, wondering why I was invited to witness this fire-and-brimstone rhetoric when I saw Tyler whisper in Trevor's ear.

"Ah, Mr. Keller," he said, glancing at me with a glitter-dome smile. "Glad you could make it. I hope my last minute request caused you no inconvenience."

"It's okay," I said extending my hand. "I was polishing my shoes."

"Well, at least you're not wasting your talents," Tyler said, trying to mask a snarl.

"Tyler, does psychiatric services know you're out of your bunk?"

Tyler tried to step forward, but Trevor put an arm in front of him.

"Come, come now. We're all brothers here." Trevor stepped forward. "Walk with me Mr. Keller."

While everyone else continued to look busy, I strolled with Trevor around the long since abandoned projects.

"What do you see here, Mr. Keller?"

"The last monument to low-income housing. The first stage in our own self-destruction," I replied.

"I'm not sure if you're kidding or not."

"There's not much around here to kid about."

"No, there isn't. You know what I see?"

I assumed it wasn't a trick question. "Why don't you tell me."

He smiled. "I see the future. Detroit is in the midst of a great revitalization, but it must not end with the downtown district. This area we're walking in was part of a future, but it became decayed. Most of our neighborhoods are in decay and unless we empower and engage our neediest denizens, the city will become a bigger caste system for those who have the most and those who have the least."

"I understand that's being addressed," I said.

"Not fast enough and without the needed conviction. The current administration is too concerned with looking good. They prefer style over substance. Detroit needs the right kind of visionary."

"Define 'right kind'."

"Someone willing to put Detroit first by building the power centers in the city. Build them right here in these neighborhoods. 'Empower Detroit' has the necessary connections and financial backing to begin a massive overhaul of these places and turn them into places where families can live in peace and children don't have to fear the night."

"Hard for me to disagree with those ideas, but what's that got to do with me standing here?"

"Straight forward and to the point," he said grinning. "Lincoln, may I call you Lincoln?"

"Linc will do."

"Do you know why I've been successful?"

"Your ancestors were cruise directors on the Mayflower?"

He hesitated a beat. "My ancestors were cramped in the same sun deprived quarters as yours. No, my success can be attributed to one thing; I can spot good talent. I know how integrate a person's talents into my organization in ways that make us all successful."

"I'm sure Tyler would agree."

"You'd be surprised at what Tyler is capable of doing since he's come to work for me."

"No, I wouldn't be surprised, but you might be."

He ignored the comment. "Soon I will be turning over the reins of Empower Detroit to Pernell. I intend to be successful in Detroit politics. First, a seat on the City Council and from there, the Mayor's seat. There's no doubt in my mind that it will unfold as I've stated. The time is now to become a part of the noble future I see for Detroit."

I stopped walking. "Mr. Stallings, this seems like a lot of effort to just secure my one vote or do I detect more behind your statement."

He grinned again. "There is more. I'd like you to become part of our team. I could use a man with your talents. I can pay you a nice salary with a few perks thrown in to sweeten the pot."

The offer came as a complete surprise. "What would I be doing for this nice salary with the thrown in perks?"

"Personal security mostly, run a few errands. Be there when I need you. But most importantly, you'd become an integral part of helping to reshape Detroit's future. You'd have a guaranteed spot by the seat of power. Think of it, Linc. No more following philandering husbands or peeping in keyholes for answers to the wretched secrets that haunt our souls."

"So, you're asking me to give up a job where the pay is sporadic, the hours are lousy and my Nova is in constant need of a tune-up, to join you."

"The obvious wisdom in that decision should be evident," He remarked, confidant in what I would say.

"Except for one thing," I said. "It's the way I like it. You see, I chose this line of work because it's consistent with how I live. Sporadic money is a problem if you're broke and I'm not. I like the hours and my Nova and I have been together longer than some people have been married. I'm happy. I serve no Master other than my own convictions. I appreciate the offer, but I tend to steer clear of loyalty to a power seat. In my experience, you have to make too many adjustments before you get comfortable."

"Does the idea of having access to power frighten you?"

"Power, like any tool, can be used to build or destroy. The issue seems to always be the people who crave it the most."

"You'd find me to be a very benevolent employer. I take care of my people," he said trying to stay even toned.

"Unfortunately, I'm not a very benevolent employee. Being at your personal beckoning is not the vision I have for my future."

"There are people who would kill for this kind of opportunity."

"People have killed for less. If this kind of job is that important to someone, I'd just as soon they got it."

He sighed. "Well, Linc, I am disappointed in your decision, but I respect your convictions. Perhaps there will be another opportunity for us to pursue some kind of alliance."

He extended his hand and gripped lamely. Trevor walked back to his waiting entourage and they moved quickly to their vehicles.

I watched as the cars and van backed out of the parking area and turned onto the street, heading east to the Southfield freeway.

Having been left alone in the abandoned courtyard with night beginning its descent, I realized that I had just turned down a bribe. It wasn't the kind of thing that could be proven in court, but it was a bribe.

"Keep your friend close, but keep your enemies closer," I said, recalling that statement being made by J.R. Ewing when the television show, Dallas, was making its run. The script writters got it from ancient wisdom.

I strolled over to my Nova more convinced than ever that I was getting close to something. Trevor Stalling grinned a little too much and didn't seem too disappointed that I'd turned him down. Now that he knew I couldn't be bought, he'd have to move to the next level of persuasion. No doubt he knew of my visit with MiShaun and as I motored onto the Southfield freeway I had no doubt as to what would happen next.

Now was the time when I needed a cell phone.

39

Moves and countermoves are what keep a game interesting. Anticipation and intuition have kept many a player at the top of their game; the issue is knowing when to bite.

The only advantage I had on the Stallings was the knowledge that something was going to happen. What I needed was an edge. Something that would keep me one step ahead and closer to finding Deborah's killer.

I motored over to the east side of town, weaving my way down the split-level home side streets until I reached the front of the Wayne Turner Community Center, haven to the NBA wannabe's. It wasn't the non-stop games of basketball that brought me to the yellow brick building, but the person who influenced the activity in the area.

The early evening hour didn't act as a deterrent to the sound of popping nets and verbal dissin'. The crowds of teenage males, who were sky walking, sliding and gracefully raining thirty-foot jump shots from their Momma's kitchen, seemed more than usual. As they contended for court respect, I surveyed the sweat drenched warriors hoping to find someone who'd be my point of contact into what I needed to know.

I saw him.

Eyes shaded with raybans and a self-made grimace designed to hide the gap in his front teeth, he was leaning against a metal pole not looking particularly enthralled by the slam-dunks. His bulky physique suggested that he hadn't turned down too many meals lately. Oddjob was a 'Smiling Jack' compared to this manservant.

Though the sparse crowd of onlookers provided some shielding, I knew he'd spot me long before I made myself known.

Survival heightens that kind of instinct in people.

When our faces locked, he only acknowledged me with a slight, almost imperceptible nod.

"You still driving that same piece junk?" he asked through unmoving lips.

"You still wiping your nose with your sleeve?" His face gave away nothing. "Your boss around?" I said emphasizing the 'boss'

"He's busy."

"So am I. Where is he?"

He pulled a black cell phone from his pocket, punched in a number and mumbled something. He smiled slightly after shutting off the phone. "Doesn't like it when people come looking for him. Usually means they want something. What you want?"

"I want to see more of him and less of you."

He turned toward the basketball activity. "Says he'll meet you. Try waiting by that junker you drive."

"How long?"

He shrugged.

I eased back out to my car and sat on the hood closest to the passenger side. Getting an audience with 'Nightlife' on short notice was more than a notion, but when people owe you a favor, they're usually anxious to clean the books so they can go back to disliking you with a clean conscious. Any alliance with 'Nightlife' could prove to be challenging in ways uncommon to the normal flow of relationships.

So I waited.

I kept spinning the elements of Deborah Norris's unsolved homicide through every vacant corner of my brain. I felt like I was bungey jumping in a hurricane. It seemed that no matter where I stretched the end of the cord, I was snapped back into the completely opposite direction. However, the one thing that seemed unmistakably clear was that my investigation had made one, or both, of the Stallings nervous.

Nervous people tend to do very nervy things.

So I waited.

The time gave me the chance to clear away the tumultuous thoughts for a moment and so I amused myself by thinking about the various lines I'd use on Malone to ease back into her emotional and superbly crafted physical space.

There's got to be something I can say. How about; "I have crawled though this tunnel of darkness in search of a beacon of light. Temporarily swayed by the artificial, when yours is the brightness that surrounds the heavens. Beam me home, baby."

Wait a minute. Voice inflection. Women are heavy into voice inflection, right? *"I have crawled though this tunnel of darkness in search of a beacon of light. Temporarily swayed by the artificial, when yours is the brightness that surrounds the heavens. Beam me home, baby."*

No, not that. "I have craaawled though this tunnel of darkness! in search of a beacon of light. *TEMPORARILY* swayed by the artificial, when **YOURS** is the brightness that surrounds the HEAVENS. Beam me home, BAABEEE."

Hmmm. "ı ɦʌve cʀʌwleð ᴛɦouɢɦ ᴛɦıꜱ ᴛunnel oꜰ ðʌʀknessꜱ ..... " Aw, forget it. My attempts at attention-grabbing love lines yielded nothing that Malone or any other woman would find romantically enticing. I may have a private investigator's license, but I definitely don't have a poetic one, voice inflection or not.

Time passes rather quickly when you're almost having fun, and it wasn't too long before the unofficial 'Don' for this section of Detroit, made his way toward me. There was the usual assortment of grimace-faced bodyguards forming a half circle around him, surveying the area, the admiring onlookers and myself as well.

One heavily muscled face smasher moved quickly to fill the space between 'Nightlife' and me. He said nothing, just near silent breathing and a menacing, glare inches from where I stood.

"You carryin'?" he asked in an even tone.

"Just breath mints 'cause I knew you'd need one," I said returning the tone.

His eyes widened slightly. "Funny man. Takes chances with things that he should leave alone."

I looked past him. "I need a minute of your time 'Nightlife'. Tell sunshine here to go study for his diplomacy certification."

Nightlife stepped forward holding up a cautionary hand to my adversary. "He's cool. He couldn't have gotten this far if he wasn't. What brings you this way, Keller?"

"Can we talk?"

He nodded and his protective entourage angled off to different areas away from my Nova. The distance allowed for a private conversation, but no unexpected moves.

Nightlife leaned against the passenger door. "You believe cars say a lot about the person?"

"They say enough."

"First time I saw you in this junker, I figured you were a low-life hustler who bummed food stamps."

"And now?"

"I know you don't bum food stamps."

I grinned. "Ever hear of a guy named Tyler Cain?"

"And why is that of interest to you?" he replied evenly.

"I have something I'm working on and his name keeps coming up. I need to know how serious to take him."

He mulled that statement for a minute. "Word has it that some years ago, Cain had a crew that could jack cars off an assembly line. They were good. Real good." There was a hint of admiration in his tone. "His crew was fast. Once a car rolled into their chop shop, they could disconnect, unhitch and unbolt faster than anybody in the business. They only jacked the high price models. Apparently they had a pretty ritzy client base. People order the parts and they usually found the car."

"What did Cain do?"

"Usually took the orders. Coordinate his crew's assignments. I hear he was an invisible middle man."

"Only special orders?"

"Mostly. Every now and then he'd do a special order."

"Which means?" I asked

"Some high level type gets himself in a jam and needs to get rid of his car. Usually it's for the insurance money. Occasionally because the car is hot."

"I thought all stolen cars are considered hot."

"Most are. Sometimes a car is hot because it's been involved in something and needs to vanish."

"Something like what?" I asked.

"Think about it, Keller. All those unsolved dead bodies in the city morgue didn't come from gunshot wounds."

"Yeah, I know. Someone driving a car runs down some people. That would make a car hot."

"So if you need to get rid of the car right away and have the right connections. Boom, no car and no evidence."

"But you'd still have to fill out something for the insurance company."

"You wait a day, file a stolen car report and life goes on."

"Except for the person who's lying over in the city morgue."

He shrugged. "Call it cruel fate."

"Sounds like business was good. So why'd Cain stop?"

"We entrepreneurs understand risk. Maybe the business was getting too risky. Maybe he found religion. Maybe a certain businessman, who wants to be Mayor of our fair city, converted him from his risky business ventures. Who knows? Whatever the reason, he hasn't run a crew in years."

"What's your take on him?"

He thought for a moment. "I wouldn't turn my back on him. Hell, I wouldn't turn your back on him."

"Dangerous?"

"Just like all of us, only quieter."

"You two ever bump heads?"

"No reason to. He knows his place."

"Any of his crew still around?"

"Maybe. The years can be hard for people living on the edge."

"I'd like to know."

He paused. "I hear anything, I'll let you know."

He stood and walked toward the recreational center, quickly being joined by his 'crew'. He stopped and turned back towards me. "You planning on taking him on?"

"I'm planning on not being taken."

His crew circled around him and followed closely as he pulled open the mouthpiece to his cell phone.

I slid behind the driver's seat and peeled back toward the highway. Nightlife had probably told me more than he wanted, but he owed me and he owed Jefferson. As a source, I knew I didn't have to question the validity of his statements. If Nightlife said it, call it a fact. He'd confirmed what I already knew and gave weight to my suspicions.

The night wasn't over.

40

This wayward path I'd been on lately started when Deborah Norris became curious about something uttered during the course of self-remorse. MiShaun regretted her involvement in an accident that took the lives of Morris Shaw and Daphne Connor. At least that's what I concluded based on everything I'd learned.

I was convinced that Deborah had arrived at the same conclusion.

Now the question centered on the extent of her involvement. Did she actually cause the accident or was she a shocked observer? If not she, then who?

Why did Trevor Stallings care? Blind loyalty to a valued employee? Or was there a lot more underneath the surface? Despite his social benevolence, did he actually move Tyler Cain from sinner to saint?

I didn't like the feel.

When I worked as a patrol officer, my partner and I were assigned to some of the tougher sections of Oakland and even among that chaos, you could always tell when there was something in the air.

The Stallings/Cain relationship had that same smell.

I had a hunch that somewhere in the middle of that relationship, Deborah Norris's life came to an abrupt end.

Despite my deep-in-thought mood, I rolled over to Artie's for an overpriced drink and salt peanuts pick-me-up, content to let the smell of cigarette smoke and sweaty leather deaden my senses before returning to my apartment.

After two drinks and three small bowls of peanuts, I left the noisy oasis of lies and motored back to my apartment.

Now that I knew what I knew, I wanted to rest.

I didn't have a strategy for the next step, but I did have my .38. It seemed to be a good time to keep it close at hand. Despite feeling drowsy, I had to stay alert. I thought a good night of uninterrupted sleep would ignite the engine. My mind was on information overload and practically screamed for time to process and download. My body just wanted to melt into the mattress. Once I'd made it inside my apartment, I didn't bother checking the answering machine, figuring that the messages wouldn't vanish before morning.

The messages were easy to ignore; it was a lot harder to ignore the ringing phone.

I groaned, "Hello."

"Look alive, brother man. It's time to celebrate."

Truman is the only person I knew who celebrated the fact that there were no official holidays in August. "What are we celebrating?"

"Didn't you hear my message? We just completed the last parts of our local agreement and all that's left is to put it before the membership for a vote."

"Shouldn't you wait until after its been ratified?"

He laughed. "It's a lock. We got what we wanted. The membership will rubber-stamp the agreement. I'm feeling like I want to howl. Let's prowl these mean streets. I'm buying."

"Actually, little bro, I'm exhausted and was just heading to bed."

"Is Malone there?"

"No, I ..... "

"Then the hell with going to bed. I'll be there in ten minutes."

He hung up before I could finish my protest.

I sighed. So much for downloading and sleeping.

●　　●　　●

The old man had often described Truman as the reason why he stopped at four sons. I once heard him look at mom and say, "If there's another one in there like him, I won't be the reason why he shows up."

Mom would smile and wave pop away.

My brother wasn't a bad kid; it's just that the star he followed couldn't be seen with the naked eye or the Hubbell telescope.

We were parked at a round oak table for seven in the middle of a bar where peanut shells were thrown on the floor to add to the décor. The red and white checkered plastic tablecloth was embedded with the round water stains of many a half-empty pitcher.

The crowd of end-of-afternoon-shift blue collars were in a joyous mood, having heard the negotiations were over. Truman was backslapped, high fived and bear hugged by most of the patrons who frequented 'Chip N Ales' on Dix Road a few miles from the famous Rouge Assembly Plant. He absorbed the body punishment in the spirit that it was delivered. Actually, you could've bounced a brick off his muscular, compact frame.

Everyone insisted on buying both him and me a drink. He declined most of the offers, saying 'let's save it for the big celebration'.

"So what's up with this case you're working on?"

I leaned forward, cuffing my hand around my ear as he repeated the question.

Over the joyous noise, I gave him a shortened overview what I'd been doing, preferring to save my voice.

"I heard you and Jeff had a run-in with some rough types. What went down?"

Again, my explanation was short, but he caught the gist.

"Tortured the brother with a blow torch?"

I nodded.

Truman shook his head. "Worst he'll do is jail time. Some of the bloods just don't get it, do they?"

"No Tru, they don't."

"We have some like that in the rank and file. Lots of noise and hot air. Strut around like they know which way is up. It's all just a front. They don't want people to know that they're runnin' scared. Most of us try to bring them along before they mess up their lives. We've saved several, but a few still slip between the cracks."

I smiled. We didn't have to say what we both knew. Truman had walked that same path for a while. During the years I was in Oakland, he walked the edge of trouble before finding himself in the Union. It was the patience and belief of an older line worker who took an interest in Truman. He brought him into Union activities and helped to focus his life. Since then, my brother's wild days haven't completely diminished, but he's a lot clearer about who he is and what he wants to be.

"So what's your next move?" he asked, breaking the silence.

"I have this offbeat angle I want to pursue, but it's going to take some leg work." I told him what I intended.

"Tell you what; let's relax and enjoy ourselves and   " he glanced at his watch " ..... in an hour or so, I'll take you to meet someone who can probably knock hours off your search."

"Oh yeah," I said. "Why can't we go now?"

He leaned back and motioned toward the bar. "Because it isn't time."

41

We left Truman's union brethren just before the designated closing time
for all Detroit area watering holes. We smelled of cigarettes, sweat and
laughter. Any intoxication we may have felt resulted from the joy in the
air and not the liquor in the glass.

Truman's Ford Explorer had a state-of-the-art CD player that made
it sound like Miles Davis was sitting on the dashboard. We small talked
our way east on I-94 until we reached the West Grand Boulevard exit and
following the street across Warren Road until we reached a two-story,
gray brick framed house on an easy-to-miss side street. Though the streets
double-sided parking seemed filled to capacity, there were a number of
cars parked in awkward locations around or near the building.

"Now this is where Detroit's other night life kicks in," Truman said
with a knowing grin.

After he parked near a Honda Accord, I followed him up a narrow
concrete walkway that led to a back entrance to the building.

Though all the windows were shaded, light filtered out the side and
occasional shadows floated past the light. We stopped at a windowless
backdoor with its V-shaped bar screen open and a large master lock
hanging from its hole.

Truman knocked twice and the door cracked open.

Whoever answered blocked the little bit of light trying to escape.

"Who knows you?" the voice asked cryptically.

"Back off 'Bone', it's the 'Sugarman'," Truman replied.

The door swung open and a figure the size of the Detroit Lion's front line laughed and motioned us in. "My main man 'Sugar'. How you been?" he asked extending a five-fingered tree trunk.

"No complaints, 'Bone'. This is my brother, Lincoln."

I extended my hand and prayed parts of it would be returned.

"Yeah, I know you. You played for the Raiders years ago. Number 44, nickel-back, sometimes played the corners. How's the knee?"

"I hobble more during the rainy season, but other than that, it's fine." I stared at him. "You played?"

"Drafted the same year as 'Refrigerator Perry'. He found fame in Chicago and I didn't hang around Houston long enough to get a number. Blew out my knee during training camp and haven't played since."

Truman interrupted. "Need to see the boss lady. She around?"

"Oh yeah. Where else would she be? Go on up."

We climbed several stairs until we reached an open entrance to a large area designed to look like an upscale bar, complete with bar stools, tables and waitresses with short skirts. The mellow jazz sound brought a quiet, distinct air to the sharply dressed and colorful crowd.

"Now this is after hours," Truman said smiling.

The real night lifers and most of the local law types were the only ones who knew of Detroit's third entertainment time zone. There were a number of after hour spots located around the city, most having an 'A' list of clientele. Unlike the 'Blind Pigs' of the riotous 1960s, many of these establishments were tolerated with feigned ignorance and an occasional slap on the hand when the neighbors complained. This one seemed like the top of the mark. Only the elite who worried little about racial make up and focused more on pleasant opportunity to just ..... chill.

Truman moved through the crowd with unconscious familiarity and I followed. He spoke to several of the patrons and I recognized a couple of off duty police officers. We made our way to a zinc-topped, crescent-shaped bar where a red-haired, cinnamon-toned woman in a multi-colored, V-neck, sequined gown had finished laughing at someone's comment and locked eyes with Truman.

"Truman Keller!" She yelled as she made her way from behind the bar. "You get over here right now and give me a hug."

He eased toward her, hugged and lifted her at the same time.

"Put me down now!" She said in mock protest while slapping his shoulders. "Where have you been, young man? You've been shamefully neglecting me."

Truman held up his hands. "My work load has been demanding as of late."

She smiled and glanced over at me. "And who is this portrait?" Her tone had that sly air of interest.

"Down girl." Truman responded while waving me over. "This is my brother, Lincoln."

"I should have known," she said while extending her hand. "He has that Keller jaw line."

Truman smiled. "Linc, you are in the presence of urban royalty. This is The Lady Flamingo Brown."

The legendary 'Lady Flame' held the distinction of being one of Detroit's best, natural resources. She'd started as a nightclub singer at the tender age of sixteen, back during the time when Detroit's 'BlackBottom' was a social, political and entertainment Mecca. During her heyday, it was rumored that she could hold a note so long that it was possible for the entire audience to take a bathroom break and order drinks before she stopped to take a breath. Along the way, she managed to acquire her own brand of wealth and property. She could have retired years ago, but what would Detroit be without its 'Lady Flame'?

"And tell me, Lincoln; is there some reason why we haven't met prior to this moment?"

"An inexcuseable oversight for which I can offer no reasonable explanation, but I hope that your reputable forgiveness is as magnanimous as your obvious charm." I kissed the back of her hand.

"He also has the Keller tongue," she said smiling. "Consider yourself forgiven, young man. Now, what brings you two to my little cabin in the sky?"

"My brother's a P.I." Truman offered. "He's working on something and I thought you might be helpful."

"Maybe," she replied. "Depends on what you need to know and the boundaries around that information."

She motioned us to a corner of the bar and shooed two of the regulars away from their barstools. Neither of the well-dressed men protested, so I assumed it was a ritual.

She popped the top of a diet beverage for me and set a small bottle of seltzer water in front of Truman.

"I hear you've been doing a lot better," she said to Truman.

"You know it."

Sensing the understood message between the two, I started. "Miss Brown ..... "

"Call me 'Flame', honey. Everyone else does."

"Flame, I'm working on something that has all the twists and turns of a daytime soap opera, only it's real. I've started developing a working theory, but need information on a few points."

"You talk," she said. "And I'll listen."

During the ten uninterrupted minutes that I overviewed the case, Flame listened intently. No one in the room seemed bothered by her lack of attention to them. Everyone seemed content to talk, drink and chill.

When I finished, she stepped away from the bar, placed a brandy snifter on the counter and poured a small amount.

"I remember that story," she said. "Pretty young girl like that. Taken out for no good reason. We lose too many of our young talent, you know. They think living hard and dying young is some great act. They don't know the real joy is in the living. I have seventy-three years of experience, so I should know."

If the Flamingo Brown I was looking at was really seventy-three years old, then she definitely made a good case for the living.

"Can I drop a couple of names and you tell me what you think?" I asked.

"Go ahead."

"Tyler Cain."

She thought for a moment. "I don't recognize the name, but one of my people might know him."

"The Stallings. Trevor and Pernell."

An amused grin complimented her knowing half moon eyes. "I don't personally care for either one of them, but what do you want to know?"

"Give me an overview and I'll focus the picture."

Truman smiled at our verbal dance and eased over to a table of people he seemed to know.

"He wants us to talk freely," she said.

I nodded.

She took another sip of brandy and leaned across the bar counter. "Trevor rarely came by any of the places I used to run. Didn't matter if they were regular hours or after hours. He always tried to keep a safe distance. From what I hear from some of the other 'operators', he tried to walk a straight line."

"Tried?"

"Lines get blurry from time to time. Usually doesn't mean anything unless there's something you want."

"What don't you like about him?" I asked.

"I can see past his high wattage smile. His eyes are tight and his soul is chained. He's someone who'd be a mean drunk. I know for a fact, he'd been that way.'

"To you?"

"His lines never got that blurry," she replied matter-of-factly.

"How about Pernell?"

She sighed. "Now there's a package in desperate need of wrapping."

The next fifteen minutes were spent on stories of a young man consumed by the blessings and trappings of a life many would kill to sample. Lady Flame's memory covered both the breadth and depth of people, relationships and the corners of closets where the truth lay hidden. Pernell seemed to be both ends of the spectrum. He easily walked the line between dashing blade-about-town and destructive knife-in-the-back. He'd made his legend in the nightspots and after-hour places around Detroit. On his path lay the hearts and souls of those who loved him a little too much. Those hearts and souls bore a resemblance to Jocelyn Kilgore.

Lady Flame talked and I listened.

"He was a wild one, alright. I thought sure he'd die at a young age, but then he suddenly toned it down. He wasn't seen in so many places. Though he still managed to come to places like mine from time to time."

"Sounds like he found religion."

She grinned. "The only thing that boy found was a cubby hole in order to hide from the havoc he caused."

"When did this transformation take place?" I asked.

She didn't ponder long. "Close to eight years ago. Not too long after the sports car of his was stolen. Word has it that Trevor really laid it on him about being a responsible citizen, serving Detroit and all that."

"He heard the call to public service?"

"Trevor heard the call, Pernell follows along because he has to. But it's not in his heart."

"I noticed that the oldest of the clan has aspirations for the Mayor's seat."

Lady Flame stopped to give instructions to the high cheek boned woman tending the bar. "Funny, we all thought Trevor would make his run for city council several years ago. He seemed primed, but then let it go in order to expand the work being done at 'Empower Detroit'. It seemed like that boy was everywhere. Neighborhoods, political functions, school board meetings, testimony to state Senate committees, social functions and anything else that would put his name and picture in a newspaper or magazine."

"Why do you think he changed his mind?"

"Part of me believes that he wanted to increase the number of people who'd recognize his name. You know how it is, just because people recognize your name, they think you actually know something."

"What about the other part of you?"

Lady Flame gave me a cat-eating-canary grin. "The other part of me says it was something deeper than name recognition and running for city council. Something happened that forced him to put his ambitions aside for a while, but only for a while."

She continued with a few more Pernell Stallings stories and offered some speculations about why Pernell is following the straight to path individual salvation. Most of what I heard made sense, given the little I'd gathered on his background. Although I still didn't buy the notion that he suddenly woke up one morning and decided to change his life, unless something happened during the night.

"How long are you two going to keep making goo-goo eyes?" Truman asked as he ambled back over.

"She's already become my light of life," I answered. "I can only hope that I am eternally worthy."

"You two youngsters may need to get on about your business and let me run mine."

I thanked Lady Flame for the talk and promised that I wouldn't be a stranger.

"I'm only open at night, honey. When the people with too much to do need time to do less," she said as she extended her hand.

I repeated my earlier kiss on the back of her hand and Truman and I made our way back through the crowd and into his Ford van.

"Was she helpful?" he asked as he gunned the engine.

"More than I hoped."

He turned onto Grand River and drove over to I-96, while the music of Miles Davis filled the cabin. "Now what, Bro?"

"You can drop me off at my apartment and I suggest you head home and get some sleep. You have a busy day tomorrow. Contract ratification and all that."

"Yes!" he said. "For the union!" I'd gotten used to his unexpected outbursts of union support coupled with an endless supply of energy. He filled up on the energy he drained from others. "And what will you do tomorrow?"

Feeling completely drained; I laid back against the headrest. "Checking on a stolen car."

42

Truman had already U-turned and was speeding back toward Seven Mile Road when the first shot penetrated the doorframe up by my left ear.

Instinctively, I rolled away from the door as two other shots riddled the area where I'd been standing. I grabbed my .38 and tried to shake the sudden piercing sound bouncing against my eardrum. My senses were back on full alert as I crawled across the sidewalk and hid behind that abandoned Ford Galaxy.

The shooter had taken a position across the street and continued firing at the door, the wall and anything else not moving. There were no on-coming cars in either direction and from my crouched position I could see across the street a pair of shoes move quickly from a darkened door area.

I quickly surveyed the area, not wanting to be caught from behind. No one emerged from the shadows and no one appeared interested in the shots being fired.

I certainly didn't blame anyone for being disinterested.

From my position I caught a glimpse of him moving toward me. My night vision had already kicked in as my adrenaline pumped new energy into my no longer tired frame.

He moved with the stealthy confidence of someone who knew his target was outgunned. I stayed low as he fired into the car where I was hiding. At the first break between bursts, I fired two shots in his direction. He'd already moved out of my line of vision, unloading another burst that had me kissing the sidewalk.

I knew he'd try and work his way around.

I rolled toward the street, still using the Galaxy as a shield. I didn't have enough bullets to hold him off and my one hope was that someone heard the shots and called 911. I didn't have time to consider the random concern of strangers.

Another burst took out the passenger windows. I kept low, crouched and slid around to the driver's side. My one advantage was being able to see his feet from underneath the car.

He tried to slide around to the other side of the car, when I fired and caught the back heel of his left foot.

He yelled and cursed loud enough to wake the night crawlers.

As he limped to one side of the car, I quickly crawled around to the other side hoping for another shot. Even during the exchange, part of me wanted him wounded and talking, if he gave me that option.

He yelled again, cursed even louder and fired wildly at the Ford Galaxy and along the wall. The deafening sound of a gun being emptied randomly may have worked to his benefit in keeping me low, but it also masked the sound of a vehicle speeding down the street.

Under the burst of gunfire, I heard tires screeching in a mad dash and caught a quick glimpse of a vehicle, minus its headlights, roaring toward my attacker.

The sound was instantaneous. A loud, jarring thud that caught him from behind before he could point his weapon.

He yelled again.

There was an immediate crunch of bones and flesh. He didn't hear it until he'd already began his helpless descent.

I stood up just as he landed several feet from where he'd been hit. He looked like a crash dummy lying sprawled in the middle of the street. Only he wouldn't get up to walk away as part of a commercial demonstration.

Steadying my gun and reluctant to breathe until I was sure this duel had ended, I approached the apparently lifeless body. I glanced over at the driver who'd just sent this guy on his last night's journey.

"You alright, Bro?" he asked as he moved slowly toward me.

"That was some piece of driving you did, Truman," I said. "What brought you back?"

He'd already pulled out his cell phone and began punching in some numbers. "When you've been in as much trouble as I have, you develop a good sense for when its about to happen."

As the silouhettes from lighted windows began to move from their protective havens, I breathed a sigh of relief and thanked my parents for the Keller instinct.

Truman had strolled back to his truck, leaning on the hood as he completed his phone call.

The sprawled body of the latest shooter told me that it would be a while before I saw the end of this night.

•   •   •

"It seems that lately my life is filled with more Kellers than actual homicides," Lieutenant Knackton growled as he stood up from examining the gunman that tried to part my hair with a bullet. "Tell me this is your fault so I can happily testify at your trial and retire a happy man."

"I'm afraid you'll have to hold on that happiness, Lieutenant. This guy tried to kill me," I said nodding toward my motionless assailant.

"Oh? And why is that? Did you sell him a bad lottery ticket?"

"No, actually it was a good ticket. But he used it to pick his teeth and ruined the edges."

Truman sat in the back of a squad car recounting what happened to a youthful looking detective with auburn hair and GQ hands. He looked out of place working homicide, but seemed at home with the attention.

"Let's hear it from the top, Keller," Knackton said to me.

"Which CNN version do you want?"

"Morning edition and don't spare me the details."

So, while the paramedics attended to my attacker and the regular patrol officers walked around the cordoned area and got statements from witnesses, I told Knackton some of what was going on. He wrote in a small notepad, stopping every so often to click the top of his pen. My adrenaline high had started to wear off and I began to feel the pangs of a body in desperate need of sleep. I yawned three times during the explanation; the last long yawn sent water dripping out the corner of my eyes.

"Try to stay awake, Keller because we'll have to do this again," Knackton said with primal glee.

"I know how it works, Lieutenant."

"We've got a pulse!" one of the paramedics yelled. "Let's move him fast."

Knackton glared over at Truman. "Looks like you and your brother just avoided a homicide charge. Now, if your story checks out I'll have to find other reasons for having your license taken." A patrol officer who whispered something to Knackton while shaking his head momentarily interrupted his joy. "Well, Keller, there's no ID on this one or nothing to indicate how he got here in front of your apartment. But he's probably been printed before, so we'll know pretty soon. Meantime, I'll have to confiscate your gun. We have to do a match on the bullets."

My .38 had already been placed in a plastic bag and marked. A couple of crime scene techs were gouging bullets out of the front door of my apartment and from the completely destroyed Ford Galaxy.

"I fired three shots, Lieutenant," I said pointing to the building across the street. "Two are located in the wall of that building and the other is somewhere in Mister Man's left foot."

"The lab will sort all that out. But you'll still have to fill out a weapon's discharge form."

"What if I promise to come fill out the form after I've slept for a week?"

"What if I bring you and your brother downtown and keep you up for two weeks?"

Before I could answer Truman wandered back over. "Hey, Linc, this detective says I have to go with him to answer some more questions. Looks like they're going to impound my truck."

"Standard procedure," Knackton said. "Your truck was used as a weapon in an assault."

"Man tried to take out my brother," Truman said crisply. "I did what I had to do. I don't like the idea of possibly having killed this guy, but he left me no choice."

I gave Truman a brotherly hug. "Thanks, Tru. I owe you. Sorry you had to get involved in this mess."

"No big deal, Bro. This will give me a chance to stop by and say hi to some guys I know who are doing county time. I'll catch you later."

Truman climbed in the back of the patrol car just as the EMS van rolled off. Though the activity started to wind down, Knackton kept asking me questions, sometimes rephrasing the same question. Fortunately, I knew it was a standard process in most police investigations. It probably made me more tolerant than I would have been.

"Any chance this may be connected to the Norris case?" he finally asked.

"Anything's possible, Lieutenant," I replied. "You find out the name of the trigger-man and I'll know if it's connected."

"You're saying you don't know this shooter?"

"He's not anybody I've dined with lately."

"Any idea who sent him?" he asked with some sarcasm.

"The tooth fairy for all I know." Though I had my suspicions.

Again, more questions, restated, but getting the same answers. I had gotten tired of the game.

"Ever hear of a Detective Wendy Brewer out of Mount Clemens?"

"Yeah," I said wearily. "She sold me a ticket to the Policeman's ball."

Knackton pressed on. "She called around about you. Wanted to know if you were just another cheap key-hole peeper or if you were really about something."

I opted to ignore that statement.

"She says," he continued, "that you've been snooping around an old case of hers. Two kids who were killed on the night of their prom in a car accident. Is that true?"

I yawned.

"She wondered if you were just bird dogging for some ambulance chaser."

"I get that a lot," I said.

Knackton stopped long enough to sign a form attached to a clipboard brought to him by one of the technicians.

He growled something indecipherable before turning back to me. "You make a habit of hanging around old cases that are none of your business?"

"Only when I can't find work as the lead violin in a string quartet."

He spent another twenty minutes asking questions and I kept giving the same answers.

"Look, Lieutenant, I've bottomed out. I'm battle-weary and the water in my eyes is starting to crust. I've been up so long that I don't know if this is yesterday afternoon or tomorrow night. You're starting to look good to me so I must be hallucinating. Now, either take me downtown so I can sleep on one of those comfortable jail bar-be-cue pits masquerading as a bed or let me drag what's left of this body upstairs where it can rest. I can provide you with a more thorough account of tonight's movie tomorrow or today or whatever-the-hell time it is."

"Don't you want to go share a cell with your brother?" he asked slyly.

"He's not going to see the inside of a jail tonight. His story will check out, as does mine. Besides, one phone call from him and all of Local 600 will ride down en mass on 1300 Beaubien." The cement fortress, located downtown, housed the first precinct and was typically referred to as 1300. "Now I'm going upstairs to bed. You know where to reach me."

I turned and walked past a crime scene technician still digging out the bullets. Another technician was videotaping the entire scene.

"Keller!" Knackton yelled. I turned back. "The day ends and I don't see you downtown, I'll get a judge to sign a warrant which I will personally serve. I got a special pair of handcuffs for you."

"Lieutenant, Knackton, please," I said grinning. "The technicians are videotaping this, you old dog."

To this day, I'm not sure how I made it upstairs to bed. Levitation, psychic transport, teleportation or maybe Scotty beamed me up. When my head finally hit the pillow, it didn't matter.

43

People who work the graveyard shift and vampires must develop a tolerance for sleeping through the day noises. Every possible sound, and sounds within sounds, all interwoven into an unending chorus ripped through every nerve ending of my body. Fortunately, my mind had disconnected from my tired torso and if not for those silly dreams, I might have actually enjoyed that half-restful morning.

That and the phone calls.

Through dry sealed eyes and a baritone Barry White would envy, I addressed each phone call with short, curt, agree-to-anything closure.

"Yes, Rosie, you're right. I shouldn't do anything that encourages Truman to get in trouble."

"You're right, Julie, I'm not in the office yet. Thanks for pointing that out to me."

"You're right, ma'am. Taking the number 3 off my phone would definitely cut my phone bills in half. I'll think about your offer."

"You're right, Rae. I should get married and settle down. Starting tomorrow."

"Yeah, Jeff, I'm fine and ..... , Jeff? You never call me at home."

"Okay, Your Honor, this afternoon at one o'clock. Fine."

"No, Truman. I'll never go anywhere with you again."

"Fine, Knackton. Just make sure it's a cell with a soft pillow."

"I know my lease said nothing about bullet holes in the front door."

"Three o'clock? Okay, Malone, I have to be downtown anyway. I'll stop by your desk."

If ever a body and mind needed to totally separate for the sake of their individual survival, mine did. The two decided to remain together and drag the remaining parts out of the bed at just past 11:30.

"Great," I grumbled. "Still time for brunch."

As my eyes focused, I saw my wayward cat, 'Free Ride', sitting on the window ledge staring back at me as if I was recent roadkill.

"Et tu 'Free Ride?'" I said as I opened the window and he sauntered into the kitchen expecting a meal. I fed him something from the fridge that looked like cat food.

He didn't seem to mind. The ASPCA hadn't called lately with any complaints about what that wandering tub o' lard had been eating.

I showered, stayed with a Khaki casual look, grabbed Deborah's journal and drove over to the office. Once inside, I took out the meticulously arranged Norris file and went through certain details to see if anything matched with some of the things she'd had written in her journal.

What I saw said very little. The world she'd captured in her journal and the one gathered after her death, were opposite ends of the universe. But it was worth a look.

I had just enough time to grab a high cholesterol meal before meeting with The Judge. I assumed he was being a typical client and wanted an update. It always amazed me how clients can wait a lifetime for something to change, a husband to give up his mistress, a wife to give up her lover, a relative to finally fade and die, yet the moment a private investigator is added to the equation, time is supposed to speed up and all answers should have been revealed yesterday.

It's what passes for nutty in a normal existence.

I grabbed a dog and cola from a downtown vendor and made it to The Judge's chambers by 1:00 p.m.

He valued punctuality.

He gave a dismissive wave to the clerk who escorted me to his office and waved me in. His massive frame was leaned back in his swivel chair, phone positioned on his shoulder, as he gave an articulate dress down to a lawyer on the other end. Apparently, the misinformed person had dared to question the legal interpretation of one The Judge's rulings. What I heard was chapter and verse of legal summaries and cross summaries finally ending with an implied 'don't ever question my rulings again or I'll have you for lunch'.

He placed the phone in the receiver and turned toward me.

"Bit of trouble last night, Mr. Keller?"

"A little, Your Honor." I replied.

"Care to fill in the details of what I don't know?"

"I'm not sure what you know, but I'll tell you what happened."

So I went over last nights events, again. Telling him only what he needed to know. Some things I still reserved for my own purposes. He listened intently and when I finished, he mulled over what he'd heard.

The quiet moments didn't bother me. Experience teaches a good investigator to sometimes let the quiet tell you all you need to know.

Finally, he said, "Is this related to Deborah's case?"

"Hard to say, Your Honor. I've worked a lot of cases. It could be related to something else. I won't know until they ID the shooter."

I lied, of course. The timing was too close and I always rule out coincidence. I didn't want The Judge intervening in matters floating around in the gray zone.

Judge Zone pulled a manila folder from the top of a small pile and slid it across the desk to me. "He's in a coma over at Harper," he said as I picked up the file. "His name is Roger Martin. Age 27, got a sheet that goes back to his pre-juvenile years. Lots of petty stuff, probation, time served and like that. Did nine months at one of our youth correctional facilities. He'd been known to run with some pretty heavy players, looking to graduate into the big time."

I read through the file while The Judge continued hitting the highlights of this lowlife.

"Mr. Martin hadn't been heard from for a while, until last night. 'Course, we didn't think he'd gone the straight and narrow; just hadn't been caught at anything lately. Figured he was just biding his time until he could find a way to add his name to the list of men helping to generate so much funding to build bigger and better prisons across the country."

I finished reading through Roger Martin's file and gave it back to The Judge. "He's no Sir Galahad."

"No. The question is; why his interest in you? Right now, he can't tell me, but I thought you could."

"I'm clueless in Cleveland right now, Your Honor, but I'll check it out."

"Knackton's already looking into it. I'll run some interference for you, but walk lightly."

"Thanks, Judge. Well, I have ..... "

"Just one other thing, Keller; my wife says that there's the possibility that Deborah kept a journal and that you were looking for it. What can you tell me about that."

"Not much," I lied again. "So far it's been a dead end."

"So you don't think there is a journal?" he asked.

I felt like I was being cross-examined. "There's always that possibility, Your Honor. Can't say right now."

"If such a thing exists, it may contain information that could expedite your investigation."

"And it might not," I continued. "Dead ends are a normal part of an investigation, Your Honor. You know that. I'll keep looking and we'll see what happens."

He mulled again. "You know, during the years I played football, I learned how to read what was coming by staring into the eyes of my opponent. Coaches teach players to react to the ball. I react to the eyes. I used the same principal as a Prosecuting Attorney and even now as a Judge. Most people don't understand that simple fact, but another player would. I hoped your eyes would tell if you were lying or not. But they didn't. So you're either telling the truth or an excellent liar."

He left it there and so did I.

Realizing he had a trial at two o'clock, he told me to keep him informed and I said I would.

As I walked out of the 36th district building, past the people filing in past the security checkpoints, I thought about The Judge's comment. As a defensive back with the Raiders, I too, had learned to read the eyes. And there was something in his eyes when he asked about Deborah's journal that made me uncomfortable. I couldn't shake the feeling, so I stored it away. Going to see Malone would require a different set of emotions and I was too tired to bring up the shield.

· · ·

Candy was at her desk on the fifth floor of the First Precinct. Clad in a light green blouse, black casual pants and hunched over her desk, she had that harried look of someone who'd pay an arsonist to set fire to that growing pile of folders.

"Hey, detective," I said. "Mind if I investigate your background?"

She gave me a half smile. "You're certifiable you know, completely certifiable."

I plopped down in the chair next to her desk. "How you been?"

"I should ask you the same question. Why does the Keller name keep coming up in situations involving shooters and other malcontents?"

"We're community activists demonstrating our concern for a better Detroit. Want to help us get funded?"

"Not funny, Linc." She leaned back and exhaled slowly. "I'm sure this has something to do with the Deborah Norris case, but, Linc it sounds like this may be a bit over your head."

"I can swim."

"But the waters are shark-infested, lover man. You're pissing off some powerful people."

"The Stallings? They aren't powerful, just power hungry."

"With some powerful friends who don't appreciate you harassing a possible political contender. Why don't you let Knackton handle it. Tell him what you've learned and back off."

I stretched. "Knackton didn't hire me. Besides he's too busy trying to right the day-to-day wrongs." I motioned toward her pile. "As are you."

She sighed. "Yeah, that's the truth. Promise me you'll be careful. Go slow with this, Linc. It has a bad feel."

"I will, but I need a favor. Actually two favors. " She glanced at me warily. "Nothing spectacular; I just want to know if Pernell Stallings ever filed a stolen car report."

"Why do you want to know that?"

"He wants to buy my Nova. I need to know if he's a good risk."

"Just a second," she said suppressing a smile. She walked over to a computer terminal and pulled up some funny looking screen. She was only gone a few moments before returning with some information she'd jotted down on a pad. "April 18th, 1990, he filed a report for a Nisson, stolen from a parking lot over on Mount Elliot. As far as we know, the vehicle was never recovered. The insurance company paid off the claim. Does that help?"

"Some, but who knows?" I replied nonchalantly. "Thanks, Malone. I'd better leave you to your work. I need to fill out a weapon's discharge form and give an official statement for Knackton's report." I stood up and rolled my neck around to stretch the kinks.

"What's the other favor?" she asked.

"Know what else I need?" I said giving her my most extreme leer.

"Not now, Linc," she said dismissively.

"I need copies of Deborah Norris's phone calls."

"Why?" she rolled her eyes at knowing why I asked her.

"I just need to see if there's anything there."

Malone sighed. "You're determined to have me back on Vice, aren't you?" I tried my most hang dog impression. "Oh, I'll see what I can do."

"Thanks, Malone."

"One thing," she said sliding away from the desk. "Be careful."

"Always, Malone." I leaned across her desk and whispered. "I miss you, too." She gave me a blank stare. "Don't think I didn't catch the lover man comment."

"Out, before I have you arrested for loitering," she said pointing toward the door.

I spent the next hour filling out reports and having my statement taped by a disinterested officer working with Knackton. I drank two cups of sludge that cost a dollar a piece and finally signed the transcribed forms. I had to wait for Knackton's approval before my gun would be released and, naturally, he wasn't around at the time.

It didn't do much good trying to argue with the officer handling the flow of paperwork from last night's episode and I wasn't in a mood to appeal to rationality.

Leaving seemed a better solution than inciting a riot in a police station.

There were other sources of information I needed to tap into and most of the day was gone.

I pulled out of the downtown parking lot and headed back to the office. With the sounds of my Sentiments tape playing in the background, I thought about the seventeen days between Pernell's stolen car and Deborah's death.

Could be nothing, but then again .....

44

"Obviously, someone doesn't like what you're into right now, Linc. Candy makes a good point. Maybe you should let this Knackton character dodge a few bullets."

Julie stood next to my desk, holding a print-out of an insurance claim filed by Pernell Stallings. Her unexpected interest in the Norris case had taken me off guard. As had her interest in my recent dangers.

I removed my feet from the edge of my desk and reached for the form. "I appreciate your concern, Jules, but I know what I'm doing."

· "It has a bad smell, Linc," she replied. "This thing could be over your head. It's been eight years, you know. A lot of things happen during that time. Lives change. People become crazier with age. The living are more concerned with living."

"Doesn't help the dead rest easier," I said as I unfolded the paper.

Julie sat on the edge of my desk and folded her arms across her chest. She looked like a school principal about to extract the truth. "Linc, in the time we've known each other I've watched you. You might think that all I do is gather information and send you a bill, but I've watched you and the man hunter work. I think Jeff's a lot more detached about his work, but even you manage to keep some objective distance. Not always, but enough to keep you sleeping at night."

I leaned back in my chair. "What's your point, Jules?"

"What makes this one so different? The crime happened eight years ago. Deborah Norris, tragically, is dead and all the Kellers in the world can't change that fact. It's possible that she was robbed and is the tragic victim of wrong-place, wrong-time. Maybe you're looking for things that aren't there. Maybe, just maybe, this is one of those times when it's best to leave things unsettled."

"Like knowing when to walk away and knowing when to run?"

"Something like that." Julie sighed. "Linc, that light you see at the end of this tunnel may be a train coming at you."

"During my brief stint in the NFL, I was sometimes brought in to play the 'nickel back' in obvious passing situations. I was taught to read the flow, follow the action and stop the play."

"What's your point?"

"This case has flowed in directions I hadn't anticipated and the resulting action has been unexpected. But I was hired to stop the play and I'm too far into it to stop now. Besides," I hesitated, "I don't think I can stop."

"Oh? And why not?" Julie asked trying to mask her concern.

"I don't think I'm suppose to."

Julie let the unspoken moment linger. She finally stood up, rubbing the creases from the front of her lavender skirt that slit on the right side. "Well, hotshot. It's your head. Even my late-paying client's beats having none at all, so you be careful. Fools rush in where wise men never go."

"Unless it's the end of the work day in Manhattan and they're cramming themselves into an elevator."

Julie waved and I focused on the print out.

BAI Insurance was listed as the company that insured Pernell's car. He reported that his Nissan was stolen from a parking lot on Mount Elliot in April of 1990. After a thorough investigation, the insurance company paid off his claim. Naturally, hiked his insurance rates and since that time, he's owned three other sport models, all heavily insured and none have been stolen. I checked the handwritten signature at the bottom of the form and saw that the insurance investigator who worked the case was named Brian Semple.

I got the number for BAI Insurance, called and asked for Brian

Semple and was transferred into his voicemail. I left a message and hung up.

What I had in my head was a working theory that fit a few facts, but left the others on the sidelines waiting for an opportunity to come in and support the theory.

Fact: Deborah Norris was killed and her purse was stolen.

Fact: Deborah Norris was killed with her own gun.

Fact: Deborah Norris was investigating the accident that took the lives of Morris and Daphne.

Fact: Morris and Daphne died as a result of a speeding car running their car off the road.

Fact: Deborah documented MiShaun's expressed drunken regret about an accident.

Fact: Deborah identified the Morris and Daphne accident as having occurred the same night as MiShaun's near fatal accident.

Fact: At the time of the accident, MiShaun's license had been suspended.

Question: Since she hadn't borrowed Deborah's car that night, how did she get around?

Question: How did MiShaun get connected with Trevor Stallings?

Question: Who stole Pernell's car?

Question: What is Tyler Cain's connection with the Stallings?

My questions were starting to run ahead of my facts and the answers were nil.

I welcomed the ringing phone as much as a unknown actor welcomes a photo op.

"Lincoln Keller, please." He sounded like someone happy to assume authority.

"Speaking," I replied.

"Name's Brian Semple," he continued. "I'm returning your call."

Semple sounded like the kind of man for whom words were a minor annoyance. 'Keep it simple Semple' I dubbed him. "Thanks for calling, Mr. Semple. I'll try not to take too much of your time." He didn't respond. "I'm assuming you already checked and confirmed that I am a private investigator."

"You assume correctly. What can I do for you?"

Stay with the facts, Jack. "I'd like your opinion on a claim you investigated."

I heard the keyboard clacking in the background after I gave him the claim number. I think he knew not to ask how I retrieved the information since investigators don't always walk a straight line.

"Got it here in front of me. What's your question?"

I sighed. "Was the car really stolen?"

"Technically, yes it was," he said in a direct tone.

"But ..... "

"But I'd stake my reputation that it was a scam. I could never prove it, but that would be my guess."

"You think he set it up?"

"You taping this?" he asked.

"No."

"Hold on a second. I want to get my personal notes from that claim." I heard the receiver being placed on a desk, then some muffled office noises before he picked up again. "Not only do I think he set it up, but I'm pretty sure who he used."

I interrupted. "A guy named Tyler Cain."

"That's the name I have written in my notes," he replied.

Damn

45

Semple explained why he suspected Pernell of using Tyler to 'jack' his car. As an insurance investigator who specialized in stolen cars, he had contacts with most of the local police authorities and their car theft units. Tyler Cain came to his attention several years ago and during that time, he believed that Tyler ran the most efficient and discreet 'jacking crew' in the area.

I thought a moment. "What was hot eight years ago?"

He didn't miss a beat. "Foreign models; mostly. Jags, Nissans, Hondas." He paused. "'Course, that's been pretty consistent across the country over the last decade. It doesn't work that way in Michigan. Our thieves are brand-loyal. Neon's, Jeep Cherokees, Explorers and Mustangs. We don't car jack em' unless their domestically manufactured."

I picked up on the next beat. "When I worked as a cop in Oakland, we regularly took reports from people claiming their car was stolen only to find out that the claimant had it stolen just to get the insurance money."

"Still happens, only more so. For a couple of hundred bucks, a person could have a real top of the line car stolen, file for the cash and no one would be the wiser."

"Where are the stolen cars taken?"

"Most jackers work with one crew, unless forced to do otherwise. It takes a while to establish their method of operation and then they stick pretty close. Even though cops do a pretty good job of shutting down those operations, they spring up double the next time and twice as hard to catch."

"Was Cain that good?" I asked.

"That good and that uncatchable. I don't know how he did it, but the crew we believe he assembled could make cars disappear and the parts sold before we could even pick up the scent."

"Tyler's working with Trevor Stallings over at 'Empower Detroit'. Apparently he likes more formalized entrepreneurial activities. You think he's found religion?"

"I think he's found a good front. Maybe Trevor did take an interest in him, but Pernell influenced him. I've been suspicious of that connection since I first heard of it."

"Yet you haven't followed up?"

"Come look at my backlog of claims I have to investigate, Keller. Car theft is a thriving business."

I thanked him.

My own suspicions were starting to grate on my nerves. I needed rest more than I needed answers. A sane man would have gone home, poured himself a half a jelly jar of bourbon and watched reruns of The Three Stooges. It was a tempting alternative, but this case was flowing and stopping to rest felt like cheating.

I stood up and stretched. Every abstraction and vaguely passing thought took on definable features. I believed those features were attached to the face of a killer with a name just beyond my investigative grasp.

In one of the corners of my mind, a looking glass had formed. I gazed inside the looking glass and Deborah's face smiled back.

"Deborah," I said. "Who shot you?"

She didn't answer.

Cradling the phone on my shoulder, I punched in the number for information, asked for the number to Harper Hospital and let the operator immediately connect me to their number. A wispy voiced woman answered and I asked to speak to the Doctor or Nurse working the Roger Martin case. I was put on hold and soothed by music that would have calmed a caffeine addict.

Another woman's voice, stern and formal, haggard to a fault, broke up the Sleeper's Concerto in minor E. Her tone suggested that I should ask my question quickly or hang up.

"My name is Keller and I'd like to know how Roger Martin is coming along."

She popped her lips. "Really, Mr. Keller. We're much too busy here for this kind of game. Now you already know how he's doing. I told you this morning. So please don't waste my time."

I paused and quickly regrouped. "Excuse me. But this is the first time I've called."

"Mr. Keller." She stopped to answer a question. "You and I talked this very morning right here at the reception desk. I told you then and I'll tell you now; Mr. Martin is still in a coma."

"What did I look like?" I asked.

"Mr. Keller ..... "

"Honestly. What did I look like?"

She gave a quick description, said she had more important matters and hung up. The description she gave definitely matched a Keller, but not me.

"Now why was Jeff interested in Roger Martin?" I muttered as I envisioned Jeff lurking around the hospital trying to get information.

The image faded as I stumbled from the office, ignoring the ringing phone and nearly colliding with the woman who suddenly appeared at my door.

I immediately apologized before recognition set in. "Jocelyn? Jocelyn Kilgore ..... Right?"

She smiled. "I didn't think you'd remember me. I'm impressed. Did I catch you at a bad time?"

"Any moment in the last decade is a bad time. What brings you here?" I asked stepping aside so she could ease into the office.

"Some things have bothered me lately, so I decided to come talk with you. I hope you don't mind?"

"Things that bother people have been my specialty of late. Have a seat."

Wearing a champagne silk tapestry jacket and matching tank dress, Jocelyn sashayed over to the ladder-back chair adjacent to my desk, crossing her legs after she sat down.

"I've never been in the office of a private investigator." She glanced around. "It certainly is ..... lived in"

"We hope to make the cover of Trash and Burn magazine," I replied. "I'd offer you coffee but what I make is only suitable for unclogging drains."

"Don't bother. I've had enough for one day." She leaned back. "You know, last time we talked, I seem to remember that I did most of the talking, but I never found out why you're so interested in Pernell."

"I wasn't interested in Pernell. I was interested in why you were upset. Just being a helpful citizen."

"That'll be the day. What were you really trying to find out?" she said as she locked her hands under her chin.

"Nothing much. I just happened to be in the area."

She gave me a wry smile. "Oh, I get it. You don't know if you can trust me. Right?"

"I'm sure you're have a trustworthiness that would make the Girl Scouts proud."

"But it's the truth. Right?" she persisted.

"It's an issue. Professionalism and all that. There's very little I can tell."

"Can you tell me why Tyler Cain is so important to you?"

I poker-faced my response. "He's not that important to me. There's little I can tell you."

She straightened. "Suppose I told you that I know where Tyler hangs out at night. Interested?"

"Possibly," I replied. "Although of late I'm developing an aversion to the night."

"I know exactly where he's going to be at ten o'clock tonight," she said knowing my curiosity was piqued.

"Care to tell me?" I asked knowing the answer.

"I'll tell you where to pick me up tonight so we can go there."

"Jocelyn, I wouldn't be very good company tonight. I ..... "

She'd already picked up my scratch pad and started writing. "Pick me up at this address at nine tonight." She looked up at me. "Dress a little nicer."

"I gave my tuxedo to a homeless penguin."

She ripped the sheet from the pad and slid it over to me. "I live in Southfield." She stood up. "See you at nine o'clock sharp."

"Exactly where are we going?" I said with some insistence.

"Nine o'clock sharp, Mr. Keller. Don't worry," she said turning toward the door. "I think you'll be surprised.

Another surprise? I thought. *How rare.*

46

As much as I wanted to be useful, I had a uselessness streak running through me that would have been the envy of any veteran Senator. The sleep I discarded from last night reared its matted head and sent me back to my apartment where I settled into my recliner and let the late afternoon traffic play a commuter's opera in my head.

I unplugged the phone, hoping I didn't have a friend on a ledge in need of counseling.

Sleep was instantaneous.

Far from a heavenly doze, it did satisfy the basic rest requirements.

When I awakened at just after 8:00, I had that uncertain feeling that comes with not knowing if it was the same evening or the next morning. When Jocelyn's image paraded across both parts of my brain, I had my bearings.

After the shower put my senses on full alert, I looked through my closet for something that fit Jocelyn's 'dress a little nicer' comment. The fact that I had no idea where we were going only added to my indecision. I finally decided on an open-collar, white cotton shirt, my black Italian-cut jacket and black chino slacks, figuring even though it wasn't quite GQ, it was a lot farther from GS (government surplus).

I plugged in the phone, checked the address and wheeled onto Livernois Avenue heading north to the Lodge Freeway and into the City of Southfield, Detroit's first post-modern city of suburban, middle-class dreams.

Silent Suspicion

•　　•　　•

Southfield grew as part of Detroit's changing social landscape, quickened by the 1967 riots. The bedroom community of ranch homes, Tudors and evenly manicured lawns became the first of several sanctuaries that sprawled north and west of Detroit. I've still never figured out why a city named Southfield is located north of Detroit.

I drove down Southfield Road until I reached Thirteen Mile Road, opting to fill up at the service station on the way back and avoid the endless wait at the stoplight. I found Jocelyn's red brick, two-level on a quiet street two blocks down from a Borders bookstore. I parked my Nova in front of her home and followed the red brick walkway up to her door.

What is this lady up to? I thought as I rang the dimly lit doorbell.

When Jocelyn greeted me at the door, she was dressed to kill. She wore a body tight, sleeveless silver and satin dress. Silver, high-heeled leather sandals were all that covered a pair of smooth exposed legs. Though I wasn't a true compliment to her style, I was acceptable on a short-term basis.

"Thanks for being on time," she said as she set the alarm and closed the door. "I'm ready."

We started down the walkway when she suddenly stopped. "Tell me we're not riding in that," she said pointing to my Nova.

"My horse doesn't work the night shift."

She tsked, reached in her purse and pulled out a set of keys. "We'll take mine. Can you drive a car manufactured in the Nineties?"

"Sure," I said. "Is the crank in the front or back?"

Ignoring my comment, she pressed a button on her key ring that disengaged the car alarm of her sleek red Chrysler Stealth.

After that annoying two-note signal stopped, I opened the passenger side door and Jocelyn slid into the seat like polished royalty.

I eased into the driver's seat, completely impressed with its aqua blue veneer and its digital front panel. Driving a sports car loaded with everything but the Brinks truck that paid for it was not part of my evening game plan.

Nor was Jocelyn.

But I was part of hers. Using Tyler as bait was a good move and she played it well. Now that the events were in motion, I had to see where it would lead.

"I take it we're not going to a mud wrestling tournament," I said while starting the engine.

Her coy smile told me all I needed to know. "No. But where we're going is just as entertaining."

The statement 'famous last words' popped in mind as I backed out the driveway.

•   •   •

Shocker's-At-Night was more than just a dance hall and watering hole. The multi-lighted nightclub sat along Eight Mile Road, the multi-dimensional, quasi border between Big City Detroit to the south and Bedroom Community Southfield to the north. The place drew the kind of crowd that would make a marketing specialist salivate. The needed-to-be-seen, already-seen-but-look-again, and demanding-to-be-seen were lined up along the extended, curving marble-topped bar, stuffed in the leather booths or standing around the crowed tables. A DJ played a combination of Rap, R&B and Bump and Grind as sharply dressed couples demonstrated the latest dance steps on a highly shined oak wood dance floor.

Shouting was the most efficient form of communication.

Jocelyn had swindled a booth that offered a good view of the bar, the dance floor, the front door and most anyone lost in that sea of low cut tops and high brow suits.

The raging hormone meter had already moved into the red warning zone when Jocelyn and I ordered our second drinks.

She ordered another Scotch and water.

I stayed with a lime chaser.

"Why are we really here, Jocelyn?" I shouted as she surveyed the crowd.

"I told you. This is where Tyler hangs out," she said without looking at me.

"And we're just supposed to sit and wait for him?"

"He'll show," she said with a dismissive wave.

"I'm sure he will," I said. "Assuming you and I are talking about the same 'he'."

I don't attribute much to fate, but I do believe in timing. So when Pernell made his entrance into the room, my role in this 'geek' tragedy was clear; Jocelyn baited my hook with Tyler and baited Pernell's hook with me. She locked eyes onto him as he strolled across the edge of the dance floor on his way to the bar. He greeted everyone he knew and some he didn't. When he settled next to a sexy number in tight sequins, Jocelyn went into her act.

"Let's dance," she said sliding out of her seat.

"Let's not," I said. "I don't want to miss Tyler when he comes in."

"You won't," she insisted.

"Bad knee. Dislocates every time I hear Rap music." I held her stare. "Besides, Pernell's coming this way."

She glanced around and watched as he made his way to our booth. She slowly sat down next to me, holding my hand and leaning close.

"Jocelyn," I said. "I gave up social games for Lent. Why don't you ....."

Pernell stood next to our booth before I could finish my protest.

"Jocelyn," he said with sugar coated charm. "Why, I certainly didn't expect to see you tonight."

"Or any night, for that matter," she said smoothly. "Have you met my date? His name's Lincoln Keller. He's a private investigator."

"Not formally. No," He replied extending his hand. "Mr. Keller."

The hottest of clubs can't conceal the coldest of greetings. "Stallings," I replied, "That was quite a showing your brother made last night at Herman Gardens."

"He wants to help the city," he replied, never taking his eyes off Jocelyn.

"How noble. And what do you want to do to help?"

"I'd like to help myself to a dance with your date." He finally glanced over at me and flashed a half moon smile. "That is, if you don't mind."

"That's up to the lady."

Admittedly, Jocelyn pulled it off with subtle grace and restraint. You might not have ever guessed it was what she really wanted.

"Well, maybe just one dance." She stood up, and with one arm already around her waist, Pernell eased her through the crowd and onto the dance floor.

I would have done the honorable thing and left her without a ride home, but timing took a familiar twist in the face of Tyler Cain. He must have strolled in after Pernell, because he found a spot toward the end of the bar and grim-faced an order for a drink. Since Jocelyn had raised a jealous streak in Pernell, I saw no reason for wasting the evening, so I wandered over to where Tyler was sitting.

I squeezed by a soon-to-be-in-bed couple and stood next to Tyler.

He sipped his drink before finally realizing that someone was staring at him. He peered up at me and flashed a surprised-to-see-you smile.

"Hello, Tyler. Read any good pictures lately?'

He glared and then his eyes widened. "Keller, you've become a bad habit I'm more than happy to break."

"Keep charming me like that and I won't tell your analyst how you used to pull the wings off flies."

"Look, man!" He stood up, quickly closing the distance between us. "I've had it up to here with you. Maybe the Stallings think you're just blowing smoke, but I'd just as soon ..... "

"Kill me," I said interrupting his thought. "That day just might come your way, but not tonight. I wouldn't want to interfere with your social conquests." I nodded toward a woman three barstools from us. "That one looks seventeen. You'd better hurry before she requires a written exam."

His eyes telegraphed what was coming long before he actually swung. I stepped aside and before he pulled his hand back, had grabbed his collar and pinned him back against the bar. Several people stood aside, curious, but not looking to get involved.

"Tyler," I said. "You and I can't seem to be in the same room without causing trouble. Now, I've had a busy last couple of days. There's a trail I've been following that stinks to high heaven and that smell keeps coming back to you and the Stallings. I don't know why, but it's just a matter of time. I'm gonna keep digging and sooner or later I'll find out if it's your face at the bottom of the hole."

I let him go just as two beefy salt and pepper security men joined us.

"What's the problem here, gentleman?" asked salt beefy.

"No problem," I said. "Just a slight disagreement over the weather. He thinks its raining."

"Tyler?" Pepper beefy asked. "Everything cool man?"

Tyler nodded.

Pepper beefy turned to me and said, "Maybe you should find a dance partner or an exit."

I'd had enough for one evening. Despite my adrenal rush, I wasn't in the mood for more games and silly distractions. "Good idea, Atlas. My dance card is used up anyway."

I looked around for Jocelyn, hoping she wasn't locked in a hot bump and grind with Pernell. They weren't in the booth we'd occupied, two other couples had seen to that. I checked every table, each spot along the bar, searched through the standing crowd as well as along the walls. The dress she wore would have made her stand out in any crowd, so I knew she'd be easy to spot. After my third sweep of the room and seeing no trace of Jocelyn or Pernell, I decided to check outside.

Several couples were milling around the front of the club, while others mingled along the sidewalk or leaned against their parked cars. Shockers-At-Night was everything I'd heard and as I passed by a car with moistened windows and a rappers rock, it was some things I hadn't heard.

I didn't see Jocelyn or Pernell anywhere in the parking lot, so I doubled back, cutting through an area behind the club when I heard a muffled conversation several feet in front of me. It didn't take much thinking to know that it was a couple having a whispered dispute about something.

I slowed to a quiet pace until I was within comfortable listening distance. The voices were recognizable and I should not have been surprised.

"So what did you tell him, Jocelyn?" Pernell asked sternly.

"I haven't told him anything. He wanted to find out something about Tyler, not you," Jocelyn replied with some defiance.

"Then what's he doing here with you?" he continued in a firm tone.

"He's my date. What am I supposed to do? Wait around until you finally decide to get around to seeing me? Other men want to spend time with me. What's your problem?"

Pernell inched forward. "Look, Jocelyn. I told you before; we had some good times, but you're too possessive. I can't breathe around you. We had to stop before we really hurt each other."

"I'm not possessive!" she yelled. Then she wavered. "I was good for you, Pernell. I could have made you happy. I've been there for you, haven't I? Why did you keep coming back? You kept coming back, baby."

She moved toward him and he shoved her back. She fell against the wall, gripping her shoulder after the impact. "Stay away from me, Jocelyn! You don't own me. You never will. Now you get that private investigator away from here or so help me I'll ..... "

"You'll do what, homie?" I said stepping out of the shadows. "Tell me what you'll do if she doesn't take me away from here."

I walked toward Pernell, stopping between him and Jocelyn. "Tell me now what you wanted her to relay to me. I'm all ears, homeboy. Try to get my attention the same way."

He went from stunned to angry and finally tepid before deciding to just walk away. I grabbed him by the arm, stopping him in his tracks. "The lady hasn't heard your apology."

He glared at me and then to Jocelyn. "I'm sorry," he murmured sarcastically.

"That much we already know, Pernell. Now be a good little Stallings and run along."

He started to say something, but I put a finger on his chest. "I think you're dumb, but do you want to go for stupid?"

He moved quickly to the front of the club while I turned to Jocelyn. "You alright?"

She nodded trying to hide her embarrassment. "I guess I made a fool of myself, didn't I?"

"Yeah, I guess you did. You want to go home?"

I took the sobbing and tears as a definite yes.

47

Jocelyn kept apologizing despite my continued assurances that it was no big deal. She saw my declining her invitation for coffee at her place as a sign that I was still angry. I kept telling her that I was tired and nothing more. I thanked her for a wonderful evening and when she promised me that we'd have the night with no expectations in the morning, I told her that it never works that way.

"Tomorrow we'd try to justify tonight's lame excuse."

"It's the lady you've been seeing, isn't it?" she asked as she stood inside her doorway.

"Yeah," I said, knowing Malone and I hadn't seen much of each other lately. Standing in front of Jocelyn made me realize just how long it had been for a number of things.

"She'll never know," Jocelyn said convincingly.

"Yes, she will. Besides, Jocelyn, wasn't it you who told me not to be a bastard?"

My 'date' only lasted a couple of hours, but it seemed like forever. Now, Tyler and Pernell knew that I was onto something. Jocelyn's attempt at induced jealousy had backfired as had her second-act seduction and Deborah Norris was in some spiritual arena pointing a finger and wondering why I had wasted so much time.

When I pulled away from Jocelyn's house, I thought about the number of bad dates I'd had prior to meeting Malone. Though Jocelyn's clearly qualified as one of those for which tomorrow was a welcome relief, it hadn't been the worst. As a late-thirties male with one foot in the new century, I hoped the next hundred years of dating would prove to be more interesting.

As I wheeled back to my apartment, I assumed that any remaining evening excitement would take the form of a fluffed pillow and an erotic dream.

My previous nights' escapade left me a little reluctant to use the front entrance to my apartment, especially since my landlord was now questioning the sanity of having a private investigator living over his accounting service.

I cruised down Livernois, passing my apartment building as I surveyed the landscape, looking for anything remotely suspicious. Once I'd gone an extra block, I did a U-turn and slowly made my way back. Everything looked calm. No one appeared to be lurking in the shadows, but the Roger Martins of the world are a dime-a-dozen, work cheap, lack a moral base and seem to multiply with every economic downturn.

Satisfied that all looked well, I parked in an area adjacent to the building and strolled cautiously to the bullet-holed front door. Now that the crime scene tape had been removed, getting in and out didn't look as silly.

Once inside, I accidentally kicked a small manila envelope lying on the floor. I picked it up and saw that it was letter size, sealed with no address. I waited until I did a complete check of my apartment before examining the contents of the envelope.

There was a hand-written note with four names and a few folded newspaper clippings. Three of the names had a red check mark at the end and the fourth, 'Richard Beasley', had a seven-digit number next to it.

"And just who are these media darlings?" I muttered.

I unfolded the newspaper clippings and their claim to fame was apparent. All I had to do was match the names with the obituary. Three names with a red check mark, three obituary columns and a fourth name with a seven-digit number.

I punched in the number and an echoed voice answered.

Cellular phone I thought. "I'd like to speak with Richard Beasley."

"Who's asking?"

"Name's Keller. Lincoln Keller."

"Yeah," he replied. "Who knows you?"

I only needed a second to put it together. "Nightlife."

"You the P.I.?"

I grunted.

He paused. "I'm giving you an address and an hour. You only got tonight and I disappear. Anybody come with you, I pop you and him." He rattled off an address. "Your hour starts now."

He disconnected as I glanced at the digital clock on the table by my recliner. "Almost midnight," I sighed. "And the night is still young."

•   •   •

As I drove to meet with Beasley, I wondered if the God of the Midnight Hour had somehow gotten his wires crossed and had me confused with Truman. Late night hours were never my strong suit. When I worked the night shift as a patrol officer in Oakland, it was all I could do to keep my eyes from rolling out of their sockets from all the water I generated from yawning.

The area, once known as the Jeffries Project, was a testament to the 1940's vision of living in the city. Towering tenements designed to hold hundreds of families on the smallest patch of land for a minimum cost and maximum gain. The red brick, rectangular monoliths were getting a face life as a commitment to that once proud vision.

The building Beasley identified was easy to find, despite the visual similarity. The area stank of abandonment and shattered dreams. Though the night provided its own cover, I kept close to the light.

The grafetti sprayed door that hung by one hinge was our designated meeting spot. I approached the door aware of the nocturnal movements of the current residents.

As I neared the door, I felt the barrel of a gun pressed against my back as I was marched through the dark covered debris to a wood patched window. The sound of scurrying around on the floor was a reminder that Beasley and I weren't the only non-paying occupants.

"I'm alone," I said.

"I know. I've watched you from the moment you parked." He backed away and told me to turn around. "Why are we talking?"

"Don't get too crazy with that thing," I said nodding toward his gun. "I have something I want you to see."

I pulled the envelope from my jacket pocket along with a penlight I carry for assistance in picking locks. He cautiously moved forward and I showed him the names on the paper and the obituary columns.

He stared a few moments before saying anything. "What do you want to know?"

"Who are the three with the check marks?"

"Nightlife said you could be trusted. That true?"

"Go with that. Do you know these brothers?"

He sighed. "We were a crew. I could break an alarm and pop the column faster than anybody. Dwight here was a spotter. He watched people and always knew when to make the move. Leon used guns to scare people and force the action. He enjoyed a good daylight 'jackin'. Fred knew how to break a car down in the least amount of time. We were a good crew."

"Who was your crew chief?"

"I tell you that, I'm a dead man."

"Not if I can be trusted," I said. "But let's try it this way; why are those three dead and you're not?"

"You can't kill what you can't catch."

"Doesn't mean you stop looking."

He stepped away and moved toward the far end of the room. As my eyes adjusted to the dark, I was starting to see his outline. He appeared a couple of inches shorter than my six foot, one inch height. His hair seemed closely matted. He didn't look rumpled. Though his clothes did need a long run in a spin cycle.

"Dwight was blown up in his car. Nobody knows who did it. Leon was found swinging from a rope in an abandoned building off Forest. There was a suicide note. Fred was electrocuted while taking a bath. They say it was an accident."

"What do you say?"

"Play dead until I can make my move."

"Why did the crew break up?" I asked.

"Crew chief got religion. He found a legit way to make his bone. He paid us and said he was out of the business."

"Why didn't the four of you continue on without him?"

"He was the man. He had all the contacts. We stole the cars and broke down the parts, but he made the deals. Along about the time we started to connect with a few of the players, Dwight's car blew up. We had a serious manpower shortage. A week later, Fred did his electro-hustle in the tub. That's when I went underground. Something wasn't right."

"What about Leon?"

"Who knows how long he'd been swinging. I only heard about it in passing. So, that leaves me."

"And you had nothing to do with their deaths?" I asked.

He turned toward me and pointed his gun at my chest. "You're still alive aren't you?"

"Yeah," I said. "And so are you."

He lowered his gun. "I got insurance."

"Tell you what. I'm going to say a name. You don't answer, then I have my answer." I waited until he nodded. "Tyler Cain." He didn't answer, but the subtle shift of his eyes answered in droves. "You were all part of his crew?" He glared and backed toward a window, peeking through the cracked wood. "I'm suppose to stand here all night asking questions that you won't answer?"

He waited several beats before turning toward me. "I'm here and that's all the answers you need. You got questions, then go ask Tyler. He's the man. He's got your back, but watch the knife across your throat."

"When did Tyler lose interest in the business?"

"Six or seven years ago. He said he had better things to do. Me and Leon said we'd keep making the runs, but we didn't have the connects and Tyler wouldn't share his."

For someone who'd granted me a limited amount of time, he spent most of it talking around what I needed to know. All I needed was a wooden booth and a white collar.

"Look, my man," I said, finally interrupting his monologue. "Confessions may be good for the soul, but I'm not qualified to grant you forgiveness." He stopped, arms folded, staring at the floor. "Your former boss is now living the good life, playing water boy to Trevor Stallings. I need to know how they became connected."

"He did the man a favor."

"What kind of favor?" I asked impatiently.

"The kind that can never be paid back."

"Meaning?"

"Life saving. If you hear me."

I sighed. "Yeah, I hear you. Now break it down for me."

"Stallings found himself in deep trouble and needed a fast way out. He came to Tyler cause he knew it would be done with no trace of evidence. He could make things disappear and no one would be the wiser. He was that good."

"What did Trevor want him to do?"

He smiled. "Who said anything about Trevor?"

48

As our shadowy outlines became less sinister, I listened to Beasley rattle off a story that reeked of low level cover-up and tabloid stench. If the story ever came out, talk show junkies would line up for their daily fix.

If Beasley could be believed.

He stated that about eight years ago, he and the other crewmembers were called by Tyler to handle a fast pick up. The call came in late one night. The car was sitting in a designated spot and there would be no trouble. They were to pick up the car, break it down and have the parts ready to go. Once that was done, Tyler would make sure that the rest of the car disappeared. They did the job as instructed and Tyler took care of the rest.

Before I could ask, he explained why there was such a rush.

"The car was hot," he said. "Not hot like stolen, but hot because of something that happened. Only we weren't supposed to know. But I knew something was up. Tyler wasn't his usual cool about this one. Every car we 'jacked' was hot, but this one was different."

"What kind of car was it?" I asked.

"Nissan 300X, light blue drop top."

A piece of the puzzle slid into place. "Where'd you pick up the car?"

"Outside an after hours place on Mount Elliot."

Another piece of the puzzle that fit nicely into its slot.

Even though he felt something was up, he went along because it was what Tyler wanted. "It didn't feel right, so I did a couple of things just to give me an edge."

I waited.

"We move something that fast, I figure it's got to be worth something, so I wrote down the license plate number."

"And?"

Reluctantly, he pulled an envelope out of his pocket. "I show you this, then you become my insurance. You gotta protect me. Can you do it?"

"I assumed 'Nightlife' had your back."

"If nobody asks, then he don't tell. He knows where to find me, if I need to be found, but I been on my own."

"He didn't like your line of work?"

"He don't trust people who worked for someone else. I made a deal with him. In return, no drive-bys on my old ladies' house. No accidental fires in the kitchen. He moved her and my sister into the neighborhood, so they're protected. Tyler can't touch them and he won't. I've been on my own ever since."

"What kind of deal did you make?"

"I show you this picture, the deal is complete and I'm your problem. Still want to see?"

Adopting a late twenties son who'd been living on the run for a while was not how I envisioned my late thirties years, but if he had a key piece of evidence that would help me solve the Deborah Norris murder, then I had to take that chance.

"Show me the picture," I said.

He did. What I saw would make law authorities salivate. Beasley was sitting on the trunk of the Nissan with the license plate number in plain view. The blue plate with white letters read PERN S2, which meant the license was easy to trace, but more importantly, in the background were two figures who seemed to be having a discussion. I recognized one as being Leon, the other was Tyler. It appeared to be a pretty cramped space, but some of the tools of the car jacking disassembly trade were in clear view. The picture told me a great deal, although it could still be argued as circumstantial.

"It's something, but it could still be argued that the car was stolen. All you're doing is proving the point."

"I got more pictures like this one. Mostly of the cars we jacked. Fred liked taking pictures of the cars. For him, it was like collecting model airplanes or something. He knew Tyler wouldn't like it, so he kept a small camera and when no one was looking, he took a picture. When everything started going down, he hid the pictures and told me that if anything happened to him, to hold onto his pictures. He died the next day."

"Where are the other pictures?"

"At momma's, but she don't know it. One time when I slipped over there, I brought the pictures with me and hid them in her house."

"Okay, so we can prove, at long last that Tyler ran a slick car jacking operation, but what about this Nissan. At best, we might be able to prove a false insurance claim, Pernell has to make restitution and that's the end of it."

"Fred had one other habit about taking pictures. Look up in the far corner."

I'd given it a passing glance the first time, but then it stood out. It was an old clock radio that numerically displayed the month, day and year in white letters. I did a quick calculation. The day and time were seventeen days before Deborah was killed.

It still wasn't much, but it was a thread. "Any idea why this Nissan was hot?"

He sighed. "I wasn't sure until I heard about an accident in which some high school couple bought it. News had it that the only witness said he thought it was a blue sports model convertible. The car and driver hadn't been found. The car would never be found since we'd taken care of that, but the driver ....., well, what do you think?"

I remembered from Detective Brewer's report that the date, time and year on the clock in the picture were exactly the same as the Morris and Daphne accident. I had another thread, loose, but starting to tighten.

"You think this car was responsible for the accident?"

"What I think and what you have to prove are two different things. I wasn't there. I didn't see it, but somebody did. Now ..... ," he pulled a one of those large plastic sandwich bags from his pocket and gave it to me. " ..... you find the person who was wearing this on that night and you'll have your witness."

I opened the bag and removed the silk contents. Holding it up against the dim light, I saw it was a light orange neck scarf with a patterned floral arrangement.

"I found it in under the back seat on the driver's side. I don't know why I kept it, but I did."

I only half heard what he said, since my brain racked each cell, searching for the memory of where I'd seen that scarf. The answer was as transparent as the embroidered initials I found on a corner of the scarf.

M L

It looked just like the scarf I'd seen MiShaun wearing that day in her office. If it was MiShaun's, what was it doing in the back of Pernell's Nissan?

The shock that was trying to set in was put off until later. Right now I had other things to do. "I need this picture and scarf."

"I need cover and back up. Nightlife said if I help you, you'll take care of me. You the man or not?"

I had enough to worry about without having bringing Beasley further into what I knew was going to be an explosive event. Still, I couldn't make Nightlife look bad either. A person's street rep, no matter what it is, happens to be their entrée in a lot of things otherwise left unstated. Nightlife had given his word on my character and I didn't need him mad at me too.

"Let me borrow that cell phone," I said.

He flipped it over to me and I punched in a number. On the third try, I remembered to hit the send button. On the fourth ring, Jeff answered.

•   •   •

Once I explained what was going on, Jeff knew why I called. He talked to Beasley in that matter-of-fact-take-it-or-get-out-of-my-face manner that our father had mastered to a tee.

It didn't take much convincing. Beasley knew his options were limited and I had to honor my agreement.

Beasley sat in the passenger's seat of Jeff's van while Jeff and I discussed my next move, not his.

"Too much stuff has been flying around this case. You sure you want to see it through?"

"Have to, Bro," I said. "The old man would roll over if he knew one of his sons left a job undone."

He nodded toward Beasley. "Once I get him set, I'm around for a while."

I nodded. "Hope this one works out better than ST."

"I'll give him the choice. It's up to him if he sees it through."

Jeff climbed into the driver's seat and I strolled around to where Beasley sat. "Anything I can do?"

"Yeah," he replied. "Get word to my momma. Tell her I'm alright." He pulled the cell phone from his pocket. "Here. You might as well keep this. Don't look like I'll be needing it for a while."

"Doesn't it belong to 'Nightlife?"

"He doesn't hang onto hot cell phones. Too easy to trace his movements."

An unanswered question popped in my head before I pulled away from the passenger door. "You familiar with a brother by the name of Roger Martin?"

He thought for a moment. "If you're talking about the one lying in a hospital dreaming of better days, then yeah, I heard of him. Word on the street is that some guy tried to run a tire track over his back."

"He had an unfortunate run-in. What have you heard on him?"

"He's been goin' for big time. Tryin' to convince people that he's a good shooter. I heard that he's done a few jobs. Mostly contract, where he could get it."

"A gun for hire?" I asked.

Beasley snorted. "Not anymore."

Jeff pulled away from the curb leaving me uncertain as to whether he was going to put Beasley on a bus or drive him all the way to his former colleague's transition home. I hoped Beasley had the good sense that escaped the late ST.

Now that my third straight late night was coming to an end, I drove back to my apartment with more pieces to the picture of an expanding puzzle. I wasn't sure if the borders were being stretched or the middle pieces were shrinking. I was in too deep to back out and unlike a contentious divorce case, the matter wouldn't be settled by an impartial judge. I had the task of bringing it to an end.

As I closed the door and clicked on the light, I caught a quick glance of someone just at the edge of my peripheral vision.

I turned quickly, shocked by the full view. "Malone?"

She sauntered out of the moonlit shadows of my bedroom wearing a red silk robe with an open V neckline that stopped just short of an unbearable tease. She wore her hair loosely draped down to her shoulders, accented by a sensually alluring perfume that I hoped was titled 'Here and Now'. Using the unexpected moment to her advantage, she wrapped both arms around my neck and planted a long, lingering kiss that smoldered my lips and singed my tongue.

We held that passion for several moments, allowing the dormant combustion to begin its slow boil. When our lips finally parted, she slowly pulled me toward the bedroom.

"Malone. I ..... "

"I don't want you to say a thing," she whispered as she placed a finger on my lips.

Realizing that I came close to talking myself out of a wonderful and much needed evening, I willingly gave in to the symphony she was about to orchestrate and she played me like the first violin with the Boston Pops.

With slow and deliberate pacing, Candy Malone seductively fought my instinctive attempts to rip my clothes off in one quick motion. Choosing instead to use her body to delicately massage and titillate those carnal parts of me awakened by the first kiss.

She removed every item I wore slowly and carefully, stopping in between pieces to both kiss and caress us into the bedroom. Wearing my birthday suit and a longing smile, she eased me down onto the bed, forcing me to watch as she stepped back and dropped her robe onto the floor.

I took in her fully disrobed figure, exhaling slowly so as not to choke.

She slid down next to me and if ever a symphony had a powerful and more pulsating crescendo, it took place in that bedroom. The buildup to the overture was a series of well timed strokes, plucks and harmonic pleas for an encore. The hour-long eternity ended with both of us ravaged and sweat-drenched, exorcised of those personal demons that live behind the wall of our insecurities.

The music we made deserved a joyous round of applause, only I was exhausted.

I wrapped myself around her until I heard the soft breathing that signaled the first phase of a needed sleep.

I rolled over, staring up at the ceiling. Malone hadn't explained this time together and I didn't ask. Maybe we both just needed the time to shut out the noise. Maybe in a world where human life is seen as a meaningless annoyance, we needed something real and something good.

I didn't know for sure. But until I brought this case to an end, the spirit that circled Deborah Norris's east-side grave would dog my soul until she could finally come to a rest.

That notion and Malone's warm body allowed me to sleep peacefully.

49

"Are you Lincoln Keller?" asked the pudgy faced man in a brown tweed jacket. Dribbles of sweat ran down the side of his combed-over-the-bald spot hair. He was a hard breather wearing brown penny loafers. He looked flushed for nine thirty in the morning.

He was standing outside my office door, leaning against the jamb wiping his forehead. I could smell the sweat stains from his shirt from the top step of the landing as I walked down the corridor to the office.

For a clear sky day, mild temperatures and my happy mood, he was not a pretty sight.

"If I say no, will you go away?" I was still reliving the previous night and the note Malone left as she tip toed out while I slept. 'And the flowers were a nice touch too!' she'd written.

"C'mon, buddy. I'm just doing a job here," he said, wheezing after each sentence.

I nodded and he gave me a very legal looking document and asked me to sign a piece of paper attached to a clipboard.

"You've been officially served," he said.

He turned and slow-walked down the hall. I waited to see if he was going to tumble down the steps, but each slow creak told me he was being deliberate in his movements.

Once inside, I unfolded the document and after glancing through the forewiths, heretofores, therebys, and aggrieved parties, I realized that I'd been served with a cease and desist document forbidding my having contact with any members of the organization known as 'Empower Detroit'. The order specified Trevor, Pernell, MiShaun, Tyler and even Helen. The official language also went on to say something about not being near the premises, not harassing other members of the organization and possibly owning my Nova. I especially liked the threat to have my investigators license revoked. These on-going attacks upon my ability to earn a living were humorous and tiring.

A high-powered law firm out of Bloomfield Hills had drawn up the document. There were enough odd sounding names listed at the top of the document to make a national spelling bee champion nervous enough to wet their pants.

I flipped through the pages until I came to the name of the aggrieved parties champion attorney. Clark Kindle had a masterfully messy signature. As I reached for the phone and began punching in some numbers, I pictured Clark Kindle with a high-pitched voice, a black pin strip suit and wearing lifts in the heels of his black wing tips.

When the female voice on the other end answered, I asked to speak to Judge Henderson.

He was already in court, as I suspected, but she assured me that she'd have him call as soon as he took a break.

The Stallings had taken their first shot. They were paper bullets from a high-powered legal chamber aimed at my ability to earn a living, but a shot is a shot is a shot, regardless of the type of gun. This was more than just firing a warning shot over the bow to get my attention, this was a cannonball descending at light speed on my poopdeck.

I liked a challenge.

There was no doubt that I'd forced their hand. When high profile people run to high profile law firms for help, it usually means there's something low down, dirty and reeking with a stench that they want to keep out of the high profile papers.

Since bribery and verbal threats hadn't taken me off the case, the next option had to be legal redress. I also knew if the legal system didn't stop a person from moving forward, then the next option would be something lethal.

"Thanks, boys," I said. "You just gave me a reason to keep digging."

I dropped the document on the desk and started thinking about my next move.

MiShaun was a weak link in this ever-tightening chain and possibly the key to breaking the whole thing open. My working theory had two more anchors in the ground and I needed for her to know.

After calling the hospital and being told that she'd already checked out, I tried her home number and after the fifteenth ring, figured she wasn't there or wasn't answering. I also wondered what happened to her answering machine.

I called her office, pretending I was an old friend from the neighborhood and was told that she was not available. Helen, though not enamored with MiShaun, still managed to protect her time and location, even after I said I was only in town for a minute.

Just as I was thinking through another option, the phone rang and the very judicial voice of Judge Zone boomed through the receiver. He didn't have time to exchange pleasantries so I told him I'd been served with a cease and desist order.

"I'll hold while you fax it over," he said. Fortunately Keller Investigations had invested in a seldom used and equally ugly looking fax machine, so after he told me the fax number I ran the document through and waited for his response. He didn't say anything while we waited and I felt no need to fill the void. Finally someone brought the faxed copy to him and I heard his brain churning as he flipped through the pages. "Very official, but pretty standard. I'm familiar with this law firm and Clark Kindle is a well paid windbag who probably had one of their law clerks draw up this document."

"But it's still quite legal," I said.

"Letter of the law perfect. So what did you do to invite the wrath of Kindle and company?"

I told him about my run-in with Pernell and Tyler as well as my meeting with Trevor during one of his photo-ops.

He sighed. "Mr. Keller, do you have something against just sleeping at night?"

"It's a skill I intend to master once I'm given the opportunity."

"Anything else?" he asked.

I didn't see a need to mention Jocelyn or Richard Beasley "Nothing that warrants your attention."

"You think the Stallings are involved?"

"I won't lie to you, Your Honor. I don't really know. But my investigation keeps leading me to their doorsteps. I consider it more than a coincidence. Beyond that, I'm not sure."

"So why not cease and desist?"

"To quote a famous philosopher, I can smell a draw play."

He snorted. "Where do you think its leading?"

"Right now, I don't know. But given your previous history with the Stallings, I felt it was best that you know. I'd like to keep digging, but you're the client. Things could get a little uncomfortable and I didn't want you and Mrs. Henderson blindsided. So its your call."

He didn't hesitate a beat. "Deborah's dead and somebody knows why. At this point in our lives and career there isn't too much anyone can do to us. So damn the conditions, Mr. Keller. Follow where the path leads and I'll run interference for you."

I thanked him and he rang off telling me to be careful.

Careful I thought. That's what drives people into accounting.

The manila folder containing information about Deborah's murder expanded with the addition of the legal document from the power seekers in Bloomfield Hills. Though it was an interesting distraction, it didn't take from the pattern that kept coming back to the door of Trevor and Pernell Stallings. Any first year law student could argue everything I had as 'circumstantial' and 'highly inconclusive'. I needed to start linking the pieces together in a way that logic could support and a defense lawyer couldn't break. So I retraced every piece of information I'd collected and spread them across my desk hoping that the picture in front of me would reveal its holes.

A half-hour later, I stepped back and looked at the linked pieces of information and came to one inescapable conclusion; there were enough holes in the chain of evidence to start a doughnut factory. If I saw the holes, so would any law school trained hole seeker.

I'd need another angle to pursue. The only thing that seemed to make sense was the silk scarf Beasley took from Pernell's missing Nissan. The initials 'ML', though not conclusive, were suggestive. All I needed to do was figure out how suggestive they were.

There was only one person who could answer that question.

Since I had nothing else to do, I decided against doing nothing. Investigators live by the credo 'when you reach a dead end, blow up something'.

On the way out, I stopped in and told Julie about the document I'd received.

"So where is it?" she asked impatiently.

"I left it in the office. Why?"

She popped her lips in that way that teachers do when exasperated by a child's inability to comprehend a simple fact. "Didn't we agree to modernize your file system? How am I suppose to scan the document in your newly created file if I don't have it here with me?

There would be no arguing the coming lecture. "Yes, we did and I meant to bring it over to you, which I will, when I return."

"Technology can add a form of efficiency to that chaos you and Jeff call an office."

I smiled, reached in my jacket pocket and took out the cell phone. When I showed it to her, she gasped.

"It's a good start, Linc. Who knows, maybe you'll move up from using an eight track tape player."

Even with a battle plan, I knew I couldn't win.

I locked up the office and headed to my car. I decided to stake out the 'Empower Detroit' offices again.

This was a time when luck would determine how successful I'd be.

50

I parked across from the 'Empower Detroit' building in the same parking lot and paid off the same sleepy-eyed attendant. It was easy to monitor the comings and goings of the people who worked there and I hoped no one spent time monitoring me.

It was sometime after one o'clock after I'd gone through the alphabet backwards for the fifth time that a blue and white Crown Victoria pulled into the parking lot, not flashing its blue, red and white lights, but looking just as menacing. The police cruiser pulled up behind me and I watched the bearded, ebony-toned officer and his glasses-wearing partner ease out of the car and slowly approach me from both sides.

He had the walk of a veteran; she couldn't have been more than two months out of the academy.

I'd already rolled down the window and kept my hands on the steering wheel as he angled his approach to make sure I wasn't hiding a weapon.

It was understandable.

None of us had ever worked in Mayberry.

He used a polite, even tone when he spoke. "Excuse me, Sir, but may I see some identification?"

My insurance certificate, driver's and laminated P.I licenses were already in my hand.

"What is this all about, Officer?" I asked, already knowing the answer.

He did the stone-face-silence act, common to most police training before giving a stony polite answer. "We received a complaint, Mr. Keller. Some folks wondering why you're sitting outside in this parking lot."

"I'm watching to see what my girlfriend bought me for Christmas."

He grunted and said he'd be right back.

While he walked to the patrol car, I glanced in the rear view mirror and watched his partner do the slow back step; eyes fixed on my every movement, her hands near her sides for easy access to her revolver.

"A little rough on her technique, but otherwise not bad," I said.

Being a former patrol officer, I knew exactly what they were doing and why they took so long. It's all part of the make them sweat game when officers make a routine stop. In this case, someone allegedly called to express concern about my sitting in a parking lot.

After a light year had gone by, he returned. His face was still stone and his partner worked on her approach-from-the-passenger-side technique.

"Mr. Keller, I can't officially order you to leave since this is a public parking lot."

"And I am paid up for the next few hours," I interrupted. "It only costs me the insurance on my first male child."

He stone faced it. "But it is my understanding that you do have a cease and desist order and you're to stay away from certain members of 'Empower Detroit'."

"Wow. Are your on board computers that updated? I thought you'd only get as far as my last known address."

"Maybe you should move along."

Realizing that he was only doing his job, I opted not to smart mouth it. "I will as soon as my paid time has run out."

"Have a good day, Mr. Keller," he deadpanned.

He strolled away and his partner did her slow back away routine.

"Needs a little more work," I mumbled.

So much for my stakeout. I knew that someone said something to somebody and one or both of the Stallings called the cops. They'd fired another warning shot.

Since the thing called luck hadn't worked well in that situation, maybe it would in another.

I wheeled out of the parking lot and zoomed along Third Avenue with the seeds of an idea. It was highly possible that I was approaching it from the wrong angle. Instead of staking out the 'Empower Detroit' building, I thought that I should stakeout the most likely place MiShaun would go.

Where would a recovering alcoholic who fell off the wagon and tried to kill herself go for comfort?

I pulled my cell phone out of my jacket and called Julie.

Julie had several things going, but still managed to take my call.

"Jules, I'd like another background check on MiShaun Lucas."

"Probably couldn't get to it until tomorrow." She paused. "Late tomorrow."

"Need it now, Jules. It won't take but a minute."

"Which is fifty-nine seconds longer than what I have available," she said with some irritation. "What do you need?" I told her and gave her the number to my newly acquired cell phone. "Before you get too comfortable with that thing, you'd better check to make sure its activation is legit."

There could be nothing legit about a cell phone given to Beasley by Nightlife that had found its way into my possession. I'd worry about activation stuff later.

Ten minutes later, as I was pulling into a local fast food joint, the phone buzzed. "Linc, I was able to find an address in town for an Ida Lucas. She's MiShaun's mother. Does that help?"

She read off the address. I thanked her and she reminded me that a bill was forthcoming.

Julie is always the persistent entrepreneur.

I bought a burger and soft drink, ate quickly and set out to meet Mrs. Ida Lucas. I hoped they were the kind of mother and daughter who at least talked to each other, even when talking is futile.

• • •

Pasadena is a tree-shaded street on Detroit's northwest side, composed almost entirely of brick two level homes, most with a large front and top porch. Ida Lucas lived in one of the few small, one-level homes, on a patched, bumpy street in desperate need of leveling.

I parked in front of the modest home with its barred windows and doors and followed the sidewalk up to her door.

"A prisoner in her home," I muttered. "Something got overlooked in the movement."

I pressed the doorbell and waited until I heard a strained voice ask, "Who's there?"

Yelling through a closed door, however uncomfortable, had become an acceptable form of communication in a society obsessed with safety and security.

Though I took great care to identify myself, it wasn't until the door actually creaked open that I caught a glimpse of the round-face woman whose raven tone, sunken red eyes and bleached blond hair reminded me of a 1940's cartoon character.

"Miss Ida Lucas?" I asked.

She gave me a hesitant nod.

I showed her my P.I. license. "I'm looking for MiShaun, Miss Lucas. Any chance she might be here?"

"She don't come round here no more." Her now raspy voice didn't mask the disappointment. "She's not here."

"I need to find her, Miss Lucas. She's not in any trouble. I just need to ask her a few questions."

"She's not here."

I needed to keep her talking because sometimes a person will let something slip. "Has she called recently?"

317

"No."

"Did you know about her accident?"

Miss Lucas open the door just wide enough to allow for her full look of surprise. "What accident?"

"She attempted suicide, Miss Lucas. She'd been in the hospital for a couple of days, but now she's checked out. No one seems to know where she went."

"Suicide!" she replied. "Why would she try to do that? Why? Is it just like last time?"

I heard the opening and callously moved in. "Yeah. Only this time it almost worked. We thought she'd gotten through it, but I guess we were wrong."

Miss Lucas shook her head. "That child is gonna be the death of me. I swear. I prayed she'd be better. Wasn't she better? She just don't listen to me. Never did. Child grew up too fast."

"Miss Lucas, we all thought she was better, but apparently not. I need to find her before something silly happens. Is there anything you can tell that would be helpful? I'd like to find her as soon as possible."

"I tried to help her. I tried. That child is too stubborn. Too good to spend time with her momma. I gave her life and she's been a living hell."

So I had her talking, but not saying anything I could use. "Do you have any idea where she might go? Friends, other family members, a church or anything like that?"

She stopped beating up on herself to think about the question. "Probably that no account boy she's been around all these years. I told her to stay away from married men, but she doesn't listen to me. I told her he'd be no good. Always promising to leave his wife and she fool enough to think that he would."

I didn't know if he was a no account boy, but Trevor was the only married one of the two Stallings. My apparent leap of intuition didn't sit well with the logic of the situation. So I pressed on.

"This man have a name?"

"I don't know his name. I just know that every time she's in trouble, she always go to him, not to me, but to him. She goes to him. That's probably where she is. Always following him, even when he left town, she still followed him. She'd meet him here and there. Always bragging about what he could do for her, but she never came to me. I'm the one that gave her life. I did. Me."

"Miss Lucas, did she ever show you a picture and talked about what he did? Any idea where he worked?"

She shook her head. "No. I just know that he was married and lived out of town. Then he came back. I remember her saying that it was nice to have him back. She helped ruin his marriage and she felt no shame about it. No shame at all."

I didn't want a long conversation with Mrs. Lucas, but she had given me something to think about. MiShaun has a friend with whom the relationship is more than just a passing notion and he's, if it is a he, currently divorced from his wife.

It smelled too much like someone who'd already lied by omission.

After I thanked Mrs. Lucas and assured her that she'd done the best job she could, I drove away wondering why Winston Hill, newly employed boyfriend of Sharron Westlake, kept surfacing during this investigation.

I didn't doubt that he'd have an answer.

I'd have to find him in order to ask the question.

51

After making a call to Sharron and her assuring me that she hadn't seen Winston since they celebrated his new job, I drove over to his residence, fully expecting him not to be home. After all, the man was supposedly employed now.

But since I'm too dumb to have confirmed whether or not he was home by making a simple phone call, it seemed to me that actually ringing his doorbell would tell me a lot more than an unanswered phone.

It did.

He reluctantly answered the door. Actually, half opened the door, signaling that I wasn't invited in. That was twice in less than an hour. A lesser person may have taken it personal.

"Hey, Winston. How goes the new job?"

"Fine," he said with no conviction. "What do you want?"

Since he was going for straight forward, I was happy to oblige. "MiShaun Lucas. She's here, isn't she?"

"Now, why would she be here?" he replied.

He quickly changed from the straightforward approach. "You already know the answer to that question. I'd like to talk to her."

"She isn't here," he said angrily. He stepped back and quickly closed the door.

My foot was already in the door and the jamb, so, when the door bounced off my shoe, he looked angrier. "Look, man ..... "

I pushed the door open, causing him to spin away as I stepped in and quickly surveyed the area.

"Son of a ..... " He stopped, caught in his own anger. "You get the
....."

"Now, now, Winston. No need to get nasty. You've been feeding
me nothing but crap since the first time we talked. I gave you the benefit
of the doubt, but the last couple of times have really shown your lying
nature. So, don't go for bad right now. Go get MiShaun. You and I both
know she's here."

"Look. I told you ..... "

"Nothing worth believing," I said. "Now, where is she?"

MiShaun stepped from an area next to the kitchen, dressed in a red
and green running outfit and pointing a small handgun. Her gaze was
steady, though her gun hand trembled.

"MiShaun!" Winston yelled. "What are you doing? I told you to let
me handle it."

I stopped in my tracks and flashed my best I'm-not-nervous-smile.
"Hello, MiShaun."

"How'd you know where to find me?" she asked.

"Your mother says 'hello'. She sends her regards," I said.

"How would she know?"

"Your mother may be confused, but she's not stupid. She has listened to some of the things you've told her. You should try it sometime."

Winston eased toward MiShaun. "Put that gun down, baby. He
doesn't know anything."

"Then why does he keep bothering me? Why am I seeing so much
of him lately? Why can't I sleep at night now that he's been to see me?"

"It's the Keller charm," I said. "You'd be surprised as to how many
people have sat up wondering what to do about it."

"Give me that gun, MiShaun. I can't help you like this," Winston
said as he walked slowly toward her. "I told you I'd help you, but not like
this. Whatever is going on here, I'm sure we can get through it. So give
me the gun."

"NO!" she screamed. "NO. He wouldn't be here if he didn't know. I can't go back to the way it was."

"You won't," Winston said. "I promise." He turned toward me and asked, "What do you want with her, Keller?"

"Should I tell him, MiShaun? Or will you do the honors?"

"There's nothing to tell," she screamed again.

The silence hung between us like a helium-filled balloon about to explode.

I finally broke the silence. "She hasn't told you about her being a witness to a double homicide."

"What?" Winston said disbelievingly.

I noticed her eyes starting to water. The gun hand shook a little more.

"It was an accident," she finally sobbed. "An accident. It wasn't supposed to happen. It was an accident."

"Two people died, MiShaun. You know it, I know it and ..... " I said dragging out the moment; "Deborah knew it."

What happened next would have made a nice slow motion segment on the six million-dollar man, only it happened much faster, in real time.

"NOOOOOO!" MiShaun yelled in a voice that echoed from deep within her soul. She then swung the gun around and aimed it directly between her eyes. Winston sprung toward her yelling for her to stop. I ran also ran toward her, my hand outstretched to try and grab the gun before she could pull the trigger. Winston and I would have collided if not for the fact that our sudden out-burst startled her just long enough for me to grab her wrist and pull the gun away, aiming it at the floor. Winston reached out with both arms and grabbed MiShaun around the waist, lifting her up as the gun finally dislodged from her hand.

"No! Don't do this to yourself," he yelled, pulling her over to a three-pillow couch. I kicked the gun away and turned around just as they both plopped down. Winston kept both arms around her and then began stroking her head as years of pent up anger or fear burst through in cascading tears.

"Not like this," he kept saying as he held her firmly and rocked gently. "It's going to be all right. We all miss her, baby. We all miss her."

I took in the scene of MiShaun and Winston, not quite convinced as to who was comforting whom. They were two people beaten up by the memories of a friend whose death forced them to face the one thing they couldn't acknowledge during her life. He rocked and stroked her head, while I picked up the gun. Though it was only a .22, a bullet taken that close would have been fatal. While they murmured to one another, I flipped open the cylinder and emptied the bullets into my hand. I checked the chamber, placed the bullets in my pocket and set the gun on the table.

No sense it taking any chances, I rationalized.

I slowly walked over to where they sat. Winston looked up, unconcerned about the tears that now trickled down his cheek.

"How about the truth now, Winston? What's really been going on all this time?"

He paused, shook his head and after years of holding in all in, he let me hear the truth as it sounded from a man who shielded his life in lies.

Most of what he said, I'd already suspected. There'd been no affair with Deborah. There had been a relationship, but not as he originally told the story. The real thing had been with MiShaun. They were the ones who did the playful sneaking around. After he was transferred, he and MiShaun met on several occasions for unbridled fun, minus the emotional involvement. After he finally divorced, he and MiShaun drifted apart, she started moving up in 'Empower Detroit', while he moved along trying to find his groove. When he finally returned to Detroit, MiShaun was hanging out with Detroit's power brokers, running with the Stallings and getting closer to Detroit's inner circle.

"But I knew something was up," he said. "It's like her whole manner changed. I assumed it had something to do with Deborah's death. I knew she'd stopped drinking and was trying to clean up her life, which I knew was good ..... " He stopped and lifted her chin and looked into her eyes. "But it was almost like she stopped living. The zest that made her so much fun was replaced with a hardness I didn't recognize."

"How'd you managed to keep Sharron and MiShaun from crossing paths?" I asked, knowing he caught my drift.

"They weren't speaking anyway, so I never brought it up. Besides, MiShaun and I weren't involved like we once were and Sharron was pretty needy."

I curled a lip.

"Yeah, I know," he said. "I was feeling pretty needy too. Sharron and I just hit it off. I was back and still a little down on my luck and we had our previous friendship through Deborah."

"Did Deborah know about you and MiShaun?"

"Naw. She never caught on," he replied.

Wrong. She never let on, I thought to myself.

I eased over and sat down next to MiShaun. Her crying had stopped somewhat and as rotten as it made me feel, I had to have answers. "MiShaun, tell me about the accident. What happened that night?"

She turned around, eyes red and starting to swell. "I ..... I ..... "

"I think I can place you at the scene and most likely I know who was driving the car." I pulled the scarf out of my jacket pocket and showed it to her. Her eyes widened as she raised a hand to touch a long forgotten memory.

"Where'd you get this?" she asked.

"It was found in the back of a car, specifically a Nissan, in which you were a passenger. And I think Pernell Stallings was the driver."

She hesitated and leaned back into Winston. Her posture and composure softened, as she seemed to search her memory for something to say.

"I think that during one of your wild nights on the town, you met up with Pernell," I continued. "I think that you two danced, drank a little, maybe a lot, and he decided to take you for a ride in his car. I think he wanted to impress you with his driving skills on backroads. I think that sometime during that night, he went streaming down a road in Mount Clemens, lights off and tires spinning and somehow, probably accidentally, caused a car to run off the road and crash into an embankment. He never stopped to see what happened and the only witness is, at best, unreliable. So, that leaves you, MiShaun. You're the only other witness to an accident that took the lives two innocent teenagers on their way home from their prom."

"Hey, Keller, ease up, man. You don't have to ..... "

"Don't interrupt, Winston. I haven't said a single thing that she's denied."

MiShaun waited and so did I. She finally broke the silence. "I wasn't as pretty back then. If it wasn't for the fact that he'd had a few drinks, he might not have ever invited me to go with him. I was such a willing fool back then. I recognized him right from the beginning. I'd seen pictures of him and his brother in some of the Detroit papers. It seemed like a good opportunity to know someone important. So he drank and pretended I was pretty and I drank and pretended not to mind."

"MiShaun," Winston interrupted.

"Let her tell it, man," I said, trying not to sound irritated.

MiShaun gently patted Winston on his knee. "It's okay. I don't mind. Most of that night is still a blur. I do remember hearing a car swerve and the next thing I knew I was knocking on Deborah's door. I guess I bumped my head and got a few scratches when he turned too fast to keep from hitting the car. I'm not sure what happened after that." She leaned forward and touched the scarf. "I always wondered what happened to my scarf. I hoped I'd left it at the club and someone just walked away with it. Yet, somehow I knew it would show up again one day. I don't know why I knew, but I did."

She leaned back into Winston, turning her head toward his chest. He held her tightly and glared at me.

Any other time I might have cared.

But not this time.

What I heard answered a lot of questions, but none of it would stand up in a court of law. All the evidence was too circumstantial and with no solid proof, it would come down to MiShaun's word against Pernell's. I already knew the jeopardy in that mix. I had a picture of his car being stripped by some now dead car jackers and the testimony of a man who'd been in hiding for a few years, whose whereabouts were known only to Jeff and his network of unknown accomplices.

What I had wouldn't hold water in a steel mug. That much I knew.

As Winston rocked MiShaun and spoke comforting words, I considered what I had to do before taking leave of this party.

I glanced at Winston. "Did you know about this?"

He hesitated a moment before answering. "Yeah. MiShaun told me what went down." He paused and said with a dismissive tone. "It's not like she could have done anything for those two kids. They were already dead. There was nothing she could do to bring them back."

"What's that suppose to mean?"

"It means don't rock the boat. Those two kid's deaths were unfortunate, but at least she got something out of the deal. MiShaun got the leverage she needed. That's what it takes, you know. You need leverage in order to stay ahead, stay employed and to stay in the game."

"Murder isn't a game, Winston," I said inching forward.

"Everything's a game and the only true winners have the leverage they need to play."

I didn't feel a need to argue metaphysical ideas with him, so I decided to shift the discussion. "Did either of you kill Deborah?" I asked, assuming I already knew the answer.

Winston was incredulous while MiShaun just shook her head. "How can you ask such a stupid question?" Winston said through clenched teeth. "I ought to ..... "

"You ought to sit there and answer the question," I said. "Did either

326

of you kill Deborah?"

"Why would either of us do something like that?" Winston fired back.

"Everybody loved Deborah," MiShaun said. "Especially us. She was our friend. A good friend. They didn't make them any better than Deb."

Apparently there was at least one person who didn't love Deborah, but I let that point slide by.

"And the answer to my question is .....?" I continued.

"No. Neither one of us could have killed Deborah," Winston said. "Now, take you and your stupid accusations out of here right now!"

I didn't mind his anger, in fact it told me a lot more about the truth than he'd care to admit. I couldn't think of a motive for either one and most likely a motive didn't exist that fit. So I was left with one last approach. A highly risky one, but I saw no other choice.

Sensing that there was little else I could do for the moment, I gazed at MiShaun and tried not to sound like a complete jerk. "MiShaun, I can't tell you what to do at this point. All I have is a scarf that was given to me by someone a defense lawyer would love to rip to shreds and what you've told me. All of which can be denied. And Winston can attest to the fact that you said nothing of the sort. It does explain how you attained such a lofty position with 'Empower Detroit' when there are so many more people with credentials and experience stronger than yours. Trevor would have never considered you for that job if you didn't have something on his brother. I doubt if he would have given you a second look."

"I've done well in that job," MiShaun said, her voice quivered with intensity.

"Not mine to measure," I said. "What I do know is you and Tyler have been milking a gravy train and normally I wouldn't give it much thought, if any at all. However, here's something for you to think about; two kids named Morris and Daphne left home eight years ago headed to their high school prom and neither returned home. Their lives were cut short and I believe it's connected to Deborah's death. I will prove it. That much you can count on. Now, I'm no priest and have sinned on more than a convenient occasion, so I have no moral judgements to throw your way. You work that through your own conscious."

I stood up, walked to the door and turned around. "But eight years ago, your friend Deborah set out to find out what happened and never got to finish the investigation. Well, half of the story has been solved, but I won't rest until it's all been brought together. Because for all the questions you've answered there's still more looming on the horizon which I don't believe either of you can answer." I put my hand on the doorknob and added; "We still don't know who killed Deborah and why." I pulled the door open and said in my most firm voice. "But I'm damn sure going to find out."

I walked back to my Nova with one thought running through my head.

"Pernell Stallings," I said. "Give your soul to the devil, because the rest belongs to me."

52

Mary, Julie's secretary, after laughing at another one of my classic come backs to her frequently annoying question of 'how's the dick business?' gladly went along with my ruse. Using her most sexy voice, which admittedly wouldn't have gotten her employment with one of those 1-800- hot lines, was still convincing enough to Helen who said emphatically that Pernell had left for the day and wouldn't return. She agreed to take a message.

"Tell him ..... ," Mary cooed drippingly. "Tell him ..... 'Feathers' called. He'll know who it is."

I could see Helen's eyes rolling on the other end of the phone.

"Now what?" Mary asked, eyes beaming in anticipation as she returned the phone to its cradle.

"Don't quit your day job, Kid," I replied in my best Bogart impersonation.

She giggled. "That was fun." She giggled again.

Gigglers are a stand-up comic's best source of support and acknowledgement that their material needs work. Fortunately, private investigators don't have an on-going need for gigglers.

I strolled back to my office, opened the far window and checked for messages. The first two were for Jeff. Someone had missed their court appearance and he was needed to insure the person's safe and timely return. The third call was for me. A male voice calling from a phone kiosk I concluded that as the sound of traffic sped by in the background.

"Lincoln Keller, there's a phone list I'm supposed to give to you. I'll

329

leave you a number where I can be reached." I noted that the call came in during the typical lunch hour around the city and the phone number was minus the area code. The caller apparently worked for the Detroit Police department and was doing Malone a favor. I checked the time and saw it was after the shift change, so whoever had called was gone for the day and most likely at home or at the number he'd left.

I punched in the number and the same voice answered after the second ring.

"I'm Lincoln Keller. You mentioned something about a list of phone numbers."

"Yeah. I got a copy for you right here. Malone said I'm to get this list to you."

"When and where?" I asked.

"I won't be too busy for a while. Why don't you come on by."

I jotted down his address. The number and street I recognized as being on Detroit's southwest side. "Sounds like a home address," I said.

"It is. It's my home address," he replied matter-of-factly. "When should I expect you?"

"Within the hour."

I was a little surprised that he wanted to meet at such an open location like his home, but being in the sneaky business tends to make one a little more paranoid than the average nosey neighbor.

The drive to the southeast would be an easy shot from the Lodge Freeway, so I took a few minutes to write down everything that had transpired that day. I became more and more concerned about the details of what I'd learned.

Facts and motives are what drive an investigation and give it a shape and direction. I had an increasing number of facts and only a few motives that might fit, but the fit was a size eleven and I wore a size twelve. The hand-written information on the yellow legal pad in combination with everything that Julie had now put on her computer was probably showing me the face of Deborah's killer in complete tone and detail.

So why the hell couldn't I see it?

I closed up the office, gave the current information to Mary to give to Julie and fired up the engine to my Nova. Driving, sometimes, is a helpful form of mental relaxation. Often times, if the physical part of driving is a rote exercise, then the rest is a mental opportunity to play with facts and figures. There were times during my days as a football player when the long plane ride from New York to Oakland allowed for plenty of time to dissect the factors that contributed to a victory or defeat. That mental exercise sometimes generated the insight needed for the next opponent. It was one of those routines that had come to serve me well as a football player and a cop.

Of course, as a football player and a cop in Oakland, I rarely had to contend with the ongoing, seasonally irritating work of the Michigan road crews. The long line of single lane traffic from the Lodge to I-75 south narrowed down my mental exercise options.

The only prevailing notion was try not to rear end the car in front of me.

•　　•　　•

Detroit's southwest side is rarely touted as a culturally diverse area where whites, blacks and browns shared living space with a tolerant under-standing of their economic cradle. Over the years, it always struck me as odd how other large cities like Chicago played up their ethnic diversity as part of what made them such a thriving city, yet in Detroit, it seemed we only talked about our Mexican-American population when there was teenage gang activity.

I guess Dickens was right; it was a tale of two cities.

The address I located was part of a gray-painted, brick two-family flat on Cadillac Street. The residential street, with parking on both sides, looked like the last reminder of a time when neighborhoods were places where fathers went to work, mothers stayed home and the elderly sat on the front porch watching the children play in the street and the neighbors play with their lives.

After finding a parking spot, I locked my 'Club' in place and walked back toward the house.

The wooden steps and wrought iron support columns represented early and post modern architecture that came together in an attempt at preservation.

I rapped on the aluminum screen door and waited several moments. When the door opened, a slender framed man of average height greeted me. His ebony straight hair was cropped short and I could immediately tell that there was a real story behind those deep set brown eyes.

"I'm Lincoln Keller," I said in front of the still closed front door.

"Ramon Gutierrez," he said opening a door and extending his hand. "Come on in."

He lived in a modest home, the furnishings being just good enough to give the impression that he'd moved beyond functional living, but not much. The room had that lived-in, bachelor look consistent with his late twenties manner.

"Have a seat," he said pointing to a cushioned armchair. "Can I bring you something to drink?"

"Whatever's easy," I said.

On the way to the back, he said. "That manila envelope has what you need."

I nodded my thanks and proceeded to empty its contents.

The gray-copied printout had a list of phone numbers that went out and came in to Deborah's home several days prior to her death. Every phone number was underlined, check marked and given some obscure coded abbreviation by Knackton. He'd also signed the bottom.

I had to admit the man was thorough.

"Find anything in that list?" Ramon asked when he returned holding two cans of light beer.

"Nothing that makes sense just yet, but I'll check later," I said. He handed me the beer and sat down on a matching couch. "I appreciate your help."

He waved dismissively. "Forget it. There's nothing I wouldn't do for Malone. Working in records gives me access to most everything and everyone who generated a record with Detroit's finest."

"She's a good detective."

"She's a tough one, I'll tell you that. But very fair. She took a chance on me years ago, and now I'm working in Administration for the Detroit Police Department and not laying on a slab in its morgue." He sipped from his beer. "I came to her as a wayward youth during her days as a patrol officer. I'd gotten into trouble. Riding around with the wrong group at the wrong time. You know the story."

I'd heard it, and seen it, during my years as a cop. Contrary to what is really known, there are more circumstances of people being in the wrong place at the wrong time than one can imagine.

He continued. "After a thorough grilling from her and some plea bargaining, I was released and told to find something better to do with my life. When I applied to the academy, I was all set to explain what happened, but for some reason it never came up. I figured I'd gotten lucky. After I put in my time on the streets, I applied for, and got, into Administration. One day I was curious as to what was written on my record, but I couldn't find it. So I tracked down my defense attorney, who now works for a firm downtown, and after jogging his memory, told me that Malone argued for a complete purge of my files. It was like it never happened. I knew one day I'd be able to thank her for her faith in me. So, when she called there was no question as to what I'd do."

"Well, I'll try to make good on the risk you took to get this information."

"Anytime."

We sipped our beers and traded a few cop stories, as cops are inclined to do. I thanked him again and he insisted that it was no big deal.

"Maybe if I ever have need for a P.I ..... ," he said with a grin.

I gave him my card. "Make sure I'm the first one you call."

Though Knackton had done the majority of the work, I believed his abbreviations were really the initials of people whom he'd contacted. The meanings were clear in his head, but wouldn't make sense to me unless he explained it to me.

I didn't think he'd be open to that conversational interaction between us.

Using my still illegally activated cell phone, I called Julie and asked if there was anyway she could pull together all the information I gathered into some kind of order.

"What kind of order, Mister Technically Disabled?" she asked.

"Names and matching addresses."

"Alphabetized?"

"That would help," I said. "How long will it take?"

"It's done," she said. "I'll slide the printout under your door."

"That was fast."

"Try paying my bill that way."

I placed the cell phone on the passenger seat and thought through a few other things I had in mind before returning to the office to begin matching phone numbers with abbreviations. I had no doubt that a few of the names and numbers were no longer relevant, but for those that were, it would mean getting a little closer to the truth.

Streams of thoughts whirled through my head as I motored back onto I-75. I knew I was guilty of the first rule of investigation; I hadn't checked my assumptions at the door. They were sitting in my lap helping me steer the Nova. Now that MiShaun told me what I needed to know about the Morris and Daphne accident, and I knew that it was something Deborah decided to investigate, I wondered if I could make the leap that Pernell Stallings was, at least, responsible for Deborah's death.

"It's a leap," I mumbled. "No hard evidence and the word of a former heavy drinker against the word of a man whose brother covets the Mayor's seat."

I wondered if a possible barrier to the Hizzoner's office would be motivation enough to compel someone to take a life.

I knew that politics made for strange bedfellows and, if given a chance, even a religious fanatic would compromise on morality to achieve immortality.

It's what makes people of diametrically opposite orientations find common ground in order to advance their purpose ..... or career.

In the middle of my speculations an unfamiliar tone echoed from the cell phone. Obviously someone was trying to reach me, but I didn't know who had the number.

"Yeah?" I said.

"So, where is he?" asked the familiar voice on the other end.

"Which he are you referring to, Nightlife?" I asked.

"Don't get cute, Keller. I arranged a meeting for you and now the man can't be found. You ice him?"

"No. No reason to."

"Where is he?"

Nightlife was a stickler for details, especially if he thought someone owed him something. "He's safely out of your hair, mine and everyone else who needs relief." I paused. "It's nothing that will come back to haunt you."

"And I believe you because ..... ?"

"Because I said so."

After he let that statement spin around in his head, I said, "You want your cell phone returned?"

He laughed. "Why? I have others. This squares us for now, Keller."

"I consider the relationship squared."

Although I knew it wasn't over. Squared maybe, but not over.

53

I drove back to the office, picked up the printout Julie had slipped under the door and started comparing phone numbers with names and locations.

In the month before her death, Deborah had made, and received, forty-three phone calls, mostly calls going out. Knackton had underlined all the outgoing calls and circled the calls that came in. I immediately eliminated the seven incoming calls that were initialed SH figuring those were from Sylvia as well as the six outgoing calls to the same number. Now down to thirty calls, I checked for other patterns. Mishaun had called six times and Sharron had called four times. Deborah returned three of Mishaun's calls and two of Sharron's. That elimination brought the number down to fifteen calls. Knackton noted a couple of calls from people trying to sell a service and I'm sure he checked both calls thoroughly. I still had thirteen calls to consider.

There were two calls made to people at newspapers, which he noted, and one call made from a photography studio and two calls returned to that number.

"Probably making the arrangements to pick up her pictures," I muttered. Not knowing if it would lead anywhere, I jotted the number on a sheet of paper.

Two days before her death, Deborah had called a number that was initialed JH. It was the city Prosecutor's office where JH, Judge Henderson had worked as an Assistant Prosecutor. She also called a number in New Orleans. I punched in that number and a woman with a thick bayou accent answered. I told her I was trying to reach my Uncle in New Orleans and if he was still at this number.

She assured me, with limited patience, that my Uncle couldn't be at that number since she'd had the number for six years now.

"You're not much of a nephew if you haven't talked to your Uncle in six years," she said and disconnected the line.

Six calls to go and nothing seemed to jump out at me. There was one phone call made to a dry cleaners, another to a clothing store, one call to a retail store and another to a restaurant.

The day before she was killed, Deborah received a phone call that was initialed GS and the day she died, she made one phone call to a camera shop.

The realization that it was the last recorded phone call of Deborah Norris was quite a sobering moment. Part of me wanted to stop and get angry with someone, anyone, who'd allow something like this to happen to someone with the world in front of her. The unfairness of life's imbalances continues to amaze me somehow. Deborah Norris, in her own way, was trying to do something good in the world and she's taken out at a young, contributing age and some of the most evil people I've ever encountered will live to a ripe, hateful old age.

Life's unfairness stinks sometimes.

The voice of Reynolds Keller, family patriarch echoed in the vast regions of my mind.

"Life is rarely fair, it just is and nothing more, so just do the best you can, Son."

Right, Dad. The best I can do is find out what happened to Deborah.

I checked the names on the printout against the GS initial. None of the names matched, so I punched in the number on the slight chance that it might lead somewhere.

After two rings, an automated voice told me that the area code had changed and to try again.

Of course I'd been lulled into thinking that all of Deborah's calls still fell within the 313 area code. The phone companies had been reassigning area codes all over the country since Deborah's death.

The new area code had to be 810 or 248, so I tried 248.

The number rang several times before an exasperated male voice answered.

I apologized to him saying I thought I'd called the funeral home where my recently deceased grand aunt had been taken.

The man's voice lightened. "No, Sir. You called the wrong number.

"I'm a little distraught," I said. "Exactly where have I called?"

"A pay phone at Anthony's Service Station in Southfield."

I paused. "Oh. How long has this been the number at that pay phone?"

"It's been here for the ten years that I've owned the place," he said as an engine roared in the background.

"Where is the station located?" I pressed on still trying to sound distraught.

"Corner of Thirteen Mile Road and Southfield."

"You're Anthony?"

"Last time I checked," he said and hung up.

GS meant gas station to those of us still use to calling liquid detergent, soap powder.

"Who called Deborah from a gas station in Southfield?"

I hate intuitive leaps. There were too many factors to consider in asking that question. People use pay phones all the time for all kinds of reasons. Eight years ago, cell phones hadn't enjoyed the raging popularity so evident now. Sure they were around and growing in popularity, but not like eight years ago. Hell, if not for the cell phone given to me by Beasley, I'd still be using pay phones when in between spots.

So why call Deborah from a pay phone? And who called?

I mentally pictured Southfield Road and its congested two-lane, end of the day nightmare. I saw the red brick, one- and two-level office buildings, the annoyingly long stop lights from Ten Mile Road onward.

There was the collection of strip malls and eating establishments along the way, both fast food and real dining. I mentally pictured the drive, crossing Eleven Mile Road and the I-696 overpass, down past the apartment complexes and a little known trailer park just past Twelve Mile Road. Once I visualized some more fast food places, I came to rest at the corner of Thirteen Mile Road and Southfield. I saw Anthony's Service Station on the northwest corner and a competitor service station just across the street. On the southeast corner was a strip mall of shops and food places and across from it a Borders bookstore.

The store's image sat easily on the front of my mind since it was just down the street from Jocelyn Kilgore.

54

I sat and considered the possibilities. There was a connection between Jocelyn and Pernell Stallings. A long connection based on the ups and downs of a relationship that hadn't found a satisfactory end point. But how that connection translated back to Deborah and whether or not it was linked to an obscure phone number to a pay phone in Southfield .....

The longer one stays around and pays attention to the everyday going ons in the world, there is a bit of wisdom that finds its way into your head, irrespective as to whether or not you're worthy of that wisdom. If you see enough, live long enough and remember what you've learned then leaps of intuitive faith become pretty commonplace and the accuracy rate increases.

As much as I tried to stay with the logic, the leap kept . . . well leaping out at me. My natural inclination is to hold intuition under a skeptical microscope and go with the facts. I hadn't seen enough to know for sure, but it seemed to me that intuitive leaps were accurate about one third of the time. Being wrong two thirds of the time is okay in baseball, but if you're throwing a football or shooting a basketball, that kind of percentage would not earn you a spot in the starting line up. I had to decide if this intuitive leap was accurate for being at bat in baseball or if its another brick shot bouncing off the front of the basketball rim.

I picked up the phone and punched in Julie's direct line. When she answered I immediately apologized since she doesn't want anyone calling her on the direct line unless it's one of her daughters.

"Sorry Jules, but this couldn't wait."

"I grant one forgiveness a year to people other than my daughters, Linc and you just burned yours. Now what is it?"

I told her I needed information on when Jocelyn purchased her home and anyplace she lived prior to that purchase. Julie jotted down the address and phone number and said she'd look into a few databases and get back with me.

While waiting for the information, I also went through the list of names of the people I'd encountered on this case. Sometimes the connections between people are so subtle and so discreet that it requires laser surgical technology to spot the gray lines and in other cases you can get your eyes poked out from staring at the obvious. As this case was taking shape, it seemed as if my eyes were being poked out with a surgical laser instrument.

The phone rang, bringing an end to my speculations.

I answered assuming it was someone looking for Jeff; "Keller Investigations, Lincoln Keller speaking."

"A most neglectful species you Kellers. Inviting an old ladies attention and then leaving her for the first young thing with bottle-shaped hips."

"Lady Flame," I said recognizing the two pack a day baritone. "Any neglect is due to unrelenting work, not unwelcome distractions. How you doin'?"

"Nights are when I'm at my best. It's the days that bring me grief."

"How can I lessen a grief filled day?"

"Don't be so neglectful in the future." She paused. "I heard about you and Truman's adventure after you left here. You two boys all right?"

"Kellers are like the truth; hard to kill."

She laughed. "Listen, someone I know is willing to talk to you about our friend Pernell Stallings. Interested?"

"You have my undivided attention."

She told me about Linda Green and gave me her phone number.

Linda worked for her a few years ago. "She's a good person. Usually worked to earn extra money while going to school. She really has her life together now. She fell in with Pernell for a while, but was smart enough to get out before she got in too deep."

"She willing to talk with me?"

"As long as you don't neglect me in the future young man."

"I'll sign it in blood," I said. I would.

Lady Flame had an infectious laugh that complimented her I've-seen-it-all-wisdom. After she rang off, I punched in Linda's phone number, waited through the three rings and into the answering machine.

I was half way into my message when she picked up.

"Hello, Miss Green. My name is Lincoln Keller and Lady Flame suggested that I contact you."

"Yeah. She told me. You want to talk about Pernell right?"

"Well I was hoping you'd want to talk about him."

"Normally I wouldn't waste my time, but for Lady Flame, I'll make an exception."

"Well, if you have a few minutes ..... "

"Not now. I just ran in from work to check on a few things. I'm headed back. But if you want to meet me at my job, come on by."

"I wouldn't want to mess with your work hours."

"Not a problem. I'm the Community Relations Coordinator at the Barnes and Noble in Grosse Pointe. We're located on Mack and Alden road. When you come in, just ask for the CRC and they'll page me."

I told her I'd be there in about forty-five minutes.

I hoped I wasn't in for another sad story of true love wiped out by false expectations. Those stories get to be pretty routine and pretty old in the P.I.business. It was one of the reasons why I tried to steer clear of those kinds of cases. However, the Lady Flame thought Linda's experience with Pernell might be helpful to my case, so I decided not to question her judgement.

The complicated pieces of this were magnetized and slowly being drawn to each other, giving the picture a shape and form. In the end, I hoped the picture made sense.

Realizing that Julie was a busy person and would get back with me when she could, I locked up the office and decided to make the drive over to meet Linda Green.

• • •

The parking lot of the mini mall with the large green and white Barnes and Noble letters over the archway leading into the bookstore was bustling with afternoon traffic. The stores reside close to the line that separates Detroit from the more established suburb known as Grosse Pointe.

Inside the mall were a couple of fast food places, a clothing store and a coffee shop. I followed the tile-covered floor to a side opening that led into the bookstore. I stood between the checkout area and the information desk, taking in the shelves of books and the number of people milling about in search of something to read.

There was a small information counter where a brown-haired woman in her early twenties was staring at a computer screen and talking on the phone.

She made a courteous comment, thanked the person for calling and hung up. We made immediate contact as she flashed a radiant smile and asked if she could help me.

After hearing my request, she smiled, picked up the phone and paged Linda on the store's loudspeaker.

It was a short wait before Linda turned the corner after coming up one of the aisles. As she approached, I understood Pernell's attraction.

She is a little shorter than medium height, nut brown tone and eyes that would have convinced Romeo to have a 'just friend' relationship with Juliet. She wore dark blue pants, a yellow collarless blouse and sweater and low-heeled dark blue pumps.

"I'm Linda Green," she said extending a manicured hand with crimson colored fingernails.

"Lincoln Keller," I said.

She smiled. "Your timing is good, Mr. Keller. I have a few minutes, but we are preparing for an author signing tonight.

"Anyone I know?"

"Actually its three female authors who write mysteries. Penny Mickelbury, Barbary Neely and Lisa Saxton. Sound familiar?"

"I'm pretty sure I've seen their books on my brother's bookshelf. He's a big mystery fan. I'm too busy living the life to read about what I'm doing."

She motioned toward a fast food pizza place just down the hall. "C'mon, let's grab a bite over there."

After ordering a thin slice of pizza and soft drinks, we slid into a booth by a window and watched as a group of women from the adjacent hospital filed past.

"Book club month," she said as she smiled at the group. "They love our discounts."

"So, how'd a nice girl like you end up with a jerk like Pernell?"

She arched an eyebrow. "Well, I see he isn't number one on your list of people with whom I'd like to be stranded on an island."

"Actually, he is. What an opportunity to inflict a daily dose of mental abuse."

She bit into her pizza. "Oh, he's not so bad. Cute in an annoying little brother kind of way. Too dependent on his brother's limelight and a little too wild for my way of living."

"But you two were involved for a while."

She wiped the corner of her mouth. "Involved. That's a nice way of saying we tried hanging together even though our tastes ran opposite of each other."

Linda went on to explain that she'd met Pernell at a book signing party for a local author who was a friend of Trevor's. She'd gone just to support the author and because she had some free time on her hands during a semester break. She'd been working full time at a bookstore in downtown Detroit, taking classes at Wayne State University toward her Bachelor of Arts degree and looking for opportunities that would keep her involved in the book world.

"I love books," she said. "There is so much you can learn through other people's words and experiences. It seems to me, we don't do enough to promote the work of authors. Books are another form of entertainment, equal to music, dance, artwork and videos. It's a more passive form, but just as enriching."

I listened to the digression knowing it's part of the interviewing process. She went on for a few more beats before she stopped, paused and smiled.

"Sorry. It seems I can't stay off that soapbox."

"It's alright. At least your soapbox has some merit."

She sipped her cola. "I broke up with Pernell about a year and a half ago. The reasons were too numerous to mention, but they all had a name. I didn't mind so much, since I didn't think we were really going anywhere. I think I was in it for the fun."

"When did the fun end?" I asked.

"When the phone calls began. It started with someone calling and then hanging up, from there it progressed to threats. This woman claimed to know where I worked, where I lived and knew how to reach me. I even went with an unlisted number and two days later, the calls started again. Finally, I decided it wasn't worth it. I told Pernell one of his lady friends was giving me too much grief, so I ended the relationship. It didn't seem to break his heart, but I started getting some sleep at night."

"You're sure it was one of his girlfriends?" I asked.

"No doubt," she said. "During one phone call, she described in explicit detail the nature of their lovemaking, complete with a description of his clutch and speed capability...if you catch my drift.'

"What kinds of threats did she make to you?"

"Only the kind a sick, unstable person would make. When it was clear to me that the caller was a loony tune, I brought that stuff to a quick end. I had no interest becoming part of her silliness and I wasn't in love with Pernell."

"I'm sorry you had to go through that, but I don't think it was any great loss."

"No. It wasn't. I'm a lot better off now and I'm involved with a man who's trying to be about something. So things have a way of working out."

I took a swig of my drink. "I'm happy for you, Linda and I appreciate your taking time out to meet with me."

"Has it helped?"

"Maybe. Most of what you've implied about Pernell, I pretty much knew. Your receiving harassing phone calls from one of his lady friends says a lot about the caller."

"Yeah. She's persistent."

"That's a nice way of saying unstable. But, she did get you out of the relationship."

"Me and several others."

I stopped and furrowed my brow. "What others?"

"The other women who were also harassed by this caller. We're thinking of forming a support group for women-who-came-to-their-senses-about-Pernell."

"How many others?"

She paused. "Six that I'm aware of, though I don't know them well enough to call them my friends. I did meet a couple of them just by chance. We found out we had Pernell in common as well as the harassing phone calls experience. They each talked about a few others that they knew who also went through that madness."

"Same caller?"

"I assumed as much. We were all told similar things."

"As far as you know, did everybody end the relationship?"

"Wouldn't you? How much hassle does a person need in one lifetime?"

Linda recalled the names of the two women she'd met. I jotted down those names as she excused herself.

"I really have to get back," she said. As she slid out of the booth, she stopped, stared back at me and added, "You know, I really haven't asked you what this is all about. Part of me wants to know and the other part says to mind-my-own-business. Lady Flame said I should talk with you and I did."

"Well, I could ..... "

She held up both hands. "Actually, I don't really want to know. Pernell was one story in my past and believe me, that chapter has ended."

I thanked her for her time and she strolled back to her job.

There was a lot to admire about Linda Green and I think she knew it without my endorsement.

As I drove back to my office, I had another piece of the puzzle to throw on the table to see how it fits.

"The question is.," I said to no one in particular. "What does a series of harrassing phone calls made by a woman and directed to women who dated Pernell Stallings have to do with the death of Deborah Norris?"

55

On the drive back through the city, I called Julie and she informed me that Jocelyn purchased her home in Southfield seven years ago.

"That doesn't help me very much," I said with some disappointment.

"However," Julie said, "she did live in an apartment complex on Evergreen, not too far from her current residence. She lived there for five years."

She had lived in the surrounding area and though most of what I was thinking was pure speculation, it did give something to think about.

I drove down Mack Avenue, half focused on the out-of-sync stoplights and recalling my initial conversation with Jocelyn. She had an on again, off again relationship with Pernell for several years and, if what I observed the other night was true, then their relationship had enough explosive elements to it to take out a sizeable chunk of Connecticut. Just how far would a person go to keep a relationship? What did Pernell have that she wanted? What did she have that he needed? Jocelyn started with and currently held a nice position with the local Telephone Company. Despite all the assurances, safeguards and threats of suspension and dismissals, it was still relatively easy to obtain someone's unlisted phone number. Who could better access a phone number than someone with time, experience and relationships in a phone company? Would someone deliberately go after perceived competition just to keep a relationship?

Psychology wasn't my thing in college and what little I learned came in handy on the football field and on the streets of Oakland. But the real depths of the human psyche I left to trained skull jockeys and the numerous Psychic Networks. I knew that what a person does can say a lot more about who they really are and not who they professed to be. Jocelyn was a woman capable of extreme mood swings. The more I thought about it, the more I realized that I'd seen several of her mood swings. They were all right there like odd named cartoon characters whistling on their way to work. Grumpy, happy, silly, testy, gloomy, misty and flighty had all been moods she'd shown me during our two encounters. What was out there had been obvious all along, and I'd missed it.

"I don't like where this is leading," I said as I gunned the engine to just make it through the yellow traffic light.

•　　•　　•

Rosie and Rae sat next to each other on their L-shaped couch while I paced. They hadn't protested the fact that I'd interrupted their dinner, however I think their designs on dessert went beyond the usual hot apple pie with vanilla ice cream. The kids were visiting their grandmother. There were lighted candles and a half-empty bottle of white wine on their glass-topped coffee table. Rosie's new videocamera was positioned on its tripod and I decided not to speculate.

I apologized for the interruption. Rae smiled and said "no problem" and Rosie wanted to know if it could wait.

They listened while I talked through every aspect of the case and where it seemed to be leading me. They listened while I broke down every detail and speculation. If I was going to do something meaningful with this case, and Deborah's memory, I had to be sure.

It took one uninterrupted hour for me to go through the details and when I finally sat down, I poured the remaining corner of wine into an available glass.

"So what do you think?" I asked.

Rosie answered first. "I don't know, Bro. There's several ways of looking at this and I'm not sure any of them is the right answer. The simple fact of the matter is; through all this, you have one eye witness account of an accident that took place eight years ago. You don't sound very confident about her and what does she have to gain after all these years? Quite frankly, the Stallings are well connected in the city and have gone to great lengths to maintain a squeaky-clean image. So trying to prove either one was involved in something like a vehicular homicide will be quite an uphill task. Even if your one eye witness has an attack of conscious, it's still her word against his and given her previous bouts with alcohol, her word is shaky at best."

"What about the other piece of the puzzle?"

"This Jocelyn woman?" Rosie asked. "It's a leap, I'll grant you, but harassing phone calls to murder over some dude. It just doesn't make sense."

"Then what does make sense?" I said taking my first sip of wine.

"The facts, Linc. The facts are what make sense," Rosie replied earnestly. "Fact; MiShaun was riding with Pernell when the two kids were killed. Fact; this guy Beasley gives you a scarf that we now know be-longed to MiShaun as well as a picture of the car he drove as it's being dismantled by this Tyler Cain and his crew. Fact; Deborah Norris found out about the accident and was investigating it prior to her death. I'll bet she was onto Pernell, but somehow he got wind of it. So, to protect his family name, he took action. Conclusion; Pernell Stallings is responsible for the death of Deborah Norris."

"You think he did it?" I asked.

"I think he's responsible somehow. All fingers point to him as the culprit."

Rosie's statement of the facts were as crystallizing to me as icicles on a gutter. Just hearing him say out loud what I'd been thinking helped in several ways.

"I hear you, Rosie, but there's something still lingering in my gut about this Jocelyn thing."

"A jealous, obviously unstable woman makes some harassing phone calls to keep her path clear to Pernell. So what? It doesn't mean anything."

Rae smiled and patted Rosie's knee. "Which is probably why you should pursue it, Linc."

"Help me understand why, Sis," I said, settling back in the armchair.

Rae stood up and walked over to one of their floor-to-ceiling bookcases. She reached down and pulled a green and white leather-bound photo album from a bottom shelf. She sat down next to Rosie and began flipping over the plastic covered pages.

I recognized the Michigan State University 'Sparty' emblem on the front cover.

"What are you doing, Babe?" Rosie asked.

Rae didn't answer but kept turning pages. "Here we go." She pointed to a picture. Rosie stared for a moment, nodded and they both looked up at me. Rae turned the album toward me so I had a full view of the picture.

It was a 1970 color shot of a woman with a wide smile, glasses and one of the biggest Afros I'd ever seen.

"Her name is Bertina Burks. Everyone called her BB. We met her in '69 when your Rosie and I started at Michigan State. She was from Detroit, graduated from Finney and majored in Chemistry. She went onto Med School and did her residency at Henry Ford. Anyway, to make a long story short; somewhere along the way she got involved with a guy who liked having a doctor on his arm...and in his bed, but not completely in his life. She had the kind of profession that was conducive to his enjoying the good life. She worked long hours, was always on call and when they were together, well...it wasn't pleasant. They'd break up and get back together, break up and get back together. I never knew why, since she had so much going for herself."

"So what happened?"

"At first, she believed that she was the reason why they kept breaking up, so she tried to change. Took on a brand new look, tried to shorten her work hours and started getting into his interests. When that didn't work, she believed the problem was the women who threw themselves at him. So she started missing her work to follow him. Whenever she'd see him with another woman, she'd cuss out the woman and argue with him later. After eight or nine times of this, he tried to break it off, but she wouldn't let him. It all came to a head one night when she finished up early and came over to his place. Only he wasn't home, supposedly. So she drove around the block and waited. After a couple of hours, he waltzed out of his apartment with some babe on his arm and before you know, Bertina went ballistic."

"Why do I have the feeling that I'm not going to like this ending?" I said.

Rae shook her head and Rosie shrugged. "Bertina ran up behind the two off them just as they were about to embrace and kiss. Bertina stabbed the woman in the back of her neck with a surgical scalpel and cut him across his throat. She stood over both of them and watched them bleed to death. By the time the EMS wagon arrived, it was too late. From what I understand, when the detectives asked why she did it, she replied 'because I loved him'."

"Do you buy that?" I asked Rae.

"Do I buy the fact that a supposedly easy-going, serious-minded, studious friend of ours from our campus days who excelled in Med school and had a promising career as a doctor in front of her, in a fit of rage, is capable of killing two people?"

"You're saying my speculation has some merit?" I said.

"I'm saying women don't think like men and that's what makes us who we are. How we rationalize and process is something you all can never get to."

I set my empty glass on the table, apologized again for my interruption and thanked both of them. As I made my way to the door, I stopped at looked back at Rae and Rosie.

"So would you ever kill for him?" I asked, nodding at Rosie.

Rae smiled in that way women smile when they know something you don't know or believe. "I'd kill for him, over him and with him if that's what it took. But I'd never kill because of him and that's the difference between me and Bertina."

"You wouldn't kill because of me, Baby?" Rosie asked amusedly.

"No, I'd kill *you* first," Rae replied flashing that same half-corner smile.

I shook my head. "You know, Rae, I believe you would."

"What's your next move, Linc?" Rosie asked.

I paused. "I've got to force the play to my side of the field."

56

My next few moves would be the equivalent of walking on a tight piece of thread across Niagara Falls. The slightest wrong move and I'd be the only one falling into the rapids without a barrel. Somewhere in the circle of suspects was the hand of a murderer. Fortunately, it was a circle in which a few had already taken their turn. If what Deborah suspected was true and MiShaun's version was on target, then Pernell Stallings was directly responsible for the deaths of Morris and Daphne as they returned home from their prom. If Beasley told the truth, then Tyler Cain was responsible for the deaths of his former crew.

None of this stuff was provable given the lack of solid evidence.

I also believed that someone in the Stallings camp was responsible for the direct attack on me. Roger Martin wasn't in a position to tell me who paid his fee since being comatose rarely allows for good two-way conversation. The sudden attack on me had the kind of smell that generally floats around men like Tyler Cain.

All I had were a bunch of wild ideas and my sister-in-law's assurance that I was onto something.

I made my way back to my apartment, parked in my recliner and gave thought to the details of my plan. Eight years was a long time to try and bring closure to a case, but I'd come to believe that Deborah Norris was pretty special.

I guess it's what Judge Zone saw in her.

Sylvia certainly knew it. So did Sharron, MiShaun, Winston and Arlan Schafer. I caught a glimpse of it in her articles and her journal.

She'd managed to touch the lives of people in her world in a way that would have made the rest of the world envious.

She died before her time and I needed to know why.

At that moment, when self-doubt and being bull-headed collide, lies a point of clarity. An abandonment of rationality in which the bombs exploding in front of you are far less painful than the ones you've endured. The only direction is a straight line to the end zone.

What needed to be done, *had* to be done, with no thought of its impact five years or five hundred years from now.

I only had the lost dreams of a woman I never knew as my guide through the murky depths of a swamp filled with desperate souls.

The first of several phone calls filled the next hour.

• • •

The things people will tell a stranger over the phone have always struck me as an interesting commentary on human nature.

First, I contacted the two women Linda mentioned during her interview, and after a few phone calls made to people with similar names, I finally found both at home, enjoying their new-found lives.

Sarah Joseph and Megan Taylor talked very openly about their brief experience with Pernell, both ending with the harassing phone calls.

"I told that sistah to get a life and if she ever called me again, I'd personally take time off from work to kick her ..... "

" ..... I'm sure you did Miss Joseph," I said, interrupting her feisty tirade.

Megan spent more time reflecting on the nature of someone who'd engage in that kind of behavior.

"I really felt sorry for her," she said. "I wasn't that into Pernell and if she wanted him that bad, she could have him."

All harassing phone calls kept leading back to Jocelyn. Now whether or not it wound its way to Deborah's grave would be a little harder to prove.

One other thought hit me. I rang MiShaun's home and wasn't too surprised when she didn't answer.

I called Winston's place thinking she might still be there.

Hearing my voice didn't elevate his already dismal mood.

"No, Keller, she isn't here."

"Any idea where she went?"

"Most likely she went home," He replied.

"I just tried her at home and didn't get an answer."

"Well, she said she was going home. Maybe she'd rather have you talk with her answering machine."

"When did she leave?" I asked, knowing he wanted to hang up.

"Couple of hours ago. Look, man, I gotta run."

He disconnected before I could tell him to have a pleasant evening with Sharron.

Even under the most adverse of traffic conditions, it wouldn't take MiShaun two hours to drive from Winston's place to her home. Detroit is a big city and there are several places she could have stopped, assuming she wasn't sitting at home not answering the phone...alone.

It was a thought; MiShaun at home alone after being confronted with an eight year old secret that's helped her career and may have possibly cost the life of one of her best friends.

"I hope she's not," I said as my internal alarm started flashing a red warning light.

I rang her number again, waited for the answering machine after the beep, yelled at her to pick up the phone. I urged her to pick up the phone for the entire minute I had before the answering machine clicked off.

Uncertainty at critical moments can get you killed or allow someone to die. I wasn't sure if I should drive over to her place and kick the door in or keep buzzing her phone every five minutes. Part of me wanted to find Winston and grind his nose through a pencil sharpener for letting

MiShaun go off by herself, but I'd have to save that pleasure for later.

Feeling a need to do something, I grabbed the area phone book and checked the listings for places where AA meeting were held. I found a few addresses in the general vicinity where Winston and MiShaun lived.

At all three locations, I told them I was trying to reach my sister because I promised to attend the meeting with her, but she left before I got home. I gave MiShaun's name and came up empty each time. There were other listings around the city, but the odds favored those calls being, at best, futile. For my own sake of sanity, I needed to know what she was doing and if she was okay.

"Dammit," I said as I stood up and leaned against the window, staring at the evening flow of traffic. "This case is getting on my nerves."

The thing I wanted to do had been replaced by my need to know where MiShaun had gone, so with the night slowly descending, I grabbed my jacket and took to the streets...again.

The next few hours were a waste of time and energy. I did go by MiShaun's place and there was no indication that she'd made it home. I waited for a while and then zipped over to Winston's place hoping he'd lied to me again so I'd have reason to continue my growing distrust of him. My options started to dwindle. I didn't know why I needed to be concerned about MiShaun, but something told me that I should. I did the obligatory call around to hospitals and received the usual 'We're a hospital, sir, not a hotel.' My remaining options were the local drinking establishments, but the number far outweighed the level of energy needed to conduct a decent search. I had to try something since this nagging feeling kept sending tremors through my gut. Of course, even more ridiculous than calling a hospital to inquire about a sick or injured person is to call several bars and ask if there is a medium height woman drinking herself into a stupor.

"No, buddy. Why would something like that be happening at a bar?" was one of the more humane comments to my obviously stupid question.

Realizing that all my effort was nothing more than my own sense of do-somethingness, I motored over to the City of Southfield hoping to catch Jocelyn at home.

During the time it took to get to her place, I'd already worked out what I wanted to say. Since I was dropping by without an invitation, I felt like I had the advantage.

Her home was mildly lit as I parked in front. There didn't appear to be any visitors or people lingering in the shadows. Once I rang her doorbell, I braced myself for anything once she opened the door.

Fortunately, it didn't take long. She peered through the keyhole and clicked open two locks before standing in the doorway dressed in a satin robe.

"What brings you to my door unannounced like this?" she asked clearly puzzled by my appearance.

"You."

"Me? What about me?"

"Couple of things, strictly FYI," I said.

Still puzzled she asked if I wanted to come in.

I declined. "I just want you to know that I know about the phone calls you've made to some of Pernell's former girlfriends."

She appeared startled for just a quick confirming moment before she regrouped. "What phone calls are ..... ?"

"Oh, don't play innocent, Jocelyn. I've looked into your eyes and seen your soul, so let's just drop the game. Quite frankly, I don't care."

She stood back, folded her arms and gave me a look of total indignation. "What makes you think I'd do something like that?"

"Who better than you, a phone company employee, can access phone numbers at will? I know a lot has changed and security safeguards are supposed to be at an all time high, but nothing beats access like people who work in the environment. And there are so many ways to access information, some of which are probably known only by people who work for the phone-company."

She glared, frowned and started to slam the door.

"Tell Pernell that I know all about the accident," I shouted.

The door was practically closed when she stopped. As she stood on the other side of the door, I could only imagine what she must have been thinking.

I continued. "I know how he got rid of his car and I know about the only eye witness. Two kids are dead because he's a hot-rodding low-life."

Jocelyn slowly pulled the door open and blessed me with a defiant glare. "Tell your boyfriend that I intend to nail him. I have all the proof I need to bring a case against him, Tyler and his brother."

"His brother?" she asked.

"Accessory after the fact. You don't think MiShaun and Tyler are working close to him because of their years of academic study do you?"

"Why should I care what happens to him?"

"Because you're a love sick poodle who's addicted to insecurity pills. Oh, you care alright or you would not have run off all his potential suitors."

"Whores! All of them," she said smugly. "I'm the best thing that ever happened to him and he knows it."

"He'll really believe you from his cell in Jacktown. You tell him that no court order is going to keep me from turning him into fresh meat for some husky lifer who likes turning men from AC to DC."

I turned, took two steps and looked back. "And by the way, the case I'm working has shown that the day before my client's sister-in-law was murdered, someone made a phone call to her home from that gas station on the corner. Now, I have to ask myself, why would someone call her from a gas station and isn't it interesting that it happens to be in the same area where you live? Eight years ago, unlisted phone numbers were easy to access and I suspect they still are for people in the know."

My statement caught her completely off guard. I knew I hit on something since her bottom lip began to quiver slightly. She stood speechless.

"I know it was you, Jocelyn. Proving it won't be that hard."

Strolling down the steps and around to the driver's side of the car, I glared back at Jocelyn still standing in the door.

She watched me fire up the engine, U-turn on the street and drive away.

I let loose a deep sigh as I motored toward Southfield Road. "It's late in the fourth quarter and the clock is winding down."

57

I eased back to my apartment and actively debated whether or not I should play the answer machine when I saw the flashing red '1'. Now that I had set some things in motion, it didn't seem like I had much of a choice.

After the digitized voice told me I had one message and that the message came in an hour ago, I heard. "I'm so sorry." The sobbing voice belonged to MiShaun. "I didn't mean for anyone to get hurt. You have to believe me!" I strained to listen for anything that might tell me where she was. "Oh, what do you care? What do you know about anything, huh! What do you know, mister high and mighty detective!" She whimpered and her words dragged along. "She was my friend, too. She was. I didn't mean to... What could I do? I'm alive aren't I? I have to live, too. She has to forgive me. I didn't mean to ..... She has to forgive me."

The line disconnected.

"Great," I said. "That's just great! Now where am I suppose to find her?"

My alarm kicked in again and I knew I'd better get moving, but I didn't want to play the aimless wanderer for the rest of the night.

I played the message again, listening for anything I could hang my hat on. There weren't enough background noises to tell me if she was inside or outside. I hit the play button again, hanging onto every syllable. There had to be something there, I thought as my chest pounded from my increased heart rate. MiShaun wasn't one of my favorite people in the world, but that had nothing to do with the price of wigs on Woodward.

She was someone in trouble and unfortunately that was the game I signed on to play.

Again, the message played and I listened. What was there that I wasn't hearing.

"Who has to forgive you MiShaun?" I said without knowing why. "Deborah? Does Deborah have to forgive you? Is that it?" I don't know why it felt right, but it did. "How can Deborah forgive you when she's ..... Holy..!"

I grabbed my jacket and raced out the door.

•   •   •

I don't know how long she'd been sitting there when I finally heard her low sobs in that quiet surrounding. She knelt on the evenly trimmed grass, arms folded across her chest, head down and rocking back and forth when I crept up behind her.

She jumped, startled by my voice and surprised to see me. "What are you doing here?" she said in a whispery tone.

"I came to get you."

"Please, just go away. I'm all right. I just need to be alone."

I stepped closer, not completely convinced she wanted to be alone. "If you wanted to be alone, why'd you come here?"

"What could be more alone than a graveyard?"

I eased up next to her and stared at Deborah's marble headstone. "I don't know if the dead are ever lonely. Though they may be forgiving."

"What do you know about forgiveness?" she asked staring blankly at the inscription that summed up Deborah's life.

"Like I said earlier, I'm no priest, but what little I know about forgiveness pales in comparison to what I know about forgiving."

"What do you mean?"

"I mean that I don't think it was Deborah's nature to grant forgiveness. I think she hung around that area called acceptance thus making it easier for others to be forgiving of their own mistakes."

MiShaun glanced up at me. "What do you know about Deborah's nature?"

"I only know her through your experiences, her words and my own speculations." I touched her arm lightly and pulled her up toward me. "What do you think Deborah wants you to forgive about yourself?"

Her eyes began to moisten as she thought about her answer. "I took shortcuts in order to promote my own ambition. I had to live with events and secrets in order to protect my sense of order and place. I was too impatient to wait for the rewards that I thought I couldn't compete for in any arena. Now, I have something, but..," she turned toward Deborah's headstone, "at what cost?"

"You knew Deborah was looking into the accident, didn't you?"

She nodded. "Yes, I knew. She made the mistake of leaving the newspaper clipping about the accident on her table. I saw her code system on the article, so I knew. I had stopped by just to pick up a few remaining items. Since I still had a key, I came in and heard Deborah in the shower. I yelled to her that it was me and I'd help myself to a cup of coffee. That's when I saw the article. I spilled some of my coffee because it shook me so bad." That explained the stain on the newspaper article. "I didn't know what to do, so I excused myself and left."

"Then what did you do?"

"Since I'd been drinking and was pretty much out of it, I wasn't sure what I'd said or how much. I knew it wasn't a coincidence, so I ran back to my condo and thought about what do to."

I didn't see a need to withhold the truth. "According to Deborah's account, you mumbled a great deal during the night. You kept referring to an accident, some guy you were with, who we now know was Pernell and how it wasn't supposed to happen."

She sobbed. "I hoped she would leave it alone or it would go away."

"That wasn't her style, MiShaun," I said.

"I know," she replied quietly.

"Did you tell Pernell about what Deborah was up to?"

"Not at first, but after I realized who he was, you know, his connections and all, I just thought I'd help my career along a little faster. I mean, after all, we had shared something. We had something in common."

"You mean you were both killers."

"I wasn't the one driving," she yelled defensively. "I was a passenger. It wasn't my fault."

"But you never said anything, MiShaun. You're just as guilty whether you were driving, riding or sitting on the hood."

"There was nothing I could do about it."

"That's not what Deborah thought," I snapped. "I met the mother of the boy who was driving. Her life has a hole that can never be filled. What do you say to her? How does she get through the days and nights of hoping he'll come walking through the door having just had a wonderful night with his girlfriend at their prom? Where are her answers. MiShaun?"

"I didn't mean to ..... "

She buried her face in my chest in order to hide the sudden outpour of tears. I held her tight and looked over at Deborah's headstone.

I whispered, "Forgive her, Deb."

MiShaun pulled away from me, but I held on. "C'mon, MiShaun. It's late. I'll buy you a cup of coffee."

58

MiShaun followed me back to my apartment, where I attempted to brew something that looked like coffee. She relaxed in my recliner while I made small talk. There were still questions that needed answering and I couldn't let the opportunity get away, not when I was so close.

She settled into the recliner like someone content to sit, staring empty-eyed at the city traffic and waiting for the model year changes. While she waited for nothing to happen, I took care of a few items.

When I finished brewing my low octane sludge, I ambled back to her and she looked like she'd aged. Her eyes were closed and she seemed meditative, like she'd just been purged of a demon from some gothic novel.

I don't like feeling sorry for anyone, but this one was hard. Since I knew I had several more questions, my shot at humanitarian of the hour was just about to be blown.

"Try this," I said. "It won't kill you, but you'll wish you were dead."

"I've already made that wish," she said as she accepted the cup of coffee with mild indifference.

"Doesn't count," I said. "I didn't include any candles."

She feigned a half smile and sipped slowly. "I've had worse."

"That puts me in the fair-to-midland-category. I'm moving up."

She asked several questions about work, family and me. I answered, figuring she wanted a digression from the thoughts that troubled her. I've never been one to elaborate, but I gave just enough information to fill the void.

After about twenty minutes of answering questions, her eyes started getting heavy and shoulders began to sag. Her body had decided to rest and my questions weren't going to prevent that reality.

She finished a yawn and said, "I guess I should be going. I do have to work tomorrow."

"Don't bother," I said. "You can bunk here tonight. While I made your coffee, I took the liberty of setting out fresh linen. My bedroom is in the back."

"Mr. Keller, I know ..... "

"It's not what you think. I'll sack here on the recliner. I think you need some undisturbed sleep and maybe I can make that happen."

"That's awfully kind."

I nodded. "I also set out a pair of unused green and white, Michigan State University cotton pajamas on the bed."

"I thought you went to Prairie View," she said somewhat amused.

"I did. My brother Roosevelt thinks that God created Michigan State and everything else came by way of the flood. Whenever he returns from one of his visits, one of us always ends up with a pair of something."

"Thanks," MiShaun said.

We stared at each other for that awkward moment when people are trying to decide just how thankful they should be with one another. Do you shake hands, hug like family, hug like friends, kiss like family, kiss like friends, or hug and kiss like tomorrow may never come.

Of course, it was a scene like this that drove a wedge between Malone and me and here I was on another late night with a woman I'd recently met, staring at me in my apartment.

I told her good night, turned around and plopped down in the recliner.

MiShaun rubbed the side of my face, whispered good night and headed to my bedroom.

Chivalry isn't dead and neither am I, I thought as I pulled a spare blanket from underneath the recliner. But some things are best reserved for knights in shining armor, not private investigators that drive a Nova. I chased that thought into my dreams.

59

Sleeping on a recliner all night isn't my idea of a walk on the beach, but I did manage to comfortably make it through the rest of the night. Even my dreams had a less hectic feel. There were no shadows or distorted images cautioning me along a certain path. All I remember is standing on a bridge watching the waters calmly flow and thinking how good it felt.

I sat up at just a little past seven, having heard the first angry commuter blow his horn to kick off the morning's episode of road rage.

The sound of my shower running reminded me that I wasn't alone. Using the kitchen sink to wash and brush, I had coffee brewing and frozen waffles in the toaster when MiShaun made her morning appearance.

"How'd you sleep?" I asked.

"Okay," she replied and sat down at the table. "Thanks for the use of your bed. I didn't realize how tired I was."

We added more morning small talk as a prelude to comfortably saying good bye. We both knew that we'd dodged those few remaining questions that I didn't bother to ask last night. There was no cover of darkness to shield the truth.

MiShaun sipped her coffee and I cleared my throat. "In the days prior to Deborah's death, did you receive any harassing phone calls?"

"No. None at all. Why?" she asked.

"How about in the weeks prior to her death? Any calls like that?"

She thought for a moment. "No, but remember I was living with Deb until an apartment opened. We used her phone, so if there were any calls like that, they would have come in for her, not me."

My mind shifted back to our first conversation in her office. She had mentioned that she and Deb lived together for a while. "Yeah, I'd forgotten that. Did you get a phone right away?"

"No, I'm sorry to say. It took a while. I was just getting back on my feet. I kept using Deb's phone until I had my own."

"How about threatening notes? Did anyone confront you about your relationship with Pernell?"

She shook her head. "No. Why are you asking these questions?"

I soft pedaled an answer and moved to another topic. "Your employers might not be too happy with you if they know we've talked."

She sighed. "We've all been walking around each other for years now because of that accident. When I confronted Pernell about it, he promised that if I kept quiet, he'd help my career. He told me his brother would one day run for Mayor and if I shut up and went along with the program, we'd all be key executives on the Mayor's staff."

"Those dreams may come crashing down pretty soon."

"From the moment I agreed to keep quiet, that dream has been one long nightmare."

"What are you going to do?" I asked.

"I'll let you know after I've cried," she said glancing at her watch. "Well, I really need to be going. I still have a job to go to." She stood up. "I have just enough time to drive home, change and be professionally late without causing too much strife."

"You've been through quite a bit lately, MiShaun. It might be in your best interest to stay home for a few more days. There's a volcano about to erupt and I'd hate to see you get burned in the spill."

"That happened eight years ago when I turned my back on those two kids. It's time to face the truth. I've lived with this thing long enough. I sure don't want to die with it."

"Well, before you do anything MiShaun, tell your side of the story to a good lawyer. Right now, your advantage is coming forward before everything breaks. In some ways, a lawyer might be able to cut a deal that would keep you from doing any jail time."

"Maybe I should go to jail," she said regretfully.

"You've already spent time in your own personal jail, don't be a martyr. The last one was burned at the stake and it still didn't improve the human condition."

"I guess you're right."

I nodded just as the top lock to my door unlatched. I stepped away from the table as the door pushed open and Malone stood in the doorway.

She quickly glanced around the room before saying anything. "Sorry, Linc, I didn't know you had company."

"Malone? I didn't expect to see you this morning."

"Obviously," she said as she strolled over to MiShaun and extended her hand. "I'm Candy Malone, Linc's ongoing point of conflict."

"I'm MiShaun Lucas," she said awkwardly. "Linc was kind enough to let me spend the night."

"His kindness rivals the saints," Malone replied. "Is that coffee fresh?"

She strolled over to the counter and pulled her cup off the top shelf. As she poured the coffee, I wondered what elements of the truth would make the most sense.

"Don't worry, Miss Malone, Linc was just being kind. Nothing happened here."

"I know," she said with a wry smile.

"Anyway, I was just leaving," MiShaun said as she walked to the door. "Thanks for everything, Linc. I'm sure I'll see you real soon."

When the door closed behind her, I turned to a still smiling Malone as she leaned against the kitchen counter. "So what makes you so sure nothing happened Miss-come-over-unannounced."

"I didn't become a detective just because I look good. The blanket on the recliner, your wrinkled pants and the fact that the apartment has the smell of fresh coffee and nothing else tells me nothing happened here last night. Now, that doesn't mean there isn't a story to tell and I'm all ears."

She sat down and I gave her a quick overview of last night. Though Malone is one of the few people I trust outside of my family, she's also in a delicate position because she's a cop and sworn to uphold the law. So I decided not to tell her those things that would further compromise the relationship.

"Nothing comes easy for you, does it, Linc?"

"Hey, I played for the Raiders. I can handle it," I said. "Besides, what brought you by here this morning?"

"Long night and I wanted to bring you this," she said as she reached in her jacket pocket. "This was supposed to go to you yesterday."

She handed me my .38 Smith and Wesson. "Hey, how'd you get this?"

"A friend owed me a favor. I know how you men are about your toys."

"Knackton might blow a gasket."

"He probably already has, so what's one more gasket?" she said as she finished her coffee. "Also, I don't like the feel of this case and well, I'd feel a lot better knowing you had something of an equalizer." She stood up, walked over to the counter and placed her cup in the sink. "Linc, promise me you'll be careful. Watch your next few steps."

"You can talk plainer than that, Malone. What's really going on here?"

"I don't know. I've just been hearing a lot of stuff, rumors mostly. Court orders, phone calls to the chief, state representatives, threats to have your license taken and the list seems to get longer. Knackton's been on a tirade since you first stumbled onto this case. He and Judge Zone have had words."

"I've been pretty busy lately. Not everyone is happy with my work."

"Unhappy people can be dangerous in their own way," Malone said as she stepped closer toward me.

I saw genuine concern in her eyes. "Depends on what they're unhappy about."

"You seem to have a real knack for making the wrong people unhappy."

"It's a talent that makes me happy," I said trying to keep the mood light.

"Don't let your talent get you killed," she said forcibly. Then she softened. "Why can't you let this one go, Babe?"

"My answer may be too trite, or sound like something out of an old western."

"Man's gotta do what a man's gotta do?" Malone asked playfully.

"Something like that, only there's more driving me here than some silly, archaic code. I didn't want this case in the first place. I tried to get The Judge to hire someone with a lot more experience. He was so insistent and Mrs. Henderson needed piece of mind. I figured I'd give it a solid few days and let it go." I paused.

"So what happened?"

"It started to matter too much. It wasn't just Deborah, but two kids who never made it home from the prom. There are so many who are grieving and no real answers. So I have to find the answers. Somehow, the grieving has got to stop." I stopped and gazed into her eyes. "It probably doesn't make sense."

Malone wrapped her arms around my neck, pulled me forward and kissed me as if we were rehearsing a passionate love scene for a movie on a pay-per-view channel. The kiss, long and wet, tongue probing with a fiery climax that I could only describe as the tail of Haley's comet, enflamed and aroused me beyond the point of resistance.

When we finally parted, I stared into her eyes while continuing to hold her close. "You know, it's unhealthy to have dessert before one has had their breakfast."

"Call it incentive. We have a lot to discover and you need to be careful or you'll never know what you missed."

She pulled away and eased toward the door. "Well, long nights and passionate kisses don't do much for my equilibrium so I'm headed home. I need to rest." She stopped at the door and turned around. "I'll see you later?"

"Try and stop me," I said.

Malone smiled and closed the door behind her.

I quickly headed for the shower.

60

Mosquitoes, bees and hornets serve a very useful purpose in nature's scheme of things. If nothing else, they are an irritating reminder that if you buzz around a person long enough, you'll get a reaction. The high-risk downside is that the reaction tends to be fatal for the buzzer.

I hit the streets with the idea of being irritating. Pernell Stallings' fast-laneing, high-speed, former life led to the deaths of two people. He'd managed to get away with it by employing the services of his friends, co-conspirators and his brother, although I didn't know to what extent.

He'd gotten away with murder and something had to be done.

It was time to buzz.

The day started with a series of phone calls from the office. I checked and rechecked with a number of people who'd had some affiliation with the Stallings, knowing that somebody in that network would be incapable of holding back information about a detective making inquiries.

I was counting on that fact.

Later that morning, the garage attendant at the 'Empower Detroit' building was more than willing to let me leave a note on Pernell's car. It cost me two Hamilton's and a Lincoln, but worth every dollar. Knowing Helen would not put me through directly to Pernell, I contacted Pat Terry at 'Terry's Enchanted Garden' and had a floral arrangement expressed to Pernell's Office.

"Tell me again what you want the card to say," Pat asked, not sure that she'd heard me correctly the first time.

"Ours souls are restless thanks to you," I said repeating the quote.

"And sign it Morris Shaw and Daphne Connor."

Pat assured me the delivery would go out right away.

Then I decided to call Pernell's office and received the anticipated grand put-off by Helen. She also told me MiShaun, Trevor and Tyler were also unavailable and that if I called again, she'd contact their lawyer.

"I just want to leave a message for Pernell," I said ignoring her comment.

She sighed impatiently and told me to go ahead.

"Tell him the price of two innocent souls will be his brother's bid to be Mayor, if he doesn't meet with me and soon. I'm one phone call away from calling a couple of sources I have at *The Detroit News* and *Free Press*."

I left the number of my cell phone and told Helen to have a better day.

It took me several minutes, but I finally managed to have someone at the phone-company direct me to Jocelyn's voice mail. After waiting through the 'leave a detailed message', I left a detailed message.

"Jocelyn. This is Lincoln Keller. I hope you find time to talk with Pernell, because either he's going down or you're going down. One or both of you had something to do with Deborah's death and I'm just a few steps away from putting it all together. I just wanted you to know. Have a nice day."

My hope was that she'd do something stupid before realizing that I'd bid a five-special with only four low cards in my hand and an unwavering hope that there was back-up in the kitty.

Just to be annoying, I called 'Empower Detroit' again, spoke with Helen and was ceremoniously rebuked.

I hung around the front of the 'Empower Detroit' building, occasionally stopping someone going in and asking them if, by chance they were going up to the Stallings office, would they be so kind as to leave a message with Helen, the office manager for Pernell Stallings.

"Why can't you do it yourself?" asked a woman wearing a matching blue skirt and jacket.

"Our family has been split up ever since we fought on our

grandfather's estate and I've been doing everything I can to get us back together, but he refuses to see me. I'm hoping his heart will eventually lead his head back to us."

The smile that followed was long on dazzle and short on sincerity. She didn't appear to mind.

"Tell him what's done is done and now it's time for restitution. His brother Lincoln has his hand out."

She smiled obligingly and headed for the front entrance.

I eased over to the parking lot and slid into traffic just as a blue and white unit pulled in front of the building. There was no doubt that they'd been called by someone upstairs. It had to be someone who had become irritated by my presence.

"Being irritating has its rewards," I said with a half-grin mumble as I slid into traffic.

Going back to the office would serve no purpose and I figured there'd be someone in a suit, with another official looking document trying to warn me off the Stallings or arrest me for violation of the first legal looking document. I decided to stay in motion for a while, using my cell phone to make contact or be contacted. There were more than enough fast food joints and watering holes for a person to hang out for several hours and still maintain that irritating spirit.

Now that the snowball was rolling down hill and getting bigger, I had to be sure that I was on the back end and not the front.

•   •   •

I decided to hang out at Artie's, the one place I knew that only closed its door once a year to throw out the stiffs. Ada hadn't made her appearance and I was content to sit in a booth in an isolated corner and think of other ways to be irritating.

I ordered the 'Thriller', a double meat burger with cheese and a special sauce that subbed as fuel for a rocket launch.

On a piece of yellow-pad paper, I jotted down the moves that needed to be made in order to draw out the truth and avoid any legal hurdles. Into a large circle, I wrote the names of the people I believed most connected with Deborah's murder and their possible motives.

Pernell's was basic; he didn't want to do jail time. He also didn't want to jeopardize his brother's political career.

Trevor wanted to sit on City Council, in the Mayor's chair or unseat the current incumbent in the 13th congressional district. People had been sent to their graves for far less.

MiShaun wanted a shot at being somebody, having spent years not liking what she was. She'd tasted success and chose to ignore its bitter after taste. She used what she knew to get what she wanted. 'Knowledge is power' I wrote in quotes.

Tyler was a thug who dressed to kill and probably had. He wanted access to power, by any means necessary.

Jocelyn wanted her shot in the spotlight. Her one chance had to come through the one person she'd met who had some spotlight to share. What she didn't want is that spotlight shared with anyone else but her. In that sense, it made her a loose cannon. Dangerous to anyone for whom she'd taken aim. I put a question mark by her name.

I wrote Winston's name, not completely convinced it even belonged on the paper. I wasn't sure what he wanted since there was nothing this case seemed to generate for him. Another question mark was placed by his name. He'd proven to be more of a liar than a reliable source. Several of his lies of omission had more to do with his relationship with MiShaun and Sharron. He didn't want me to know and I hadn't taken the time to pursue the reasons why.

Maybe he had more to hide than he let on. I put an exclamation point next to the question marks.

Content to mull through the possibilities and wait, I wondered how long it would be before someone made the call that would set everything in motion.

It took an hour, maybe less when my cell phone rang and interrupted my doodling.

"Yeah," I said.

"Keller. We need to talk," Pernell said irritation laced in his tone.

"Why, Pernell. I'm touched. You and I have done so little of that lately."

"I don't have time for games, Keller."

"Neither did Morris and Daphne," I replied. "Not that you were overly concerned. So let's move on. Where do you want to meet and when?"

"Tonight preferably. I know a spot."

"Today, as in now, and I know a better spot."

I sensed his reluctance, but let the silence work to my advantage. I assumed he was talking with someone like Trevor or Tyler, or even his lawyer. I knew it wasn't anyone connected with law enforcement. So I waited.

"Where do we meet?" he said.

I told him.

"How do I know you can be trusted, Keller?"

"You don't know, that's the beauty of the relationship. But you have no choice but to find out." I gave him a moment to soak it in. "And Pernell, I see your little watch dog anywhere in the area and I head straight to the cops. There's a Mount Clemens detective anxiously waiting to meet you. See you in an hour." I disconnected, checked the time and sighed.

Pernell had responded to my buzzing.

I knew he was stupid enough to try something, but I didn't think he had the nerve.

Even though an hour wasn't a lot of time to plan and coordinate something major, it was enough time to put something in place.

I had to take my chances.

61

I raced over to our arranged meeting area having had the advantage of picking a spot closer to me than to Pernell.

Trust was so nonexistent in our relationship, that trying something underhanded, sneaky or just plain low-down would not have been above his character. Choosing a busy spot where things could be overheard, but not really, made the most sense to me. I could watch both he and the crowd.

The drive to Chene Park took less than fifteen minutes, but afforded me time to park and check things over before Pernell arrived. I sat on a bench that gave me a full view of the area in front of me and the soothing sounds of the Detroit River in back of me.

There were more than enough early afternoon people cruising around the waterfront or lounging on the grass for me to find a strategic spot and wait to see whom he would bring with him.

Chene Park was a revitalized area along Detroit's downtown shoreline. The open, well-manicured area contained an amphitheater where numerous summer musical acts came through to add to the summer entertainment menu.

I caught sight of Pernell approaching from the side street where he'd parked his white and black trimmed sports car. He looked around the crowd, finally catching sight of me waving to him. He wasn't dressed to kill, but rather casual in black slacks and an open collar blue shirt.

"Keller," he said through tightly drawn lips.

"Where's your brother?" I asked.

He sat down, unmoved by my question. "You said come alone."

"And did you?"

"Look, Keller," he said ignoring my sarcasm, "I don't like these allegations and innuendoes you've been throwing around. I could sue you for defamation of character and slander on top of the court order we already have on you. We could make a lot of noise and you wouldn't be able to get a job working security for a corner gas and snack shop."

Another threat to my employment fell on deaf ears. "If you want to involve your lawyer, go right ahead. I have more than sufficient evidence to pull you off the streets. That little accident you drove away from eight years ago left a permanent mark on two families who did nothing more than try to raise two good kids."

"I don't know anything ..... "

"Can it, Pernell. I know all about the incident. You took MiShaun on one of your joy rides in your fast little Nissan, just as you'd done with so many others, only this time there was a car coming in the opposite direction that didn't see you until it was too late. Those two kids are dead and you're sitting here, so don't play the innocent with me. I know how you got rid of your car and I know why MiShaun is employed with your organization. Both of them saw you as a gravy train for their own personal agendas. So they used what they knew to become part of the Stallings inner circle."

"You're crazy."

I smiled. "I just might be at that. Everything might have worked out just fine, except for one thing; Deborah Norris, the late friend of MiShaun, got wind of what happened and decided to look into it. The more she looked, the more she realized that MiShaun's love of drinking and partying had gotten her into something she hadn't expected. When Mishaun realized what Deborah was doing, my guess is that she told you, thinking you'd advise her on how to handle it, but not knowing just how sinister it was until after Deborah was killed. I think that's when MiShaun took out an insurance policy of sorts. She was smart enough to leverage what she knew with what she wanted. I think it cost the life of her friend Deborah, but she was somehow convinced that it was the most practical course of action." I stopped to let it sink in. "How am I doing?"

"You're guessing and hoping I'll say its true," he snarled. "Well, you won't get me to admit to an incident in which there is no proof I was involved. My lawyer will rip apart any arguments you present regarding my car, that scarf or any alleged night I supposedly spent with MiShaun."

I leaned back, pretended to clean a fingernail and rubbed my tongue across the front of my teeth. I hoped I looked pensive. At least that's what I hoped he thought. I saw a confident, gotcha, smile working its way up from the corners of his mouth.

Finally I said. "That's interesting. I never mentioned a scarf to you."

The smile quickly faded. "Of course you did."

"No Pernell. I know who I've talked to about an alleged scarf and you weren't one of them."

"Well, it must have been mentioned in another conversation," he said trying to cover his tracks.

"I don't doubt that. The question is; with whom did you have that conversation."

He stopped and rolled the thought around. He looked like the errant husband trying to explain to his wife why a pair of half eaten candy panties happen to be in the jacket of his sport coat.

"Okay," he said. "Let's get down to business."

"What business is that?"

"You think you have something, fine. You'll never be able to prove it, but fine. I don't have time for this constant going back and forth. So let's find an agreeable end to this lie. How much do you want?"

It took a second for the statement to register. "How much do I want?"

"Yeah. Name your price. I'm sure we can work this out."

The idea of meeting with me had nothing to do with doing the right thing, but finding the one tried and true way of suppressing a secret.

Every man has his price and Pernell had been sent to find mine.

"Pernell," I said, "I'll be honest with you, draining you for money was the farthest thing from my mind when I set up this meeting. I'm surprised it didn't occur to me."

He blinked. He, too, was surprised. "It didn't? But I thought ..... " He let the sentence trail off.

"Thought what?"

"Never mind," he said recovering quickly. "Well, what the hell do you want?"

"Preferably your head on a stick. Falling short of that, I want you to call Detective Wendy Brewer of the Mount Clemens police force and tell her that you're responsible for the deaths of Morris Shaw and Daphne Connors."

Pernell smiled, then laughed. The sound of his laughter increased in a matter of seconds. When he finally gathered his wits, he stared at me defiantly. "You are one piece of work, Keller."

"Think so?" I said.

"Yeah. You are. I'm not sure if I should laugh myself silly or have you arrested for character deficiency."

"Maybe I can help you make up your mind." I backhanded him and watched as he toppled from the seat to the ground. A few people stopped and stared as Pernell jumped to his feet.

I'd already stood up. "Does that help get you closer to doing the right thing?"

Pernell backed away. "This isn't the time, Keller, but it's coming. Believe me, it's coming."

"But know this, Stallings; I don't like the fact that two families have been denied the opportunity of holidays with their kids because they happened to be on the road the same time as you. I don't like the fact that Deborah Norris isn't writing articles about whatever she has as an interest." I stepped closer. "And most of all I don't like you. Now, the best thing for you to do is to stick your tail between your legs and go crawl into a hole because what's really coming is something you can't handle."

Pernell wiped his mouth and glared at the few onlookers. "What are you all looking at?"

Some of the observers turned and moved on, a few stayed and smiled, anticipating more action.

"I'll be calling Detective Brewer at the end of the day. I'd better hear that she'd heard from you," I said as he moved back through the crowd. He watched me closely as he backed away, occasionally bumping into someone.

He finally disappeared into the crowd and I sat down.

I knew Pernell wouldn't go to see Detective Brewer. If anything, he'd go see his brother, probably consult with their lawyer and ask Tyler for some assistance. In any event, I'd drawn first blood and he wasn't going to take it lightly. There was too much on the line.

Calling 'Empower Detroit' was another effort in futility, since Helen continued her block and roll interference. I hoped MiShaun had authorized her to let my calls through, but it had not happened that way.

Figuring MiShaun had talked with Pernell about the missing scarf, I wanted her to know that she'd compromised the little leverage I had. Given her guilt-driven mental state, I would not have been surprised if she'd told Pernell everything I shared with her.

I hoped I could use that information to my advantage. There was still a little more irritating that needed to be done.

In the time Pernell had left, I made several routine moves just to make sure I wasn't being followed. The crowd had been given my standard check for people engaged in activities that looked out of place. During the drive home, I routinely switched lanes, made unexpected turns which did not endear me to battle-weary drivers and took to the highway for a long stretch drive just to see who would hang with me.

Once I was convinced that there was no one on my tail, I headed home to think through my next steps.

Back at my apartment, I leaned against the window, sipping a light beer and watched the late afternoon traffic. The congestion of drivers and pedestrians on Livernois were immediate reminders that what I think is important is nothing more than a minor annoyance to people wrapped up in their own lives. Deborah, Morris and Daphne were long since gone from the rock and rhythm of Detroit's driving cadence. They were documented memories trapped forever in the subconscious catacombs of their mourners. They were gone. For the living, it should have been enough that they came through when they did and stayed as long as they could. That should have been enough.

In my heart of hearts, I knew it wasn't enough. Perhaps it was some unknown force that threw me in the middle of a story without an ending. I hadn't played the role of a self-appointed moral avenger and I couldn't honestly say why I cared so much. Deborah Norris should have been nothing more than a case with a number that I'd file under 'gave it my best shot'. Morris and Daphne were still Detective Brewer's concern and none of my business. Yet, they were all connected in ways that kept me searching.

Staring out the window, with my .38 cleaned, loaded and holstered, I sensed that something was about to break. In much the same way horses can feel the first wind of a sudden thunderstorm and instinctively run to shelter until it blows over, I had that same sense of foreboding.

Something was in the wind and I knew the Stallings were going to make a move.

62

My musing came to an abrupt end when the phone rang and Julie tore into me before I'd completed my greeting.

"You know someone named Winston Hill?" she asked not waiting for a confirmation. "He came by your office twice today looking like someone needing to finish a race. He seemed insistent on getting in touch with you and after Mary calmed him down, I said I'd see what I could do."

"Did he say what he wanted?"

"No. Just that he needed to reach you right away. He left a number."

I wrote down the number and thanked Julie. She stopped me before I could hang up.

"Hold it. Did you read the report I submitted on him?"

"What report?"

"The one you obviously didn't read. His name was on that list you gave me, so I did my standard search on him."

"Anything I should know?"

"Hold on." I heard those magic fingers working the keyboard. "Here it is. If he's the same one, he has an interesting work history."

"He said he'd been downsized two or three times."

"Maybe, if I dug a little further I could probably access his personnel record, but the real interesting thing is how he's been able to sustain a living despite having those periods of unemployment."

"I assumed his wife handled the big stuff during his down time."

"If she did, she's the best divorced wife I've ever heard of. They were divorced in '92, she moved to Dallas while he stayed in Ohio, then on to Indiana and finally back here. Meantime, there are no records of debt accumulation on his credit reports. He bought several things in which he paid with cash and based on what I saw, he doesn't appear to be hurting. Now, unless he's had a few sugar sweeties along the way, this man is very good at budgetary living."

"I just saw him recently and he says he's found a new job," I said while the gears turned in my head.

"Good. When you find out, let me know so I can make it part of your official file."

I thanked Julie again and punched in the number Winston left with her.

When he answered and heard my voice, he went ballistic. "Keller! Where the hell is MiShaun?"

'It wasn't my turn to watch her' was the first quote I toyed with, but decided to go with a straight answer. "She said she was going to work."

"I tried there and no one's seen her."

"I was told that she wasn't taking messages."

Something clicked in my head that I immediately set to the side.

He paused. "Damn. I hope she hasn't decided to hit the bars again. You know she's recovering."

"Yeah, I know. Did she have certain places she favored over others?"

"A few. We have to find her. Something tells me she's in a bad way."

I sighed. "Look, Winston, she's probably sitting somewhere reevaluating her life and will come home soon." I hoped she was sitting with a lawyer, but I couldn't be sure.

His tone became insistent. "Last time she experienced some emotional crap, I found her asleep in her car outside a bar on the eastside. I tell you she's hit the bars again. We have to find her."

"I'm kind of busy right now, but let me know if ..... "

"No good, Keller," he said firmly. "You're the one who stirred up all this mess in the first place. If you hadn't come around asking all those questions about Deborah and stirring up old memories, MiShaun would have been all right. She's not as stable as she lets on. You should know that by now. You have to help me find her. In some ways, you're responsible."

'You're confusing me with Judge Zone' I thought, knowing I couldn't say it out loud. "I don't agree, but I'll argue the point later." That seemed to calm him somewhat. "Tell me where you are and we'll go looking together."

"I'm back at my crib. Hurry up, okay?"

"Yeah, yeah. Okay," I muttered.

When I called the 'Empower Detroit' offices, Helen answered and I asked her why did she lie about MiShaun being there.

"She's not available," she said and disconnected.

I put on my jacket, cruised down the steps and out the door. There were too many other things I needed to do to bring some form of resolution to this case and it seemed that every step forward resulted in three steps to the side and one at an angle to the left.

It was the way of investigations.

MiShaun's worrisome antics had taken their toll and I was starting a personal 'dislike Winston' campaign that would rival the Heat and Knicks in intensity.

•   •   •

After we struck out at the obvious places, her home, the job...again and a few AA meetings that were in session, Winston and I cruised the bars, both the seedy and shiny, uptown, downtown and everything in between, in what I knew was a waste of time. Though he seemed appeased.

The late afternoon became early evening, which then became late evening and as my impatience grew, so did his misplaced concern.

"Just how many places was MiShaun known to frequent in the old days?" I asked as we pulled away from 'The Latin Lounge', a mid-scale bar located off Woodward.

"MiShaun got around back then," he said as he crossed off the Latin Lounge from the last minute list he'd put together. "I know she's in one of these places. I just know it."

"Maybe she went home," I said.

"Then why doesn't she answer her phone?" he asked as he checked the next name on the list.

"Look, Winston, this is getting us nowhere. This is a big city and MiShaun is a big girl. She can take care of herself, no matter where she is."

"Let's try this one last place and I promise to let it drop for the night."

There was an admirable aspect to his persistence. One more stop on an already wasted trail didn't seem like too much to ask. Despite the annoyance of the activity, it had bought me some time and distance from the Stallings. When we finished, I promised myself I'd return to buzzing.

The last place on the list was an out of the way relic of a cabaret called 'Fast Nights'. The gaudy looking, two-level building still had the iridescent blue lights shaped like handwriting. Located on a street where small homes, corner stores and two-sided parking had gone the way of urban renewal, the few reminders of that bygone era stood like haunted structures in a 1950's ghost movie.

"You can't be serious," I said as I parked the car.

"She and I came here a few times," he said slamming the passenger side door.

"Obviously for the scenery."

"It wasn't so bad back then." As we walked toward the front entrance, Winston motioned to a walkway leading to the back. "MiShaun and I discovered that the best drinks are served in a lounge area upstairs in the back."

I followed him past the barred windows, hearing only a hint of life coming out of the building. There was a set of stairs located in the back leading up to a door where the shadows on the windows suggested that there was life, or some aspect of it, going on inside.

We headed for the steps and as I turned to walk up, I heard a familiar click that I didn't think was a twig snapping.

I turned and saw Winston stepping back pointing a familiar looking gun at me.

"This place that dangerous?" I asked.

He frowned. "Sorry to have to do this, Keller, but you couldn't leave well enough alone."

"Winston," I said, lacing my tone with mock surprise, "are you mad at me about something?"

"Ease your gun out of the holster, real slow, place it on the ground and slide it over to me."

"Aren't you afraid someone might come out and see us?"

"Just do it," he said evenly.

"And now you're a Nike spokesman," I said easing my gun out of its holster. "Your talents are endless." I placed my gun on the ground and slid it over to him.

He motioned me to step back. He held his gaze and aim as he knelt, picked up my gun and placed it in the pocket of his jacket. "Now toss me your car keys."

"Can you drive a stick?" I asked while I reached in my pocket. I tossed the keys to him. "She's temperamental you know. Only runs when the mood suits her."

"I'm used to temperamental women," he said catching the keys in his free hand. He stepped back and pointed to an adjoining alley several yards from where we stood. "Walk slowly."

"Should I put up my hands?"

"Just walk," he said, his voice growing sterner.

I walked toward the alley, slowly, my head spinning and my eyes looking for anything that might be an advantage. "You know, MiShaun almost killed herself with that gun."

"I know, but I'm less temperamental and a better shot."

"So as long as we're out walking and talking together, you want to tell me what's up? What is it that I couldn't leave alone?"

"I had everything going just right until you showed up and damn near spoiled my gravy train."

"Meaning; because MiShaun told you about the accident and who she was with, you saw an opportunity to make a little money by milking the Stallings for a steady supply of cash."

"When did you figure it out?" he asked.

"Actually, just now. It explains the lifestyle of a man with periods of unemployment, no credit purchases worth noting and cash payments for several items." I stopped and turned around. "After all, Winston, you're no Denzel clone. It figures no woman was going to take care of you. I doubt if a rich relative kept dying in between your unemployment periods, so it was a guess, but it seems to make sense."

"You're a smart guy."

"Thanks. Can I go now?" He motioned for me to keep moving. I shrugged, turned and walked toward the alley. "Tell me something, Winston; are you doing this on your own or are the Stallings paying you extra?"

"They don't know what I'm doing. They don't know it's me. Working in the automotive industry taught me a great deal about keeping secrets and how to keep from being known. Once I let them know that you're out of the picture, they'll be happy to pay a higher fee for my silence. It's not like they can't afford it."

"What about MiShaun?" I asked.

"She was part of the package, the fool. She wanted a prominent position, so that's what she asked for. Me, I just wanted something to fill the gaps from time to time. MiShaun and I decided to make her my insurance. If anything happened to her, I'd go straight to the police. She was the link between us. At first it was easy, but somewhere along the way MiShaun actually started believing that she was of some worth to them. She forgot her true value to us, and them."

We stopped at the edge of the darkened alley. Though my eyes were starting to adjust to the light, I was unfamiliar with the turf and running out of options.

"Don't bother looking for a way out, Keller. I've already taken the liberty of checking out this area. Besides, I'm not going to kill you here. I just needed an out of the way place to knock you senseless, pull up your car, load you in and make sure you take an unexpected plunge into the Detroit River. Careless driver that you are."

"Couldn't you just shoot me? That way I won't have to think about the water," I said, stopping mid-step.

He stopped and backed away. "Bullets are too easy to trace. Besides, a killing would just arouse the authorities, should your body ever be recovered. This way, it looks like you just took a wrong turn."

"Never did do well on my drivers test."

"Now, turn around please. I promise you this won't hurt much."

"How about if we try it on you first," I said as I quickly surveyed the area. "One other thing before I become fish bait; do you know who killed Deborah?"

"No. I don't. I wish I did, but I don't. Besides, knowing wouldn't bring her back. She's dead and I'm sorry, but I have to look out for me," he stopped, looked around and then back at me. "Now turn around."

It was now or never. Everything I'd learned so far had come down to this one gambler's moment. "I'm not going to make it that easy for you, Winston. You're going to have to shoot me or turn your butt around and hurry home. I'm through playing."

His eyes widened for that unexpected moment when the realization of something deeper sets in. He started to recover when I took a step toward him.

"Are you out of your mind, man? I'll shoot you right here and right now."

"Then you'd better," I said. "I don't like the idea of being fish food and the closer I get to you I'm forced to remember that I'm allergic to scum."

Though he backed away, he pointed the gun and glared. "Don't force me to take you out, Keller."

"May the force be with you," I said.

The sudden rush of movement was an adrenaline moment for both of us. I rushed him just as he clicked the trigger. A loud thud erupted as our bodies collided. The force of my shoulder being driven into his chest drove him backwards causing his feet to leave the ground and the gun flew from his hand. He landed on his back, holding his chest. He tried to immediately sit up, but found himself gasping for air. The difficulty of breathing caused him to plop back down. A look of fear and puzzlement crossed his face as I stood, rubbing my shoulder and finally walking over to where the gun had flown.

I stepped over to him as he sat on the ground, still struggling for air.

"You just had the wind knocked out of you," I said. "One of the advantages of playing football is knowing how to take out someone without having to kill them."

He sat still, heaving his chest in and out and looked up at me. He couldn't say anything. I didn't take his forced sighs as a sign of fan admiration.

"The gun? It was a ballsy move I'll grant you that, but I figured you hadn't bothered to make sure it was loaded."

A few more forced sighs.

"Once you confirmed that this was the same gun MiShaun used to try and renew her relationship with Deborah, I gambled that you hadn't seen me remove the bullets. At the time, I thought I was doing it for your own good. Funny how things work out, isn't it?"

I pulled Winston up by his collar. As he stood wobbly on his feet, I took my gun from his pocket and returned it to my shoulder holster. His gun was placed in my pocket and I finally released the bubble of air I'd held in my lungs since Winston first showed me his gun.

I turned him around and pushed him back toward the front. As we approached the Nova, air had started to flow through his lungs although I didn't think he was in much of a talking mood.

He sat down in the passenger seat and leaned forward, burying his face in his hands.

"Now Winston," I said after starting the engine. "I figured you were up to something. Your display of concern was a little too showy. You're going to make a phone call."

"To who?" he asked.

"The Stallings. You're going to contact them, only this time it's to arrange a meeting. You're all going to finally meet."

"Why can't we just keep it the way it is? Hell, I can set it up so there's something in it for you, too."

"That's already been tried." I took out my cell phone. "Call them now. Tell them you want to arrange a meeting for tonight. It's a one time, end of the relationship meeting. You're going for the big score."

He reluctantly took the cell phone. "Look, Keller, maybe we can ..... "

"Make the call now, Winston. You're already looking at charges of assault, attempted murder, blackmail and anything else I can think of to put you away."

"It's your word against mine," he said shakily.

"Winston, you don't want me dedicating the rest of my life to making you miserable. I will personally give up this glamour life to chase you down every street, alley and back road in this country, or around the world just for the pleasure of seeing that look on your face whenever you think you've gotten away."

He pressed the power button. "What am I suppose to say?"

I told him what I wanted, where to set up the meeting and the time it should take place. He did get through to Pernell Stallings. I couldn't hear Pernell's reactions, but they were predictable. He couldn't take the chance now that there were two of us in the picture. His perfectly arranged cover-up had taken a few dramatic turns. It took eight years, but the turns were happening.

Winston's voice lacked the commitment of the greedy leech that he was, but he did convince Pernell that meeting with him was in his best interest. I still marveled at how he and MiShaun had pulled it off for eight years.

I didn't like what had triggered their collusion.

His manner lacked any joy or relief of conscious as he powered off the cell phone. "Now what?" he asked returning the phone to me.

"My turn. I have a few calls to make." I started punching in a phone number. "Don't look so disappointed, Winston. Just think of all the time you'll have to contemplate the new direction that your life has taken. Relax, we're about to have a party."

He leaned back against the headrest and sighed slowly.

We motored up to Gratiot Avenue. The timing of my original plan had been moved up and I wasn't going to wait for the Stallings' next move. The chapter had closed on the lives of Deborah Norris, Morris Shaw, Daphne Connor and several others since then, but the story wasn't over. Its ending had laid dormant for several years. It was time to close the book and the key to its ending came down to the next few hours. Winston was already an unwilling partner and, at best, his help would be minimal, but I needed him with me just so I'd know he wouldn't do anything stupid again.

I'd been directed to awaken an irritable sleeping giant and not get crushed by its rampage. The complexity of issues and personal entanglements seemed overwhelming, but I was motivated to resolve this thing and find the truth.

That luxury of this final gamble was mine to see through.

So was its high-risk outcome.

63

On a cold December Sunday, during my second year with the Raiders, our team was locked in a scoring free-for-all on the home turf of our bitter rival. Both offenses seem to score at will, in spite of some outstanding defensive efforts by both sides. Finally it came down to who had last possession of the ball with the clock winding down. The final two minutes of a football game exists only in the minds of scientists. For the rest of us, two minutes is stretched into fifteen minutes, sometimes a half an hour, if all timeouts are in place and the team on offense is working the sidelines. Time can be both enemy and friend. It can collapse around you like an imploded building, unconcerned about anything lying underneath, or it can be stretched like a bungy rope, delaying the outcome until it snaps backward, or breaks and hurtles forward. In either case, death is a likely outcome, if one isn't careful. We won that game by stretching those last two minutes into fifteen until with time running out we kicked a field goal that sailed through the uprights as the final seconds ticked off and the gun sounded.

Memories of that foggy-breath afternoon served as a reminder that I had to stretch time taut enough to finish what Deborah started eight years ago and not have my face snapped off by the backlash. Events were set in motion that I hoped would finally bring the pieces of the puzzle together. It all came down to a meeting in two hours for which my short career as a private investigator would flourish or falter.

I'd seen the same thing happen in the last two minutes of a game.

Winston was a reluctant participant in a game where the rules didn't favor his unique brand of competitive mayhem. The simple fact that he'd been so good at being so elusive spoke to his ability to stay out of the limelight and milk the audience.

He understood my desire to keep him close.

When the last phone call was made and all parties had agreed to the informal meeting location, I motored over to a gas-and-guzzle station, ordered a jumbo cup of coffee, snack items, and a large styrofoam cup. The proprietor smiled politely from behind his glass barrier. Given what I'd just shelled out for those few items, I figured he'd use the over price to buy a stretch of land in Florida.

"What do we need with an empty cup?" Winston asked as we slid back into my car.

I held up the large cup of coffee. "You'll know after we've sat for about an hour."

We still had ninety minutes before it all came crashing down or all hell would break loose. I couldn't risk anyone getting there before we did.

Everyone had to show or my plan would have too many indefensible holes.

•   •   •

A black sedan and a red two-door, mid-size car rolled to the meeting location about twenty minutes before the actual meeting time. As the four doors swung open, I had a good view of all the occupants; it looked like something out of a 1970's black cast movie with a Curtis Mayfield sound track.

True to form, Tyler showed up with Pernell and Trevor and deployed two of the three men he'd brought with him to hide in strategic areas close to the meeting spot.

I watched both of them scurry to the right and left, disappearing behind a moonless cover of darkness. Winston, breathing hard and wiping away nervous sweat, looked at me as if to say that there had to be a better way.

I whispered that everything would be just fine, and seconds after I made that statement I noticed a familiar face sitting in the back seat of the car next to a third man who I assumed was part of Tyler's new crew.

We'd found MiShaun, and from the look on her face I gathered she hadn't volunteered to ride along. They'd brought along their trump card, but they didn't know if it was a four- or six-card kitty.

We still held the advantage, but not by much.

Winston recognized MiShaun about the same that I did and grabbed my left arm. "Now what?" he whispered in a tight voice.

"We still go through with the plan. They probably brought her along to guarantee your cooperation."

"Which you so conveniently provided for them now that I'm out of the shadows. We could have milked this for all it was worth. Maybe even had a shot at some big money if Trevor made it to the Mayor's seat."

"Just follow the plan," I said.

"Suppose they decide to kill us."

"We'll save a bundle on Christmas Cards."

I watched Tyler move several yards from where Pernell and Trevor were standing. He tucked his right hand underneath his jacket and I took that to mean that he wasn't cold. The third man stayed in the car with MiShaun. He'd been brought along as additional incentive for Winston to cooperate.

Trevor and Pernell were standing exactly where they'd been instructed. Pernell nervously checked his watch while Trevor was ice cool.

Everything was set. It was now or never.

"Okay, playboy. Go do your thing," I whispered to Winston. "Play it exactly as I told you and this will be over in no time."

His face didn't brim with confidence, but he reluctantly walked toward the Stallings.

I drew my gun.

"Shouldn't he be here by now?" I heard Pernell say to Trevor.

Before he could answer, Winston stepped into the clearing. "I'm here," he said, though his voice lacked conviction.

Pernell started to move forward, but Trevor held him back. Forever the one in charge, he stepped in front of Pernell and stared into Winston's soul. "So you actually do have a face. You're not quite as abominate looking as I expected, but close enough."

"As long as you paid on time, what do you care how I looked?" There was a noticeable tremble in Winston's tone.

Trevor stepped forward, extending his hand. "Interesting meeting arrangement Mr.... what is your name by the way?"

Winston stepped back, refusing the greeting. "That's not important right now," Winston replied. I moved through the shadows to a spot closer to where they were talking. "I thought this was the perfect spot for us to finally resolve our situation."

"Why here?" Trevor asked, still restraining Pernell.

I glanced over to where Tyler was standing. He wasn't ready to make a move.

Winston pointed to the marble headstone that signaled Deborah's resting spot. "Because she's here. Deborah Norris was a friend of both MiShaun and me. She's dead and I know why. I think its time we settled on all accounts so we can all move on to what we really want to do."

Trevor intensified his gaze, but his voice remained calm. "Why would your friend's death be of concern to us?"

"Because the reason why she's dead has everything to do with you, Pernell, and that man over there," he lamely pointed to Tyler. "Her death meant your brother would avoid a vehicular manslaughter charge. Deborah got wind of the deaths of two high school seniors by listening to MiShaun's dribble one night after a binge with a guy later identified to be Pernell Stallings. She pursued the story and I think she was killed because of it. I know MiShaun was the passenger the night that Pernell ran those kids off the road."

So far, Winston had done well. Some of the nervousness had left his voice. I kept a close eye on Tyler knowing he was the random factor. He remained steady and fixed on what Winston was saying while Pernell seemed to become increasingly agitated.

Trevor turned and whispered something to Pernell. I watched their exchange to make sure that neither one had passed a weapon.

He turned back to Winston. "Go on."

Winston moved further into our rehearsed speech. "That meant he wouldn't go to jail and upset your plans to be Mayor. I mean, how many folks would actually vote for a man whose brother spends more time in front of the law and not in support of it?"

"That's a lie!" Pernell shouted.

"Tell that to a jury of your peers in the event I should decide to go public with this information. You know, newspapers are always looking for these kinds of stories, whether they're true or not. Plus, I do have proof that I'll be happy to sell to the most needy bidder. Everyone wondered why you dropped out of the race eight years ago. Most people thought it was your concern for the community, but it really was about allowing enough time to go by, forcing the attention on yourself and less on your brother so that people would be so in love with you that your brother would be tolerated as a nice addition to the mission of saving Detroit."

Winston had done a good job of staying with the script.

"What proof?" Trevor asked.

I'd worked my way past several large headstones and crouched behind a small mausoleum. The moment was fast approaching and I wanted to be ready.

"You'll see my proof soon enough." Winston said, mildly confident. "Of course, with the right kind of offer, the bidding can end tonight."

"Don't bid with him, Trev," Pernell said angrily. "He'll just try and suck us dry later on. Let me handle it my way."

"Be quiet," Trevor said in a restrained tone. "My brother is right, you know. If you're who you say you are, then we've made cash payments to you for several years now. And in each instance, the price went up. We've provided your friend over there with a good life as well and in each instance, she wanted more. You can sense the pattern, can't you? Now you want to meet for one final offer and then you'll go away. You'll forgive me if I am untrusting of that as a final outcome."

"I don't think you have much of a choice," Winston said. "It's one thing for your irresponsible brother to cause the death of two high school seniors, but it's another thing to murder the one person who would have blown the whole thing wide open." He nodded toward Deborah's headstone. "She was close to figuring out what happened. Somebody, probably one of you, got nervous and took her life."

"That's a pretty strong accusation, Mister. I hope you have plans to back it up." Trevor said coldly.

"He does," I said, stepping from the shadows with my gun drawn. "He has all the back up he needs right here." I moved closer to the group, keeping my gun aimed at Tyler. "Drop the piece, big man and come on over."

Tyler smiled, showed both hands and eased closer to us.

"I want to see that gun on the ground, Tyler. Now, before I decide that I don't like you."

What fell to the ground was something compact and powerful enough to take out a small tank.

After it hit the ground, I said, "Do you use that thing for deer hunting?"

"Keller! I might have known," Trevor said as his voice lost some of its calm. "You two are in this thing together. I didn't think you were much of a detective, but I didn't figure you for a blackmailer."

"It's been a bad year," I said all the while keeping an eye on Tyler. "Now that we're all here, the negotiations can begin."

"Well let's see what we all have to offer," Tyler said. He snapped his left fingers toward the car where MiShaun was being held. His view had been blocked somewhat, but Tyler stepped aside and let him take in the whole picture. "Bring her out of the car," he yelled.

MiShaun was pushed out and held onto by her arm. The burly-looking third man marched her forward and kept a gun aimed at her side. Tyler motioned for him to stop a few yards from where we were standing.

"We caught her packing luggage. She probably thought she had some place to go," Tyler said. "Now, you drop your piece on the ground and let's see who has what to negotiate."

I threw my gun on the grass. It was a calculated move, but I couldn't take a chance on MiShaun being hurt.

Trevor appeared calm, but I knew what they'd planned was now being compromised and he didn't like it. "Easy Tyler. I'll take care of this." Trevor turned back to Winston. "What do you think you want from us?"

"Two hundred and fifty thousand would keep me quiet for a lifetime," Winston said.

"So would a bullet," Tyler noted.

Pernell's anger began to show through by way of a self-confident, slack-jaw sneer as the events moved in their favor. "Don't give this loser anything, Trev," he jawed. "He's lived off us long enough."

Trevor ignored him. "And you, Mr. Keller; what do you want?"

"I want to know who killed her," I said pointing to Deborah's headstone. "Although I figure it wasn't you, Trevor. You've got too much polish and class to resort to something like murder. You wouldn't ruin a good suit just to save your neck." I looked at Pernell. "You could have done it, but don't know how to clean up the mess you make. That's Trevor's job. I even thought your lady friend Jocelyn might have had a hand in it, but she's too emotionally dependent and unstable. She would have blabbed after finding you with the second or third woman that she managed to run off." I turned my attention to Tyler. "But you'd do it, wouldn't you, Tyler? You'd snatch the false teeth from an old lady if you thought they could be sold somewhere. Shooting someone less powerful than you would be consistent with your style. You're sneaky and treacherous when it comes to protecting your interests. I wonder if my man back there knows how wonderful you treat people who use to work for you. Your man Beasley gave you such a wonderful recommendation."

Tyler's eyes widened. "Where's Beasley?"

"Out of harms way for now," I said.

"Too bad we can't say the same thing about you." Tyler replied.

"Who was Deborah supposed to meet that night Tyler? Was it you, Pernell or Jocelyn? Who set her up so that you could pull the trigger?"

"He's guessing," Pernell said to Trevor.

"Maybe, but it makes sense. My only problem is trying to decide who gave the order. You see, I think Tyler is incapable of making those kinds of decisions unless it concerns his own crew." I looked at Trevor. "I think Deborah presented a problem for both you and Pernell. Yours, of course being more political and his involving jail time. So if she couldn't be bought off, she had to be eliminated." I moved sideways away from Winston until I was directly in front of Tyler. "Who gave the order, Tyler?"

"No orders were given for anything!" Pernell shouted. "Come on, Trevor, let's get rid of these pests."

"I'd like you to shut up for just a minute," Trevor said to Pernell. "Just once, would you keep your mouth shut or I'll have to clean up another mess."

At that moment of clarity, all the pieces fell in place and I knew. "You gave the order, didn't you, Trevor?"

His manner remained calm and his voice even. "Tyler, check to see if either one of them happens to be wearing a wire."

Tyler stepped forward and began to frisk Winston. He hadn't realized what the entire action signaled. He was a foot soldier obeying the commands of his leader. He was following orders just as he had back when Deborah was in pursuit.

After he finished with me, picked up my gun and stepped back, I glared at Trevor. "He follows orders real well."

"Mr. Keller, you've proven to be more annoying and persistent than she was. Naturally I couldn't move forward until enough time had past and her death was a distant memory sketched along Detroit's violent landscape. A landscape I intend to change, by the way."

"Detroit's doing fine without your assistance," I said.

Trevor smiled. "But it can do so much better and I'll see to that." He pointed toward Deborah's headstone. "She threatened my political future. There were a number of things I did to misdirect her because I didn't see her as much of a threat despite her persistence. I suggested to Jocelyn that her status with Pernell might improve some if she helped advance my cause. So I did have Jocelyn arrange a meeting under the guise that she'd receive confirming information to help her story."

"If she wasn't' much of a threat, then why is she dead?" I said trying to control my anger.

He sighed. "Sadly, mistakes happen. She was not the threat I needed to have removed."

That piece of news circled around my brain like a communications satellite looking for a compatible connector. The jolt from the realization nearly buckled my knees. I looked past Tyler and over to MiShaun, frightened and uncertain as to what was going on and very much...alive.

"She was the threat, but MiShaun was the target," I said trying to keep my voice even.

Pernell looked away while Trevor continued his story in dispassionate neutrality. "Jocelyn made the phone call to entice MiShaun to come and discuss how we could help one another, but it was this woman who showed up."

Jocelyn must have called during that time when MiShaun and Deborah had stopped being roommates, but still using Deborah's phone. Jocelyn would not have known MiShaun's voice from Deborah's and Deborah could smell a story.

It all started running through my head faster than I could comprehend. Deborah went in MiShaun's place hoping to get to the bottom of what happened to Morris and Daphne. She was the one at the arranged meeting and she was the one killed in place of MiShaun.

"How'd you get her gun from her, Tyler?"

He smiled. "That was easy. Once I got the drop on her, I checked to see if she was carrying some kind of tape recorder or something. Women tend to do that a lot, so when I saw her gun, I thought it would be funny. You know; killed by the very thing she thought would protect her. I wore gloves so it couldn't be traced back to me." He looked back at MiShaun. "I think she figured out what happened and hid out for a while."

Trevor interrupted. "Imagine my surprise when she showed up one day and demanded a job. That led to the further surprise of these intermittent messages from someone demanding money and reminding me that he also knew what happened and that he was MiShaun's insurance."

"That's a policy that's about to run out," Tyler said.

When the first scream ripped through the air, everyone turned to see the man holding MiShaun toppling forward onto the grass, holding his head while a lone figure, holding a crowbar in one hand, grabbed MiShaun and yanked her back toward the car. They took cover on the side of the car, before anyone had time to react.

Truman had done his part.

In the second that Tyler turned his attention away from me, I rushed him, crashing my shoulder into his chest and driving him into the ground. Even with the wind knocked out of him, he managed to lock an arm around my head and tried to roll me over. I swung my body across his chest and dropped an elbow into his solar plexus. He gasped and I shook myself loose.

A shot was fired and I rolled away from Tyler unable to find my gun, or his. Another shot ripped across the grass and when I got my bearings, I saw Pernell running away from the spot where he'd tried to pick up Tyler's gun. A quick glance at Trevor revealed his surprise at the escalating events. He seemed hypnotized by the heightened activity and unable to decide whether to run or fall down.

While Tyler attempted to stand, I saw my gun just off to the left. Aware that there were still two others unaccounted for, I picked up my .38 and ducked behind a large concrete headstone as two more shots were fired.

Another scream followed the second shot. I turned toward the sound and saw Winston curled up on the ground holding his shoulder as blood seeped through the bullet's opening. He lay there rocking and moaning in pain.

"Somebody shot me," he cried out. "Oh, God! I've been hit."

"Stay down, Winston." I yelled out.

"Help me Keller," he said in a voice of exaggerated anguish.

I looked around, hoping to get some bearing on the flight of the last bullet. Only a second or two had gone by when I heard someone yelling and cursing. Down by the second car, Truman had tackled Pernell and driven him into the ground.

It was a perfect takedown for an automatic three-count.

When I'd gotten my bearings, Tyler had somehow made it to his feet and, with his gun in hand, staggered over to where Winston had fallen.

He was about to steady his aim when I called out, "Drop it, Tyler."

He turned toward me with a look of savagery. "You're a dead man, Keller," he said as he swung the arm holding the gun towards me.

I didn't hesitate and fired off three rounds before he had a chance to aim.

He fell back on the grass, holding his stomach and gasping for air. The first shot hit him in the stomach, followed by holes to the right arm and leg. I'd seen the gun drop from his hand and as I took cautious steps toward him, he rolled over and slowly crawled to where Trevor was standing.

Trevor remained standing as Tyler wrapped a blood-soaked hand around his ankle. Trevor tried to pull himself loose, but Tyler kept a strong grip. Tyler moaned and murmured defiantly at Trevor's shoes.

I knelt beside Tyler and rolled him over. Blood flowed from all three wounds as Tyler labored for air.

"Don't just stand there," I said to Trevor. "Pop that cell phone from your jacket and dial 9-1-1."

He seemed momentarily disconnected from the sight of Winston's yelling, the now silent graveyard and me trying to stop Tyler's bleeding.

I yelled at him two more times before the sounds of approaching footsteps caught my attention. I turned and saw Truman escorting a pro-testing Pernell back to where we'd gathered. Truman had one of Pernell's arms bent behind his back, so all he could do was protest.

"You all right, Bro?" Truman asked as he pushed Pernell next to Trevor.

"Yeah, I'm fine," I said. "But this one's in bad shape. Grab that cell phone and call for an EMS unit."

Truman looked down at Tyler. "Oh, he'll live. Though he may not want to."

"MiShaun?"

"Scared, but okay. She's sitting on the other side of the car," he said as he punched in 9-1-1.

By now, Pernell was yelling for Trevor to do something, but he continued his disconnected trance. Pernell's prolonged barking almost drowned out the approaching sound of something being dragged along the grass.

Using the back collar of their shirts, Jeff was pulling along the two men who'd been deployed in opposite directions when the meeting first started. He moved along with confident ease, pulling each man as if he were a sack of cotton candy. The only evidence of any strain showed in the arm muscles of his sleeveless, blue jean shirt. He stopped a few feet from us, let each man fall to the ground and stepped forward. I didn't doubt that they were probably connected with the break-in at Sharron's.

Just following orders.

"I hoped you'd be able to stop both of them," I said as he stood next to Truman.

"They voluntarily resisted," he said "What about this one?"

"Wounded, but I think he'll be okay. We've called for an EMS unit." I nodded toward Winston. "Check him out for me."

Jeff moved over to Winston, stared at him for a moment before kneeling down and helping him to his feet. "Easy man. It's not bad." He pointed to the two unconscious men. "One of them managed to squeeze off a shot before I could get to him."

Winston stopped moaning and looked to Jeff. "Thanks."

In a move that caught us completely off guard, Jeff punched Winston in the face with such force, that he ended up on his butt, holding his nose and moaning again.

Jeff dropped down to one knee and pulled Winston's chin forward. "Next time you get any ideas of trying to kill any one of my brothers, I'll personally put your face in a grinder."

He stood up and walked back to us.

"What was that about?" Truman asked.

"I did some checking around. Somebody who fit Winston's description hired that guy you took out with your van. One of my sources got a positive ID for me. I was looking for him when Linc called with this hairbrained plan."

In the distance, we heard sirens rushing hard to our location and I wondered if anyone could legitimately sort through the chaos that had come to resolution in Detroit's Memorial gardens.

Pernell went on the offensive. "We are going to have a good time suing all of you. Just wait till the papers get a hold of what really happened here." He glared at me. "Especially when it becomes known that you had a court order placed on you, Keller. You can kiss your private eye days good bye."

I looked up at him and then over to Trevor. Through it all, I think Trevor saw a world he'd built for himself crumble as quickly as the clay

support he'd built around him. Pernell had visions of escaping justice .....
again.

"Hey, Rosie," I yelled to a corner of the yard.

He came from underneath a long patch of shrubbery, his new high
tech video recorder on his shoulder and grinning like a 'B' movie director.

"This camera can do so many things," he said as he walked forward. "The lens adjusts to pick up clear night images, the microphone
can pick up conversations from as far away as ..... "

I interrupted; "Did you get it all?"

He held up his left hand with his thumb and first finger in the
classic 'Okay' gesture. "I got it all."

64

The events of that evening hung like backstage theatre wires, pulleys and ropes of a Broadway musical. Every piece was connected to some aspect of the show and all the players were about to become their own audience. Though it didn't seem possible, the winding trail of the Deborah Norris murder was about to come to an end in a place where endings were a common practice.

Long nights and short naps had become a critical way of life over the last few months. Despite my obvious look of fatigue and luggage eyes, the bustling masses seemed intent on stretching the night into a taunt pull through the waning hours.

The fact that I was bushed didn't matter. There were too many questions from too many on-the-scene experts about things they'd just screw up in the later hours. As I later explained to Julie when she expressed interest in my secret diet that caused my weight loss, I told her to just get enough people pissed off at you and by the time each finishes taking a piece of your ass, you'll be thigh slim and booty short.

The reigning chaos did little to shield me from the onslaught. Everyone at the crime scene wanted a piece of Lincoln Keller's torso. Now that two of Tyler Cain's henchmen were handcuffed and bullets from my gun wounded Tyler, I had a lot of explaining to do or like the Titanic, I was going down.

Homicide's emissary of mirth and good cheer; Lieutenant Knackton, strolled over to greet me as I sat with my brothers on a grassy knoll, surveying the activity.

His Cheshire grin would have made the current Speaker of the House quite envious. "Kellers!" he proclaimed. "My world is plagued with Kellers." He ignored my brothers and glared directly at me. "Give me one reason why I shouldn't rip your license into little pieces."

"It's laminated Lieutenant, you'll have to use your teeth." Truman and Rosie laughed while Jeff surveyed the officers and EMS people who filled the landscape. "If you'll wait a few minutes, Lieutenant, I can explain everything."

"Take two minutes."

Though my explanation took longer than two minutes, the job of replaying the events felt like years of mentally draining activity that finally came to an end. My monologue seemed clearer to me as I talked through it than it did while I wrestled with how the pieces fit.

Knackton listened intently, occasionally stopping me to ask a clarifying question, but never stopped taking notes. By the time I'd finished, Truman had wandered over to console MiShaun and Rosie had snagged some uniformed officer who'd made the mistake of asking about his video camera.

Jeff stayed nearby.

I completed my story and sat back, folding my arms and yawning.

"Anything else?" Knackton growled. I shrugged. "I want the video tape from that camera and Deborah's journal and those pictures given to you by this alleged unknown car jacker," he said closing his notebook. "I'm going to check this story out closely. You'd better hope this all means something or so help me Keller ....."

"Yeah, I know; I won't be able to get a license to chauffeur a rich widow lady on Sunday afternoons down a sparse back road. Right?" I said suppressing a grin.

"Something like that."

His gloating was short lived as Trevor Stallings, fresh out of his trance, came storming forward.

"Lieutenant!" Trevor yelled. "I demand that you arrest this man.

Now!"

"If you'd like to come down to the precinct and press formal charges, that's your right as an individual citizen. Right now I have more important matters."

Knackton pivoted and rambled back toward the crowd of uniforms engaged in gathering stories and evidence.

Stallings glared at me. He was a shark in search of a leg to bite. My blood was a nectar he craved, my head was a trophy. He sauntered forward. "Your preposterous accusations will not go unchallenged, my friend. Rest assured. When my lawyers finish with you, being a water boy for your former team will seem like a gift from the Gods."

Actually, given the Raiders' recent fall from football grace, being their water boy would have been more like a curse from the Giants. "Self-delusion is a common disease among the politically inept. Try taking two aspirins and sticking your head in a bucket of ice."

"You ready to go, Bro?" Jeff asked locking eyes with Trevor.

"Just one last thing," I said.

I turned and walked toward the marble headstone that marked the final resting of Deborah Norris. When 'War Zone' first pulled me into this case, I thought I'd give it a few good days and tell him what everyone else had been saying for eight years. I hoped to make a good showing, but I wasn't convinced that I'd make a difference. Deborah was supposed to be just another name on a folder marked 'unsolved' and filed away in a far corner, out of sight. But I hadn't been afforded the chance to just move on to the next case. Deborah became a life to me. She was a choral voice with definable features, yet kept her suspicions silent.

I knelt in front of the headstone, muted the surrounding noise and whispered. "We got 'em Deborah. I hope you can hear me. We got 'em." I stood up; glancing at the star lined sky and released a pent up sigh. "Rest in peace, my friend."

65

Judge 'Zone' and Sylvia listened in awe as I recanted the events from earlier that evening. I talked through every point as if I needed to purge the details from mind. They'd already retired for the evening when I came ringing their chimes.

I couldn't think about the lateness of the hour. I was only a few steps ahead of the local media and I didn't want The Judge answering questions before answers were known. They'd soon swarm around their door like predatory birds looking for road kill. Knackton granted me the time, knowing it was all going to break loose.

Sitting together on a deep-tufted couch with plush cushioning in a room of cherry veneers and hardwoods, they held hands while I paced. A second wind of energy kept my mind working and my tongue moving. No one asked questions or interrupted for clarification.

They listened.

I talked.

"And so," I said finally sitting down in the matching armchair, "Deborah was never the intended target."

"My sister is dead because she was mistaken for someone else?" Sylvia asked.

"Your sister is dead because of what she didn't know," I replied. "Deborah didn't know the depths that friends and foes will sink just to preserve their own well being."

Judge Zone listened, dispassionately trying to create some distance from my statements. He'd spent the latter third of his years enforcing the law and handing down judicial pronouncements. Now all he could do was listen.

Sylvia seemed less tense; her shoulders slumped as if some giant weight had just been fallen off. I wasn't sure if she fought back the tears or fought off the disbelief. I should have been more concerned with how the information was being received, but I had a tight clock. The local media would show up in mass and I didn't want to be there for the assault.

"Lieutenant Knackton will probably be here very soon and he can punch in all the details. I won't say this with too much fanfare, but Tyler Cain, an associate with the Stallings, pulled the trigger that ended Deborah's life. He acted on orders from Trevor Stallings. Deborah found out that Pernell Stallings was responsible for the deaths of two people and was close to gathering the evidence she needed when her life was ended. I just picked up the trail from there."

The look that crossed Judge Zone's face would have thrown fear into fanatical terrorists. Though he fought to restrain the anger, I knew that the wounds Tyler currently had would seem like mosquito bites if The Judge were anywhere near him.

"Your Honor, any moment now, your door is going to be filled with satellite vans and network wannabes. Maybe you had better prepare for the bombardment."

The Judge looked up from his embrace of Sylvia. "That would appear to be a wise course of action for now."

The tears Sylvia tried to restrain slowly made their appearance from the corner of her eyes.

As the messenger, the news I'd brought couldn't be classified as bad. Judge Zone hired me to find the answer to a trouble-plagued question and that's what I'd done. Deborah's killer had been identified and the motive, with some time, would be easily established.

I'd earned my lunch money.

There was nothing left to do but file an official report, fend off a million questions by Knackton and prepare for the unending court appearances and public allegations. It wasn't going to light up my life, but at least I had a life.

It didn't seem like enough.

"I'd better be leaving, Judge. I'll put together a report and send you a bill later on."

Judge Zone nodded.

Sylvia brushed away a tear. "Mr. Keller, I want to thank you for all you've done. I'd all but given up hope, but now, well I just want to say ....."

I held up a palm. "Glad to help, Mrs. Henderson. I wish I could do more."

The picture of Deborah on the corner of the mantel slowed my hasty departure. It seemed like yesterday when I first gazed at the face with the elfish grin and look of mischief. She'd managed to leap her way into the fabric of my life and I wasn't sure if I'd ever be able to let go.

I fixated on the necklace hanging around her neck. Having come to know Deborah, the fact that she'd give her sister such a special gift was consistent with her unique character. She was also very good at elaborate pranks.

I continued to stare at the picture, remembering Sylvia's description of the last time they dined together. My thoughts ran through the described movements of that evening, specifically during the dinner and after.

Deborah wore a turtleneck blouse that evening. She was with Sylvia most of the time except for a few minutes when she stepped away from the table.

I walked over to the picture, picked it up by the frame and shook my head in disbelief.

"Deborah. You didn't!" I said turning the picture frame over.

"Mr. Keller, may I ask what you're doing?" The Judge asked in a puzzled tone.

"A moment, Your Honor, please," I replied as I pulled the back cover down through the slots.

"Mr. Keller, please," Sylvia shouted.

Once I had the back cover in my hand, I saw a thin envelope taped to the brown piece of cardboard in back of Deborah's picture.

"She's still a gamester, after all this time," I said as I pried the envelope loose.

"What do you have there?" The Judge asked.

"I believe this is for you, Mrs. Henderson," I said handing her the envelope.

She stood, puzzled, held out her hand. "What is this?"

"The last thing you expected to see."

She opened the envelope and emptied the contents into her hand.

Sylvia gasped at the familiar piece of jewelry that fell into her hand along with a small hand written note.

"This looks exactly like the necklace I'm wearing." Sylvia said. "But why would Deborah put another one in back of her picture."

"I don't think it's another one, Mrs. Henderson. I think it's the original one."

Sylvia opened the note and after a moment began to chuckle. "I don't believe it. I just don't believe it."

"Believe what?" The Judge asked equally confused.

Sylvia handed the note to him as her chuckles turned to hearty laughs.

The Judge unfolded the note and read out loud. "Happy Birthday, Sis. I know you always wanted my necklace, so take it with my blessings." He stared disbelievingly at the note and then at Sylvia who'd sat back on the couch, clutching the necklace to her chest and laughing. "I don't understand."

"It's simple, Your Honor," I said amused by the irony. "Deborah wanted to give Sylvia her necklace, but not before getting another one just like it. Deborah bought the one Sylvia is wearing for herself, knowing she'd be giving up the first one to Sylvia for her birthday. When Sylvia was contacted about the new necklace, she assumed Deborah was having it made for her. Since the first necklace was never found, because we assumed it was taken in the robbery, Sylvia just naturally thought the new necklace was meant for her."

"But Deborah was wearing her necklace the last night she was here."

"I know, your honor, but remember, she left the dinner table for a few minutes and you said she was wearing a turtleneck blouse. I think she slipped the necklace in back of the picture when she left the table, knowing the neither of you would notice if she still had on the necklace."

"But she tapped her necklace just before she left me that evening," Sylvia said.

"Force of habit. Probably done to let you think that she was wearing the necklace. It was never stolen because it was here all the time."

Sylvia engaged in an odd mixture of laughing and crying, while Judge Zone stood shaking his head.

"She loved a good prank," he said.

I nodded, turned to Sylvia and said, "Happy belated birthday, Mrs. Henderson."

As they continued to think about the strange twist of irony left undiscovered for eight years, I let myself out and aimed the Nova toward...well; I didn't really have a destination in mind.

If I were a boozer, I would have swung over to the nearest watering hole, stuck my head in a bottle and stayed there until I was able to play double dutch with my intestines. Instead, I motored home to my apartment.

Once inside, I called Arlan Schafer and told him how the case has unfolded.

"I think there's a story there Deborah would have wanted you to finish," I said. "I have all the background material if you're still interested in writing that hell of a story."

He managed to fight off the sadness, but agreed to write the story.

I channel surfed, hoping to find something a little more amusing than looking at my brain through rolled over red eyes.

And there it was, in humorous irony, being replayed on a late night newscast.

'Tommygun' Harper's, Detroit's version of a punk-faced, know-it-all, opinionated sports broadcaster had been captured on tape in the studio. His guest was a local hockey player for whom Tommy had been particularly brutal in his column and on his weekly radio show. Saladimir Boulchevsky had endeared himself to Detroit hockey fans because of his tendency to start fights with opposing players. After the fighting was over and he was penalized, during the post game interviews, his face was typically scarred so badly that you never knew if he actually won the fight.

Tommy started the interview by referring to Saladimir as 'Salad Bowl'. Saladimir told Tommy not to call him 'Salad Bowl, but by the name his mother gave him.

Tommy didn't listen and gleefully taunted him again. Saladimir calmly insisted again and Tommy ignored him, choosing to go with 'Salad Bowl'.

That's when the fun began. Saladimir jumped up from his chair, grabbed Tommy by his jacket lapels and dragged him across the interview table. He lifted Tommy over his head, twirled him around and rammed him into the studio set. The canvas set ripped as Tommy slowly descended to the floor and the studio crew did what they could to restrain Saladimir.

In between laughs, I said, "Who said God doesn't have a sense of humor?" The echo of my own laughs drove me to pick up the phone and punch in a familiar number.

Hope does spring eternal.

Epilogue

Despite the uneasy feeling of not being alone, there were no shadows, shafts of white light or shrill winds blowing across the Douglas MacArthur Bridge. In fact, the morning qualified as the most peaceful and serene I'd ever experienced. Picture perfect, the way Norman Rockwell might have painted it if he could capture the preciseness of the blue sky.

I walked across the white stoned arching bridge, realizing the emptiness of traffic moving onto or off Belle Isle. The image wasn't consistent with the predictable traffickers who often escaped to the island for various forms of respite.

The lack of noise was also unsettling.

An explanation seemed lost in the serenity.

I had no real sense of the time since I couldn't see the sun and I couldn't explain my own presence.

I kept walking until I reached the apex of the bridge and noticed, to my right, a figure, back turned, staring at the calm waters of the Detroit River. Since we were the only ones, I walked over, hoping my newfound companion could offer some insight.

"Excuse me," I yelled as I paced faster to where the person stood.

It was only after I'd come within a few feet when the person turned around and flashed a warm smile.

I blinked.

Impossible I thought. "Ma?"

"Hi son," she said, opening her arms in anticipation of a hug.

I ran toward her and squeezed for all eternity.

When we finished our clinch, I stood back and gazed at the five foot, four-inch woman who bore four sons of six feet, plus inches. She looked no more than thirty years old. Black hair pulled back in a ponytail and those embracing brown eyes.

"Ma. What the devil are you doing here?"

She laughed. "Believe me son, my being here has nothing to do with the devil."

"No. I mean what are we doing here?"

She nodded toward the brilliant island green slowly being enveloped by a descending mist. "I always liked Belle Isle and the visual symbolism is important in helping you understand what's about to happen."

"But Ma. You're. . .wait a minute. Am I . . ? "

"No Linc," she interrupted. "It's not your time. But I am waiting on someone."

"Who?"

"All in time," she said, smiling.

I never questioned her 'all in time' statement in life and it still didn't feel right, especially now. "So where's Pop?"

"You know your father. When I left him, he was busy arguing with DuBois about his talented tenth notion."

I shook my head. "The old man is still the eternal agitator."

"Well he is now. Anyway, he wanted to be here, but only one of us could come. He sends his love."

I had a thousand and one questions, all swirling in my head like debris in the tail of a hurricane, when my mother nodded toward the middle of the bridge. I glanced over and saw two figures I immediately recognized, strolling hand in hand, peacefully looking ahead.

"Morris and Daphne?" I said with some confusion.

"That's right Linc. Their souls are at peace now. They can cross over now. They have resolution, thanks to you."

Still confused, I turned back to my mother. "They should be thanking Deborah. She figured out what happened long before I came along."

"True, but she was taken before she could follow through. What you're seeing is their completion."

"I'm not sure I understand."

She put her arm around my waist and nodded toward the river. "The water is unusually calm because of the souls that have been freed from those sweeping currents. They can finish their completion now because someone decided to help. There are a lot of souls waiting beneath the surface for someone to take an interest."

I turned and watched as Morris and Daphne strolled over the arch of the bridge toward the growing mist. They stopped and turned back toward us.

"Why'd they stop?" I asked.

"They're just waiting on their escort," Mom replied.

"Is that you Mom?"

"No," she said softly. "It's the same person who's anxious to meet you."

"That would be me Mr. Keller," a voice behind me answered.

Mom and I completed our half turn back toward the bridge and the person who greeted me was someone I would've known anywhere in life. Had that chance not been taken away.

"Deborah?"

"In the flesh," she said. "Figuratively, speaking of course."

She extended her hand and I unconsciously returned the gesture. I was amazed by her touch.

"Surprised huh?" She laughed. "Don't worry, your hand won't pass through mine. In this place, we're all quite solid." She nodded toward my mother. "You were right Mrs. Keller. He is quite persistent."

"He gets it from his father. We're quite proud of our sons," Mom replied.

Despite the uncertainty of what I was experiencing, I knew what I had to say. "Deborah, I'm sorry we didn't know each other before now. I like to think I would've been there for you. It's too bad we didn't get to know each other over there, out there or wherever there happens to be. I have a feeling we would have been good friends."

"We may still find out one day," she said whimsically. "Anyway, I just wanted to meet you and say thanks." She leaned forward and flashed an elfish grin. "For a while there, I didn't think you were getting my messages."

I paused a moment. "The dreams! Of course, the shadows and distorted images, that was you."

"Yeah. I tried with Sharron for a while, but her memories kept getting in the way, so she never clearly understood what I was trying to tell her."

"Why me?" I asked.

"Warren had a previous encounter with you. It was easier convincing him to hire you and your mother was quite persuasive."

Deborah looked liked she'd just stepped out of one of the picture frames. A mischievous look that signaled an on-going prank. Where the uncertainty came from was not knowing if you were in the middle looking out or on the inside looking across. Deborah was the consummate prankster whose commitment to the elaborate detail of a joke always left a person scratching his head. If this was a prank or an elaborate illusion, then David Copperfield should have been with me taking notes.

"You've been guiding me right from the beginning haven't you?"

"More or less. It became easier once you decided to commit."

"Your reputation precedes you Deborah. An elaborate prank played from beyond the . . . , I don't even know where we are."

Deborah smiled and glanced toward the mist. "Well," she said without hesitation, "I have to go now. Morris and Daphne are waiting to get fitted and I'm their escort. They've waited long enough and so have I." She walked over and hugged my mother. "Thank you Mrs. Keller."

Mom smiled.

"Mr. Keller, may I impose on you for one last time?"

"Call me Linc. Sure what is it?"

"Tell my sister. . . tell her I'm doing fine. Tell her to live her life embracing each moment and not to mourn for me. We'll see each other again. Tell her that when it's time, I'll meet her right here on this bridge."

I nodded.

She turned and walked toward the mist. When she reached Morris and Daphne, they each hugged and then looked back at us.

"Linc, it's time for me to go."

"Wait Mom. Time for you to go where?"

"Why with Deborah," she said matter-of-factly. "I'm to see to her completion."

Anxiety raced through me. "But do you have to leave now? Can't you stay a little while longer?"

Mom leaned forward and hugged me. She pulled away and held me at arm's length. "I'll stay until you wake up Linc."

The words seemed to echo across the bridge.

"Until you wake up Linc."

The voice started to fade and then grew louder.

"Wake up Linc. C'mon baby, wake up."

I bolted upright, blinking my eyes against the darkness, looking around for something I recognized.

The light from the shaded lamp next to my bed clicked on and I turned to see Malone's concerned face staring back at me.

"Were you having a bad dream?" she asked while she gently stroked the side of my face.

"What?" I asked as I slowly worked through the confusion.

"You were talking in your sleep. You mumbled something about 'staying awhile' and started breathing rapidly," she said as she wrapped the blanket around the top of her chest. "Were you having a bad dream?"

I leaned back against the headboard and rubbed my eyes. "I'm not sure if it was a dream at all."

Malone moved closer to me. I put my arm around her as she nestled her head against my chest. "Want to talk about it?"

"Yeah," I said looking over at the clock. The red digital numbers displayed 4:30 a.m. on what would have to be a sleep in morning. "But I don't know if you'll believe it."

She would.

Lincoln Keller returns in
Silent Rage
Soon to hit the bookstores
or look for it on www.proctorpublications.com

Read this exciting preview of Chapter 1

Vandella Kincaid's serene expression offered few answers to the questions that plagued our relationship. She lay motionless in the sterile, brightly-lit room, seemingly unaware of the attentive chaos that filled the uncontaminated moments or the constant beeping of the life-support machinery that kept her breathing.

She also wasn't aware of the fact that I'd put her there.

I don't know what hound from hell dogged my heels and chose my car as the one she'd step in front of seven nights ago as I returned to Detroit.

Her reasons were anybody's guess. And I never earned a penny or won the heart of a true love by guessing.

As a private investigator, I don't guess. I look for facts. The facts tell the story and reveal any lurking truths.

Leaning against the green-striped wall of her hospital room and staring out at the multiple colors hanging from trees in the full bloom of Fall, I thought of a popular blues lament penned by an author unknown to me, but sang with convincing sincerity by Ray Charles; *if it wasn't for bad luck, I'd have no luck at all*, I whispered melodically.

With both sides of the luck coin flipping evenly that fateful night, I could have just as easily been home in bed playing 'ring around the rock' with my love interest Candy Malone. Instead as I returned from Portland

Oregon, having found my client's missing husband, I debated whether to take the Southfield freeway from I-94 east or just stay on to John C Lodge.

I took the Southfield freeway and the backhand of bad luck slapped me across the face with all the force of a happy dominatrix. In doing so, I nearly killed Vandella Kincaid.

*   *   *

Fall is a busy time for P.I.'s. All the Spring flings that led to Summer Sizzles become Fall fallout. The longer it stretches into Fall, the more intense it becomes. Business was good, which meant a lot of things were bad and all I had to do was see that it was all wrapped up, tied in a nice bow and delivered to the nearest divorce lawyer by Christmas.

I was Santa Claus with a short barrel .38, delivering messages of pain in a 1987 Nova with just enough horsepower to outrun eight tiny reindeer going downhill on a slick mountainside. I was working the kind of cases that I'd be ashamed to tell my priest, but love to tell my barber.

Professional ethics prevented either from knowing.

I really didn't need another case.

When Mrs. Laura Bradford first contacted me, I knew she would be a difficult client to turn away. There was a quiet desperation in her tone. She had an ache that wasn't going to end until she had some answers. Her base was shattered and she desperately wanted to stand on something solid.

Her slumped shoulders had carried the weight of a thirty year marriage complete with all the frills and frauds that came with sustaining something for the long term. In her pale expression, I saw the life tracks that had etched their way across thousands of planned meals and a million civic activities. She paid her dues as a dutiful wife, nurturing mother of three above average children and part time van driver for all those neighborhood kids whose parents were too busy trying to make up for sleeping through the disco era. She'd done all that with a forced smile and enough restraint to settle a wild mustang. Her payment was supposed to be an early retirement with her husband Gordon in a condo on a beachfront in Wilmington, North Carolina.

Three months ago, Gordon skipped out on his end of the bargain.

"The police say that technically there's nothing they can do." She said as she slid a color wallet photo across my desk. "He didn't commit a crime. There's no law that says a person can't walk away from their responsibilities. At least no man made laws."

I glanced at the wallet photo of Gordon Bradford. The fifty-five year old husband-turned-apparition.

"How old is this picture?" I asked.

"That was two years ago at our youngest son's graduation from Bowling Green State University." She replied softly as she placed the other items I'd requested onto my desk. "Here's the note, the recording from the answering machine, phone records, bank statements and the name of his boss from work."

"Mrs. Bradford, your husband left you with no bills, a savings, a home with no mortgage, all the furniture, both cars and all the credit cards. Obviously he cared enough to leave you with solid support."

She sighed. "All those things mean nothing. I married and built a life with Gordon. This was our life, our home, our credit cards, our kids. Now it's just mine. I don't see any real joy in that. When did he start not wanting what we had?"

I leaned forward. "If I can find him Mrs. Gordon, what is it that you want?"

"Last week I would have said that I want him back home. I want us back together having dinner at 6:30 on those nights when he didn't have to work late. But I know that won't happen. So for now, I just want answers. I want to know why he bailed out. Why did he really leave me?"

She knew the answer to that question long before she called me. I was being hired to have the answer confirmed. Any investigator on the trail of a middle-aged man, who left home, with no forwarding address, knows to start with the question, "who is the other woman"?

"Let me see what I can do Mrs. Bradford." I said. I opened the side drawer of my desk and handed her my standard contract. "I'll look over what you have, make a few phone calls and see if I can get a lead."

She read quickly through the contract, signed and slid it back over to me.

"Give me a few days. If anything turns up, you'll be the first to know."

"Thank you Mr. Keller." She said. She slowly rose and I eased from behind my desk to walk her to the door.

She paused just before I turned the doorknob. "You know, in some ways this would be a lot easier if he had been accidentally killed or been kidnapped and held for ransom. That's not what I want, of course, but at least I'd know. It's the not knowing that keeps me awake at night."

I spent the rest of the day going over the information I had and making phone calls. Gordon had left a nice three page, handwritten note that explained his sudden flight from fancy. He offered no excuses or long winded explanations. He told Laura how he'd changed the bank accounts so that everything was in her name, he made sure all the bills were paid and that she had a substantial savings. They'd paid off the mortgage three years ago and none of the kids were living at home. As he stated, it was time to go.

The weekend that he disappeared was supposed to be spent in Chicago visiting with her in-laws, but a last minute meeting that carried into the week-end kept him from taking the trip. He told Laura he'd meet her there on Saturday. She flew out on Friday evening and he cut out an hour later. Before leaving he did a couple of interesting things. He changed the message on the answering machine so that if Laura called home, she would get his voice apologizing for not being there and assuring her that he was working as fast as he could. He also left a similar message on his voicemail at his office. Gordon was kind enough to leave the company car parked on the lot, and the calling card, security key card and expense card were left in an envelope on his Director's desk.

He also left a nice note. He thanked his company for the wonderful job opportunity and hoped they would continue to do well. He left instructions for his stock options to go to his wife, and to extend her insurance coverage for another six months.

Again, he made no apologies, but insisted that it was time to go.

Gordon hadn't embezzled, stolen company property, launched a virus into the computer network or destroyed anyone's personnel file.

Sometime that Friday evening, Gordon turned his back on the well-ordered life he'd spent thirty years building.

And no one knew why.

"Hanging around until the wee hours won't bring her around any faster Mr. Keller." Grace Casey said as she came in to check the monitors.

I shook off thoughts of Gordon and Laura Bradford and watched as she patiently went through her ritual movements of attending to Vandella's care. Grace Casey's twenty-plus years of nursing expertise cascaded Vandella like a blanket of herbal tonic. All she'd seen and done as a nurse in the wards of several Detroit hospitals came together as smooth as a player's rap. If there was any stress or distress in her compact frame, it lay hidden beneath the flush bronze skin of the late forties care provider. She brought with her an unblemished record of never losing a patient who came under her care. She wasn't about to let Vandella ruin her streak.

"I could say the same to you." I said after noting that it was three hours past her shift.

"I work here."

"And I work for her." I said nodding toward Vandella.

Grace ignored my comment, choosing to concentrate on the dials, green lines and low hums that came from the machines monitoring her life signs. Over the course of the days and nights I'd spent hanging around her room, Grace and I had managed an unstated agreement. A common concern and unwavering interest in her survival linked our mutual pact. At the bedside of anyone walking down the long hall between life and death, you hope that there is someone who cheers loud and long enough to pull you back.

Grace and I were her only cheerleaders.

I watched Grace write down information on a form attached to the clipboard that hung on the bed rail.

"You know. You've done all you can do for her. Any number of people would have just left her lying beside the highway to be another unidentified body to be buried in the county graveyard. You have gone above and beyond what anyone could have reasonably expected. Just finding out who she was would have been enough. That would have satisfied most people."

"I'm not like most people."

"You're definitely not like anyone I've known." She said. "Don't you think you've done enough?"

"I don't know." I said.

Grace smiled. "That's what you said when you came in here with her and we asked you who she was."

It's also what plunged me into Vandella's world.

Lincoln Keller series:

Silent Conspiracy
Silent Suspicion
Silent Rage